Out With The Tide

Out With The Tide

A Novel

Paul Ehrenreich

Out With the Tide is a work of fiction. All incidents and dialogue, and all characters with the exception of some well-known historical figures, are products of the author's imagination and are not to be construed as real. Where real-life historical figures appear, the situations, incidents, and dialogues concerning these persons are entirely fictional and are not intended to depict actual events or to change the entirely fictional nature of the work. In all respects, any resemblance to persons living or dead is entirely coincidental.

ISBN-9781797646275

For Ellen, Elise, Alison, Raelle,
and my mother, Tema.

ONE

Umbrellas and Seals

"Again?" Rob Crosley mumbled as he made his way down the steps to the beach. This was the fourth day in a row that the interlopers had returned to the exact same spot, lined up under their beach umbrellas. Rob never saw them coming or going. They were there when he arrived, and they were there when he left. They were not technically interlopers—there were no private beaches on the bay, but the stretch of sand fronting Rob's property was a quarter mile away from the access road and parking spaces that allowed public access to the beach. Occasionally, some determined bunch would set out in search of a secluded spot further down the beach, away from the clot of vacationers who, by virtue of their indifference to crowds, or the fact that they just had too much crap, chose to stay close to the parking lot. This group of three, though not at all noisy, had a regimented approach to their beach-going adventure that added to the irritation Rob already felt at having his privacy invaded. Each of them sat under identical blue umbrellas, evenly spaced, a few feet from the water. Their chairs matched as well, though they were red, the same color as the two coolers that sat on either side of the middle chair, doubling as side tables. Were there no red umbrellas available?

Rob tried to think why he should feel irritated by these people on such an otherwise ideal afternoon. The breeze on the bay was from the south. A windsurfer darted away from the shore while boats motored out from the harbor, rushing to keep up with the tide. The air was so clear that the shoreline wrapping to Provincetown looked like a pen and ink drawing. Even the Plymouth coastline was visible across the bay. Rob decided it wasn't so much that his privacy was being invaded, but more a sense that he was being taken advantage of. "We understand you own the house at the top of the dune there, but we're going to sit here anyway," they might be saying. Or perhaps the irritation was caused by the possibility that these people were becoming attached to this spot, and might come back every day for the rest of the summer, and future summers, as well.

There were forty-two steps down to the beach. Rob counted them most of the time, as if to make sure none were missing. They were in good shape despite the seasonal poundings of the elements. There was a healthy crop of poison ivy beneath the steps, which Rob wanted to spray—he was severely allergic—but Helen Shantz, his annoying neighbor who also used the steps, would have none of it. "God knows what else it would kill," Helen Shantz said, waving to the other vegetation.

"What if the poison ivy kills me?" Rob said to her.

She rolled her eyes.

He was not kidding.

Rob arrived on the beach, with Sidney close behind, more or less. Sidney was Rob's fifteen-year-old Australian Shepherd. Sidney was no longer able to race down the steps the way he once did, which saddened Rob. On the other hand, he wasn't able to bound through the poison ivy anymore either. Sidney took the steps one at a time now, in a measured fashion, as if he was counting them, too.

Rob decided to walk past the group, traversing the narrow strip of sand between their feet and the water, and see if they made eye contact. As he got closer, he was struck by how still they were. They weren't talking, and though they brought books, they weren't reading them. The first two were attractive females, in good shape, maybe in their thirties. The other was a man, probably similar in age, maybe a bit younger. They were not particularly tanned, but the fact that they stayed under their umbrellas gave Rob no clue how long they had been on vacation. The women were fidgeting with their paperbacks, looking more like they were sitting in an airport terminal than at the beach. The man was studying the water, a pair of binoculars in his lap, poised to witness something. They could have been on a reconnaissance mission. Rob passed in front of them, affecting some form of expression that conveyed both suspicion and congeniality. Sidney ignored them, his nose to the sand, sniffing what the tide had pushed in. Rob nodded and said, "Hello."

Neither of the women looked up, burying their faces in their books instead. The man pushed the binoculars up to his eyes and continued his surveillance. Rob mumbled to himself, turned away, and headed past them. They behaved as if it was their beach and Rob was the intruder.

After setting up his own chair, and dropping his book on the seat, he walked to the water where Sidney had started rolling in the wet sand. Why couldn't they have said hello? If they had been in the city and passed each other on the sidewalk, it wouldn't have been surprising if they kept to themselves. But on the beach, on vacation, when no one else was around, and they were supposed to be relaxed and unthreatened, why wouldn't they say something? Then again, this bunch had hiked down the beach to get away from the crowds. Maybe they didn't like other people. Maybe they had nothing to say to anyone. Maybe they behaved that way to drive Rob as far away as possible. Or maybe they were just assholes.

Rob stuck his foot in the water and tugged at his bathing suit which had become wedged between his buttocks. He wondered whether he was an asshole. Maybe at times, he decided, but not generally. He could be thoughtful if he wanted to be. If he was a real asshole he would have sprayed the poison ivy under the steps and told Helen Shantz to get lost. But he didn't, because she was his neighbor, and he didn't want to have an uncomfortable relationship with someone he ran into on a regular basis.

When Rob's son, Danny, was eight years old, he heard a man yell "Jesus!" as he went into the water. Danny asked his father why the man was angry with Jesus, and Rob explained that he was reacting to the cold water. "He could have said "Wow!" or "Holy cow!" too," Rob said, glad the man hadn't said, "Holy shit!" From that day on, Danny yelled "Jesus!" whenever he went into the water. Eventually, the days on which the water was legitimately cold, meaning the bones in your legs felt like they were turning to ice, became known as "Jesus! Days." Today was not a Jesus! Day, Rob decided, once he got far enough into the water for the more sensitive parts of his body to become submerged—the tide was going out, and he had to travel thirty yards before his nuts were under water. Sidney waded in, too, but went no further than where he could stand. He was not a swimmer, and he no longer had any nuts. He cocked his head to one side and watched Rob disappear under the water. Rob was not much of a swimmer either but he liked being in the water, if only to get wet, and he liked sitting in the sun to dry off afterwards.

When Rob came out of the water, he tugged at the front of his bathing suit to keep the material from clinging to his crotch. Maybe the thing to do was to wear some kind of waterproof undergarment to keep the suit from wandering. Or he could take the thing off altogether. Would anyone mind? The umbrella people certainly wouldn't notice. And if they did, and were offended, they could move. Rob toweled off, covered himself in sun block, thinking about the sun-burn he would get if he was nude, then sat down and opened his book. After a few minutes Helen Shantz wandered by.

"Oh my, what a gorgeous day," she said. Helen Shantz was wearing a large sun hat and a robe. She was a short, skinny woman, but always seemed to be draped in oversized apparel. She carried a small beach chair.

"Hello, Helen," Rob said. She never called Rob by his name. She never called him anything, in fact. She just started talking, usually to complain about something.

"How is your family?" she asked.

"All well, thanks."

"Are they here?"

Rob raised his eyebrows and had the notion to look behind him just to be sure, but he figured she was asking whether they were on the Cape. "Yes. Katie and Danny are here," he said. He liked using names with her in the hope that maybe, one day, she might remember them. Sidney had returned from the water. Sidney didn't much care for Helen Schantz either.

"Oh that's wonderful. And there's your dog! So well-behaved! You know, I noticed you left your porch light on last night. I don't mean to be a pest but it really does shine into my bedroom window."

Rob cringed. "Christ, I'm sorry, Helen. Danny must not have turned it off when he came in last night. I went to bed early myself." The first time Rob met Helen Shantz she lectured him about outdoor lighting and in what circumstances it was a violation of town ordinances.

"Yes, well..." Helen said.

Rob seized the opportunity to change the subject, and perhaps swing Helen Shantz into his corner. "Do you know who those people are over there?" he asked.

"I don't," she said, continuing to look at Rob. "But then I'm not wearing my glasses. I'm really blind without them. Is there anything I need to know?"

Rob considered whether he should fabricate some story of reckless behavior that might spur Helen Schantz to action. He had no doubt that she would walk right over and confront them with whatever charges Rob brought.

"They've been here for three days," Rob said in an ominous way, lending some doubt.

"They sleep on the beach?"

"I think they go home at night."

Helen briefly looked over at the group one more time, and then searched the sky. "Such a gorgeous day, I can't see how anyone could possibly complain about anything." With that she headed several yards away and unfolded her chair. Sidney followed her for a few steps while emitting a low growl.

Rob growled under his breath, too, watching Helen Shantz, under her enormous sun hat, settle into her chair. "What about the porch light, Helen? That wasn't a complaint?" He probably said this a little too loudly. Helen looked up. Rob shifted his attention back to his book and pretended he hadn't said anything. Sidney abandoned his pursuit, satisfied he had chased the woman away, and lay down under the umbrella.

A short time later Rob looked up from his book and noticed that Sidney was intently watching something behind them. Rob turned to find the two women, freed from their umbrellas, each standing on one leg, slowly rotating their torsos with their arms extended in front of them, in some kind of rhythmic exercise. The man was still under his umbrella, oblivious to the oriental shenanigans going on behind him. Perhaps he had already seen it.

Rob had a hard time not staring. The women had beautiful legs and great skin. He had recently decided that a woman's most attractive quality was her skin; clean, unblemished, free of wrinkles and hair. These women had skin that seemed to glow in the sunlight. Rob's skin did not glow. It was brown and leathery and had started to sag in places, particularly around his midsection. There were more discolorations, too, now that he was spending more time at the beach. He meant to go and see a dermatologist.

"I think that's Tai Chi, Sidney," Rob said. Sidney looked back at Rob. Was he panting from the heat? "Easy, old boy."

At some point Rob decided he should probably stop ogling the women, though he was beginning to worry they were getting too much sun. Like pie crusts browning in the oven, he had the urge to cover them with aluminum foil. He turned around, in time to see a small dark object pop out of the water.

"Oh, shit," Rob said. Sidney was watching, too. The object disappeared, but after a couple of seconds it resurfaced, further along, it's snout pivoting around like a periscope. "They're here, Sidney."

The night before, Rob had watched a national news segment about the Cape's seal problem. He seldom watched the national news on any channel, and after watching for twenty minutes, he was glad he didn't. The first fifteen minutes of the newscast focused mostly on death and destruction. After that came short pieces about less depressing oddities, interspersed among drug commercials aimed at the aged and dying. Had he become part of this demographic?

Close on the heels of an ad about an older couple who had discovered the wonders of Cialis, came the story about the Cape Cod seals. Rob was concerned that the news anchor was not conveying the appropriate level of concern in his demeanor. Seals had too long been the darling of films and the media. This needed to change.

The opening shot was from a plane flying over the Monomy Islands, a stretch of sandy outposts south of Chatham. The sand, however, was not visible, having been blanketed by thousands of seals. "Look at all those fuckers," Rob said. The correspondent rattled off statistics—nearly twenty thousand seals on the Cape and Islands, growing at a rate of twenty percent annually, each one eating forty pounds of fish per day.

"They're eating more fish than all of us can catch," a local fishermen said. "It's time to lift the ban and cull the herd."

The correspondent looked distressed. "You want to kill seals?" he asked.

"Yes, sir," said the fisherman.

"Don't they have as much right to the fish as we do?"

The fisherman became more animated. "Every one of the ocean beaches on the Cape is now shark infested. They're hunting seals, but every now and then they'll get confused and take a chunk out of a swimmer. The seals eat our fish and the sharks eat our children. We're under attack here."

"Not just the ocean beaches anymore," Rob said as he watched the seal disappear under the water. Soon the sharks would arc around Provincetown and start hunting for seals in the bay, if they hadn't already.

Seals also attracted little kids, two of which now came sprinting down the beach, pointing toward where they had last seen the seal. "Where did he go? Come back, seal!"

Rob thought about how one would go about killing seals. He pictured a speed boat zipping along the shore of the Monomy Islands. A man could position himself in the bow and strafe the beach with a machine gun. This was bound to upset some people, though. Anything involving high-powered weapons was generally frowned upon. Perhaps the females could be trapped and neutered?

The overexposed Tai Chi women finished their calisthenics and returned to the umbrellas. They were talking to the man now. He was stirring and seemed liable to get out of his chair. Were they leaving? If not, what? Would they play whiffle ball? Toss a Frisbee? Frolic? The man forced a laugh and Rob imagined one of the women had made some joke about the consequences of standing on one foot in the hot sand too long.

The man put down his binoculars and picked up what looked to be a camera.

With that, the three of them emerged from under the umbrellas, in all their pastiness, and headed for the water.

"Probably not a good idea to go into the water when you've just seen a seal," Rob said to himself, wanting to say it louder. Sidney apparently agreed. He started to follow them toward the water, one ear straight up, the other flopping around uncontrollably—that ear had never been right—and started barking. Sidney was not a barker.

"Sidney, shut up!" Rob said. The three of them were wading into the water. The tide was still low but had started coming in. They were chatty now, talking as they trudged to a point where the water was deep enough to swim. Rob could hear every word. The calm, cool surface of the bay was an excellent conduit for sound waves. It was every eavesdropper's dream. Rob had once heard a young couple discussing the effects of cold water on their genitals. Mostly, people discussed what they had eaten at their last meal or were planning to eat at the next, or how they had just urinated in their bathing suit.

Here is some of what Rob and Sidney, who had stopped barking and lay down to nap, heard them say:

"You have the camera?"

"I do."

"The water's colder today."

"It's fine."

"Something just pinched my toe."

"Make sure it isn't bleeding."

"Today's the day."

They moved out of range, swimming south, until all that was left was the sound of the gulls and the swollen rush of the tide pushing back toward shore. The water sparkled as the sun stretched toward the horizon. Rob wondered what the one swimmer had meant when she said, "Today's the day." The day for what? Were they going to perform some kind of aquatic stunt and capture it on camera? He reached over and patted

Sidney. The dog slept so deeply now it was not always clear that he was still alive. Rob checked for signs of respiration. Sidney's flanks were still, but soon they rose and fell. "Good boy." Rob reclined the back of his chair, taking another look in the direction of the swimmers, figuring they were going to take a picture of the seal, and fell into his own deathlike sleep.

* * *

Rob was awakened by Sidney's low growl. Helen Schantz had packed up and was on her way to the stairs. She had a hand on the brim of her hat—the wind had kicked up—and she looked as if she was tipping her cap goodbye.

Despite the turn in the weather, the three umbrellas were still there, flapping in the wind, but no one was under them. The wind had whipped up three foot waves, helping the tide roll toward shore. There was no sign of any swimmers. The wind had shifted out of the north, and the temperature was dropping. Clouds moved in. People at the public beach were packing up and heading for their cars.

The three umbrellas began to struggle against the wind, and Rob wondered if he should take them down before they cartwheeled down the beach. Though there was no one left for them to impale, Rob decided that because he was not an asshole, he would get up and collapse the umbrellas. As he did so, he noticed the swimmers' towels neatly folded over the backs of the three chairs. He touched one of them, and found it was completely dry. He looked at the water. They might have folded their towels after drying off, but they would still be damp, wouldn't they? No one was in the water. He looked down the beach in both directions, hoping to see a trio of walkers, but there were none. The wind gusted now. Sidney sniffed at the coolers.

"Let's go, Sidney," Rob said. "Time for scotch and crackers."

As he headed up the stairs he looked back at the beach, wondering what he would do if the umbrellas were still there later that evening. Should he call the police? It occurred to him that Helen Schantz would have seen the three swimmers return, if they had returned. She might have seen them heading off on a walk. As much as he didn't want to, he decided to stop at her house and ask. Somehow he felt responsible for the people on the beach that was his but wasn't, the beach that was now narrowing by the onrushing tide.

TWO

Turkeys and Kittens

Rob adjusted the hose nozzle to full force, then pressed the trigger and let the turkeys have it. Sidney lay sleeping on the deck, oblivious to the assault.

"Run you fuckers!" Rob yelled.

The turkeys had wandered into the yard, where they were becoming a bit too comfortable, as far as Rob was concerned. Definitive action was required if he was to reclaim his yard. Like the seals, the turkey population on the Outer Cape had exploded over the last two years. Before, you might have seen the occasional depressed, scrawny-looking turkey wandering aimlessly through the brush, waiting to get taken down by a coyote. Now, entire families paraded down the middle of the road, venturing into whichever yard offered whatever it was they found pleasing. For some reason, the turkeys found Rob's yard particularly pleasing.

Some people encouraged the turkeys' visits by feeding them, fattening them up for Thanksgiving. Unlike the seals, turkeys were not protected. The sporting method of slaughter was a bow and arrow. It was also a cleaner death, and didn't send the neighbors scrambling for the phones when a gun went off next door.

The turkeys scampered back to the trees to dry off. Rob expected they would be back. He hoped they weren't so stupid that after a few soakings they wouldn't get the idea that maybe it was time to move on. He had no interest in shooting them.

Finished clearing the yard, Rob went inside and poured another scotch. Sidney woke up and followed him inside, looking for another cracker.

"All you do is sleep and eat," Rob said, feeding him a Wheat Thin.

Danny came into the kitchen wearing his running shorts and shoes, no shirt. Rob always marveled at how lean his son's body was, ideal for running long distance. Had Rob looked like that when he was in his twenties?

"You mostly sleep and eat, too, you know," Danny said.

"Don't forget drinking."

"That's part of eating."

"No, it's not. Two separate activities. You don't have to do them together."

Danny looked out the window. "Those swimmers are probably drifting out to sea by now."

"Stop," Rob said. He took another swallow of scotch. The weather conditions continued to deteriorate. The wind had strengthened and the light that managed to seep through the clouds was fading. "I'm sure they swam with the current for a while and popped out of the water somewhere."

"They all do eventually," Danny said.

"Look, I'll call the police if their stuff is still there in the morning, okay?"

"Was anyone else down there?"

"The Schantz woman was there for a while."

"Well, did she see them?"

"No idea. She wasn't wearing her glasses anyway." Though Rob suspected she could see just fine without them.

"You should ask her."

"I was going to stop at her house but couldn't bring myself to step into her yard. She would have accused me of trespassing."

"Those poor people."

"They're fine. Swimmers don't die in the bay."

"Sure." Danny tossed a cracker to the dog. Sidney made a half-hearted attempt to grab it but it fell harmlessly to the floor. He watched Danny, expecting him to throw another. Danny pointed to where the cracker was and Sidney tracked it. "Remember when he caught anything you threw at him?" Danny said.

"Those days are over."

"Hey, after you call the police in the morning, come running with me."

Rob glared at his son. "Those days are over, too," he said.

"What are you talking about? You still run."

"About half as fast as you do. You're training for the Olympics for Christ's sake. You don't want to run nine-minute miles, do you?"

"It's an easy day tomorrow. Just a few miles. I need someone to make sure I keep an easy pace. That's you."

"Hey, I bought some bluefish for the grill," he said, trying to change the subject. "That okay?"

"We'll go at nine. We can run five miles. You'll be back by ten."

"You go ahead. I need to pull the weeds in the driveway tomorrow."

"Jesus. Come on, Dad. Being retired doesn't mean you lounge around doing nothing all day. You said you were going to pick up some hobbies. Running is a good hobby."

"I'm not retired. I'm moving in a new direction."

"You're not moving at all."

Rob had been meaning to find some new hobbies. He had to decide what he enjoyed doing first. "Maybe I could raise turkeys," he said.

Danny dropped to the floor and began stretching out his hamstrings. Rob leaned to one side, giving some group of his own muscles a little flex. He didn't like running. He did it more out of habit, and also because it gave him an excuse to stand under a hot shower for thirty minutes, and then go out and eat hamburgers and French fries. Eating was a good hobby, too.

"Tomorrow morning, five miles," Danny announced, popping up.

"Go and start the grill," Rob said, taking the bluefish out of the refrigerator. He still marveled at his son's determination. Where did that ability come from? Was it something Rob had done? Could he take credit? He suspected Danny's ability to run as fast as he did was due in part to that determination, though his coaches said it had more to do with Danny's lung capacity, and that he had one of the most efficient strides they had seen in a distance runner.

"We are running tomorrow morning, right?" Danny said flicking the grill lighter at his father.

"Not if you set me on fire."

* * *

After dinner, Danny cleaned up, and Rob went across the road to visit his wife. Katie lived in a small two-room cottage she had built five years ago. The cottage sat on a lot that she and Rob had bought along with the main house. They had planned, one day, to build a small vacation home, and rent it out to the summer tourists who flocked to the Cape to lie in the sun and swim with the sharks. That idea was squashed when Katie's fear of other people, a phobia she had lived with for most of her adult life, became so severe that she couldn't even tolerate being with her husband for more than a few minutes at a time. "How could you be afraid of me?" Rob asked, as if she was leaving him for another man. But he knew there was nothing rational about the fear. People terrified her, and when she was around them she became convinced something dreadful was going to happen. Drugs dulled the fear but they also dulled everything else. "I can't live like this," she told Rob. "I may as well be dead." But she couldn't entirely abandon her family either, so she built the cottage across the street and lived there.

She had learned how to build houses from her father, who himself was a home builder. He would take her to job sites and teach her how to swing a hammer and cut two by fours. She had no fear of the furious noises and sharp spinning teeth of the power tools. These were things that were under her control. She had only to watch out for other people's missteps, which worried her even in her late teen years. One day when she was on summer break from college, she was helping two men frame the second story of a house. They were assembling one of the walls, when the two men started horsing around. One of them lost his footing and stumbled toward the edge, waving his arms to keep from falling fifteen feet to the ground below. Katie was closest, and she reached out to grab him. He yanked her arm so hard that she lost her balance, and went over the side, the man beneath her. He broke her fall, but broke his neck, too. Katie lay on top of him, watching the man gasp for air, his lungs no longer able to take instructions from his brain. He died on the way to the hospital. After that experience, a trauma that stayed with her through years of therapy, she mostly worked alone.

Katie was now effectively off the grid. The cottage got its power, what little of it she needed, from the solar panels on the roof. Water came from a well, and waste flowed into a septic system. Katie took care of any maintenance work herself. The only thing she couldn't do, and preferred not to, was clean out the septic tank. For that, a man rolled up in his truck and pumped out the tank. Katie didn't have to see him.

The bill came to the main house, where Rob took care of paying it.

She grew her own vegetables, and caught fish in the bay. At low tide she dug up oysters and clams. Rob wanted to bring her food from the store but she refused it. She didn't want to be reliant on other people when she didn't need to be. Rob offered to buy her a bow and arrow so she could pick off a turkey or two, but she refused to kill anything other than fish. Her only vice was a cell phone, which she used to talk to Rob and Danny.

Rob called to let her know he was coming for a visit. He knew not to show up unannounced. Katie was particularly sensitive when caught off guard—she became unresponsive, forcing Rob to circle the cottage, peering through the windows to make sure she hadn't lapsed into a catatonic state.

"Katie, I'm here," he announced. He brought a glass of scotch with him. There was a time when he brought the whole bottle, hoping he could convince her to share a drink with him. She had mostly given up alcohol, though. It only exacerbated her fears.

He had left Sidney at the house. As the dog had gotten older and slower, Rob stopped taking him out for walks after dark. The coyotes kept their distance for the most part, but they seemed lately to be getting bolder. Last week a neighbor up the street had watched helplessly as a coyote dragged her schnauzer into the woods. The dog had gotten away, but lost a leg in the process.

"You can come in, Rob," she called. He could tell from her tone that she was in reasonably good spirits. Her voice dropped an octave when she was not.

Rob stepped inside. Katie was on the other side of the main room, fussing with something in the kitchen. Rob sat down on the couch, knowing not to approach her. She would come to him when she was ready, or maybe not. She might stay at the kitchen sink for the entire visit.

"How are you?" she asked. "How's Danny? Did he run today? Well, of course he did. He runs every day, doesn't he?"

"Take a breath, Kay. I'm happy to sit."

"No, I want to talk. I'm glad to see you." She was shucking oysters. It helped to have something to distract her.

"Danny wants me to run with him tomorrow."

"Really? That's nice. You always like doing that, don't you?"

"Sure. I'm like one of those old retired nags that trot alongside the racehorses, to cool them down."

"You're not old. Just retired. Do you want some oysters?"

"Yes, please," he said, always happy to share anything she offered. "Can I give you a little of my scotch?"

"Oh, no, no," she said as she came over with a plate of oysters. She took measured steps. It was easier when he was sitting down. Generally, she had no more than fifteen minutes before the anxiety built to uncomfortable levels. She knew Rob liked to push his visits each time, trying to extend the threshold.

Rob slurped down an oyster, wishing he had some cocktail sauce. He looked at the oak beams that spanned the open ceiling above. The wind was still whipping around outside, fluttering the curtains as it pushed into the room. He thought to mention the umbrella people to Katie, wondering if she might have seen them, but he was reluctant to heap his problems on her. She had enough dealing with her own.

Katie ate an oyster and stared at a spot on the floor. He could tell she was trying to keep her mind from racing. "You look great," he said, meaning it. Though she had given up people, she had not given up on herself. Her hair, no longer at the mercy of chemicals, had grown long and silver. Despite a few wrinkles her face was still youthful. Her shorts gave way to slim, smooth legs, tanned by her days in the sun. There was seldom a spot of hair on her legs or under her arms. As with her power tools, Katie would not sacrifice her hygiene.

"Did you go anywhere today, besides shell-fishing?" Rob asked. He wanted to keep her distracted, but knew, at the same time, that his voice might threaten her, slashing across her veil of security. He wished she would sit down, but knew she wouldn't.

"Still too many people out there. Where do they all go?"

"They drive up and down Route Six all day, looking for a place to park."

Labor Day couldn't come soon enough for Katie, when summer vacationers went back to their jobs, and let the Cape return to its preferred state of laxity. In the off-season Katie could get on her bike and ride along the back roads for hours, and not see anyone.

"Are you okay?" Katie asked mustering the courage to look at him.

"Me?" Rob was taken off guard when anyone showed concern for his well-being. "I'm fine."

"You're keeping busy, not missing work?"

"Danny wants me to find a hobby."

"You should. Why don't you build something in the workshop like we talked about?" Katie's workshop remained in the basement of the main house. She would only use it when both Rob and Danny were away. She asked them to call her when they were coming home so she could clean up and leave. Rob did this most of the time, but sometimes he would sneak in while she was there. The noise of her machines, grinding and whirring, masked any noise he might make upstairs. If she didn't know he was there her phobic monsters stayed in their cage.

"I'd cut off my hand."

Katie managed a smile. "Maybe just a finger," she said. He tried to hold her gaze for a moment longer but she looked away. The fear could come back gradually, or it could come back in a flood of panic. One day, perhaps, it wouldn't come back at all.

"The workshop is yours, Kay. I'll find my own thing." Katie buried her face in her hands and began to rock back and forth. Rob wanted to go and comfort her but he knew this would only send her rushing to her bedroom. "Focus on your breathing," he said. He said this a lot when he was with her. It made him feel like a shit, somehow, as though he resided in the pantheon of those higher beings who had mastered the art of dealing with irrational fear.

"I know. I'm okay," she said. Somewhere outside came a high-pitched feral scream, nearly human-like in its howl of despair, like a small child being ripped from its mother and carried off into the night. The noise served to pull Katie back from the edge of her bottomless pit.

"What the hell was that? Rob said. It was not the first time he had heard the howling. He thought to get up and look outside, but didn't want to unsettle Katie further by moving around.

"Probably a fox, or someone's cat being gutted by a coyote," Katie said. Her hands were still over her eyes, but her voice had returned to its higher octave.

"Coyotes eat foxes?"

"No. That's their mating call."

"You're kidding."

"Don't let Sidney out at night anymore, not without a leash."

"Yeah, that's why I didn't bring him down here. Why don't the coyotes eat the turkeys? They've got to taste better than cat."

"They probably do, but turkeys don't scream when they're being killed."

"I hit them with the hose today," Rob said. "Sent them running off into Helen Schantz's yard."

"How is Helen?" Katie asked. Her hands were hanging at her sides now.

"I saw her on the beach this afternoon. She yelled at me about the outdoor light again. Do you think if she walked outside at night a coyote would gut her?" Rob reached for another oyster. "Hey, you should be proud of yourself. You managed the anxiety without needing me to leave."

"The dead cat did that."

"Should we buy some kittens?" Rob said, smiling, thinking he might be able to stretch the fifteen minutes to twenty. But Katie stood up, shook her head, and headed for the bedroom.

"Take the rest of the oysters," she said, closing the door behind her.

"You okay?" he called.

"It's time for you to go, Rob. I'll be fine once you leave. You should go now."

Rob slumped back on the couch and stared into his scotch glass. With each visit he hoped she would improve a little, stay with him longer, feel more at ease. When they were living together in the main house, and her fears of other people became more prevalent, Rob had worried that her condition might progress to the point where it threatened their relationship. He woke one night to find her lying on her back, eyes wide open, blankets thrown aside, her arms folded over her stomach. She had one foot on the bed and the other squarely planted on the floor, ready to bolt. He asked her what was wrong. "I can't," she said, and tore from the room, fear conquering reason. She fled to the basement where she locked herself in her workshop. Rob stood outside the door, trying to coax her back to the bedroom, but his voice only made things worse. He retreated to the living room where he sat up all night wondering what to do. Should he call one of her doctors? Should he call Danny who was away at school? In the end he did nothing, falling asleep on the couch after convincing himself that things would be better in the morning. But by the time he woke up, Katie had already pitched a tent on the empty lot across the road, and started digging foundations.

* * *

Rob walked back to the house, worried he would either be attacked by a coyote, or stumble on the remains of a disemboweled cat. Back in the relative safety of the kitchen, he finished the oysters, then sat down at his computer and punched "Hobbies for Men" into his web browser. The sites that came up included, *Manly Hobbies, Best Hobbies, Cheap Hobbies* and *Masculine Hobbies Every Man Must Try*. He immediately dismissed *Cheap Hobbies,* as the fun of doing anything in life lay largely in buying gear. *Best Hobbies* was too subjective, and *Manly* sounded too pretentious. The last one, though it begged the question of whether there were feminine hobbies every man should try, sounded just right, inclusive of every man and asking only that you try. He clicked on the link and a list of suggestions came up with a description and illustration for each. Among them were blacksmithing, high power rocketry, survival prepping, woodworking, whisky tasting—something he was pleased to learn was a hobby—and knife throwing. Also on the list was something called parkour—an unfamiliar term. The illustration showed a man jumping over a stone wall. Reading on, he learned that parkour was a sport devoted to jumping from buildings, presumably to other buildings, and vaulting obstacles. He wasn't sure why someone would want to do this unless he was running away from something, like Nazis or a tsunami. He supposed it was an outgrowth from the movies or reality TV. Though there were certainly plenty of walls and fences on the Cape he could vault over, there were few buildings. Parkour seemed to be more of an urban challenge, best suited to men who healed quickly.

Having discovered he was a whisky tasting hobbyist, he poured himself another glass of scotch and, returning to his computer, searched for sites on how to avoid shark attacks. The first site he opened actually advised him to stay out of the water if he saw a shark.

"Genius!" Rob announced loudly.

"Everything okay, Dad?" Danny called from his room.

"I just learned that you should stay out of the water if you see a shark!"

"Write it down so you don't forget."

Rob read on and was further instructed, in the event he was already in the water when the shark swam by, to keep his eyes on the animal at all times. Sharks were animals? Rob read aloud, thinking Danny was still listening. "Always know where the shark is," he said. "Remain calm. No sudden movements or splashing. Most sharks aren't interested in biting you and will likely swim away."

He came to the part he was looking for—what to do if the shark attacked. "Punch the shark in the eyes or gills. Then swim away using the breast stroke so as to minimize any splashing and reduce the spread of blood. Get help."

Rob wondered if shark fighting could be classified as a hobby all men should try. Shark hunting certainly was, as a form of fishing, but Rob did not want to kill sharks, just scare them away. For now, sharks were the only predators who were allowed to kill Cape Cod seals. If anything, more sharks were needed.

"We must learn to coexist with the sharks," Rob said to Sidney, his only audience now, and logged off.

As was becoming the norm, Rob slept well for the first part of that night, until he had to get up to relieve himself. He meant to get his prostate checked. After falling back asleep, he dreamt of a massive tidal wave that engulfed the outer Cape. Hundreds of YouTube videos showed tourists and their coolers tumbling in the surf. Half the real estate washed into the bay. The Pamet River swelled to a navigable channel, leaving North Truro and Provincetown as an island, approachable only by boat. The main house survived but the cottage did not. Whether or not Katie had been inside was unclear, but her isolation rendered her a casualty nonetheless. Rob heard reports of people perched on top of their homes, floating in the bay. If any home would float, certainly the one Katie built would. She sat huddled on her roof, shivering in anticipation of salvation.

THREE

Running Shoes and Answering Machines

Like a tidal wave rushing back to sea, the images of devastation receded from his dreams, leaving behind the debris of his subconscious. Then an alarm, sharp and precise, a blast of foreboding, jolted him from sleep. Rob wondered if it was another horny fox, but it sounded more like a prehistoric bird on the roof. A few seconds later, the alarm repeated. It had come from inside the bedroom—the bedside table, in fact. Months had passed since Rob last set an alarm for anything. Perhaps he turned it on accidentally. He picked up his phone and found that it was not an alarm, but an incoming text. This was not the sound his phone made when he got a text, though. Was there a different tone reserved for emergencies? Rob read the text.

"Get up. Time to run," it said.

"Christ," Rob muttered. "Are you right outside the door?"

"More or less," Danny answered. "You've got fifteen minutes. The weather is perfect so you don't have to put on a lot of clothes. You do have to brush your teeth."

Sidney was in his usual spot on the floor, stretched out on his side. Rob studied his midsection for signs of respiration. Some dark part of his brain hoped for Sydney's death so that he would not have to run. But Sidney's eyes were open now, and he was looking at Rob with a half-hearted gaze, curious to see what his master would do next, but knowing he didn't have to move if he didn't want to. Unlike Rob, Sidney's running days were well in the past.

"What did you do to my phone?"

"You like that? I changed your text alert last night and cranked up the volume."

Rob studied his phone wondering how it could betray him in this way. "Bitch," he said. In addition to getting his prostate checked he would also change the pass code on his phone. He swung his feet to the floor. His bare legs looked like they belonged to a cadaver. "How far did you say?" Rob called. He knew his son was still close by.

"Five miles. Easy pace."

"Did you go see your mother this morning?"

"I had breakfast with her."

Rob had started to get up but now slumped back into the mattress. Somehow Katie was better at managing her anxiety where Danny was concerned. Her maternal instincts overruled her fears. Danny was a part of her in a way that Rob was not. He got up and opened the door. Danny was right outside.

"Shorts, shirt, socks and shoes," Danny said. "You can do this."

"Go somewhere else. I can dress myself. Take Sidney outside, why don't you? Come on, Sidney. Outside?" Sidney stirred and struggled to get his hind legs under him. He stood, swayed a bit, and shuffled toward the door.

"Ten minutes," Danny said. "Then we go."

"I might have to cut my toenails. They're pretty long."

"Your toenails are fine."

Rob did as he was told, brushing his teeth and pulling on his running clothes. There was a time when running, independent of the hot shower and food that followed, had been agreeable, but as his body continued its long slog into decrepitude, it was becoming more of a struggle to find any point in the exercise anymore, other than stopping. He often wondered if Danny still enjoyed running, or if it had become a way of life for him now, an obligation to his enormous gift. He wanted to ask him about it, but was afraid to put any negative thoughts in his head. "You're right, Dad," he would say, "Every day I wake up and think about slamming my foot in the door so I don't have to do this shit anymore." But that wasn't Danny. He had set a goal of running in the Olympic 10,000 meter final. He would pay no mind to anything that might distract him from accomplishing this, including an apathetic father.

Rob laced up his running shoes—black with red stripes on the outside, orthotic inserts on the inside. He supposed this was another reason he kept running, so that he could buy new shoes every six months. Opening a box of new running shoes was an exhilarating event, hearkening back to his younger days when his mom would buy him a new pair of sneakers, and he'd wear them out of the store, anxious to get home so he could start climbing on things. Like the sneakers, the running shoes—there was really no difference—were full of promise, and foreshadowed greatness. But the exhilaration left quickly after the first time on the road, when it became apparent that he was still the same unremarkable runner. When the shoes were spent, the soles ground down, he threw out the left shoe and kept the right one, writing the date of retirement on the tongue. He had fifty right-footed running shoes saved in his closet. One day he planned to nail them to a wall in chronological order, a tribute to his insanity.

Rob grabbed a bottle of Gatorade from the refrigerator and wandered onto the deck. Danny and Sidney appeared, having returned from their short walk.

"The stuff is still there," Danny said.

"What stuff?"

"Their stuff. The umbrella people."

"Shit. I forgot about that. Really?" Rob looked at the water. The house was on a hill that lent expansive views of the bay, but not the beach below. The day was calm, no wind. On days like this one, the water was smooth, clear, and undisturbed. If there was anyone floating around out there they would be easily seen. "You sure they didn't arrive this morning?"

"No. But the umbrellas are still down."

Rob sighed heavily, sensing an ordeal. "So, I guess we call the police, huh?" he said, needing affirmation. His only experience with the police involved moving violations. Everything else was fictional, except for what he read in the papers, and he wasn't so sure that wasn't fiction either.

"Yup."

"Listen, you go ahead on your run and I'll call."

"You're not getting out of it that easy, Dad. Call and then we run. It'll take you five minutes."

"They're going to ask questions."

"I'll wait."

Rob had left his cell phone in the bathroom, so he called the Truro police on the land line. A woman who identified herself as a desk sergeant answered. He explained the situation and what little he knew. Like Helen Schantz, the sergeant became concerned that the people had slept on the beach. "That's not allowed," she said.

"No, I think they disappeared," Rob said.

The sergeant didn't say anything. Rob sensed she was writing things down. She asked if Rob knew the missing persons.

"No," he said, a hint of disdain in his voice. She asked for his name, phone number, and address. He gave his cell phone number, then remembered he was on the land line, so he gave her that number, too.

"Will you be at home later today?" she said. "We'll need to ask questions. We may need you to go with us to the beach." The term "we" sounded ominous. Would they send a platoon of officers and detectives in several marked cars, sirens screaming?

"Yes, what time?"

"Not sure. I can call you when we are on the way."

"Who will be coming then?"

"Not sure yet. Probably Detective Hill and an officer."

"Not you?"

"If I came, who would answer the phone?"

"Of course. Listen, is it okay if I go out for an hour or so, or would you rather I stay close to the phone?" Rob looked over at his son who was now glaring at him and mouthing the word, "putz."

"Do you have an answering machine?"

"Yeah, sure," Rob said, looking down to make sure it was still there. He hadn't used the land line in a while. He was thinking of getting rid of it.

"I'll leave a message to let you know when they will arrive. Nothing will happen this morning since the detective is in Barnstable. But will you do me a favor?"

"Sure."

"Please call me if they come back, okay?"

"Oh, yeah, sure will," Rob said, praying this would be the case. "You bet." Rob hung up the phone and shrugged his shoulders. He was now a person of interest where the police were concerned. His name was part of the desk sergeant's log and would figure prominently in the case file. If there was any kind of permanent record for him, this incident would become part of it. If there wasn't, there would be one now, for sure. He was a person who noticed things.

*   *   *

The run turned out to be one of those rare occasions when both his brain and his body didn't mind the effort. Rob's legs, looking gray and lifeless just minutes ago, sprang to life and strode easily, like those of an animal bred to run.

"You're looking good, Dad," Danny said. "How old are you?"

Rob was at a loss to understand the reason for these epic performances. Was it what he had eaten? The amount of sleep he had gotten the night before? The consistency of his morning shit? Or was it his state of mind? Now that he had quit working, and was free from the egoistic, soul-sucking battles for work-place supremacy, it was easier for him to focus on one thing at a time. When he was working, he always seemed to be in a rush to get to whatever came next, meaning that whatever he was doing at the time suffered. He drove too fast, ate too fast, and talked too fast. He became aggravated at work, and sometimes brought the aggravation home with him, where he found himself losing patience with Katie and her irrational behavior. When her phobic behavior worsened, Rob started to wonder if his work-driven behavior had somehow contributed to her condition. So when she announced, one summer, that she would not be returning to Boston with him—there were simply too many people—Rob had his own epiphany. He resolved to quit work, sell their house and live on the Cape year-round, too. They had plenty of money. He would tend to his wife, and he would run with his son.

Rob triumphantly sprinted the last hundred yards. Danny stayed with him, looking much more relaxed than his father, who was breathing harder now, and perhaps leaning a little too far forward. When they got to the house, and Rob's hands dropped down to his knees, Danny decided to keep going.

"Too feeble of a pace, huh?" Rob said.

"No, but I want to run some more."

"Are you allowed to do that?"

"I just approved it," he said, and disappeared up the hill in a burst of speed. The US Track Team had not been thrilled with the idea of Danny training on the Cape, isolated from other elite runners and coaches. Danny's own coach was more of a traveling secretary, mapping out Danny's race schedule, arranging travel and hotels. Danny had devised his own training regimen, one that had served him well so far. In his last race he finished two seconds off the American record for the 10K. He knew what was best for him.

Inside the house, the answering machine was beeping. Rob had a hard time believing it could be the police station. Nothing on the Cape ever happened sooner than expected—time was only a suggestion. But when he hit the play button, there was the voice of the desk sergeant again, informing him that Detective Hill had returned early from Barnstable—again, unheard of—and would come by at 11:00, assuming the missing sunbathers hadn't returned.

"They weren't sunbathers," Rob said, leaning in close to the machine as if the desk sergeant were listening. "They were umbrella people."

Rob found Sidney curled up inside Katie's old closet, which still held much of her clothing. Sidney had a foot fetish where Katie was concerned, and loved being surrounded by her shoes. Rob asked if he wanted to go outside. Sidney raised his head and looked at Rob as if he was out of his mind. At this stage of his life Sidney spent most of the day sleeping. He went outside in the morning and then slept until the cocktail hour. "Fine," Rob said, and headed to the beach.

The collapsed umbrellas and chairs were still there. The fact that they were in the same place wasn't remarkable since the three people had set up in the same spot every day that week. Rob arrived on the beach, and looked in both directions to see if any walkers were in sight, but it was still early. Nobody was on foot, and there were only a few blankets spread at the public beach. There was no one in the water either, but Rob was amused to find a seal perched atop the large rock that jutted out of the water in the hours straddling low tide. So little of the rock was visible at this point that it almost seemed as if the seal was floating on top of the water.

Rob scanned the area around the rock, anxious a fin might pop out of the water.

"Fucker," Rob said, looking for a rock to throw. It was not beyond range of his right arm. But while the shark was free to attack, Rob was not. If he knocked the thing unconscious, the police would have a whole new set of questions to ask him. Rob watched another few minutes. The seal did not move. More of the rock became visible as the tide headed out. The seal now looked like a trophy.

"What the hell happened to you guys?" Rob mumbled as he walked up to the three chairs. He knew from watching too much TV that he probably shouldn't touch anything. It became even more apparent that no one had been here since yesterday afternoon. The chairs and towels were covered by a coat of sand kicked up by yesterday evening's winds. One chair had been blown over altogether. A paperback lay open on top of a clump of damp seaweed. There were no footprints.

When Rob looked up the seal was gone. He had missed seeing it slide back into the water. As more of the rock became visible, he considered the possibility that the tide might also serve up a body, or parts of a body. The water took on a sinister tone. A gull screamed. Something had happened here.

FOUR

Footprints and Helen Schantz

It was eleven-thirty when the car pulled into the driveway. Rob had put off taking a shower because he didn't think there would be time before the scheduled eleven o'clock meeting. *Have you been sweating, sir? Can I ask why?* Rob believed that if he added up all the time he had waited for contractors and vendors to show up at the house it would be more than a full day. One day, of course, he would hop in the shower, and that would be the day when the contractor was on time. *Why are you in a bathrobe, sir?*

Rob looked out the window. A uniformed policeman, who could not have been more than twenty-five, and an older man wearing plain clothes, were coming up the drive. He assumed the older man was the detective. The cop had probably come along to subdue anyone who needed subduing. Rob could see he carried a gun and handcuffs. That's when he panicked, realizing he had not bothered to check the house for anything incriminating. Being detectives, they would be keenly aware of their surroundings. *Is this marijuana, sir? Were you under the influence at the time in question?* Figuring the police wouldn't need to come into the house at all, he went outside and met them in the yard.

"Good morning," Rob said, adding, "I think it's still morning," and immediately wished he hadn't, since it sounded like an indictment of their lateness. The he said, "Welcome," and wondered why anyone who wasn't somehow culpable would welcome the police.

The man whom Rob assumed was the detective introduced himself as Don Hill and quickly added, "It's all Don Hill from here!" The boy police officer rolled his eyes while Don Hill chuckled. "This is Officer Grainger."

Rob thought to shake their hands but stopped himself. This was another peculiar Cape custom—people didn't generally shake hands as a form of greeting, and there wasn't anything that served as a substitute other than nodding and saying, "How are you?" Or as the locals would say, "How ah yah?"

"So where would you like to start?" Rob asked. "Should we go down to the beach?"

"Are you Mr. Crosley?" Don Hill asked.

Rob cringed whenever someone called him Mr. Crosley, which wasn't often. "Yes, of course, sorry," he said and again thought to shake hands. "How are you guys?"

"Just fine, I suppose," Don Hill said. "You've got a beautiful place here. And I'll bet you've got nice views off the back, too. I envy you. I always wanted a place with water views. I could never get tired of looking at the water, or listening to it for that matter. I got an app on my phone that plays the sound of waves breaking on the shore. I sit outside, turn on the app and close my eyes. Feels like I'm at the beach."

This was why no one on the Cape was ever on time. People loved to talk. And they would talk at great lengths about anything, regardless of what they were doing or where they needed to be.

"There was a baseball park in Cincinnati called Crosley Field," Don Hill said. "Named after the owner at the time. The guy who manufactured Crosley cars. The Reds played there for years. Now they play in something called the Great American Ballpark. Sounds a little pompous doesn't it? You related?"

"Don't think so," Rob said. "Never heard of the guy."

"Still, there's something about your name that rings a bell. You getting anything Grainger?"

Grainger looked at him, a pained expression on his face, and said, "No."

"Who else lives here with you, Mr. Crosley? If you don't mind my asking."

Rob considered whether to mention Katie, but thought better of it. Technically, she did not live here with him, and Rob preferred not to mention her in the event Don Hill wanted to talk to her, too. "Just my son, Daniel," he said.

"Daniel Crosley. Danny Crosley?" Don Hill asked. "The runner?"

"Yes, the runner," Rob said becoming mildly annoyed now. How much more of his time would be wasted?

"I read the article in the Gazette about him. Going to the Olympics, right?"

"Not yet. He has to qualify first."

"What's the competition like?"

To Rob's relief, Officer Grainger cleared his throat and said, "We should move on with the investigation, detective."

"Of course. Of course. We're taking up too much of your time, Mr. Crosley. Tell your son good luck for me."

"I will."

Don Hill looked up at the sky and then whirled around, surveying the landscape. "You live here year round?" he asked.

"Yes," Rob said, wondering if Don Hill was going to ask how much he paid for it.

"So you know the area pretty well?"

"I guess so."

"Well, lead on, Mr. Crosley. Let's have a look at the beach."

Rob led the way to the stairs, passing the turkey family in the process. Don Hill said hello to the turkeys, as though they were Crosley pets. Rob felt sure Don Hill would share some anecdote about the turkey population on the Cape, but he didn't. Perhaps the turkeys had become so commonplace they were no longer a subject for digression.

Don Hill stopped at the top of the stairs and admired the view. "Wow," he said. "You can see the whole Cape. You're a lucky man, Mr. Crosley." He smiled and inhaled deeply, almost as if he was taking a hit off a joint. Rob was now sure his bag of pot was in a dresser drawer. "Is that the site in question?" Don Hill said pointing at the three umbrellas."

At last! Rob thought, *a pertinent question*. "Yes, sir," he said.

"And you say it has been there since yesterday?"

"I believe so, yes."

"You're not sure?"

"Well, I collapsed the umbrellas around five last night and they're still down, in the same spot. There's sand all over their stuff, too."

"Why did you collapse the umbrellas?"

"It got real windy. I didn't want them to blow away."

"Which explains the sand."

"Right."

"Let's go, Grainger," Don Hill said, bounding down the steps. Grainger obeyed, leaving Rob to wonder whether he was meant to follow. He stood for a moment, vacillating, when Don Hill yelled, "You, too, Mr. Crosley."

The tide was now all the way out. Rob checked the widened shore for bodies. There were more vacationers at the public beach now, but they were all alive. A biplane flew overhead, hauling a banner that advertised car insurance.

"Get some pictures, Grainger," Don Hill said, "then check the grass along the base of the dunes."

Grainger pulled out his smartphone and started taking pictures. Rob wondered why he wasn't using a more substantial camera. Don Hill walked around the beach chairs then plucked one of the paperbacks out of the sand.

"I don't think I read this one," he said, and dropped it on one of the chairs. "Well, I agree, Mr. Crosley. It doesn't look like anyone has been here since yesterday." Rob felt vindicated, no longer a crackpot who liked to cry wolf. "What time did they go in the water?"

"I'm not sure, maybe around four."

"But you didn't see what happened to them?"

"I took a nap. I was asleep, and when I woke up they were gone."

"What time was that?"

"Around five."

"And then it got windy?"

"It already was."

Don Hill continued to poke around, now checking the contents of two small backpacks and a beach bag that rested against the chairs. "Had you seen them down here before?"

"They've been here every day since Saturday," Rob said. "I think they walked down from the public lot, setting up in the same spot every day."

"You were down here every day, too?"

"Yeah, for a few hours."

"Was anyone else down here who might have seen them?"

Rob paused for a moment, thinking it might be wise to give the impression that this was a tack he had not previously considered himself. "Actually, yes," he said. "A neighbor, Helen Shantz."

"I'd be down here every day, too," Don Hill said. "God, I love the water. We'll need to talk to Ms. Schantz, if you can direct us to her house. We'll also check to see if there's an abandoned car in the lot, though I don't see any keys or wallets here. Two women and a man, right? How old?"

"The women looked to be the same age, maybe in their thirties. The man might have been a bit younger."

"That's an odd mix, don't you think?"

"I guess." Rob shrugged. It didn't sound odd at all.

"Were they in good shape?"

"Sure."

"Did you see them swimming?"

"No, only wading. The tide was coming in but they still had a ways to go before it was deep enough to swim."

"And then you went to sleep?"

"Uh huh. Oh, and I saw a seal."

Don Hill frowned. "You're not supposed to go in the water if you see a seal," he said.

"I know," Rob said, thinking he and Don Hill were establishing a bond now. Then it occurred to him that perhaps Don Hill wanted to ask why he hadn't alerted them to this fact.

"Did you hear them say anything?"

"Yeah, it was still pretty calm at that point. They had a camera and were talking about swimming further."

"Further than what?"

"Further than yesterday? I don't know."

"You think they were trying to take a picture of the seal?"

"Could be, I guess. You think I should have warned them?"

"If you had seen a shark, yes. You didn't see a shark, did you, Mr. Crosley?"

"No, no!" Rob said, too loudly. "I hope I never do."

"Well, even if there was a shark in the area, it wouldn't have cut up three swimmers." Don Hill folded his arms and looked at Rob directly. "You know what I think, Mr. Crosley?"

"What do you think, Detective?" Rob said, relieved the shark theory had been dismissed.

"I think they were out too far, started drifting, thought they could get back to where they could stand, but with the wind coming up and the tide coming in full bore, they couldn't."

"You think they drowned?"

"No. We would have had reports of bodies by now. I think they either got picked up by someone in a boat, or got swept onto shore well down the beach."

"So why didn't they walk back?"

"Probably cold and scared. There are plenty of houses on the beach south of here, which was most likely the direction of the current last night. I'll bet someone saw them come out of the water and brought them inside. Maybe let them warm up for a while, then drove them home."

"So you think they'll be back for their stuff sometime today?"

"Hopefully. If not, then we have a mystery."

Grainger returned from his dune survey with no news of anything unusual. "Should we haul their stuff out of here?" he asked the detective.

"Take the bags," Don Hill said. "We'll need to take a closer look at the contents. You can come back for the umbrellas and chairs." He turned his attention to the stairs. "Who is that?" he said. Helen Schantz had come halfway down and stopped. She was staring at them. Grainger's police uniform was sure to have grabbed her attention. Helen Schantz could see quite well when she wanted to. Rob expected she had quickly concluded that the police were there to take him into custody for some egregious violation of town zoning laws.

"That's Helen Schantz," Rob said.

"Wonderful!" Don Hill said.

"Would you like me to leave?" Rob said, hoping the answer would be yes.

"You don't like Ms. Schantz?"

"Oh, no, she's okay," Rob said, becoming more and more impressed with Don Hill's detective abilities. "I mean, I wasn't sure if you wanted to talk to her alone."

"I don't like any of my neighbors, either," Don Hill said. "You try and be friendly but they're really only interested in having you go away."

Helen Schantz resumed her descent and walked toward them. She had picked up her pace, as though there was something she was anxious to share. Still twenty yards away, she called out, "Is everything alright here?"

"Just fine, Ms. Schantz," Don Hill said, introducing himself and Officer Grainger.

"How do you know my name?" she asked.

"Your neighbor here told us," Don Hill said. Helen Schantz glared at Rob, looking for all the world as though she had never seem him before.

"Hello, Helen," Rob said. "Nice to see you." He lied.

"You must tell me what is going on," she said. "We have never had police on the beach before."

"Oh, policeman love the beach, Ms. Schantz," Don Hill said, trying to make a joke. He quickly saw this was futile. "Though not in uniform, of course."

"You're not in uniform," Helen Schantz said.

Don Hill shrugged. "Did you happen to notice three people sitting under those umbrellas yesterday, Ms. Shantz?" he asked, not wishing to engage her in further attempts at pleasantry.

Helen Schantz peered over at the umbrellas and then looked back at Rob in an accusing way. "What happened to them?" Her eyes did not leave Rob's face, making Rob feel entirely responsible.

"That's what we are trying to figure out, Ms. Shantz. Did you see them yesterday?"

"I have seen them every day this week."

"Do you know who they are?"

"And why would I know who they are? Did my neighbor say that I did?"

"I only said that you were down here yesterday afternoon, Helen," Rob said, wishing it had been Helen Schantz who had disappeared.

"Well, I don't know them."

"Did you see them go swimming?" Don Hill asked.

"Yes," Helen Schantz said looking out at the water. "They went out quite far. I would never go out that far."

"Did you see them come out of the water?"

Helen Schantz continued to stare at the bay. Rob realized this was probably the closest he had ever been to the woman. She was careful to keep her distance, as if Rob carried some form of virulent disease. He noticed now that she seemed younger than he thought she was, and probably more attractive, too, at least when she was made up.

"No," she said. "Did they drown? I wouldn't be surprised. They were out much too far."

"Can you describe them?"

"No, I cannot. I don't wear my prescription lenses on the beach and don't see that well."

Don Hill arched his eyebrows and nodded. "Well, I believe we have everything we need for now," he said. "You sure have a lovely beach here. You don't get much erosion on the bay, do you?"

"Very little," Rob said, eliciting another death stare from Helen Schantz, as though he was divulging a vital secret that might induce Don Hill to move into the neighborhood.

"I might need to ask you folks more questions. In the meantime, please call me if you think of anything else." Don Hill fumbled through his pockets and produced a couple of business cards, which he gave to Rob and Helen Schantz. She quickly deposited the card in her bag, probably incapable of reading it anyway.

"We're not going to have any bodies washing up on the beach here, are we?" she said.

Don Hill pawed at the sand with his foot. "I certainly hope not, Ms. Schantz. But if you see any, please give us a call."

Rob laughed nervously, thinking Don Hill had been making a joke. The detective and officer now stared at him, too, along with Helen Schantz, who hadn't stopped staring at him. "Sorry," Rob said. "Not funny, I guess."

"You've got to have a sense of humor," Don Hill said, and with that, he was off, Officer Grainger in tow. Once again, Rob was not clear on whether he should follow. He wasn't sure he wanted to stay on the beach with Helen Schantz either. Oddly, he was still fixated on what she looked like without the big hat and sunglasses. She continued to stand next to him, watching the policemen climb the stairs. Rob was relieved she was not glaring at him anymore.

She was quiet for a time, perhaps still processing what was happening on her beach, and then said, "I hope there wasn't heroin involved." Rob didn't know what to say to this, so he said nothing. "Have you heard about the heroin epidemic?" she continued, intimating perhaps that Rob might be totally ignorant of the issue.

Rob wondered if this was the correct use of the term. He thought of an epidemic as being the spread of a contagious disease, like the flu.

"I guess it's become a real problem," he said, though he had no idea how it had any bearing on the three swimmers disappearing.

"I should say so. You know I watched this documentary about the heroin calamity on Cape Cod and it seemed to me that everything happened at the donut shops. If the police staked out the donut shops they would catch all of them." Now the epidemic was a calamity, and donuts were somehow to blame. Helen Schantz looked at Rob in a prodding way, as though she expected him to take immediate action.

"So, how do you think heroin is involved here?" Rob asked, not expecting to get a logical response to the question but curious to hear her hypothesis, nonetheless. Helen Schantz looked at a seagull picking at the wet sand. Her expression, what Rob could see of it, softened a bit and she said, "I felt sad when I was watching the heroin documentary. I feel sad now."

FIVE

Cesspools and Canoes

Katie's boat was a single-person ocean scull that she had built herself. She liked to row south to a secluded spot that she called her secret beach, where she could spend the day swimming, reading, and digging for shellfish. There were no people at the secret beach except for the rare long distance beach-walker who wandered by. When she saw someone approaching she went into the water, or pretended to be asleep. A few of them stopped to admire her boat, which from a distance looked like a rowboat, but up close was found to be something different, something sleeker, it's internal workings similar to those of a racing boat.

During the summer months she left early in the morning, before the beach-goers arrived, and returned late in the day after most of them had gone. She rowed out quite a ways, a few hundred yards, and paralleled the shore. Depending on the currents she could row the five miles to the secret beach in an hour. This stretch of beach, protected by the Cape Cod National Seashore, was undeveloped. She could sit on the beach and feel safe there.

She had not been able to grasp why she was so fearful of other people. She had thought that the fall from the second floor of the house she was helping to build, and the death of the man who pulled her off, had something to do with it, but years of therapy prompted no revelation. One of the therapists told her she probably wasn't afraid of people at all. He believed it was more likely that she had an unrelated panic attack at some social occasion, and absent any probable cause, projected the fear onto the people around her. After that, other people became a trigger for further attacks. It was possible, she learned, to have an attack for no reason at all. Still, the mind searched for a cause just the same. Katie wasn't so sure of this reasoning. If she had a panic attack in bed, could a fear of linens ensue? Sitting on the secluded beach and watching the sunlight jump off the water, she wondered what would happen if she had an attack while alone. Then what? She decided it wasn't possible to be afraid of both. If you were afraid of other people you couldn't be afraid of being alone.

Though she reveled in the solitude, she knew that the excursions to the secret beach were a form of flight, and served to further entrench the harmful patterns in her brain. She felt safe here, but felt shame, too. A woman who could build a house, harness the sun, and live off the land should not be victimized by irrational fear. She did not want to be a coward, full of fear and self-loathing. She wanted to find ways to disrupt the harmful patterns. Without medication.

The first time a stressful situation caused her to run was when she was fourteen, and was sent by her parents to a sleep-away camp. The all-girls camp sat on a lake in the western part of Massachusetts. It rained steadily most of the time she was there. The weather made it impossible to see or do much of anything. Katie had not visited the camp beforehand. Her parents had told her that they knew people who had sent their kids to the camp, and said it was spectacular.

On arrival, her counselor, a small girl with a long ponytail and mud-caked shins, led her and other campers to their tents. As they passed the bathrooms, the counselor told them to watch their step. The rain had caused the cesspools to back up, and shit bubbled to the surface, flowing down the hill toward the lake. This elicited several shrieks from the campers. Katie wondered if what she had seen on the counselor's shins was actually shit, not mud, or maybe a mixture of the two. She looked down at the mucky ground. Little rivers of brown water were indeed carving their way downhill. She flared her nostrils trying to determine what she was smelling.

Katie's tent was empty except for her trunk. Her counselor told her that there would only be three girls in the tent. The other two hadn't arrived yet. This was good news, the counselor said, because Katie would have her choice of bunk. "Have fun," the counselor said. "Use your bug spray."

She left and Katie was alone in her tent. There were two bunk beds on either side. The air was dank and smelled of canvas. She tied back one of the flaps, hoping the wind wouldn't blow rain inside. Aside from two small armless chairs, there was no other furniture. Katie settled on one of the lower bunks, shoving her trunk under the bed. She put her pillow under the blanket to keep the dampness off it. She thought about going outside to explore, but it was raining so hard now the drops were ricocheting off the mud. She got out one of the four books she brought with her, and started to read.

Late in the afternoon, just before dinner, two trunks were shoved into her tent by two counselors-in-training, soon to be followed by two giggly, long-legged girls who looked considerably older than Katie. They were, in fact, older, as Katie quickly learned. "We're fifteen," the dark haired girl said. The lighter haired girl put her arm around the dark haired girl and said, "Some people think we're sisters but we're not. Did you think we were sisters?" Katie shrugged. They didn't look anything alike. "Is that a book?" one of them said. "I hate school."

They talked incessantly, but mostly to each other. If they talked to Katie at all, they didn't wait for or particularly care about her response. Walking to dinner that first night, they hurried ahead of Katie, splashing through the shit-filled puddles. The light grew dim now, and as darkness settled into the sodden pines, a sense of distress filled Katie's chest.

At bedtime the older girls, who had taken the two top bunks so they could see each other in the glow of their flashlights, talked about boys. Katie burrowed under her blanket with her flashlight and read, though it was difficult to tune out the conversation overhead. It was also difficult to concentrate on what she was reading, as the anxiety that had gripped her earlier in the day was not letting go. She hoped she might grow tired and fall asleep, but that seemed a remote possibility, too. Her mind was racing, and she could feel her heart pounding in her chest. The rain, which had let up on the way back from dinner, was now battering the campgrounds again.

The older girls began talking about boys they wanted to kiss, and how they would do it. Neither of them had actually kissed a boy before, and they decided to practice on each other. They hopped out of their bunks and, standing right next to Katie, began kissing. As the girls shared notes on technique, Katie worried that she would be pressured to join them. As with everything else though, the girls ignored her, keeping their carnal proclivities to themselves. Eventually their mouths grew tired, and they climbed back into their bunks and fell asleep. Katie remained under her blanket, the flashlight off, staring into the darkness, wishing that time would pass more quickly.

The next few days brought more rain, more discussion of boys, and more kissing practice. The girls had taken to kissing with their eyes open, and would often stare down at Katie while she lay in her bed, trying her best to shut them out. One evening, as they disengaged, one of the girls scowled at Katie and told her that if she said anything to anyone about their kissing she would "kill her." Katie shuddered. She hadn't been threatened by another person before, other than her parents, and certainly not with death. She expected the girl had used the word figuratively, but her mind filled with graphic images of her mangled body lying dead in the muddy-shit grounds of the camp. The girls climbed back into their bunks, and Katie pulled the sodden sheets over her head, struggling with her pounding heart and images of death.

Katie went to her counselor the next day and asked if she could switch tents. The counselor asked why. Katie didn't know how to explain the circumstances of going to bed each night. She didn't say anything about the kissing—she was doing her best to block it from her mind. She mumbled something about the other girls being older. "Well you can learn a lot from the older girls," the counselor said. That was the problem.

When the weather finally cleared the girls were able to go down to the lake. The camp director didn't want them to go in the water yet, though, because the shit from the overflowing cesspools needed time to settle. Instead, they paired off and went out in the canoes. It was Katie's first time in a canoe. She was put in the front, and told her job was to paddle. The girl behind her, who had dark curly hair and a mouthful of metal, would paddle, too, but her primary responsibility was to steer. Katie worried the girl didn't know how to steer, judging by the way she held the paddle. "We'll tell you everything you need to know," one of the counselors said. "Just don't stand up when you're in the canoe. We don't want to lose anybody."

After a brief lesson on getting a canoe to go where you wanted, they pushed off, and were told to head for the island in the middle of the lake. Katie found herself having to look behind on several occasions to see what the curly haired girl was up to, since they were heading on a course away from the island. Katie shouted instructions, and the girl eventually figured out how to rudder the canoe. For the first time since she arrived at the camp, Katie felt in control. Though they were now heading for the island, she would have been happy to stay off-course and find a new destination, far from the camp. Katie easily pulled the paddle through the water, and they ended up being the first canoe to reach the island. The counselors rounded them up and talked more about J strokes and the proper way of entering and exiting a canoe. Afterwards, they were allowed to explore the island on their own. "Do you all know what poison ivy looks like?" a counselor asked, pointing out an example close by. "Watch out for snakes, too," she said.

Katie didn't care about either of these things. She took off, and managed to get clear of the other campers. She found a secluded spot on the side of the island that faced away from the camp, and sat down on a fallen tree trunk. The air was rid of its humidity, and the trees had shaken off their watery coats. The opposite side of the lake was undeveloped—only trees and a thin stretch of sand lined the shore. Katie filled her lungs and slowly expelled the toxins that had accumulated under her ribs. For the first time since she arrived at the camp she felt at ease.

Over the next several days, Katie snuck down to the lake at lunchtime, and took a canoe out to the island. Though she expected she was not allowed to do this, no one told her she couldn't. The counselors didn't keep track of her. Only one of them knew her name, as far as she knew. She wouldn't be missed. She brought food from the care packages her mother sent, and paddled out to the island, where she sat on the far side with her book. One day she paddled around the entire lake.

Eventually someone saw her, and she was hauled in front of the camp director. "Do you not like it here, Katie?" the director asked in an aggressive tone. The dread rushed back in and Katie was nearly driven to tears. "You need to make more of an effort. There are lots of friendly girls here. They come to camp to meet new people, make new friends. That's what you need to be doing. Under no circumstances are you to go canoeing on your own. If you do it again, we will call your parents. Is that clear?"

"Will I have to go home?" Katie asked, seeing an opportunity.

"Starting today the paddles are going to be locked up. You're not going anywhere."

The next day, Katie broke into the shed where the paddles were stored, and took out the canoe. The day after that her parents came and took her home.

SIX

Pilgrims and Bounties

The next morning Rob was awakened not by the digital squawking of his cell phone, but by sweat. A warm front from the south had brought high humidity along with it. Generally, Cape evenings were cool. Bathing suit weather became sweatshirt weather, and sleeping was comfortable. This was becoming less the case as the planet heated up. At one time, Rob had thought the hotter weather was an anomaly, but after five or six years of enduring frequent bouts of sweat in his sheets, he wasn't so sure any longer. He had thought of air conditioning as being for people in Florida. Maybe Cape Cod now, too.

"It's going to be hot today," Danny said when Rob came into the kitchen, Sidney weaving behind him.

"It already is," Rob said, pouring a cup of coffee. He had remembered to set the machine the night before. Danny didn't drink coffee and never made the stuff. "Let's go, Sidney." He opened the door onto the deck and walked outside with the dog. The turkeys were in the driveway, pecking at the seashells around the car. Rob considered grabbing the hose and opening fire again, but given his frustration from the heat, and not having drank the coffee yet, he ran at them, emitting a low-pitched scream. The turkeys responded by flapping onto and over the car, one of them emptying its runny bird bowels all over the windshield.

"Son of a bitch," Rob said. Sidney had followed, curious to learn what the fuss was about. He snooped around the car and decided to relieve himself as well. Rob ended up with the hose after all, rinsing the bird shit off his car.

As he recoiled the hose, he heard a whirring noise overhead that grew in intensity. He looked up and spotted a helicopter making its way up the coast line from the south. Someone had gone missing, he thought, his mind still struggling to come to terms with the start of another day. And then he realized he knew exactly who was missing. So it was official, he thought. The umbrella people had not returned after all.

Danny came outside with a pair of binoculars and got a closer look. "Coast Guard," he said. "There are a bunch of boats out there, too."

"I wonder if they got any other reports," Rob said, uncomfortable with the responsibility for such a vast commitment of resources.

"What, yours isn't good enough?"

"Well, they don't know who the hell I am," Rob said. "I could have planted all that shit on the beach and made the whole thing up."

"The Schantz woman saw them too, though." Danny was now watching his father through the binoculars. "You spilled coffee on your shorts," he said.

The stain, another consequential damage of the turkey attack, was nearly as dark as the coffee. Rob redeployed the hose, and turned it on himself.

"You want me to get you a towel?" Danny said.

After he was done spraying himself, Rob hung his shorts on the line and took down the bathing suit that had been drying from the day before. During the exchange, he enjoyed a few brief moments of outdoor nudity. The feeling of sun and wind on his groin was surprisingly enjoyable, and he waited to pull on the suit, until some insect bit him on the ass. He slapped at it, awkwardly spanking himself, and then worried that Helen Schantz, the only neighbor with a view of his yard, might be watching. She would surely call the police if she spied him with his pants off. He rubbed his ass and pulled on his bathing suit.

After breakfast Rob decided to have a closer look at the search and rescue effort. Coming down the steps, he became curious about a small group of people huddled around something that the incoming tide had pushed up on shore. There were no signs of panic or distress, so he assumed they weren't inspecting human remains. Probably just a dead fish.

The humidity hung over the bay, blurring the coastline. Rob could still see the helicopter, however, now circling over Provincetown. There was also a group of boats trolling close to shore. One of them had Coast Guard markings. The rest were probably volunteers. It was now more than thirty-six hours since the umbrella people had gone into the water. If they hadn't come out, he wondered, could they still be alive? Were the boats looking for swimmers or bodies? Rob grappled with thoughts of whether the circumstances might be different if he had called the police that evening, rather than the following morning. He couldn't be sure they would. Don Hill hadn't seemed bothered by the timing. Police didn't usually become concerned about missing people until twenty-four hours after a disappearance, right?

On the beach, he walked toward the group of people gathered on the wet sand. From a distance, he caught site of what they were looking at but couldn't determine what it was. The shape of the thing didn't take on any recognizable form. One end was tapered, but the profile on the other end was much harsher, as though there was a piece missing. This turned out to be the case. What they were looking at was the upper half of a seal. The rest of the animal had been shorn away.

The mood of the group was somber. They looked down at the remains as if they were watching a casket being lowered into the ground. Rob glanced at the spot where the rock sat in the water but it was entirely engulfed at this point. Could this be the trophy seal from yesterday? It seemed likely, he thought.

"Probably a shark," a man said, assuming Rob was naive. "Looks like they already got boats out looking for the monster."

Monster? Rob scanned the water for bobbing body parts. He remembered what Don Hill had said, that a shark wouldn't carve up three swimmers.

"We called the police," a woman said, wagging her cell phone. She and the rest of the group were looking at Rob now, hoping he might add something useful. A group of sea gulls circled overhead, sensing the opportunity below.

"Better a seal than one of us," Rob said. He could have added that the boats weren't looking for a shark, but he didn't want to take the conversation in that direction. He expected they would run back to their rental homes that evening and hunt for *Jaws* on the cable.

"I guess they'll close the beaches," the monster man said. "And on the hottest day of the summer!"

"How long since you called the police?" Rob asked.

"Maybe a half an hour," the woman who had called said. Had they really been staring at the seal head for half an hour? Rob supposed they wanted to be here when the police arrived so they could each give their account of the gruesome discovery. People loved cooperating with the police when it was clear they were nothing more than a witness.

An SUV appeared further down the beach, having entered from the parking lot. The car stopped, and out came Officer Grainger. A woman emerged from the passenger side. She carried a suitcase and a camera. Apparently dead seals warranted professional photography equipment, where missing humans got smartphones.

The woman headed straight for the seal, set down the suitcase, and started snapping pictures. The onlookers, who had probably already taken hundreds of their own pictures and videos, pulled out their phones and began to chronicle this latest development.

"Thanks for alerting us," Grainger said to the group. "Now why don't you folks go about your business and let us take care of this. There's nothing more to see here." He smiled, giving the impression that this was the first time he had been able to use this line.

"Was it a shark?" The monster man asked.

"We won't know for sure until after the examination is completed," Grainger said.

"Are the boats out there looking for the shark?"

"Go on home now," Grainger said. "Thank you again."

After a few more close-ups of the seal and the woman, who was now putting on a pair of rubber gloves, the group went their separate ways. Rob remained.

"Hello, Officer Grainger," he said.

"Mr. Crosley? I didn't see you there."

"So, I guess the swimmers never turned up?"

"Right," Grainger said.

"Did you find out who they are?"

"Not yet. There were no ID's in their things, no car keys or phones. Weird. All we can do is hope someone reports them missing."

"You think the shark that did this might have gotten them?"

Grainger shrugged his shoulders. "Doesn't seem likely. Maybe a shark bites one of them in the leg but he still gets to shore, especially with two other people there."

The woman pulled a large plastic bag from the suitcase. Grainger went over and held the bag, while she lifted the seal head and placed it inside. Grainger hauled the bag back to the car. The woman closed the suitcase and followed. Why did she need a suitcase for a plastic bag and some gloves? Must be other essential marine forensic equipment in there, Rob figured.

The seagulls dispersed as well, and Rob was left alone. The helicopter swung past again, a little further from shore this time. Feeling the need to participate in the search effort, he decided to take a walk. Perhaps he might find a bathing suit or something. He wondered how he would react if he came across a severed limb. Would he vomit or pass out? He felt sure he would do one of these if a head was involved. The helicopters would see him lying in the surf and assume he was one of the missing. They would land and revive him and stuff the severed head into a plastic bag.

Rob walked for half an hour and saw nothing more than rocks and seaweed. At one point, a man on one of the search boats took a look at him through a pair of binoculars, trying to decide if he was someone who needed rescuing. Rob waved and gave a thumbs up sign. He couldn't remember ever giving a thumbs up sign to anyone before. He thought it must have seemed idiotic to the man in the boat. People waved to boaters all the time, but who ever gave them a thumbs up sign?

A single fisherman was on the shore casting a line into the water. Rob had once thought fishing might become one of his retirement hobbies. There was plenty of gear involved, and as long as you were surfcasting, you didn't have to do much advance planning. On the negative side, people always stopped to ask if you had caught anything. Not wanting to be one of those people, Rob waved to the fisherman and said hello.

"They're biting pretty good today," the man volunteered, not waiting to be asked. He appeared to be older than Rob, and had a crusty, provincial look about him. Still, it was hard to tell if he was a local or a summer visitor. His clothes were plain but neat. There was nothing on his tee shirt or baseball cap that lent any clues. He hadn't shaved in a day or two.

"What have you caught?" Rob asked resignedly.

"Striped bass mostly."

"That's great," Rob said. He had no idea if it was great.

"The seals must have taken the day off," the man said, throwing his line into the water.

Rob nodded. "I hear they can eat up to forty pounds a day."

"Can you imagine eating forty pounds of anything a day when you're a hundred pounds to begin with?"

Rob told the man about the seal head and guessed that this was the reason the fish were more plentiful.

"Too bad sharks can't eat forty seals a day," the man said. We need more sharks. They're the only ones allowed to kill seals right now."

"You think that will change?"

"No. We've gotten too soft. Pretty soon we won't be allowed to kill cattle or chickens either. We'll all be a bunch of vegans." The man pulled in his line and checked his lure—*or was it bait?* —before throwing it back out again. Rob thought about asking what type of lure it was, but knew he would get a cryptic response. "Why it's a blue dilly-boo jigger" or something like that, leaving him to fumble for an appropriate follow-up.

"You know," the man said, "My dad used to kill seals, back when they had bounties. Dollar a nose. I remember him bringing the noses back from the hunts. They'd take them into town and get their money. Never had a problem with seals and sharks back then. My friends and I would hang out by the trash, and when the clerk dumped the noses we'd grab them and turn them in again. Made a lot of money."

Rob imagined someone carving the nose off the washed up seal head, maybe the woman in the rubber gloves. He winced. Clearly, he was one of the soft ones.

"Who do you think they're looking for out there?" the man asked, gesturing toward the search boats.

"How do you know they're looking for someone?"

"Four boats and a helicopter, that's all they could be doing. Wouldn't commit that many resources for anything less."

Have you ever seen this before?" Rob asked, sure that the man would say yes.

"Sure. They'll never find them, though," the man said. "Dorothy Bradford got them."

"Who?"

"Dorothy Bradford. Or her ghost, I should say." The man chuckled. "You haven't heard this one, I guess?"

"Uh, no," Rob said. The Cape was full of stories about apparitions and floating objects. There were guest houses, ghost ships, and graveyards rife with paranormal activity.

"You know about William Bradford, right?"

"The pilgrim?"

"Came over on the Mayflower. Governor of Plymouth Colony. His wife was Dorothy. She came with him."

"Wait, I know this," Rob said. "She drowned, right?"

"That's it. The Pilgrims landed out here first and anchored in Provincetown Harbor. They explored the outer Cape to see if this was where they wanted to set up camp. William went out on the expeditions. While he was away Dorothy fell off the ship and drowned. It was supposedly an accident, but some people think she did herself in. She's haunted the bay ever since. Anyone goes in the water and doesn't come out, it's because of her."

"I see," Rob said. "Where does she take them?"

"Who knows? People have claimed to see her. There's even a Dorothy Bradford Society. You ever heard of Maggie Mason?"

"Nope."

"She heads it up. Used to be a psychiatrist. Lives up in Provincetown. Collects troubled women and teaches them the ways of Dorothy Bradford."

"What ways?"

The man shrugged. "How to survive, I guess."

"But she didn't survive."

"Maggie Mason thinks she did."

Rob wasn't sure about his next question but he asked anyway, sensing the man wasn't completely taken in. "You haven't seen Dorothy Bradford, have you?"

"Hah! No," he said. "Not yet anyway. Probably shit myself. Not a fan of ghosts."

This reminded Rob of the turkey shitting his car. He was close to telling the fisherman about it—he felt somehow that this was a person he could share things with—but decided it was probably a little too innocuous, up against puritanical ghosts and butchered seals.

"Name's Tim, by the way," the man said. "You can find me out here most days."

Rob introduced himself, no last name, and he didn't shake hands. "You like fishing?"

"Been doing it all my life. Become a habit, I guess."

"Well, I hope your luck continues."

"Thanks. Keep an eye out for Dorothy Bradford. She's sure to be close by."

Rob said that he would, and headed for home. He liked Tim the fisherman but thought it was strange when he said you could find him out there most days. Rob walked this stretch of beach at least twice a week, and couldn't remember seeing him before. Or perhaps he had, but wasn't paying attention. The beach had become thick with drama.

SEVEN

Hobbies and Journalists

Rob received a call that afternoon from Steve Ridgeback. Ridgeback was the journalist who had written the piece about Danny for the Cape Cod Gazette. The article received a great deal of attention, touting Danny's unique abilities and his potential to become a medal winner in the ten thousand meters at next year's Olympics. Other papers and news channels, both on and off the Cape, picked up on the piece, and ran stories about Danny's training runs along the back roads of the outer Cape. "We've got plenty of writers, artists and shrinks out here," one columnist wrote. "How cool would it be to have an Olympic Gold medalist?" Danny paid no attention to the articles, but Rob enjoyed reading them aloud while he and Sidney ate breakfast. As quickly as the notoriety swelled, however, it ebbed just as quickly. There was still a year until the Olympics, and news cycles, like most places, tended to be short on the Cape. So Rob was pleased to hear from Steve Ridgeback again, at first thinking he was calling to do a follow-up piece on Danny.

"No human interest story this time," Steve Ridgeback said. "I was hoping to talk to you about the swimmers who disappeared."

"Oh, right," Rob said. "How did you hear? I didn't think it was out there yet."

"Of course not! It's not out there until I write about it."

Rob told Ridgeback he could stop by that afternoon though he confessed there wasn't much he could tell him. "I assume you heard about it from Don Hill?" Rob said, wondering for a moment whether Helen Schantz had alerted the media.

"Of course!" Ridgeback said. He was fond of saying "of course" or "of course not" usually in a big voice, as though he were astounded by the inanity of the question. "We help each other out all the time."

When Ridgeback arrived, Rob was on the deck reading surfcasting articles on his laptop. Ridgeback shouted hello, and Rob told him to let himself in. Ridgeback had been to the house a couple of times before and knew his way around.

"Do you fish, Steve?" he asked as Ridgeback sat down.

"I've done it," he said, "but it's not a hobby."

"I'm looking for a hobby. Fishing seems like a good one. Do you have any hobbies?"

"I look for stories."

"That's your job."

"Of course! But it's what I enjoy."

"Nothing else?"

Steve Ridgeback narrowed his eyes and thought for a moment. "Did you offer me something to drink?

"Tell me your hobby and I will," Rob said.

"Body surfing."

"I'm not sure that's a hobby."

"Golf then."

"That takes a lot of time, doesn't it?"

"Only if you stink," Ridgeback said, taking out his notebook.

"You're going to take notes about my hobbies?"

"You don't have any, apparently."

"I didn't say that. I just need a new one."

"Why don't you get a job?"

"I'm retired, remember? I'm done with that part of my life."

"What do you like doing now?"

Rob considered this. There were plenty of things he "did," but did he like them? "I run. I cook. I watch World War Two movies."

"World War Two movies?"

"My son pointed out to me a while ago that I only watch movies with Nazis in them. You know, *Schindler's List, Marathon Man*, stuff like that."

"Why?"

"I don't know. Good versus evil, I guess. It's hard to watch or read anything anymore that doesn't have Nazis."

Ridgeback jotted something down in his notebook. "Interesting hypothesis," he said.

"See, I just gave you an idea for another story," Rob said. "Our culture's infatuation with fascists."

"Iced tea," Ridgeback said.

Rob went into the kitchen, and came back with an iced tea for his guest and a beer for himself. It was never too early to drink on Cape Cod. Some people did it all day, and not just those on vacation.

"So tell me what happened," Ridgeback said.

"About the swimmers?"

"Of course!"

Rob recounted the events of the afternoon, now two days ago. Somehow the day seemed planted further back in time. Details were already becoming hazy. Had the swimmers actually talked about going for a swim, or just wading around for a while? How soon before they went in the water had he seen the seal? Was he even sure he saw a seal? Could it have been a bird? Still, he gave a confident account of the incident. All of Ridgeback's questions Rob had already asked himself, or he had heard from Don Hill. There was one exception. Toward the end of the interview Ridgeback asked Rob what he thought of them.

"The swimmers?"

"Of course!"

"I never talked to them."

"I understand, but you must have formed some kind of impression. You said you saw them every day this week, in the same spot. Were they loud? Were they talkative?"

"They were quiet and kept to themselves. I walked right by them once and none of them looked up."

"They were reading."

"They had books but they weren't reading."

"What else?"

"I didn't care for them."

"Because they were intrusive?"

"I guess. They set up their chairs and umbrellas the same way every day, and sat in the same order. I got the impression they were there for some other reason."

"Like what?"

"No idea. But if one of them started sweeping the beach with a metal detector it wouldn't have seemed odd."

Ridgeback nodded and closed his notebook. He smiled at Rob in a way that suggested he had already figured out what had happened to the umbrella people. Rob squirmed. Did Ridgeback know something he didn't? Had he come to the interview with the story already written, just needing a few quotes from Rob to round out the narrative? Ridgeback got up and thanked Rob for the iced tea.

"So, when do you run the story?" Rob asked.

"Tomorrow. Hill is getting the media on board, hoping to generate a response from someone who knew them. You'll probably see some TV cameras. Reporters on the beach."

"You think they'll want to talk to me?"

"Entirely possible. I did."

"Right." Rob's brow tightened. He had not considered the possibility that this could become a media event.

"How's your wife doing?" Ridgeback asked.

Rob almost said, "Katie?" but stopped himself in anticipation of getting belted with another "Of course!" Instead, he said, "She's fine."

"Still living across the street?"

Rob didn't answer. He didn't want Ridgeback poking around where Katie was concerned.

"I never got the whole story from Danny on his mom. You'll have to tell me one day." Rob was certain he wouldn't, no longer sure of Ridgeback's intentions. He seemed to be a person whose chief interest in life was finding stories, or perhaps even generating them. And when he golfed, he probably only did so with people who might be good for a lead or two.

Rob watched Ridgeback leave to make sure he didn't wander across the street. "He's a reporter, not a friend," Danny had reminded him more than once. Rob had told Ridgeback that he and Katie were separated. "We're working through some issues," he said during one visit, after which Danny told his father to shut up. His mother was none of the reporter's business. Could it be that Rob was looking for someone whom he could talk to about his wife's condition? Katie had encouraged him to see someone. "This can't be easy for you either," she said. But Rob didn't want to pay someone to listen to his problems. "It hasn't worked for you. All they do is prescribe drugs anyway. You're hardly the best advocate for the psychiatric profession." Katie said that just because therapy hadn't helped her didn't mean it wouldn't be good for him. "I'd much rather internalize," he said. "Besides, these doctors don't really care about you. You pay them for conversation. They're whores."

What he really wanted to do was talk to his wife, but he knew that several minutes of venting his frustrations would only serve to make him more terrifying than he already was.

"It makes no sense," he said, too loudly, the night Katie ran from the bedroom. "I'm your husband. I love you. How could you think I would hurt you?" Katie was too frightened to cry. Fear was the much stronger emotion. She could offer no explanation. She needed to get out.

He did go to a therapist once, but only to learn more about his wife's condition. "Think of it this way," the doctor said, "If you step into the street and turn to see a speeding bus bearing down on you, your brain screams, 'RUN!' That's what happens to your wife sometimes when she sees another person or persons. It makes no sense; it's totally irrational. It's an important survival function of the brain, but in Katie's case it is triggered at the wrong time." Rob asked why, and the doctor shrugged his shoulders. "Some say it's behavioral, some says it's genetic. Probably a combination of the two. It is curable, though."

But drugs and therapy hadn't worked for Katie. The side effects of the dosages she needed were too severe, and she couldn't even get through the door to see her doctor, much less meet with a group of other panicky people.

"So what do we do now?" Rob asked her the day after she pitched a tent in the empty lot across the road. "Don't give up on me!" was all she said, fighting back tears. Rob would not.

* * *

Rob did not sleep well that night. The heat and humidity persisted, and he had dreams of waking up in the morning to find an array of news vans and dish antennas surging into his yard. Once or twice he got up to look outside, thinking he heard tires on the shell driveway. Lying awake in bed, a certain foreboding hung over him, a heaviness in the air that spread into his limbs. He kicked off the sheets and massaged his thighs trying to relieve the restlessness in his legs. It was not unlike the feeling he had when he was still working, and a client made unreasonable demands, threatening to yank his business if Rob couldn't meet them. His head spun with so many disjointed strategies that it soon became clear the only solution was to walk away. Quit. Go lie on the beach and look after your wife. Travel around the world with your son and watch him run ten thousand meters faster than any other human. And so he did, and life loosened its shackles. Now they were tightening again.

*   *   *

The next morning was peaceful, and the air was cooler. Danny had gone on his training run. Sidney was more alert than usual, smiling and panting on the deck while Rob ate breakfast. The Gazette did not have an online version of its paper, so after breakfast he drove into town to pick up a copy at the store. As he headed off, he came across a man combing the bushes along the driveway for blackberries. There were a number of wild blackberry bushes that grew in the area, a number of which were on Rob's property. People would occasionally wander off the street to help themselves. Though Rob seldom picked the berries himself he was outraged that certain people felt entitled to trespass and effectively steal from him. How was this any different from someone walking into the house and helping themselves to whatever was lying around? Rob pulled alongside the man and said, "Can I help you?" sarcastically. The man wore headphones and was eating the berries as he picked them. He looked at Rob and smiled. "Just grabbing some lunch," he said. Rob informed the man he was on private property and asked him to pick his berries on the street. The man flashed a peace sign and moved on. What the hell did that mean? Rob wondered. Did the peace sign make it okay? "How about an apology, asshole?" Rob muttered, considering what the ramifications would be if he ran over a trespasser on his property.

The store in town was nothing more than a glorified convenience store. It stocked most essentials, but the prices were extravagant since it was the only place within five miles to get any groceries. Rob only went in there to buy local papers like the Gazette, which was published twice a week. Most of the news was sorted onto separate pages, one for each town. Major stories got front page coverage. That is where Rob found the story on the missing swimmers.

He sat on one of the benches in front of the store, and instead of reading the story from the beginning, scanned through it, looking for his name. He hoped he wouldn't find it until the story wandered deeper into the paper, but there it was on page one, second paragraph. Ridgeback referred to Rob as a local resident who lived on the beach. A voice in Rob's head told him not to read any further, to stuff the paper in the trash and continue life in the comfort of his ignorance. He pictured Ridgeback from the day before, sitting opposite him, a smug smile on his face. Rob read on.

"Mr. Crosley waited until the following morning to call the police," Ridgeback wrote, and further on, *"He saw a seal in the water but did not warn the swimmers about the possibility of sharks."*

Rob slung the paper to the ground, nearly hitting a woman in the leg. "Are you serious?!" he bellowed. The woman quickened her pace and widened her berth. Rob could only glare down at the paper, unsure what to do with his rage. "That dick!" he yelled. Aware now that he was on the verge of creating a scene, he snapped up the paper and got in his car. He read the entire article, which also included news of the seal head—undoubtedly the result of a shark attack according to Ridgeback—then fumbled for his cell phone. Steve Ridgeback's number was in there. He pressed the call button.

"Hello, Rob," Ridgeback said, sounding too much at ease.

"What is this?" Rob said, yelling into the phone.

"What is what?"

"This hatchet job, bullshit story of yours!"

"Sorry you feel that way, Rob. Just doing my job. This isn't a feel-good story."

"And it's not my fault! You're saying it is! I didn't call *until* the following morning? I didn't warn them about sharks?"

"Did I misquote you somewhere?"

"I guess I was wrong about you."

"Anything else?"

"Yeah! Guess who doesn't get an interview when Danny comes home with a gold medal next summer."

Ridgeback let out an amused laugh in response, leaving Rob unsure of whether he and his son were being mocked. He wanted to slam down the phone, but cell phones weren't built for this, so he slung it at the passenger door. "Shit," he said, his anger giving way to panic. He snatched the phone off the floor and inspected the screen, opening and closing a few apps. The phone had survived.

Rob sat in his car and watched people go in and out of the store. How many of them would read the article about the swimmers, wondering what kind of an asshole would wait until the next morning to call the police? He gripped the steering wheel with both hands, and rested his head between them. News cycles tended to be short on the Cape. Was it Ridgeback who had told him this? Perhaps no one would care. The swimmers would turn up sooner or later, one way or the other. If they were sliced up by a shark, then the story shifted to the shark. If they had gotten kidnapped, then it became about the kidnappers. And if they wandered off on their own, then it became a story about their irresponsibility. Rob *had* called, after all. He could have said nothing. Who would judge him that harshly?

He drove home, his mood improving, until he saw the news van parked in front of the house. It was almost as he imagined it in his dream from the night before, except there was just one van. "Oh, joy," Rob said.

He didn't pull into the driveway. Instead, he kept going past the house and turned onto the dirt road that led to the cottage. He wasn't sure what he would do next. Even if Katie was home, which was likely, he wouldn't be able to stay there long. If he had to, he could drive up to Provincetown and hang out at a bar. He had resolved never to talk to the media again.

He and the car were now shielded by the scrub pines that fronted the road. He would not be seen by whoever was in the van. Rob called Katie on his cell phone, still working despite the abuse he had inflicted earlier. She picked up.

"Can I come in for a little?" he asked.

"There's a news van parked in front of the house. Is it about that?

Rob went inside and found Katie sitting at the kitchen table wearing a blindfold.

"What are you doing?" he asked.

"Trying something new."

"Blindness?"

"It's a technique I read about. If you can't see what triggers the fear, assuming it's something visible, then maybe you don't get as scared."

"But you know I'm here. You can hear me. I could try anything and you won't see it coming. That doesn't make you more uncomfortable?"

"I guess we'll see. So far so good. Tell me what's going on. Does it have to do with Danny?"

"No, me," Rob said. He watched several small fluttery things stuff themselves on seed in the bird feeder outside the window. He had thought to look on-line and find out what these winged things were, but bird watching seemed a bit too geriatric, as far as hobbies were concerned. He shifted his attention to Katie and told her the story of the missing swimmers. Katie said nothing and Rob began to worry that the anxiety was getting the better of her. He was at a disadvantage not being able to see her eyes—they were a sure gauge of her level of discomfort. Still, the rest of her seemed relaxed. No tensing of the shoulders or quickening of the respiration. Her voice remained calm.

As he began to tell her about Steve Ridgeback's visit Katie said, "Three swimmers? Was it on Monday?"

"What's today?"

"Thursday."

"Jesus has it been that long? Yes, Monday."

Katie cocked her head to one side. "I think I saw them."

"Two women and a man?"

"Yeah. I was rowing back from the secret beach and nearly ran into them. They were pretty far out. The wind was coming up. I asked if they were okay, not sure what I would do if they said they weren't. They said they were fine, but it looked like they were swimming toward me. I got scared and started rowing faster."

"Did you see where they went?"

"They kept going. It was a long way from our beach. Maybe it wasn't them?"

"Were there any seals around?"

"I didn't see a seal," she said. Rob told her about the seal head that had washed up the day before. "You think it was a shark?"

"Probably. Something chomped it." One of the birds flew into the window, making a dull thud. It had not been going fast enough to stun itself or break its neck, and flew off unharmed.

"So the police came by, and then the newspaper guy?" Katie asked. She sensed what was coming. Rob told her about the story and how he had been vilified in the Gazette.

"You think I should have called that evening?" he said. "I really thought they had swum down the beach and were walking back or something. It's the bay for God's sake. People don't get swept away. And the tide was coming in. I never should have trusted Ridgeback. Danny didn't trust him." Katie took a deep breath and smiled. Rob rarely saw her smile anymore. He rarely saw her at all anymore. He was both annoyed and thrilled. "What are you smiling about?"

"I think this blindfold thing is working," she said. They had been talking for nearly twenty minutes. It was the longest they had been together since Katie moved into the cottage.

"Maybe I should borrow it when I go back outside," Rob said. "Or put a bag over my head."

"You didn't do anything wrong, Rob."

"Yeah, but people are going to think I did."

"I saw the umbrellas and chairs when I got back, too. I thought the renters from next door had gone back to the house before the weather turned, and hadn't gotten around to going back for their stuff."

"I wish I'd said that."

"I wonder if I should talk to the police."

"No! Are you nuts?"

"Do I look like I'm nuts?" she said, holding her hands up to her masked face.

"Funny. Why is it you're having a breakthrough on the day I'm being crucified?" Rob got up from his chair, and walked slowly to the couch, sitting down next to her. He took her hand and held it in his. He had forgotten the scent of her, the smallness of her hands. "This okay?" he asked. She nodded. Was she breathing? "Let's forget the police, Kay. Okay? You can't tell them anything they don't already know. And they'll want to come meet with you. Then the press will try to get to you and make the story about your condition."

"I didn't really get a good look at them."

"All you can do is say there were two women and a man. They know that."

"They were coming at me." Katie let go of Rob's hand. "It felt like they were stalking me."

"But you feel like that about everyone," Rob said. Katie didn't respond. From what he could see of her expression, perhaps the comment had been a little too harsh. "Sorry," he said. "That was a shitty thing to say." He got up and went to the window at the front of the cottage, thinking he might be able to see if the van was still parked across the road, but the foliage was too thick. "So what should I do, Kay?" he asked.

"About what?"

"The story. Should I write a letter to the editor?"

"No," Katie said. "You're not the story here. Don't fall into their trap."

Rob stepped in front of the screen door. "It's been three days. How could they not have found them yet?" He opened the door and said, "I'm going to go take a closer look at that van."

"Don't talk to them, Rob," Katie said. "Don't let them film you either."

"I know." He started out the door but stopped and stuck his head back inside the cottage. "Hey, I'm really happy the blindfold thing worked. You're okay?"

"I think so," she said, nodding her head.

The van was still parked across the street. Rob got behind a tree and watched. After a minute, he realized there was no one in the front seat. Were they in the back performing electronic surveillance? That made no sense. If they were waiting for him, they would be up front where they could see him coming. Rob expected they had left the van and walked up to the house, taking up a position outside the front door. Could they do that? Was it legal? The station name—a local Boston network—was printed on the side of the van. Rob figured Ridgeback had tipped them off, in exchange for a lead on some other poor, unsuspecting schmuck whom he could defame. How soon before the other trucks arrived?

He snuck up to the van and looked inside the window. He could see to the back as well. No one was there. A copy of the Gazette lay on the front seat. Rob's name was highlighted in yellow, with his address written in the margin. "Assholes," he said. He decided to walk up the access road which bounded his property and led to the neighboring houses, Helen Schantz's not among them. If he walked up her access road, she would be outside waiting for him.

"I'm spying on my own house," Rob mumbled to himself, crouching down behind a bush. He was now twenty yards from the deck, and could see into the yard. Standing in front of the retaining wall that ran along the front of the property was a cameraman. He appeared to be filming the house. Rob moved further up the road and now saw a clean looking man in a suit, standing outside the front door. He was speaking into a microphone while looking into the camera lens. The turkeys were there, too, off to the side, trespassers all. Rob fumbled for his cell phone and snapped a few pictures of the news crew, hoping he would have the chance to use them as evidence in court.

When they had finished the report, none of which Rob could hear, they sat down on the retaining wall. The cameraman wasted some film on the turkeys, surely not news. From where Rob was positioned, he could see up to Helen Schantz's deck, and sure enough, there she was, up at the rail peering down at the intruders. She had her phone in her hand, but was not speaking into it. Rob assumed she was getting ready to call the police. It was the one time he was glad of her prying nature. But Rob didn't need Helen to call. He could do it himself. He found the police department's web site on his phone, and was ready to enter the number when Danny started yelling.

"What do you think you're doing?" Danny said forcefully, having returned from his run to find the news team camped in the yard. The cameraman swung the camera around toward the runner, and the newsman raced over with his microphone. Danny put his hand over the camera lens. "No way," he said. "No video. Get off my property."

"It's the son," the cameraman said to the newsman. "The runner."

"I'm not sure this is *your* property," the newsman said. "Can we speak to your father?"

"No. You can leave is what you can do," Danny said.

"Is he home? We'd like to talk to him about the swimmers who disappeared."

"Not happening. Leave."

"Dude, can you take your hand off my camera?" the cameraman said, pulling it away. Danny sprinted away, disappearing inside the house before the cameraman could return the camera to filming position.

"Calling the police now!" Danny yelled from inside.

"C'mon, let's go back down to the street," the newsman said to his partner. "Crosley's gotta show up sooner or later."

Rob watched the newsmen make their way back down the driveway. The turkeys followed. Rob checked on Helen Schantz. She too had retreated, perhaps satisfied that Danny—did she know who he was?—had things under control. Calm having been restored, Rob headed back to the house. He rarely walked into the yard from this direction, and, as a result, missed the poison ivy that now brushed against his bare ankle. He might as well have stuck his foot in a bear trap. He raced over to the hose and doused everything below the knee, using its most powerful setting. Danny came outside and found his father watering his foot.

"Did the turkeys shit on you this time?" he said.

"I stepped in some goddamn poison ivy."

"Where were you?"

"With your Mom. I left the car down there and walked up the road next door to see what was going on. I didn't want them to see me."

"So, the media is onto you."

"I have Ridgeback to thank for that. I left the paper in the cottage. That bastard screwed me."

"Ridgeback? What did you expect? The guy blows everything out of proportion." Though the newsman had written glowingly of Danny, many of his accomplishments had been embellished. Danny did not appreciate being proclaimed a shoo-in for the Olympic team by anyone, much less a local writer who had never written about track in his life.

"He said I didn't call the cops right away."

"You didn't."

"Don't be a shit," Rob said, his foot having disappeared in a small pond of hose water. "Your mom's wearing a blindfold now, by the way. Seems to help. I was with her for nearly half an hour."

"I know. She told me about it this morning."

"She wasn't wearing it?"

"No," Danny said. "You should stop with the hose, Dad. You're going to flood the basement."

Rob stepped out of the puddle, moved to drier ground and resumed spraying his ankle. "Go see if they've left."

Danny walked to the side of house. The truck was still there. He returned, shaking his head.

"So what do we do?" Rob asked.

"Just ignore them. They'll go away. I'm turning off the water now. Go wash your leg with soap."

"It's already starting to itch," Rob said.

"You're being ridiculous."

Rob walked to the side of the house and turned on the outdoor shower. He intended to only wash the leg, but in the end, stripped off his clothes and covered himself with soap. The water was soothing, and he thought he might stay in the shower for the rest of the day, or until the hot water ran out. By then, the mystery of the swimmers would be solved and the ordeal would be over.

When the hot water started to fade, he turned off the shower and went over to the line to grab a towel, first checking to make sure Helen Schantz hadn't come back out on her deck. As he unpinned the towel, the cameraman emerged from behind a tree, his camera shouldered and recording.

"Shit. Really?" Rob said, quickly covering himself.

"Mr. Crosley!" The newsman called, close behind the cameraman, "May we talk to you?"

Rob froze for an instant, wondering if he should confront them about their tactics and the fact that they now had film of him with his pants off. The two men continued toward him, walking faster now, in that frenetic way journalists move when bait is dangled in front of them. In fact, Rob did want to talk to them, to set the record straight, to send them on their way. If he ran off and avoided them, then certainly he must be hiding something. But run off is what he did, hurrying into the house and slamming the door behind him.

Inside, he went to the window. The newsmen had stopped their pursuit and were now conferring in the yard, probably devising a way to coax him out of the house, Rob thought. He then remembered he had left his cell phone in the pocket of his shorts, which were hanging by the outdoor shower enclosure. Would they rifle through his clothes, find the phone, and search for clues in his contacts and web browser? He tried to remember the last thing he pulled up on his phone's browser. Probably something about seals.

The newsmen headed back to the van where they continued their vigil. A few seconds of nudity was not going to be enough to satisfy their editors. They needed audio.

EIGHT

Snow Cones and Hydrocortisone

That afternoon Rob snuck out of the house and went down to the beach. The news team was still planted at the foot of the driveway, but from there, they couldn't see the path to the stairs. Rob planned to stay on the beach until five o'clock, by which time he hoped the van would be gone. How much time could a network waste on a guy whose only crime was picking up the phone?

Another atypical crowd had assembled on the public beach. Rob wondered if a second seal carcass had washed up. Instead, the crowd's attention was focused on yet another news team, this time a woman and a cameraman filming a segment from the waterfront. And then there were the boats. The Coast Guard patrols had now been joined by a flotilla of amateur detectives and thrill-seekers, paddling, sailing, and motoring up and down the shore, hunting sharks, lost swimmers, and any clues that might be floating in the seaweed. It was the first time Rob could remember when there were more people in the water than there were on the beach.

Rob sat down in his chair and examined his ankle. He was sure it was beginning to itch. Soon a rash would form, and the skin would begin to bubble up in furious welts. The ankle would swell and leak, and he would need to visit the doctor for antibiotics and steroid treatment. He buried his foot in the sand to keep from poking at it, then decided to go stick it in the water. He waded in with no hesitation—it was not a Jesus! Day, at least as far as the water temperature was concerned, but the hoard of watercraft cluttering the bay might have justified an expansion of the definition. There were so many people on the water that he wondered if somebody had posted a reward. A group of three teen-aged girls on paddle boards drifted by. "Oh my God!" one of them shrieked, pointing in the water, "What is that?" Her friends screamed, too, but quickly stopped when they saw it was just another piece of seaweed. Their attention shifted toward shore. They were looking at Rob now.

Do they recognize me? Rob wondered. There was no picture of him in the paper. Had the news channel already posted his outdoor shower scene on the internet? The girls started waving. Did he know them? He thought about waving back, and then realized there was someone behind him. He turned around and found the news team hovering—the clean reporter and his not so clean cameraman.

"Mr. Crosley, is this where you saw the swimmers go into the water?" the reporter asked, shoving the microphone in his face. The guy had actually waded into the water—in his shoes. The cameraman, he of the scraggly beard and greasy ponytail, was recording the inquisition. Rob could see a red light glowing on the camera. The three girls had paddled to shore and were now bouncing around behind him, in view of the camera.

"Are we on TV?" one of the girls squealed, striking what she hoped would be an alluring pose.

Rob snarled at the newsman and shook his head.

"Is that a no?" the newsman asked. "Where then? Were they looking for the seal? Did you warn them not to go in the water?"

Rob turned away from the newsman and waded further into the bay. Maybe one of the boats would pick him up and take him away. The other film crew had taken notice of the competition, and were now hustling down the beach to make sure they didn't miss any important developments. The beachgoers followed close behind, determined to add to their digital vacation memories. Rob was still wearing his sunglasses, but went ahead and submerged himself anyway. He planned to stay underwater for as long as his lungs would allow. He wished the seal would swim by and create a distraction. It would have to be a new seal though. The old one had been cut up by a shark.

He figured he had been underwater for a minute, maybe long enough to instill some panic, make them worry that he, too, had now vanished. When he emerged, gasping for air, he was greeted by a resolute mob of people on the shore, each pointing a cell phone or news camera at him. One or two women had their hands over their mouths, as if they were witnessing some unspeakable calamity. A family of five were eating snow cones. The bright red and green colors of the frozen sugar stood out against the sandy backdrop. Rob wondered where they had gotten them. There were no concessions at the public beach. Maybe that had changed now that the beach was in the news. He turned around, wanting to swim further out, but there were three kayaks and two motor boats hemming him in. He was trapped.

Both of the news reporters were talking into the cameras while pointing at Rob. Someone in the crowd asked loudly, "Who is he?"

"He's the guy who didn't call the police!" someone answered.

"Oh, come on!" Rob yelled, slapping at the water. Everyone looked up from their devices, not sure the man in the water hadn't just been clipped by a shark. Rob decided that if he spoke to them, they might leave him alone and go hunt entertainment somewhere else. Maybe life could return to normal.

"He's coming out!" someone shouted. "Are you getting this?"

Rob came out of the water, and walked to his chair to towel off. The crowd followed him.

"Okay," Rob said, looking at the reporters. "Here's the deal." Both microphones were in his face now. The crowd huddled together, straining to get a clear line of sight. Two of the kids from the snow cone family were right next to the reporters, furiously licking their slush before it splashed into the sand. He had thought to make a statement, but stopped. Perhaps it would be smarter to answer their questions. "Fire away," he said.

"Is this where you saw the swimmers go into the water?" the male reporter asked.

"Yes."

"Do you live here?" the female reporter asked. Rob wasn't going to answer this question. The other team had tracked him down. She could, too, if it was important to her.

"And you saw a seal?" the male continued.

"I did, but it was well before the people went in the water."

"How much before?"

"Maybe half an hour."

"And you didn't see what happened to them?"

"No, I fell asleep."

"And when you woke up they were gone?"

"They hadn't returned. Or maybe they had returned and went for a walk. That's what I thought anyway."

"But you waited until the next morning to call the police?"

"I didn't think anything was wrong until then." Someone in the crowd hissed at this, general murmuring ensued. Here is where they lynch me, Rob thought.

"Do you think they were eaten by a shark?" the female reporter asked.

"I have no idea," Rob said.

"Did you see the half eaten seal that washed up yesterday?"

"Yes."

"That was a shark, wasn't it?"

"I don't know, was it?" More murmuring.

"Did you know them?

"Who?"

"The swimmers."

"No. I would have told the police if I did. Their names and pictures would already be out there."

"But you had seen them before?"

"Once or twice."

"Had you ever talked to them?"

Rob thought of the time he had tried. "No," he said.

"What do you think happened to them?"

Rob paused, losing patience with the reporters' idiotic line of questioning. All the same, he pretended to give the question careful thought. The crowd leaned in. With a hint of drama, he cleared his throat and said, "Dorothy Bradford got them."

This created a stir. "Who?" the male reporter asked. He looked at the female reporter, who shook her head. But Rob was done. Let them google her. He was going to sit in his chair and watch the search parties.

"Who is Dorothy Bradford?" the female reporter asked as he sat down.

"It's an old wives' tale," someone in the crowd said. And just like that, everyone shifted the attention to this other person and continued the inquisition there. Rob was left alone.

* * *

That evening Rob and Danny sat in front of the TV and watched the local news. Each of the network affiliates carried the story of the swimmers, who had now been missing for three days. Rob was featured in two of the reports. To his relief, both of the stories only referred to him as the guy who called the police, not the guy who *waited* to call the police. There was also mention of the maimed seal that washed up, and the general assumption that a shark was involved. The only consequential audio that was used in the segments was Rob's opinion of what had happened to the swimmers. In serious tones, the reporters explained who Dorothy Bradford was and the local legend associated with her. They left the viewers to form their own opinions. They also spoke with Don Hill, who encouraged anyone with information about the missing swimmers to call as soon as possible. When asked about the Bradford story Hill said, "Dorothy Bradford died four hundred years ago. Let's keep our eye on the ball here."

Danny looked at his father and shook his head. "Where did that come from? Did you make that up?" he asked.

Rob was busy with a large tube of hydrocortisone cream, slathering the stuff on his ankle. "A fisherman told me that."

"You were fishing?"

"No. Since when do I fish? I ran into him on the beach yesterday. He seemed to know a lot about her."

"You know, I think you like the attention," Danny said.

"Listen, they're off my back."

"Don't you think it's weird that they still don't know who they are? Wouldn't you think their families would have called?"

"People like to be left alone when they go on vacation. Nobody calls."

"I think you're putting too much of that stuff on," Danny said. "What does it say on the tube?"

"It says apply liberally," Rob said. "Leave me alone. I know what I'm doing." Rob's cell phone rang. He thought it might be

Katie but it was another local number, one he recognized. "Shit, it's the police again."

"They probably want to question you about the death of Dorothy Bradford."

Rob answered the phone. Don Hill was on the other end.

"I hope I'm not calling in the middle of dinner," Don Hill said.

"Actually we were just watching the news," Rob said.

"Listen, would you be able to come down to the station?"

"Now?"

"If it's not too much trouble."

"What's it about?"

"Someone found a waterproof camera. A nice one. Washed up on shore. We're pretty sure it belonged to the swimmers. We need you to look at the pictures. Shouldn't take long. You know where we are?"

* * *

Rob hated going anywhere after five o'clock that didn't involve eating or drinking. No one should have to be responsible for anything after five o'clock. When he retired, people told him that he could now be irresponsible all day. But this sounded too much like dereliction to him, and he was not going to be a derelict. Not yet anyway.

The police station was only a few miles up Route Six toward Provincetown. The traffic that strangled the two-lane thoroughfare during the day eased as the sun went down. People were back in their rental homes by now, mixing cocktails and tending sunburns. Pulling onto Route Six, Rob wondered what was in the pictures that Don Hill wanted him to see. He figured there would be shots of the swimmers in the water, and that he would be asked to confirm that they were the people he had seen on the beach. Maybe there were shots of the now slaughtered seal, too, bounding through the waves. "Was this the seal you saw, sir?"

The irritation he felt when he left the house gave way to a sense of civic pride as he parked in front of the station. He was not just another visitor looking for some sort of registration form or other, but someone with vital information that might lead to an important case being solved. He was someone who should be given special courtesies, or at least a reserved parking space. There were plenty of parking spaces, though. No one else was there.

The desk sergeant who greeted Rob was the woman who had taken his call three days before. She told him to have a seat, but Rob was not interested in taking a seat. He had no interest in waiting at all. And why should he wait, when there was no one else there? He wanted to get on with it, before the cocktail hour ran out, so he could go home and fix a drink and feed his dog crackers. He remained standing instead, and suffered the desk sergeant's glares.

"He's on the phone, Mr. Crosley," she said with a huff. "As soon as he gets off you can go back."

"I see," Rob said, still not willing to sit down. He folded his arms and wandered over to look at the bulletin board. There was a posting of the hunting schedule for the upcoming season. In particular, Rob took note of open season for turkeys, which began on October twenty-fourth. There were also important safety tips listed, the stated purpose of which was "to prevent tragedy during open season." The first such tip advised residents and visitors not to go into the woods. One should choose activities around town instead.

"He's ready for you now, Mr. Crosley," the desk sergeant said. She motioned behind her and said, "You can go into the conference room through that door there."

In the conference room—a bleak affair with no pictures or windows—Rob was greeted by Don Hill and Officer Grainger. Both seemed a little distracted. Rob imagined that being a cop on the outer Cape must be pretty easy during the off-season, whereas during the summer, when the population increased ten-fold, the force had to adjust to the demands many big-city cops faced. He knew they were paid well, though. The tax base, thanks to all the high-priced summer homes, was substantial.

"Thanks for coming in on short notice, Mr. Crosley," Don Hill said. "We appreciate your cooperation. This is the first break we've had." He opened a folder that contained several enlarged photographs. "Before we take a look at the photos though, I have one more favor to ask."

"Sure," Rob said, not so certain he was. Grainger's stern expression seemed to indicate that some sort of admonishment was coming.

"I have to ask," Don Hill went on, "that you please not spread idle rumors about these people." He paused to make sure Rob understood what he was referring to. "I know you thought you were having fun with the press, but there are a lot of people out there who will believe anything they hear."

Feeling an immediate sense of guilt, Rob apologized. "The questions were just so stupid," he said. "Strange things come out of your mouth when someone sticks a camera in your face."

"No more Dorothy Bradford?"

"No. Definitely not."

"Not that I don't like Pilgrims. I'm something of a history buff, myself. Did you know the Pilgrims weren't supposed to settle in Massachusetts? They were supposed to go to Virginia." Don Hill sat down and motioned for Rob to do the same. Officer Grainger, relieved that the detective had not continued with the history lesson, remained standing—a cautious observer.

"So where did you find the camera?" Rob asked, hoping to ease the tension in the room.

"A woman picked it up on the beach this afternoon. Called right away." Rob winced when Don Hill said "right away." Was this another dig? He felt his stock slipping. "Pretty expensive camera," Don Hill added. "Waterproof. I guess people use them to take pictures of fish and coral reefs. No coral around here, of course. Plenty of shipwrecks, though. They'd be great for that. The camera washed up almost a mile south from your place."

"Wow," Rob said idiotically. He fumbled for something insightful to say, but could think of nothing so he fell back on the relative safety of asking more questions. "Who was the woman?" Somehow Helen Schantz had come to mind.

"Local. Writer. Told me about her new book. Something to do with dogs. She brought her own dog right into the station. Never been a dog person. Had a hard time shaking her."

Don Hill spread out three pictures on the table, each showing two women in the water. Their faces were not immediately visible in the first two, but the third showed the women mugging for the camera as they tread water. They were both smiling and pointing toward something out of the frame. They had beautiful skin.

"Were these the women you saw on the beach?" Don Hill asked. Rob remembered the women performing Tai Chi. In the picture they were only visible from the chest up, and their hair was matted down by the saltwater. Still, he remembered that one of the women wore a bright orange bathing suit, and he could definitely make out the same color suit on the woman on the right.

"Yes," Rob said, mentioning the bathing suit. "What are they pointing at?"

"Hang on a second," Don Hill said, pulling out another photo. "How about these two?"

Rob looked at the picture. Initially stunned, he looked again wondering if perhaps he had misinterpreted what he saw. The picture was of one of the women pulling the other woman out of the water. She could have been dead or unconscious. There were no visible signs of trauma.

"I guess so," Rob said, swallowing hard. "I can't see their faces. Is that woman dead?"

"Can't tell," Don Hill said. "This was the last picture taken. We wish there had been one or two more. The date and time stamps match the timeframe you described." Don Hill paused, then collected the photos and placed them back in the folder. "Maybe she was just exhausted from swimming back to shore."

Rob's palms were sweating. Did they suspect him? He fumbled for something to say. All he could think of was not to go into the woods during hunting season.

"We have one more picture we're hoping you can help us with, Mr. Crosley," Don Hill said. Rob worried it would be of him. Had they taken his picture with the water-proof camera? "Maybe this is who the women were pointing at. Can't tell, really. But they took a whole series of this person." Don Hill laid the photo in front of Rob. "Any idea who this is?"

The picture was of a woman in a row boat. The woman was Katie.

NINE

Panic Attacks and Porta Potties

Even before her first full-blown panic attack, Katie had never been comfortable in crowds, and tended to avoid them when there was a choice. She hadn't said anything about the discomfort to anyone, even to Rob, and so far had been able to mask her symptoms. And since the anxiety tended to get stirred up in public places, there was usually a restroom nearby where she could hide until her discomfort subsided—a couple of minutes usually, not long enough for anyone to ask if she was okay when she returned. So, before the day she went to see Danny run in the high school state championship, she didn't have a phobia; she simply didn't like crowds. Lots of people didn't like crowds, the same way lots of people didn't like turbulence on an airplane, or getting into a crowded elevator. She didn't dwell on her discomfort. She managed the circumstances and then moved on.

Danny was in his junior year, and had won every race he had run that season, usually by a wide margin. He already owned the outdoor state record for two miles. That he would win the state title was a foregone conclusion. What drew the large crowds to the event was to see whether he would break the American record.

"How big a crowd are they expecting?" Katie asked Rob as they drove to the stadium. The championships were being held at a state college in the suburbs west of Boston.

"The stadium has a few thousand seats," Rob said. "Danny's coach said there might be some news crews there, too."

"Oh," Katie said, pressing her bunched up hands into her stomach. She was already starting to feel anxious. She had been to most of Danny's races, but there were typically less than a hundred people at any of them.

"He said he feels good today. I think he's going to do it."

"Yes. Me, too. What's the record?"

"Eight twenty-nine something. I've got it written down."

Katie looked out the window and watched the trees fly by. The landscape seemed particularly grim and forbidding. She wanted to be excited for the race, but was unable to escape the feeling of being trapped. Her stomach tightened, her shoulders tensed. Thoughts of jumping out of the car reared up. Terrified she would act on them, she shoved her right arm under the shoulder harness, restraining any movement toward the door handle.

The stadium parking lot had the frenzied atmosphere of a pre-game tailgate party. People were eating and drinking out of the backs of their SUV's. Some kids tossed around a football, which was caught about as often as it bounced off of car roofs. There were even a few cheerleaders from participating high schools. Katie and Rob were familiar to most of the Boston area track families, as well as the scouts who frequented Danny's races. As the parents of a star athlete, they were famous by association. On their way from the car to the stadium, Katie did her best to greet the well-wishers, but most of her energy was spent battling her nerves. The throng of people and the aluminum bleachers in the distance loomed ominously. She couldn't understand why she felt so on edge, so isolated and closed in. She reached over and took Rob's arm but somehow that only made matters worse. She needed to remain untethered.

Katie hoped she could lure Rob to the upper tier of seats, away from the crowd, but there were so many people even the back rows were full. Every step was painful as they made their way up the steps from the track level. Katie insisted on sitting in an aisle seat as close to the stadium entrance as possible.

"You okay?" Rob asked. Katie closed her eyes. The symptoms of her anxiety were leaking out.

"Just nervous about the race, I guess," she said.

"He's a lock, Kay. Even if he trips and falls he'll have plenty of time to get up and chase down the field."

Katie lasted fifteen minutes before the weight of the crowd became too much to bear. She had not been so terrified in her life. Her heart was pounding and she was having trouble focusing on the track. All she could see was a sea of assassins waiting for her to show her face so they could pick her off. She leaned into the aisle, knowing that once she got up to leave she wouldn't come back.

"I've got to go," Katie said to no one in particular. Rob was talking to another track father sitting next to him, and didn't hear her. She got up and headed down the stairs.

"Where you going?" Rob said.

"Bathroom," Katie said. "Be back."

"Hurry," Rob said. "Danny's race is coming up."

She couldn't bear the thought of missing Danny's race. Her son was about to run the biggest race of his life, and she was running away to go hide in a porta potty. There was a line of green boxes at the open end of the stadium, and though there may have been facilities closer, she headed for the temporary johns because few people were around them. She got there quickly, and the anxiety drained away, only to be replaced by feelings of shame and confusion. She stepped inside one of the johns and locked the door. The shit and urine floating in the plastic bowels of the porta potty made it hard for her to take deep breaths, the one thing she found helpful when she was anxious. She stared down at the soupy feces, stewing in the heat, and thought of the percolating shit at camp, running down the hill to the lake. It had been easy to run away then—there was nothing she wanted to stay for. "What the hell is wrong with me?" she said. It seemed like there was someone else inside her—some invasive being that was wreaking havoc with her innards, poking at the fear-inducing parts of her brain. Her cell phone rang. It was Rob.

"Hurry up," he said. "They just announced the two-mile. Danny is on the track getting ready." Katie opened the door and peeked outside.

"I'm coming," she said. There was open field between the porta potties and a chain link fence that bounded the track. There were a couple of people hugging the fence, watching the races from there. Katie locked her eyes on the ground in front of her and headed for the fence. She put her hands on either side of her eyes to block out the site of the crowd in the bleachers on either side. She found Danny and kept her eyes only on him.

"Are you there?" Rob said, still on the phone.

"I'm down at the fence. Can you see me?" she said. "I'm going to watch from here."

"What?" Rob said.

"There are too many people up there."

"Did somebody say something to you? One of those recruiters?"

"No, nothing like that. It's okay."

"They're lining up. The race is starting."

"I see him. I've got a great view."

The gun sounded and the runners set out on the first of eight laps. Katie was at the first turn, and by the time they zipped past her Danny had already taken the lead. When they came around again, Danny had opened a ten yard gap on the second place runner. Katie was ten yards away herself at this point, and could see the calmness in her son's expression, no hint of strain or exertion. For the next seven minutes she forgot about her inner turmoil and watched Danny fly by six more times. By the last turn he was a half lap ahead of the nearest runner, and had started to kick, in an effort to break the record. Katie could not see the race clock from where she stood but knew he was on pace, judging by the growing roars from the crowd. People clapped and shouted, "Run!" He crossed the line and was mobbed by his teammates and other people on the infield grass. Several photographers crowded around. Katie had not remembered falling to her knees, but there she was, kneeling in the grass, watching through the chain link. Her phone, which was still in her hand, started to vibrate. Rob had sent a text. Danny had broken the American record by a half second. In a second text he said, "I'm heading down to see Danny. Come meet us!" She could no longer see her son. The finish line had turned into a mob scene. She typed in a reply. "Tell him how proud I am." Then, "See if you can get a ride home, okay?"

Katie ran to the car, got in and drove. She needed a reset. If she could have a few hours to herself, away from the crowds, she felt she would be alright. Walden Pond was not far, but she knew there would be plenty of people there, too. She drove to the sculpture park instead, parked the car and walked into the woods on the east side of the neighboring pond.

Her phone vibrated several more times as Rob tried to reach her. "The crowds really put me off," she wrote back. "I'm sorry I left you guys." She told him where she was, and that she would be home later. He didn't need to worry. She received messages from friends, too, offering their congratulations on the race. Would there be some kind of celebration? She left those unanswered, though, and eventually turned off her phone.

She found a secluded spot by the pond and sat down on a rock. The thing inside her, whatever it was, was at bay now. But for how long? Would it rear up every time she was in a crowd? Could she go to the movies, or the theater again? The grocery store? And what about Danny's races? He was sure to draw more attention now, and larger crowds, too. Katie closed her eyes and tried to quiet her thoughts. She pictured herself paddling a canoe across the pond, then back again. The water was calm, and the bow of the canoe cut cleanly through the water, making no noise. Maybe she could buy a canoe and find places where she could put it in the water. Or, maybe she could build one herself. She would not be defeated by this. She opened her eyes and stood up, resolving to jump back into the middle of a crowd as soon as possible.

She got back in the car with the intention of stopping at Walden Pond first—to test herself—and then going back to the stadium. But as she entered the pond's parking lot, choked with cars, the fear started to rise within her again. "God damn it," she said, gripping the steering wheel so tightly her fingers hurt. In a moment of panic, she somehow managed to turn on the windshield wipers. Then she honked the horn. People in the lot turned to look at her, wondering what the problem was. Had someone snatched her parking space? The panic was even more intense than it had been at the stadium. She was trapped again, only this time she was behind the wheel of a car. "No!" she yelled and made for the exit. She had to get out as quickly as possible, but somehow couldn't manage to get the car to go more than five miles an hour. She inched along, while cars behind her became impatient and honked at her now. She turned onto Walden Street and then Route Two, headed west, now managing the speed limit, but no faster.

She drove with the thought that she might never turn around. The further she got, the better she felt. When she reached Greenfield, Route Two ended, and she found herself merging onto Route 91 North, heading toward Vermont. Not wanting to leave the state, she exited onto Route 10 and headed east. She found a road that dead-ended at the Connecticut River. There was a small, empty parking lot there, where she left the car and walked down to the river. She brought her phone, which she had now remembered to turn on. There were a slew of calls and texts from Rob. "Where are you, Kay? We're getting worried! Call!" She would call him back, but not yet. She walked along the river, headed south, away from Vermont, or was it New Hampshire now? She walked for an hour, maybe two. She wasn't sure. Time was no longer her enemy. There were open fields beyond the trees on either side of the river, with no roads or people anywhere. She was safe here. Her mind cleared and she contemplated the ramifications of the days' events. Rob and Danny would need to be told something. What would she tell them? What excuse could she make? She would have to tell them the truth, of course. It was a panic attack, she'd say, induced by the crowd. Rob would look for a reason, some rational explanation. Did you sleep okay last night? Did you not eat breakfast? And, why did she drive to Greenfield? Why didn't she go home? It had nothing to do with Greenfield, though, she just needed to find someplace where there weren't so many people. Where there weren't any people. It was a fluke, Rob would say, a one-time thing. You'll be fine tomorrow. She hoped so, but sensed that anything that could cause such a violent reaction would not lay down so easily.

Katie came to an inlet that was too deep to cross. Her shoes had been beaten up by the hike. They weren't intended for this kind of thing. She took them off and waded into the water, wishing again that she had a boat. There was nowhere to go now but back to the car. Back to her newly compromised life.

TEN

Fartleks and Blue Priuses

That morning, Danny ran earlier than usual. He wanted to get back to the cottage before the police came by to question his mother. His father had told them there was no way around it. Rob had tried to persuade Don Hill to interview Katie over the phone, but Hill said no—she was too important a witness. He would have to meet with her, though he did agree to come to the cottage, as opposed to dragging her into the station. Rob also convinced him to wait until the next morning. Don Hill was ready to go over there that night, but, having explained her condition, Rob said there was no way she would talk to him after dark. Katie believed that she could get through the questioning so long as Rob and Danny were there with her, and so long as she could wear the blindfold. She also asked that Don Hill come alone. It was beginning to sound like a hostage negotiation.

Danny thought about none of this while he was running. His thoughts were entirely on his stride and the cadence of his breathing. He was running intervals, or fartleks as the Swedish liked to call them. After a five-mile warm-up, he began running four-minute miles, interspersed with two minutes of easy jogging.

The sun had not yet cleared the treetops, and the light on the road remained dim. Danny was flying along Old County Road churning out quarter-miles every sixty seconds. He ran on the left side of the road, so he could see the traffic coming toward him. When he ran at race pace, his speed approached that of a slow moving car. Oncoming drivers were sometimes startled at how quickly he approached them. It was far from ordinary to see someone running at a rate of fifteen miles per hour on the street. He might have been mistaken for a cyclist riding on the wrong side of the road. By the time the driver saw him it was almost too late to react. For this reason, Danny had to stay vigilant when running on the street. His coaches preferred that he run on a track, but Danny didn't enjoy running in circles, unless it was a race.

Three miles from home, as he was finishing up his last speed interval, a Prius came quickly around a turn just ahead. It wasn't clear whether the driver, an older man, hadn't seen him or was too challenged to be able to turn the steering wheel any further. Or perhaps he just didn't care. In any event, Danny darted off the road to avoid the car. With his first wayward step his foot found a tree root, and he vaulted head first into the brush. He skidded to a stop, his arms and legs collecting scrapes and burns from the sticks and pine needles. He lay flat on his stomach, breathing heavily both from the intensity of the intervals and the near calamity with the Prius. He looked behind him to see if the car had stopped, but the driver continued on his way, apparently oblivious to having nearly killed someone. Danny sat up and took inventory of the damage. Most of it appeared to be cosmetic—no open wounds, no punctures. He popped back up, figuring he could go straight to a cool down, running a slow three miles back to the house. But as he put weight on his right leg, a sharp pain shot through the inside of his right knee. "No," he said, like he was speaking to a misbehaving child. He massaged the area, then flexed the knee and put weight on it again. He took a few steps, then jogged easily. The pain did not go away.

* * *

Katie sat on the couch, her eyes covered by the blindfold. Rob was next to her. Across from them sat Don Hill. Officer Grainger remained outside in the squad car. Rob didn't understand why the two of them travelled everywhere together. There was none of the chatty cop-drama repartee between them. They didn't seem particularly close. He supposed it was department protocol. Or maybe Don Hill didn't drive.

Katie clasped her hands in her lap. Rob knew she was uncomfortable, but that was to be expected. She had decided to go ahead with the questioning despite Danny's absence. If she waited, the anxiety would start to build to intolerable levels.

"It's not like him to be late," Rob said. "I'm sure he'll be along shortly."

"Well, I'm going to try and make this as brief as possible, Mrs. Crosley, though I've never really been accused of being brief." Don Hill smiled, but didn't get the response he was looking for. Given the blindfold, it was hard for him to gauge what sort of emotion the woman was betraying. "I played poker once with a guy who wore sunglasses. I could never tell whether he was bluffing. Lost a hundred dollars that night."

"The quicker the better," Rob said, now wishing Officer Grainger was here to keep Hill between the white lines.

"Your husband explained your condition to me last night, but would you mind telling me?" Don Hill said. He had a notepad. Rob couldn't remember seeing him with a notepad before.

"Is he carrying a gun?" Katie whispered to Rob. Don Hill wore a polo shirt and khakis. Pretty much what he had worn every time Rob had seen him. There was no sign of any firearms.

"No, I don't think so."

"What's that?" Don Hill asked, leaning forward. "I didn't hear."

"You don't have a gun on you, do you?" Rob asked.

"No, no. I don't carry a gun. I'm only a detective. The last thing they want me doing is shooting a gun. I ask questions and look for clues. That's about it."

"I have a panic disorder, Mr. Hill," Katie said. "It's triggered by other people."

"You're afraid of other people?" Don Hill said. "Some kind of phobia?"

"Right," Katie said.

"And that includes your family? You're afraid of everyone?"

"Yes. Not so much with my son, though." She reached over and grabbed Rob's hand—a form of consolation.

"Sorry to hear that," Don Hill said. "I'm sure it's tough. Are you on any medications for it?"

"I was. Not now. They didn't help."

Don Hill next asked Katie to describe the events of the Monday before. She told him about her trip to the secret beach, how long she was there, and what she saw on the way there and back.

"How often do you go to this beach of yours?" Don Hill asked.

"Three or four times a week."

"Did you go on Wednesday?"

"No. Too many boats out there." Don Hill asked her to be as specific as possible about her encounter with the swimmers. He showed her the pictures. She lifted her blindfold just enough to get a look at them. "That's them," she said.

"Why do you think they took your picture, Mrs. Crosley?"

"I have no idea. I never saw them before."

"Did you notice that they were taking your picture?"

"No. I didn't see a camera."

"And after you passed them, they continued swimming in the opposite direction?"

"Yes."

"And you were able to see them since you were facing that way in your rowboat, right?"

"Yes."

"How long after they passed by were you able to see them?"

"Couple of minutes."

"Two, three?"

Katie took a deep breath then got up from the couch. She pulled up her blindfold and headed to the kitchen. Rob knew this meant she was losing her grip. The front door opened and Danny came in. His thighs and forearms were covered in scrapes. The right leg of his shorts were ripped.

"Sorry I'm late," he said. "Mom, you okay?" He went over to where she was standing in the kitchen, something Rob wasn't able to do. He put his arm around her, something else Rob couldn't do, and spoke to her quietly.

"Is she alright?" Don Hill asked.

"We may be done," Rob said.

"Yes," Danny said. "You guys need to leave."

"What happened to you, Danny?" Rob asked. "Did you fall?"

"I'll be right out, Dad. You guys really need to leave." Rob got up and motioned for Don Hill to follow.

"I have more questions," Don Hill said.

"Come on, Inspector. You'll get another opportunity, but not today."

They went outside. Officer Grainger greeted them rather urgently. "Just got a call from the station, Inspector," he said. "Someone saw the pictures we posted and called in about the missing women. Said she knows them."

"There we go," Don Hill said. "Local?"

"Yes."

"Maybe now we'll get some answers." Don Hill opened the door to the patrol car, then paused before getting in. "Mr. Crosley, have you ever known your wife to get angry when she has one of her panic attacks? Does she lash out?"

Rob thought this was a particularly stupid question. "Of course not," he said. "She doesn't attack people, she runs away from them."

"I see. Makes sense. Please thank your wife for me. And tell her I apologize for making her feel uncomfortable. I can ask the rest of the questions over the phone." With that he got in the car. Grainger hopped in and they left.

Rob reached down to scratch his ankle, wondering why it was now okay for Don Hill to talk to Katie on the phone, when it wasn't initially. The skin on his ankle was beginning to bubble up. Despite the liberal use of hydrocortisone cream, the itching was now approaching the violent stage. The only real relief came from pounding the ankle with scalding hot water, which replaced the itching with an unimaginable ecstasy. But the bigger relief at the moment was having learned that the missing swimmers could now be identified, shifting the media attention away from him.

Danny came out of the cottage, moving slowly. He was limping.

"Jesus, Danny, why are you limping?" Rob said.

"I had to jump out of the way of a car. Tripped over something and crash-landed. Listen, I need to have my knee checked. I may have strained something." Danny reached down and massaged his knee.

"I'm sure it's just a sprain or something," Rob said, immediately going to a place of denial. He had done the same thing when Katie began to complain about her increasing anxiety in public places. He couldn't accept that anything bad ever happened to his wife or son— that they would ever be in distress. "It doesn't hurt, does it?"

"A little. It still works, though. Hopefully, it's nothing serious."

"Did the person stop?"

"No. I walked for a bit, then someone gave me a ride."

"Son of a bitch!" Rob said, wanting to exact vengeance. "Did you get a look at the guy? Maybe we can find him."

"Forget about it, Dad. He didn't hit me. Let's focus on the knee, okay?"

"Right, of course. I'll drive you. Where do we go? Hyannis Hospital?"

"There's an orthopedic guy in Chatham who works with the team. I'll call him. I need to get some ice from the house, too."

"You stay here and sit. I'll get your stuff and the ice, and be back with the car. Mom okay?"

"She's fine. She went into her room and closed the door. That cop was a little too aggressive with the questions."

"Yeah. I think that was intentional. I think he wanted her to have an attack."

"Why?"

"To see how she behaved. See if she became violent."

"You're kidding? What does he think, that she clubbed the swimmers over the head with an oar?"

"I don't know. Hopefully he's done with us. Get off that leg." Rob watched his son sit down on the front step of the cottage. The act of bending the knee was clearly painful. This was the first time his son had ever suffered any type of injury. "Don't worry. This isn't going to screw up the Olympics," he said. "You'll be fine."

"Plenty of time to recover," Danny said.

* * *

Rob was back on Route Six, driving south towards Orleans. Danny was in the back, making calls, his leg stretched out on the seat, his knee wrapped in ice. Danny first called his coach to let him know about the accident, and was promptly subjected to a tirade for running on the street. Danny thanked the coach for his concern, and told him he would call after seeing the doctor.

"I'm getting a new coach," Danny said, "That guy bugs the hell out of me."

"Didn't show the appropriate level of concern?" Rob said.

"No concern," Danny said. "He even said I told you so, at one point."

"Did you tell Mom about the accident?"

"No. She had pretty much shut down by the time I got her to her room."

"The guy should have stopped," Rob said, still stuck on the driver. "How does he not stop? What kind of car was he driving?"

"Blue Prius," Danny said, now texting. Rob immediately spied a blue Prius on the other side of Route Six. He would see seven more of them before reaching the doctor's office in Chatham.

"The world is going to shit," Rob said.

"Oh, wow," Danny said.

"Wow what?" Rob said, looking at his son the rearview mirror.

"Your video went viral."

"My video? I don't have a video. What are you talking about?"

"Your news video on the beach. Jesus..."

"I don't understand, why would it go viral?" Rob wanted to pull over and see what Danny was looking at.

"Because you look like a lunatic. Your hair is sticking out at crazy angles, you haven't shaved in a week, you're going on about Dorothy Bradford, and you've got seaweed hanging from your ear. Oh, and there's three little kids with snow cones, staring at you. It's pretty funny actually. They're chanting your Dorothy Bradford line over and over. Dorothy Bradford got 'em!"

Rob stared hard in front of him, looking *at* the windshield rather than through it. His infamy would not wane.

* * *

Forty-five minutes later they were in Chatham. The Priuses gave way to BMW's, and the Red Sox logos were replaced by yacht club insignias. Lawns were tended here, kept green in the sandy soil by in-ground sprinkler systems. Golf clubs were everywhere and boasted a full eighteen holes, as opposed to the quaint nine-hole courses in Truro and Wellfleet. Rob hit the brakes hard as a golf cart wandered into the cross walk, heading for the beach club across the street. "That's for pedestrians," Rob said, gesturing at the oblivious driver of the cart.

The doctor's office was in a medical building that also housed a pharmacy and an imaging center. Rob parked and helped Danny into the reception area. A nurse came out to greet them, and took them straight back to an exam room. "The doctor will be right with you," she said. Rob helped Danny onto the exam table.

"I guess you must be a big deal," Rob said. "No waiting. Does the doctor call you by your name, too?"

"Go wait outside, Dad. They're going to need to do x-rays before they know anything. I'll ask them to get you when they do.

Rob took a seat in the waiting room. The office had free Wi-Fi for family members and those less fortunate patients who had to wait to see the doctor. He joined the network, opened YouTube and clicked on trending videos. It didn't take long for him to find his. There had already been 120,000 views. He shaded his eyes with his free hand, as if to hide from the three other people in the waiting room. Danny was right—he did look and sound like a lunatic, particularly when he named Dorothy Bradford, shouting her name into the camera. And perhaps he was a lunatic, he thought. Unemployed or retired, whichever, he wasn't much into grooming anymore, and rarely looked in the mirror. He also wandered around the yard in the nude, and sprayed turkeys with a hose. At least the network had somehow held off on airing the nude footage. That would have made a wonderful second act for the video.

Rob took his hand away from his eyes. A younger man, perhaps in his thirties, had come into the waiting room, on a pair of crutches. His right leg was missing below the knee. The man sat down two seats away from Rob and said hello. Rob nodded and smiled in a reserved manner, trying not to look like a lunatic.

"What are you in for?" the man asked, leaning his crutches on the seat between them. "Since this is an orthopedic practice, I figure it's okay to ask, but if you don't want to answer, I understand."

"No, that's okay. I'm here with my son. Knee," he said, patting his knee, as if to indicate it wasn't missing, only damaged. He didn't think it was necessary to ask what the amputee was in for, without seeming like an asshole.

"I get my prosthetic today," the man said, patting his own leg, or what was left of it. "Doctor says I'll be walking in a few weeks."

Rob tried not to stare at the missing limb. "Can I ask how you lost it?" he said.

"Shark took it. Most of it, anyway. They couldn't do anything with what was left, so it had to come off."

"Wow. Really?"

"Just north of here. Three feet of water. Came up from behind and clamped onto my leg. Knocked me over. Didn't even know what had happened until I saw the blood."

Since they were talking about it now, Rob went ahead and stared at the wrapped stump. "Were there any seals close by?"

"Yeah. My mistake, I guess. I saw two of them, actually, and wandered into the water to have a closer look. I learned my lesson the hard way. Won't do that again. Can't afford to lose the other one." The man looked up at the wall clock in the waiting room, a pained expression on his face. Rob wondered whether the cheerfulness was really a façade for the discomfort he was feeling.

"I wouldn't mind losing my lower leg right about now," Rob said, pulling his right ankle onto his left knee to display his rash. The man looked at it and made a face. "Sorry," Rob said, realizing his attempt at sympathy was probably misguided. "I guess that was an insensitive thing to say."

"Jesus, you should have someone look at that," the man said. "Looks infected."

Rob nodded. He wondered if there might be a dermatologist in the building who would see him. "So, I bet you know a lot about sharks now?" he said.

"Too much, really," the man said. "I just got this app that tracks shark activity. Good thing to check before you go in the water. It sends you alerts, too." The man pulled out his phone and opened the app. "Here's the number of reported shark sightings around the Cape in the last month. Pretty amazing, huh?" There were small shaded squares for each sighting. The outer Cape, from Chatham to Provincetown, was littered with sightings up and down the coast. There was only one sighting in the bay, from a couple of weeks ago.

"Did you hear about those swimmers who disappeared in the bay?" Rob asked, confident no one could possibly recognize him as the wild-haired freak in the news.

"Yeah," the man said. "Weird, isn't it? People don't usually disappear in the bay."

"You think that might have been a shark attack?"

"No. Little or no shark activity in the bay."

"So what do you think happened to them?"

The man shrugged. "Guess they could have drowned. Maybe it was some kind of suicide pact or something. Still, you'd think they would have found a body or two by now."

Rob nodded and loaded the shark activity app onto his phone. He spent the next half hour reading about each of the thirty shark sightings over the course of the last month. Some even had pictures. While he was sitting in the waiting room, a new sighting was reported at a Chatham beach, less than a mile away. Most of the sightings were off Chatham, given its proximity to the seal enclave on Monomy. Rob became so engrossed in the app that he didn't notice he was now alone in the waiting room. How had he missed the one legged man being taken back to the exam rooms? Had he imagined the whole thing? No, he thought, someone had to have told him about the shark app.

His phone beeped, signaling the arrival of an email in his inbox. He thought it might be a welcome from the shark app people, but it was from someone named Maggie Mason instead, a person he didn't know. He assumed it was junk until he read the subject line, which read, "Dorothy Bradford."

Rob scratched his ankle, checked to make sure he was still alone, and opened the message. There was an attachment, too. The email read,

Dear Mr. Crosley,

My name is Maggie Mason, and I am the President of the Dorothy Bradford Society. We saw your interview about the missing swimmers in Cape Cod Bay. Though hardly anyone ever disappears in the bay, when they do, people sometimes say that Dorothy Bradford was responsible, like Davey Jones or something. Dorothy Bradford is not Davey Jones.

Dorothy Bradford doesn't receive much attention, something the DBS has been working to correct by raising awareness of her presence on the bay. As you know, I expect, many people believe that Dorothy drowned in Provincetown Harbor in the winter of 1620, having fallen from the Mayflower into the icy waters. There are many theories about how she fell. Some people believe it was an accident. Some people think she was drunk and stumbled into the water. Some people think her husband, William, was drunk, and shoved her in the water. Then there are people who think she took her own life, overcome by the harsh Atlantic crossing and the dim prospects for a life in a desolate place, without her children whom she was forced to leave behind. There is a new theory now that is becoming popular with a number of our members, myself included. We think that Dorothy was simply fed up with her demanding husband and the people on the Mayflower. Dorothy was not a separatist in the same sense that the rest of the Pilgrims were. The Pilgrims sought separation from the Church of England—Dorothy Bradford sought separation from everyone. She was a true pioneer, longing for a life apart from her husband and the derelict society that she lived in. At her first opportunity she escaped from the Mayflower in a small row boat, landed somewhere on shore and disappeared into the wilderness. She was never found.

The majority of our members, regardless of their opinion about how she left the boat, believe that Ms. Bradford is still alive and continues to live somewhere on the outer Cape, routinely patrolling the bay in her row boat. They believe her purpose is to find peace through solitude, like most hermits. Many of our society members spend time on the bay looking for her, hoping to learn from her experience. Some, in fact, have seen her. Most recently we secured the attached photo of a woman we believe is Dorothy. Perhaps you have seen her as well?

I would be pleased to hear back from you about your experiences. Perhaps we will meet one day soon. I live in Provincetown and am often on the bay myself. Meanwhile, please visit our website at www.dorothybradfordsociety.org.

Rob squinted at his phone, wondering how the woman had gotten his email address. His finger hovered over the icon for the attachment. He had been told not to open attachments from people he didn't know, but he didn't care—his curiosity outweighed any concern for viruses. He clicked on the attachment, and there it was again, like an image from a recurring nightmare—the picture of Katie in her boat. "What the fuck?" he muttered. He looked around to see if anyone had heard him, but there was no one to hear. He was still alone in the silent waiting room, with no TV and no piped-in music, just the hum from the recessed light fixtures overhead. He got up from his chair and walked over to the reception counter. No one was there either. He leaned over the counter and called out. "Anybody here?" he said, but no one answered. Needing assurance that he had not entered some peripheral level of hell, he opened the door into the public corridor to see if he could find someone. He just needed to see one human being, preferably with their limbs intact. Not seeing anyone in the corridor, he kept going, out of the building and into the parking lot, where the sight of an elderly couple getting out of their car settled him down. *This is why people smoke or do drugs,* he thought. He wondered if his moment of panic was similar to what Katie experienced when she had one of her attacks, though, of course, she ran in the opposite direction, away from people, not toward them.

Rob took out his phone and looked at the picture again, thinking for a moment that perhaps his mind had played a trick on him, reproducing an image that wasn't actually there. But there was no mistaking that the picture in the attachment was the same one Don Hill had shown him at the police station. How had it gotten out? Did Steve Ridgeback have something to do with it? Rob consoled himself with the thought that the Dorothy Bradford Society, clearly an organization of cranks, could not have more than a handful of members. But even one member looking at a picture of his wife was too many. He couldn't allow anyone to focus unwanted attention on her, attention that might drive her further away, further into the wilderness. He had to squash this Dorothy Bradford nonsense quickly.

*　　*　　*

That evening, back at the house, Rob and Danny sat in front of the TV, waiting for the local news to come on. Danny had gotten good news from the doctor. He had suffered no structural damage to the knee, only a small tear in the medial meniscus. The doctor told him he could clean it up arthroscopically. Danny would be back on the track in two months. Rob asked if this meant his son would be good as new. The doctor said he didn't know what "new" meant.

"What is RICE?" Rob asked, leafing through the materials the doctor had given them.

"You know what it stands for," Danny said.

"No, I don't. Are you going to make me look it up?"

"Rest, intoxication, cruelty, and extermination," Danny said, adjusting the ice pack on his knee.

"I can do the first two with you," Rob said, searching for the term on his laptop.

"Rest, ice, compression and elevation," Danny said. "You've never heard that before?"

"It could be ERIC, too."

"Sure. Next time you get injured say you're doing ERIC."

Done reading about RICE, Rob pulled up the Dorothy Bradford Society web page. On the home page there was a drawing of Bradford, looking vigilant and pilgrim-like in her bonnet. Rob was relieved that the photo of Katie was not displayed, at least not yet. He clicked on a tab called "sightings" and was further relieved to find that there were several pictures of women in boats, Katie not among them. A membership page discussed the benefits of belonging to the Society, including a newsletter and a Dorothy Bradford beer mug. Why a beer mug? Rob wondered. Not a tee shirt or a bonnet, maybe?

"So, apparently, there is a Dorothy Bradford Society," Rob said to Danny. He had not told him about the e-mail from Maggie Mason. The drive home had been a long hard slog through the vehicular chaos on Route Six. Rob was too aggravated to talk. He hated driving, even when the roads weren't plugged up with cars. Every time he hit the brake pedal, which was often, his infected ankle throbbed. The only words out of his mouth were the special terms of endearment he reserved for other drivers.

"They should make you an honorary member," Danny said. "You can be their spokesman. How did you find them? Are you googling Pilgrims?"

Rob told him about the email from Maggie Mason.

"You're kidding. Really?"

"She thanked me for plugging them on the news."

"See. Ask her for a job," Danny said. He pitched a cracker to Sidney, who had ambled into the room, looking for his evening appetizer.

"Somebody sent them the picture of Mom in her boat. Maggie Mason attached it to her email and asked me if I'd ever seen her."

"Jesus. Why?"

"They think she's Dorothy Bradford."

"Dorothy Bradford is dead."

"They don't think so."

"How did they get the picture?"

"I don't know."

"I wouldn't worry about it. They have no idea who she is."

"They know where to look."

"So write them back. Tell them you know her, and that she isn't Dorothy Bradford."

"I'm sure they'll drop it immediately."

"Make something up."

"What?"

"Tell them she's a lawyer, a real bitch. Say that you told her about the picture and that she said she'd file suit against them if they used it."

"Nip it in the butt," Rob said.

"Bud."

"What?"

"Nip it in the bud, not butt."

Rob began working on his reply to Maggie Mason. He decided to go with the litigious attorney story. As a small organization, the Dorothy Bradford Society would probably shy away from the threat of legal action, and go find themselves some other picture of a woman in a boat. He finished the email and sent it off before the six o'clock news came on. He added a postscript asking if Maggie Mason could say who sent her the picture.

They did not have to wait long for news of the missing swimmers. The two women were a married couple identified as Elizabeth Tanner and Roberta Stevenson. They had come to the Cape on vacation, though it was not clear where they were staying. The male swimmer remained unknown. The newscast reported that the Coast Guard had discontinued their search and rescue operation. It was now four days since the disappearance. The police investigation, however, continued, now focused on the area where the camera had been found. They had a brief shot of the woman—the dog writer—pointing to the spot where she fished it out of the bay. Then Don Hill came on.

"We'll find them," he said, "one way or another."

"One way or another?" Danny said. "Hill needs to work on his public relations skills."

Rob's phone emitted a ping, yet another new sound he had not heard before. This time it was the shark app reporting a new sighting, this one in the bay, two miles off the Truro beaches.

ELEVEN

God and Zoning

The next morning was a peaceful one. There were no helicopters buzzing the shoreline. The boats on the bay trawled for fish, not bodies. No clouds, no wind, no noise from the neighbors' houses. Even the turkeys had wandered off. Rob and Sidney slept in, though they slept in every day. Danny had gone down to his mother's to have breakfast and tell her about the injury. He hoped to spend most of the morning with her. The break in training would allow him to spend more time with Katie. Perhaps the two of them could heal together.

Rob got up and checked his emails. He was curious to see if Maggie Mason had responded, but his inbox was empty save for the unending barrage of spam. He was pleased to see, however, that his video was no longer trending. The number of views had dropped off sharply from the day before. Perhaps, his fifteen minutes of fame were over.

Rob swore at the coffee machine—despite programming it the night before, the pot was empty and the machine was dormant—and let the dog outside. Sidney seemed less lethargic today, so after making coffee in a more reliable fashion, Rob decided to take him for a walk on the beach. It was Saturday, change-over day on the Cape, the day when weekly renters packed up and left, and the next wave arrived. As a result, Saturdays were generally good days to go to the beach. They were notoriously awful days to be on the road.

Before leaving the house, Rob went into the bathroom and put his foot on the toilet seat to inspect his ankle. The rash didn't look quite so angry today. The itching had subsided as well. He decided that he had come through the worst of it, and that a trip to the doctor would not be necessary. He applied a layer of hydrocortisone for now, though he planned to switch treatment to salt water when they got down to the beach.

Rob carried Sidney down the steps, not wanting the dog to sap his energy too soon. The beach was deserted and Rob hoped that life might now return to some sense of normalcy. He and the water were no longer the culprits in the case of the missing swimmers. He suspected all the attention would now be on the third swimmer—the unidentified man whom no one seemed to know anything about. He was also, presumably, the one who took the picture of Katie. But why was the guy taking pictures of Katie in the first place? He thought about what Maggie Mason had said in her email, that members of the Dorothy Bradford Society went out looking for the four hundred year-old woman. Were the swimmers members? Were they not hunting seals, but Pilgrims instead? If they were, they would have certainly forwarded the picture to Maggie Mason, but they had lost the camera, and the police had found it. Someone at the police station was responsible for leaking the photo to the society. Maybe Don Hill was a member, too.

"Jesus!" Rob yelled as he stuck his foot in the water. He couldn't be sure if the water was actually that cold, or if his foot was so worn down that it just felt that way. In any event, the water was numbing, and the itching in his foot subsided further.

Despite his condition he maintained a healthy pace, sloshing his ankle through the water. Sidney kept up. When he was younger, the dog would sprint out ahead of Rob and then wait for him to catch up. Rob wasn't sprinting, but now the roles were reversed.

A number of dislodged buoys had washed up. Rob couldn't recall any overnight storms—the usual cause of beach debris. He picked up the buoys and tossed them farther onto the beach where someone would come by and pick them up eventually. He wondered if he should collect them himself, and fashion some kind of abstract sculpture—a styrofoam horse or cow, maybe. He could set it on the front lawn and see if it scared away the turkeys. He wasn't about to drag a trail of buoys behind him, though.

Further on, he found a clean length of rope, sealed at each end to keep it from fraying, perhaps used by some poor slob who had lashed himself to the mast of his boat during the phantom overnight storm, but used the wrong knot. Rob coiled it up and threw it over his shoulder. It was sure to come in handy.

After a few hundred yards he decided to give the dog a rest, and sat down in the sand. He poked around for rocks and tossed them in the water. Sidney watched but was not inclined to give chase. He knew Rob wasn't chucking food.

After a few minutes of peace, a woman and her dog appeared. The dog was much younger than Sidney and was bouncing in and out of the water. Dripping saltwater he galloped along the sand and gave Sidney an obligatory butt sniff. Sidney looked back at Rob. Rob expected that if dogs could roll their eyes Sidney would be doing so now. The woman was overdressed for the beach. She wore a long cotton dress and a long sleeve shirt with the sleeves rolled up. She wore sandals and carried a shoulder bag of some kind. She was not wearing sunglasses. Perhaps this was Dorothy Bradford, Rob thought. She certainly seemed out of place. But then he noticed she was smiling—he didn't think Dorothy Bradford would smile—and was now making her way toward where Rob was sitting. "Oh shit," Rob mumbled. Apparently, he was going to have his butt sniffed, too.

"Hello," the woman called, striding purposefully now. She waved. Rob didn't wave. He forced a smile and said hello. This was all that was required when crossing paths on the beach. You didn't have to engage in conversation unless there was something lying dead in the surf.

"Your Aussie is beautiful," the woman said.

"For an old man," Rob said.

"How old is he?"

"Fourteen."

"But he's in marvelous shape for fourteen, isn't he?"

"Sure," Rob said. "I guess so." He asked the woman about her dog, since he figured that was what she really wanted to talk about, and the woman proceeded to tell him not only about the dog, but the dog's parents, too, and the vigorous way in which they copulated when the dog was conceived.

"Don't most dogs copulate vigorously?" Rob asked.

"Not always," the woman said. Rob wanted to ask her if she spent a lot of time watching dogs copulate.

"Well, he is a beautiful dog, too," Rob said diplomatically, bringing the dog conversation, he hoped, to a merciful conclusion.

"Can I give you this?" the woman said, reaching into her bag. She produced a flyer and handed it to Rob. He expected it might be about dog mating. He was half right. The flyer was a promotional piece on a book entitled, *Finding God With Your Dog*. The author's name was Betty Whitman. Rob remembered the woman from the news segment, the one who had found the camera—the dog writer whom Don Hill had had a hard time shaking.

"I guess you're Betty?" he said.

"I am," she said, nodding her head proudly. "Since you love dogs, I thought you might find the book interesting."

"Aren't you the person who found the camera in the water? The one with the pictures of the missing swimmers?"

"That's me, too," she said. "I was walking along the beach, not far from here, and saw it rolling around in the surf. I figured it had fallen off somebody's boat, or been left on the beach by mistake. Then I remembered the swimmers from the news. I went to the police. They seemed very happy that I had found it and brought it to them so quickly."

Another responsible citizen, Rob thought. "Did you look at the pictures before you took it to the police?" he said, suspecting she might have been the one who sent the picture of Katie to Maggie Mason."

"How would I do that?"

Clearly, the woman was not technologically adept. She was still smiling, keeping her attention entirely on Rob. He could understand Don Hill's point about shaking her.

"You know," he said, looking for an out, "I have always thought there must be some significance to the fact that God spelled backwards is dog." He smiled, to make sure the woman knew he was making a joke. He was risking she had a sense of humor.

"Yes!" she barked. "I get that a lot. Very good. I considered calling the book, *Finding God with Man's Best Friend*, but it was too long."

Rob was glad that Betty Whitman didn't take herself too seriously, but he was not in the mood to be proselytized. "Where can I buy it?" he asked in an attempt to forestall any further marketing efforts.

"On my web site," she said pointing to the flyer. "There are some excerpts there, too."

"Wonderful!" Rob said.

"You've heard about any number of miracles involving dogs, I'm sure," she said.

"Sure," Rob said. "Getting my dog not to crap in the house is a miracle."

"Yes, I'm sure it is," Betty Whitman said.

Sensing her tone was becoming serious, Rob popped up and said, "Well, I'll be sure to check out your web site. Thanks." And he waved the flyer around for good measure. "Come on, Sidney, let's go!" Sidney was still planted in the same spot, ignoring Betty Whitman's God-fearing dog, who had resumed sprinting in and out of the water for no apparent reason.

"Have you found God?" Betty Whitman asked, not to be deterred.

"Never lost him," Rob said, heading down the beach. Sidney took off after him, moving faster than Rob had seen the dog move in some time.

Rob folded the flyer and stuck it in his pocket, saving it for the kitchen trash. He looked behind him to make sure Betty Whitman and her dog were heading in the other direction. When he had gotten plenty of distance between them he sat down in the sand again, letting Sidney recover from their escape. Rob had started picking through a clump of dried seaweed, when he came across a small plastic tube of some kind. The seaweed fell away and revealed a syringe, with the needle still intact. "Finding heroin with your dog," Rob muttered. He picked up the syringe, careful not to touch the needle. The plunger was fully depressed. The syringe was empty.

"What am I supposed to do with this, Sidney?" Sidney yawned and lay down in the wet sand, beyond reach of the surf. Rob looked around, making sure there were no other needles nearby. He held the syringe at arm's length, like one of Sidney's turds plucked off the kitchen floor. This wasn't something he could shove in his pocket, like the dog book flyer, to be flushed down the toilet or added to the trash. He couldn't toss it in the water either as it would just wash up on shore again, waiting to be stepped on by some unlucky bastard. He thought about burying it in the sand, but then a little kid would dig it up and stab his sister in the eye. Rob stared at the needle wondering whose arm it had been in. Would a junkie toss his syringe in the water? Maybe a rich junkie. Rob sighed, got up, and walked toward the dunes. Like most of the dunes along the bay the ones behind him were covered by a thick bramble of beach roses. He could toss the syringe far into the bushes and it would stay there for eternity, undisturbed and out of reach of any human hands or feet. He shrugged his shoulders, looked around to make sure no one was watching, and heaved the syringe into the shrubbery. It landed far up the dune but did not find sand. It lodged on top of a bush instead, remaining visible. "Shit!" Rob yelled, hoping it hadn't fully settled. It had. He stared at it for a while, feeling defeated, then ran down to the water and collected some rocks. Returning to the base of the dune he started heaving the rocks at the syringe, trying to knock it off its perch. Each attempt missed the mark. The follow-through on his last throw took him a few feet up the dune and he realized something leafy was brushing his leg. Mortified, he jumped away, but it was just more of the bushes. No poison ivy.

As his arm tired, Rob decided to leave the syringe alone. The next storm or high wind would dislodge the thing and drive it into the underbrush. Once again, he looked around to make sure no one was watching or pointing their cell phone at him. "Bradford lunatic tosses heroin needle into dunes!" the headline would read and another video would go viral.

*　　*　　*

Further down the beach, clear of sermons and needles, Rob came upon Tim the fisherman. Tim looked up from his fishing pole as Rob approached. He was fixing a chunk of some sort of fish meat on the hook. There was a pail of the stuff next to him.

"Rob!" Tim called, smiling. Rob wasn't accustomed to being greeted so enthusiastically, but he was pleased Tim remembered his name. He waved, and nearly asked how they were biting. "Saw you on the news this week," Tim said.

"A lot of people did apparently," Rob said. He looked behind him and found Sidney fifty yards back, making slow progress.

"I thought it was great," Tim said. "Guess you liked that Bradford story, huh?"

"I needed something to get the news guys off my back. She came in handy."

"Yes, sir. Deflection is very effective with the media. That your dog back there?"

"Yeah, doesn't move as fast as he did, but he keeps going."

"Old guy, huh? I had a dog. Got into a fight with a coyote and we had to put him down." Tim looked down at the sand. "I haven't caught a damn thing today."

Rob looked out at the water, expecting to find the reason. "Good days and bad days, right?" he said.

"Yup. It was probably all those damn boats going back and forth. Scared the fish away."

"They identified the two women," Rob said.

"I saw that," Tim said. "Whoever the guy was, he's the one behind whatever's going on. I'll bet he's got the two women locked up somewhere. The cops were poking around the Desmond house yesterday."

"What's the Desmond house?" Tim pointed back behind the dunes, which were much lower on this section of beach. "That's it there," he said. The recently completed house was low slung and modern, a design more typical of the Hamptons than the Cape. Rob had watched it being built on his beach walks. He knew many of the neighbors in the area were unhappy with the style, given its visibility from the beach. Still, it was not monstrous like many of the new homes being built on waterfront property.

"The new one? Why were the police looking there?"

"It's still vacant," Tim said. "There's a demolition order on it."

"Why? What did they do wrong?"

"Built it too close to the beach, violated zoning regulations. Have to knock the whole thing down, or at least the part that's encroaching. Until then they can't live in it."

"Seems fine to me," Rob said.

"That's what I think," Tim said, sounding dejected. "I guess the owner figured no one would call them on it."

"They must not be from around here. I thought it was just the design people didn't like. Seems a shame to have to knock it down."

"I don't expect it'll come to that. My guess is the town levies a fine on the owners and that's the end of it."

"So why would the police think the swimmers were in there?"

"Empty house right on the beach, close to where they were last seen." Tim cast his line in the water and worked the reel, drawing it back in.

"Are they your neighbors?" Rob asked.

"No," Tim said, turning back to look at Rob. "They're me." He smiled sheepishly. "Sorry to be evasive but there are a lot of folks around here who get pretty worked up about that house. I've had too many people in my face—neighbors, journalists, zoning commissioners, town selectmen. I wanted to be sure you weren't going to lay into me, too."

"How far over the setback is it?"

"Three feet."

"They're making you knock it down over three feet?"

"The contactor screwed up. The drawings show the house right on the line. That's the other thing working in my favor. The contactor has been around for a long time and has a lot of friends on the town board. If he has to knock down the house and rebuild it he'll probably declare bankruptcy. He'll be out of business and I'll be out of a house. You want to see it?"

"Now?" Rob said, motioning toward Tim's bait bucket.

"Sure. I'm not catching anything anyway. Besides, it looks like your dog could use some water." Sidney had arrived and was lapping at the pools of saltwater.

"Sidney, don't drink that shit," Rob said. Sidney looked at Rob and then honed in on the pungent odor coming from bait bucket.

"That's not for you, boy," Tim said, picking up the bucket.

"What do use for bait?"

"Menhaden."

Rob had never heard the word, and wasn't even sure it was a fish. He would look it up later.

"Where do you get it?"

"I have a guy who brings it in for me. I get it for next to nothing, so if you ever need any let me know.

Tim led Rob and Sidney into the house. There was no furniture inside. Most of the first floor was open, with the kitchen opening onto a great room. The side of the house facing the bay was all glass. The ceilings were high, and large ceiling fans hung from the wooden rafters that stretched across the length of the first floor. Tim got a plastic bowl from the kitchen and filled it with water for Sidney.

"I can't offer much else," Tim said.

"Water's fine," Rob said, standing before the windows overlooking the bay. "Great view. So it's this three feet here?" he said, pointing down to where he was standing.

"That's it," Tim said. "That's what got me in trouble. Hey, I've got some vodka in the freezer. Is it too early?"

"Not for me," Rob said.

"Good man!" Tim said and poured two glasses.

"Where do you live now?" Rob asked.

"Across the street," Tim said, pointing out the kitchen window. My parents bought the house sixty-five years ago. When this lot became available they bought it, too, but never built on it. When my wife and I saved up enough money, we hired an architect and designed this place. We wanted something modern and we didn't want it to be covered with cedar shingles like every other house around here."

"Sure," Rob said, thinking of the shingles on his house. Storms sometimes blew two or three of them off the north face, and Rob had to hunt through the bushes to find them, then climb a ladder and put them back.

“Most people think I’m some rich prick from New York City who doesn’t give a shit about the zoning laws. I’ve lived here longer than most of my neighbors for Christ’s sake.” Tim drank down the vodka and poured another glass. Rob sensed Tim needed someone to share his frustrations with but couldn’t find a sympathetic ear. “People are too quick to judge. They hear something and assume it’s true.”

“Some people think I’m to blame for whatever happened to the missing swimmers,” Rob said. “Because I didn’t call the police right away.”

“I read that cocksucker Ridgeback’s article in the Gazette. That guy should be locked up.”

“You know him?”

“He wrote about my house. A real hatchet job. The whole article stunk of his opinions. He glossed over the contractor error and wrote mostly about what an eyesore the house was, like he was reviewing a movie or something.”

“I’m not a fan either,” Rob said.

“No, you don’t understand,” Tim said becoming more vehement, his voice louder. “This guy is a real scumbag. He decided to make my life miserable for no other reason than to stir up controversy. The last straw was when he attacked my wife, saying that she couldn’t be interviewed because I had somehow forbid her to say anything. He flat out made stuff up. I found out he has already been sued for libel once. I may sue him, too, before this is done.”

“So what would happen if you just went ahead and moved in?”

“Believe me, I’ve thought about it,” Tim said. “I’d get evicted. Ridgeback would write another scathing article and the town would burn me in effigy.”

“So when the cops came did they have a warrant to search the house?”

"No. They just asked if it would be alright to take a look. I wanted to say no. I'd know if someone was hiding in my house, for Christ's sake. But why give them the impression I was hiding something? They're a pain in the ass."

"They seem alright. I've been dealing with Don Hill."

"Don't know him," Desmond said gruffly. "Don't want to know him."

Rob figured it was best to change the subject.

"You know how you told me there was a Dorothy Bradford Society? Well, the president contacted me after my story aired."

"Maggie Mason? I'll bet she loved the publicity. What did she say?"

"She thanked me, and then went on about their search for Dorothy."

"They haven't found her yet, huh?"

"They're working on it, apparently." Rob didn't want to tell him about the photo of Katie. The less people who knew about it the better. He took out his phone to see if he had gotten any emails. There were two, one junk and one from Maggie Mason. "She just sent me another one," Rob said, feeling he could confide in Tim Desmond. "How the hell did she get my email address?"

"That's not hard," Tim said. "All you need to know is the person's name these days." Tim shifted his attention to something outside. "Will you excuse me for a minute? I've got to go talk to Sammy real quick. Help yourself to more vodka."

Rob looked around and saw a young man, probably about Danny's age, coming onto the deck. He had on work boots, and wore a vest that was stuffed with paraphernalia. He carried a tool box. "Is that your son?" Rob asked.

"Oh, no," Tim said, chuckling, as if the idea of children was preposterous. "Sammy does work for me around the house. Both houses now. Real handy. He's the one who gets my bait. Maybe you know him? He grew up in Truro. Sammy Boland. If you ever need any work done at your place, he's your guy."

Rob nodded. He had his own handyman, or woman, right across the street. While Tim was outside, Rob poured some more vodka and read the follow-up email from Maggie Mason.

Thank you for your email about the picture of the woman in the boat. We certainly don't want to spread false rumors about Dorothy Bradford, but because a lot of our members believe she is still alive we can't dismiss any new evidence too quickly. The picture has become even more vital as we just learned the names of the two missing swimmers, and they are both members of our society! We also understand that the picture was likely taken by the man who was with them. So you can see that the woman in the picture is now of great interest, as is the fate of our missing members. The society is having a special meeting on this matter tomorrow at my home. I would like to extend an invitation to you, and to the woman who you say is in the photo, to attend the meeting so that we can determine if, in fact, she is Dorothy Bradford and how we want to publicize the matter. My address is 84 Bradford Street in Provincetown. The meeting is at 7:00 pm on Monday. I hope you and your friend can come. There will be plenty to drink. Thank you.

"Fuck," Rob muttered. She had called his bluff. And what was worse, the missing women were society members. He was sure now that the women had been stalking Katie, perhaps seeing her on her boat sometime before, and returning each day to the same spot, hoping to see her again and take her picture. But if the women were society members wouldn't they live here like Maggie Mason, and not be renting a vacation house? How big a following did Bradford have?

Sidney had wandered off into the great room and was staring up at the high ceiling as if trying to determine whether he was still indoors. Tim came back inside, while Sammy Boland headed to the front of the house.

"We've got to go," Tim said.

"Go where?" Rob said.

"I mean we have to leave the house. Sammy said that one of my more annoying neighbors is nosing around the property.

I'm not supposed to be here. If he sees us in the house he'll call the cops."

They walked back to the beach. Feeling Tim needed a distraction, and understanding all too well the frustration of dealing with annoying neighbors, Rob told him about the invitation from Maggie Mason.

"Where's the meeting?"

"Her house, I guess."

"Which one?"

"She has more than one?"

"She has a big house in town, but also has a small place somewhere in the dunes. I believe she lets a few of her disciples live in the house, so she lives in her other place."

"Kind of like you."

"I don't have any disciples." Tim said, sounding dejected. "Are you going to go?"

"I don't know. You think I should?" Rob already knew he would go, to throw the Dorothy Bradford Society off his wife's trail. Were there other reasons?

"She's something of a folklore celebrity up there," Tim said. "And I hear she throws great parties. You should go. Did you say you were married? Bring your wife. If not, bring me. I'll go."

Rob would not bring his wife. What he needed was a pugnacious attorney who looked like his wife. He would have to go alone, and find some explanation for the fictitious attorney's absence.

"Hey, maybe we can fish together sometime," Rob said, worried Tim Desmond might start asking more questions about Katie. He was never quite sure how to explain their situation to other people.

"I'd like that," Tim said. "Anytime."

"I'm not much of a fisherman."

"You'll learn."

"I've never heard of Menhaden."

"It's not for eating. Don't ask for it at a restaurant."

"Right."

"And I want to hear about your meeting with Maggie Mason."

Rob said goodbye, and even shook Tim Desmond's hand.

TWELVE

Armpits and Beer

On his way to the Dorothy Bradford Society meeting, Rob stopped at the store in town to pick up the new issue of the Gazette. He knew there would be an article about the identity of the missing swimmers, but he was more concerned about the picture of Katie finding its way into the paper. In the checkout line, he flipped through the paper quickly and was pleased to not see any images of his wife.

The article was, of course, written by Steve Ridgeback. One of the pictures of the two women was published. Rob read the article in the car this time so he could react to Ridgeback's reporting slant without creating a scene. The article mostly talked about the two women. They had grown up together in western Massachusetts and had been partners for most of their adult lives. They still lived in Massachusetts and vacationed on the Cape. Ridgeback reported that the identity of the man remained unknown, as were his motives. "Motives?" Rob said. Was the man already guilty of foul play?

Just as Rob had been before, the missing man was now fixed in Ridgeback's crosshairs. Ridgeback also reported that the police had searched the *"vacant Desmond house, which is expected to be demolished."* Rob could imagine how Desmond would react to this. The house was not expected to be demolished. The courts had yet to decide the fate of the home. Ridgeback had struck again.

Rob was startled to find a short piece about the Dorothy Bradford Society, also written by Ridgeback. The journalist had learned that the swimmers were members. He had also learned that Maggie Mason was one of the people who called the police after they released the pictures of the women. "They were here on vacation," Maggie Mason was quoted as saying. "They were planning on coming to our meeting in Provincetown this Monday." The article described the society's mission and the plight of women from Pilgrim times to the present. Maggie Mason dismissed the local lore about Bradford being responsible for people who disappear in the bay. "I don't think she's in the business of rescuing souls," she said, "or doing them in. If anyone thinks differently they should come to our meeting." Ridgeback also mentioned that many society members believe Dorothy Bradford is still alive, and some of them go looking for her, including, possibly, the missing swimmers. "They very well could have been looking for her that day," Maggie Mason said. "The fact that they were in the water with a camera would seem to support this." Ridgeback referred to the missing women in the article as *The Dorothy Swimmers*. The name stuck.

Mercifully, there was no mention of Rob in the article. Perhaps Rob's threat about barring Ridgeback from future access to Danny had made a difference, though he doubted it. He flipped through the paper again to make sure there wasn't anything about Danny's injury. There wasn't.

Rob agonized about whether to go to the meeting or not. He had not mentioned it to Danny or Katie—Katie still didn't know who Dorothy Bradford was—though he knew they would have told him not to go. But he believed the best chance of nipping the thing in the butt, or bud, was by confronting the women directly. Even though he didn't have a hostile female attorney to go with him, and certainly not one who looked like Katie, he wouldn't abandon his ruse. "She's not a friendly person," he'd tell the society. "I don't doubt for a minute that she'll sue if you use her picture. She's the last person I'd pick to be Dorothy Bradford."

The only thing that could dissuade him from going to the meeting was the Provincetown festival schedule. Most every week during the summer, the town was overrun by one special interest group or another. Fishermen, bikers, gays, lesbians, bisexuals, transsexuals, queers, people who were into leather—all of them had their own festivals. The festival-goers piled into the shops, bars, and restaurants, which were already mobbed by the usual throng of tourists. This made getting in and out of town a daunting task, and Maggie Mason lived right in the center of it.

Rob went on line and checked the calendar of events for Provincetown. He learned that this week was Bear Week. He had never heard of Bear Week and suspected it had nothing to do with bears. After a bit of research he discovered that bears, in this case, were large, hairy, gay men. He figured that large, hairy, gay men couldn't possibly account for more than a small minority of the gay population, and that it was probably safe to go, at least from a traffic standpoint. Rob was neither large nor hairy.

Fittingly, Maggie Mason lived on Bradford Street, otherwise known as Route 6A, the long two lane road between Route 6 and Commercial Street that ran the length of Provincetown. Since street-parking was out of the question during the summer, Rob parked in a public lot and walked to the address Maggie Mason had given him. The house looked like Dorothy, herself, could have lived there. The two-story, rectangular structure had a steep gabled roof, shingle siding and a central chimney. But the most striking thing about the property was that the Pilgrim Monument was right behind it, perched ominously on a hill not more than a hundred yards away. Rob had not been to the monument, or seen it this close. If the thing ever blew over in a storm, it would crash down on top of Maggie Mason's house, crushing everything and everyone inside.

A sign was posted on the front door that said the DBS meeting was in the backyard. Rob circled the house, coming even closer to the monument, and found a group of around forty people milling around the yard. He noticed immediately that all of them were women, many of whom were stocky, in a healthy, intimidating sort of way. Curiously, each of them wore a bonnet, similar to the one Dorothy Bradford wore in the web site image. They also held large mugs of what Rob assumed was beer. In the center of the yard was a keg. It appeared to be the beverage of choice.

Rob was soon greeted by an imposing, bonneted woman—an amazon with blond hair and dark eyes. Like many of the women, she was solidly built, but larger, perhaps six feet tall. She reminded Rob of one of those big-breasted figureheads you might see on the prow of a ship.

"I haven't seen you before," she said. Her voice was remarkably gentle for such a large person. "My name is Rachel. Are you a new member?"

Rob smiled, trying to make a good impression. Normally he hated mingling at parties, but since his purpose was to gain support for disqualifying Katie's picture he needed to be affable. "No. Not yet anyway," Rob said. "I'm a guest."

"You're Rob Crosley!" Rachel said, excitedly.

"I am," he said, sounding delirious. He needed to tone things down. Maintaining this level of congeniality would be impossible.

"You're our new hero, Rob Crosley!"

"I am?" Rob sensed trouble. He did not do well being the center of attention.

"Your news segment was wonderful. It gave us all kinds of free exposure. Our website crashed yesterday from all the hits. Everyone wants to know who Dorothy Bradford is. We're going to talk tonight about how we make sure we don't miss out on the opportunity you gave us. I'll tell you a secret, Rob Crosley, Maggie is going to give you an honorary membership."

Rob's eyebrows shot up. He was inclined to protest but knew he had to play along. Would he have to wear a bonnet?

"What an honor," he said. "I'm not sure I deserve it, though. I don't know anything about what you do here."

"You'll learn! Let's start by getting you a beer. I see you didn't bring a mug, but why would you? I'll get you one you can use until Maggie gives you your own."

"I get a mug?"

"How else are you going to drink beer?" Rachel said. "Come on." She grabbed him by the arm and jerked him toward the keg. Fortunately, he was leaning that way, otherwise his shoulder might have come right out of its socket. Rachel was as strong as she looked.

There was a line at the keg. People didn't seem to wait until their mugs were empty before getting on line for a refill. Rob was not used to seeing so many women pounding down beers.

"Was Dorothy Bradford a big beer drinker?" he asked Rachel.

"Um, don't use the past tense when you're talking about Dorothy," she said.

"Sorry," he said, cringing.

No, it's okay. Just educating you, right? Anyway, all the Pilgrims were big beer drinkers," she said. "It's all they drank. Beer was the reason they landed here in Provincetown." Rob pictured the Pilgrims anchoring in the harbor and rowing into town to bar hop.

"I guess I don't follow," Rob said.

"They were supposed to go to Virginia, but they ran out of beer so they landed here to start brewing more."

"Beer was that important?"

"Oh, yes. Most of them drank a gallon a day. How else could they have made it across the Atlantic in that little boat? Beer helped prevent scurvy, too."

Rob watched Rachel fill a mug for him while he tried to remember how many ounces there were in a gallon. He was pretty sure it was around a hundred and twenty. That meant the Pilgrims were drinking the equivalent of ten beers a day. He hoped he wouldn't be expected to drink that much during the meeting.

"Drink up!" Rachel said. "I'm going to go find Maggie. She'll be so happy you came."

Rob was left alone. He sipped his beer, expecting it to taste like it did when the Pilgrims made the stuff, but it was actually very good. The mug also fit comfortably in his hand, a must if you were going to drink a gallon's worth.

He became aware that other members were staring at him. Some nodded, others had hard expressions, like they were trying to remember if they had seen him before. He wondered if men were treated equally in the Dorothy Bradford Society. Wouldn't they be blamed, in part, for Dorothy's suffering? The fact that he appeared to be the only male there seemed to support this. He worked to keep smiling, and nodded at the members who didn't have scowls on their faces. Soon, Rachel returned with another woman, also with a beer in her hand—Maggie Mason no doubt. She, too, was a solidly-built woman, though not nearly as tall as Rachel. She also wore a white bonnet, the same model as everyone else's.

"I see you have your beer," the woman said. "What do you think of it?"

"Very good," Rob said, waiting for an introduction.

"We make it ourselves." The woman drank down the rest of her beer and handed the empty mug to Rachel, who made for the keg line.

"Are you Maggie?" he asked sheepishly, unsure of whether it was allowed to call her by her given name. Perhaps there was some exalted title.

"I am. We're not big on formalities here."

"I'm..."

"I know who you are!" She looked behind him. Rob turned, too, curious to see what Maggie Mason was looking at. "Where's the attorney?" she said.

"Oh, she's not coming," Rob said. Maggie Mason's tone was assertive. He wondered if she thought he posed a threat. But then, she wouldn't give him an honorary membership if he was a menace.

"I'm sorry to hear that. There are a lot of us who were looking forward to meeting her."

"You don't want to meet her," Rob said. "Here or in a courtroom."

"We must be talking about two different women," Maggie Mason said. "It appears there's only one decision we can make." She cocked her head and gave Rob a knowing look that made him uncomfortable. Rachel returned and gave Maggie Mason her refilled mug. She smiled adoringly at Rob, and went to stand next to him.

"I think Rachel likes you, Rob," Maggie Mason said.

"She's a very nice person," he said, and quickly added, "as everyone here seems to be." He smiled again and watched Maggie Mason chug down another mugful of beer. These women didn't seem to know how to nurse a drink. "What do you mean when you say that there's only one decision you can make?" he asked her. Maggie Mason's mug was so large, ornately inscribed with what looked like the Mayflower, that most of her face was obscured when she was drinking from it. The mug must have held at least sixteen ounces. That meant she only needed around seven refills to reach a gallon.

"Most of our members will believe she's Dorothy Bradford unless the woman comes here and proves she isn't. They won't just take your word for it. And they won't be intimidated by threats." She handed Rachel her mug again. Rachel peeked down into Rob's mug and decided he needed a refill, too.

"Finish that, Rob, and I'll get you another," Rachel said. Rob worried that if he kept drinking at this rate he would be too drunk to make any kind of coherent argument about Katie. In any case, he let Rachel have his mug.

"I hope you don't think I'm being too harsh," Maggie Mason said. ""I tend to get a little gung-ho when I've had a few." Rob wasn't sure how to respond to this. She had announced her drunkenness like it was something to be proud of. "I'll bet you were surprised to find a bunch of beer-swilling women," she said. Rob shrugged. "The Pilgrims believed that beer was a gift from God."

"Is that why they drank so much?"

"Partly. They also believed it gave them the strength to face the hardships in their lives. Which it did, of course."

"So why Dorothy Bradford?" Rob asked, hoping to find a new angle he could use to convince Maggie Mason that she was chasing the wrong woman. He was beginning to feel lightheaded. He hadn't seen any food yet. He would have to eat something soon, or end up on the ground, which now seemed much further away than usual. The grass looked intensely green all of a sudden, and undulous, too, like broccoli flowers.

"She is our country's first female survivor," Maggie Mason said.

"Because she jumped off a boat?"

Maggie Mason shook her head and said, "Because she escaped an abusive situation and learned to survive on her own. In a very desolate place."

Rachel returned with their beers, like an overworked barmaid, holding both mugs in one hand and a box of crackers in the other. "You want some?" she asked. Maggie shook her head but Rob grabbed a handful. "I'm going to get another keg," she said to Maggie. "This one is getting low." Rob wondered how many kegs they went through in an evening.

"Good. We're going to start soon." She guzzled more beer. Rob suspected it gave her the strength to run the meetings. "Any other questions I can answer for you?" she asked.

"Uh, yes, actually. I was wondering how you got the photo."

"That's a good question. It was sent to us anonymously. Whoever sent it, though, said it was from the camera that washed up on the beach, so we know it was taken by the missing swimmers."

"And they're members of the society?"

"The women are. We don't know who the man is, but he couldn't be a member. We only have two male members and they are accounted for."

Rachel came from the house shouldering a fresh keg of beer. Rob watched as she grabbed the empty keg with one hand and replaced it with the one on her shoulder.

"Jesus," Rob said. "She is a strong woman."

"All women are strong," Maggie said. "Time for business."

A table and three rows of folding chairs had been set up in the yard. Maggie went to the table and starting ringing what looked to be a ship's bell. Rob thought it sounded like one. The tone was remarkably clear, and even after Maggie stopped striking the bell he continued to hear the sound echoing through the yard. The women who weren't on line for beer sat down on the folding chairs. Regardless of where they were, they turned to face Maggie Mason. Rob thought they looked like large shore birds in their white bonnets—seagulls, perhaps, waiting for one of them to take flight so they could all follow. She thanked everyone for coming and immediately introduced Rob, catching him by surprise. Before he knew what was happening, a few women started clapping. Most did not. He waved and set down his beer, figuring he would soon be called on to speak.

"Rob has done us a great service," Maggie said. "Though I suspect he may not have been a true believer at the time, we are confident he will become one. He is a gentle soul and means us no harm." This elicited a more enthusiastic response. The hands of the women who were clapping seemed to move much too rapidly, like hummingbirds dancing in their faces.

Rob was reminded of the bird feeder outside the cottage. Was he really a gentle soul?

"Before heading back for more beer," Maggie said to Rob, "please come up and accept your own mug and an honorary membership in the Dorothy Bradford Society!"

The women who had sat down now stood up again and continued what was becoming an overblown show of appreciation. They were clearly drunk. Rob joined Maggie at the front of the assembly and accepted his beer mug. He held it up for all to see like it was a trophy or something. He needed to connect with the members if he was going to convince them Katie wasn't Dorothy. They held up their mugs, too. Rachel snatched Rob's mug out of his hand and went to fill it for him. As people settled down, it became apparent they expected Rob to say something. He looked at Maggie for direction, wondering if this was his opportunity to speak his mind about the picture. She smiled and nodded for him to go ahead.

"Well, I don't have my beer!" he said cleverly. This remark seemed to win over the rest of the members. They turned to exhort Rachel, who was ushered to the front of the keg line. She hurried back to Rob with the full mug. Rob took four or five swallows to everyone's great pleasure. He, too, now had the strength to continue. Here was his chance to clear his wife.

"I have always been a great believer in women!" he said. "And beer!" He looked at Maggie to make sure he was hitting the right chords. She nodded, though her expression remained stern. Whereas Maggie might show signs of fervency, Rob was an altogether ingratiating drunk. "I very much look forward to meeting Dorothy Bradford one day soon!" he continued. The applause fell off a bit and Rob became anxious he had said something he shouldn't have. He was sure he hadn't referred to the great woman in the past tense.

"We thought you were going to bring her with you!" someone said. Rob was prepared to answer but Maggie cut him off.

"She decided not to come," Maggie said. "It was her decision. We'll have to accept that."

"More beer for the rest of us!" another member said, setting off another round of applause.

Rob steeled himself and said, "She isn't Dorothy Bradford!" Maggie Mason quickly stepped in front of him and gently pushed him away. The applause ended, replaced by an uncomfortable silence.

"Not now," Maggie Mason said. "Please sit down, Rob." Rob drifted toward the rear of the assembly, but did not sit down. Had he already blown his chance?

Maggie set up an easel in front of the members and placed an enlarged photo on it. Rob's spirits lifted—the picture was not of Katie, but of another woman instead, this one paddling a kayak.

"We're going to start off by talking about recent sightings," Maggie said. "First up is this picture taken by Elaine Snow. Elaine, come up and tell us about it." Elaine Snow was small by Bradford Society standards, almost meek. Rob overheard someone in the back row whisper that she was an idiot. Elaine Snow believed the woman in the kayak was Dorothy Bradford because she had an unusual paddling style. That was her entire justification. There was nothing unusual about how the woman was holding her paddle, but Elaine argued about how vigorously the woman paddled, attacking the water with each stroke. When she finished making her case, Maggie Mason frowned and asked if anyone had any questions. Without looking to see if anyone had raised their hands, she thanked Elaine Snow and pulled the kayaker off the easel.

"Anyone believe this woman is worth pursuing?" she asked, tossing the picture off to the side. No one said anything. Elaine Snow looked down at her picture lying in the grass and apologized. She was clearly distraught.

"You don't have to apologize, Elaine. It's a fine picture," Maggie Mason said.

"We love you, Elaine!" someone shouted, not the woman who had called her an idiot.

The next picture was of a woman walking through the woods. The one after that was a woman on the beach, eating what looked like a raw fish. Somehow the vivid color of the watery flesh made Rob feel hungry. In both cases the photographer got up to explain why she thought the subject was worthy of consideration. Again, the evidence was thin. The woman on the beach ate raw fish, obviously and didn't shave her armpits. The woman in the woods was seen peeing behind a tree. Rob was hopeful there was a high bar for approval. He didn't see where Katie's picture could be interpreted any differently.

"The last picture," Maggie Mason said, "was sent to us anonymously, but we know who took it." The picture had been placed on the easel backwards. Maggie had her hand on the enlargement but was not going to reveal it until she finished her introduction. "We were told that this picture was taken by one of the swimmers who disappeared in the bay last week. Some of you know that two of the swimmers, Elizabeth Tanner and Roberta Stevenson, are members of the society." This produced a gasp from the assembly, followed by murmured discussion. It sounded like no one was aware the missing women were members. Maggie let the talking die down, then continued. "Moreover, our special guest tonight, Rob Crosley, claims to know who this woman is." With that she turned the picture around. This elicited an even louder gasp. Two of the women in the front row fell out of their seats and dropped to their knees. Another woman shrieked. In an instant everyone was rushing up to the easel to get a closer look at the photograph. Even the line at the keg vanished.

Rob's heart sank. The members were pawing Katie's picture like it was the Holy Grail. But how was this picture any different from the one of the woman in the kayak? He dropped his head and walked across the broccoli lawn to the abandoned keg. He guessed this was his fourth refill. He was approaching a half gallon. He couldn't remember drinking this much beer, except maybe when he was in college. Soon he would have to go to the bathroom, and then he would be pissing all night. He looked up at the monument—the lights had come on—he could swear it was swaying.

"Rob Crosley!" Maggie Mason called. Rob turned around and was startled by the mass of people clustered around his wife's picture, all of them staring back at him. He was reminded of the episode on the beach when the news crews were bearing down on him. "Rob, now you can come up here and explain to us what you know about this very brave-looking woman." She beckoned for him to come forward and asked everyone else to return to their seats. Half of them did. The other half headed back to the keg. The uncomfortable silence returned.

He was reminded of his school days, when a teacher would summon him to come before the class and make a presentation. There was still a chance, he supposed. He would find a way to convince these people that Katie was no more deserving of being Dorothy Bradford than any of the others. He organized the thoughts swirling around in his briny beer-brain, and reminded himself not to refer to Dorothy in the past tense.

"Hello again," Rob said confidently. "Sorry for speaking out of turn earlier." He looked at the picture and was oddly empowered by Katie's expression. He hadn't really gotten a close look at the photo when Don Hill showed it to him at the police station. Enlarged now, as it was, he could clearly see the alarm on her face. Her posture, though, was more an expression of action than fear—a call to arms, as though someone were threatening her and she was bracing for battle. There was something thrilling about the way Katie sat in the boat, her knees up, the muscles in her arms tensed, her hair flying in the wind. She looked nothing like a lawyer. Rob could still hear the ship's bell ringing. He peeked up at the monument to make sure it hadn't snapped off at its base. "Some picture, huh?" he said.

"It's her!" someone shouted. "We found her! Go sit down."

"Let him speak," Maggie Mason said.

"I don't want to be the one to toss a wet blanket here," Rob said, flinching at the choice of such a lame metaphor. He pictured a massive dripping quilt hanging over the sea of sodden white bonnets below. "This woman, though she certainly looks very heroic in the picture here, is…" He paused and looked over at Rachel, probably the only person beaming at him, her hands clasped in front of her. She would have seemed like a young girl if she wasn't so damn big.

"Dorothy Bradford!" a woman shouted.

"Listen, I know this woman," Rob said, "and she is not Dorothy Bradford." Booing now. "She shaves her armpits! She pees indoors!"

"What's her name then!?"

"I wish I could tell you. I mean…she knows I came here tonight. She's married and has a kid."

"Why didn't she come!?"

"That's a good question," Rob said thinking he might have found an opening. "If she were Dorothy Bradford wouldn't she have come? To be with you? I mean, I asked her to come and she said no." General silence at this. Rob guessed everyone was too drunk to make sense of what he had said. He wasn't sure *he* could make sense of what he had said. The bonnets looked like radioactive eggs.

"She doesn't know who she is! We need to bring her back!"

"Or maybe she does know who she is but doesn't want to be brought back," Rob said. "She escaped the Mayflower to get away from the others, right? To live a life of solitude?"

"She was forced off the boat!"

"They shoved her in the water!"

"They raped her!"

Rob looked over at Maggie Mason, sensing a growing beer-fueled hysteria. The enormity of persuading forty drunken feminists began to weigh on him. Where were the other two male members? If they were there, were they not allowed to talk? Maggie shrugged her shoulders and motioned for Rob to finish with his defense. Rob looked up at the monument, still swaying, the beams of light darting through the trees, and looked for some divine clarity. If Betty Whitman were here she would tell him he should have brought Sidney along. Some of the women had started chanting "Dorothy, Dorothy," as if they were at a sporting event. Having learned from his recent experience with the press, he knew it was time to pivot.

"Listen to this!" he said. The crowd refused to settle, so Rob went over to the easel and stood in front of the picture of Katie. He thought about turning it around again but feared this might incite a riot.

"Hey, we can't see Dorothy!"

Rob pressed ahead. They hadn't gotten much quieter but at least their attention was on him, now. "A couple of days ago I was walking my dog on the beach, when I ran into this woman, who handed me a flyer about this book she had written called *Finding God with your Dog*."

"I found God with my beer!" someone shouted.

"Did you take her picture?!" someone added.

"No," Rob said. "But it just now occurred to me that she could be Dorothy Bradford."

"Take her picture!"

"She didn't look like anyone I had ever seen before," Rob said. Then Maggie Mason walked over to join him at the easel, and he sensed his time was up.

"No one is allowed to discuss a new sighting at these meetings unless they are a member, which you are now, of course, but you have to submit a picture in advance. The woman's appearance can be more important than her actions."

"I'll send you her picture," Rob said.

"I don't think that will be necessary after tonight," Maggie Mason said, cutting off the discussion. "Show of hands, please. Who thinks this woman is Dorothy Bradford?"

Everyone raised a hand. Some of them raised two.

"Well, looks like we've found her!" Maggie said. A loud cheer went up. Maggie smiled broadly. The roar sounded as though it had come from a much larger audience than the forty people in the yard. "Let's take a beer break, and then we can talk about how to take advantage of all the great publicity we've gotten, thanks to Rob and the article in today's Cape Cod Journal. For those of you who haven't read it yet we have copies up front."

Everyone got up, and those who weren't already in line at the keg, quickly joined. Rachel scurried over to Rob and hugged him.

"You were wonderful," she said, squeezing so hard he vomited some beer in his mouth.

"I wasn't," Rob said. Rachel released him and he thought he might collapse to the ground. "I was supposed to convince them she isn't Dorothy Bradford."

"You made your case, Rob. It's hard getting up in front of people. Look what happed to Elaine Snow. I could never do it."

"Do you think she's Dorothy Bradford?" Rob asked. Rachel was looking over at the keg, checking to make sure the flow from the tap was still adequate.

"People need to believe in something," she said after a moment, now sounding introspective. Rob wasn't sure this was an answer.

Maggie Mason walked over and joined them. "Sorry, Rob," she said, throwing her hands up in the air. "Like I said, without your friend there wasn't much you could do."

"So what happens now?"

"Her picture goes on our web site. She is Dorothy Bradford."

Rob tensed. He saw flashing lights now, but wasn't sure where they were coming from. He felt he needed to get angry but wasn't sure. "But it's not true," he said. "Jesus, how can it be?" His voice rose, and his tone became more combative.

Rachel shrank, as best a woman of her size could shrink, sensing the rising tension.

"You think she's dead?" Maggie said.

"Of course she's dead!" Rob said loudly. This got the attention of a few of the nearby members. Rachel crept away.

"Rob, you need to keep your voice down," Maggie Mason said.

"Okay, sure, but this is a person you're dealing with. You're putting a target on her head."

"No, we are putting a crown on her head. In this case, a bonnet." Maggie looked around for Rachel. She had not ventured far, and Maggie signaled for her to come over.

"Everything okay?" Rachel said.

"Fine," Maggie said. "Go and get me a bonnet, would you please?" Rachel nodded and headed into the house.

"But you're going to hunt her down, aren't you?" Rob complained.

"We don't hunt people down. Since you won't tell us who she is, we'll do what we have been doing, which is to watch for her. We know where the camera washed up, so we'll start there. A lot of our members are watching the water anyway. Most of our sightings are in the bay."

"And when you find her, what do you do?" Rob hated to think of what chance Katie would have trying to break free from the clenches of Rachel or any of the other substantial women.

"Take more pictures. Try and approach her. Pretty much what the missing swimmers did. We're not going to grab her and throw her in a cage." Rachel came back from the house with the bonnet. It looked like the one everyone else was wearing. Rob thought it might have had some special embroidery. "Here, Rob," Maggie said, taking the bonnet from Rachel. "I want you to tell your friend what happened here today and give this to her. Ask her to come meet with us. You can imagine what kind of reception she'll get when she does."

"She's not coming," Rob said, emphatically. "And she's not my friend."

"Isn't she? Have her put this on. She'll feel differently."

"I don't think so."

Rachel was beaming again, relieved that civility had been restored. "More beer?" she offered. She didn't wait for an answer, grabbing both their mugs and making for the keg.

"Tell me, Maggie," Rob said. "What happens when you find out she isn't Dorothy Bradford?"

"But she is, Rob."

"Let me put it this way, was there another Dorothy Bradford before this one?"

"None. Listen, you'll have to excuse me, I've got to get ready for the rest of the meeting. Give her the bonnet, okay?"

Rob didn't answer. Feeling defeated, he stuffed the bonnet in his back pocket, and thought about leaving. Rachel delivered his beer before he could.

"I have to go help Maggie," she said. "Drink up." And she left.

Rob stood by himself near the edge of the property, watching the women pound their beers and bellow at each other in full voice. He tried to picture Katie standing among them, trading stories that beer-drinking women shared. "Leave her alone," he said, gesturing to the women who were clustered around his wife's picture. "You have to leave her alone." His attention was diverted by a lone figure standing off to the side, someone who was not wearing a bonnet—another man! The man looked at Rob, raised his glass, and headed towards him.

"They'll mostly ignore you now," the man said. "They're not much for men. They know they can't exist without us, but would rather we kept out of the way."

"Are you a member, too, then?"

"Yes. Honorary like you. I think there are two or three of us now. My name's Jeff Hansen. I wrote a book about the pilgrims a few years back, and devoted a page to Dorothy Bradford. Not much more to say about her really. Still, they liked it. I raised some question about whether her death was an accident. Since then they haven't said more than a couple of words to me. They came to me once, wanting to know what Dorothy would typically eat. Anyway, I mostly come to the meetings for the free beer. Best on the Cape." He took another drink from his glass.

"How come you don't have a mug?"

"I got one, just don't use it. Those fuckers are too heavy, and I'm sure I saw one of those carved animals grinning at me once." Rob had noticed his wrist was becoming a little stiff. He studied the adornments on his mug. Nothing was grinning at him, but a wolf-like animal appeared to be moving.

"Did the Pilgrims really drink this much beer?" he asked.

"They did," Jeff Hansen said. "Water was dangerous. Too much bacteria. And it was easier to survive with a buzz on. Just like now." Hansen laughed at this.

Rob reached into his pocket and pulled out the bonnet. "Maggie asked me to give this to my friend, and tell her she is really Dorothy Bradford."

"Yeah, don't worry about it too much. They'll move on to someone else in a month or two."

"Really?" Rob said, his mood brightening.

"Sure. Another picture of a strong looking woman in a boat will turn up, and they'll decide she's the real Dorothy. Your friend will be quickly forgotten. Maggie Mason is all about publicity. She's always looking for some way to get attention from the press. She keeps throwing stuff out there until something sticks, as they say."

"Well, that's a relief," Rob said. "Maybe I should leave the bonnet with you."

"Don't give it to me," Hansen said. "In my condition, I might put it on."

Rob and Jeff Hansen spent the rest of the meeting seated under an oak tree—Rob had checked for poison ivy first—drinking beer and telling Pilgrim stories, though Jeff did most of the telling. Rob was tempted to tell Jeff about the real identity of the woman in the row boat but knew this would be a mistake. Jeff could easily have been one of Maggie Mason's operatives, sent to commiserate and elicit information about the woman's whereabouts. Still he enjoyed Jeff's company.

After the meeting they staggered to a bar and ate fried clams and drank more beer. Rob was in no shape to drive anywhere—he had long surpassed the one gallon threshold—so Jeff invited him to spend the night. Rob gave his new friend a hard stare, and before he could blurt out anything idiotic, something he was good at even when he wasn't drunk, Jeff said not to worry about his intentions.

"Not everyone in Provincetown is gay, Rob," he said.

"You should have your own parade," Rob said.

THIRTEEN

Sharks and Suicide Alley

Katie was on the water early that morning. Rob had left early, too, driving Danny to Hyannis for his surgery. Katie kissed her son, wished him luck, and asked Rob to call her once the procedure was finished. So it was that she had her cell phone with her when the shark popped out of the water, right alongside the boat. It looked to be a white shark, perhaps eight feet long—the length of the boat.

"Oh, boy," Katie said uneasily as the shark swam by. She stopped rowing and pulled one of the oars out of its lock, ready to club the animal over the head if it got too aggressive. The shark swam off and then circled back. Katie grabbed her cell phone and took a few pictures on the next pass. Rob had shown her the shark app on his phone, and she had downloaded it, too. Now she could not only report a sighting but post a picture, too.

The shark swam off a second time and was gone. Katie waited a minute then opened the app on her phone. She had only to report how many sharks she saw and their condition. Live? Dead? Distressed? How would you know if a shark was distressed? The app used GPS for the location, and provided the date and time. She hesitated about adding her name and phone number, but they were required. She posted the pictures she had taken and hit send. Next she called Rob, knowing he would still be in the car.

"What?" Rob said after she told him about the shark.

"I got pictures, too!"

"Where?"

"Maybe halfway to the secret beach. It came right up alongside the boat."

"Jesus, Kay. Get out of the water!"

"Relax, Rob, it wasn't Jaws. I reported it on the shark app. Very exciting."

"Katie, you need to get out of the water."

"How's Danny?"

"We're not there yet. Are you heading for the beach?"

"Does his knee hurt from sitting in the car?"

"He's fine. He says you should get to shore now and stay out of the water for a while. I agree!"

"I guess." Katie wasn't too sure about this. The shark didn't bother her, but the prospect of landing in an unfamiliar spot, where she was more likely to encounter other people, toyed with her anxiety level.

"You'll be fine, Kay. Use a towel as a blindfold if you have to."

"The shark is gone."

"Look, I've got to worry about Danny right now. I'd rather not have to worry about you, too. Row to shore and wait an hour. Then, if you don't see the shark again, you can go the rest of the way. How's that?"

"Okay."

"Use the towel."

"I will."

"I'll call you after the surgery."

Katie ended the call and looked around the boat. The water was peaceful. No sign of any sharks. She played with the oars, not yet convinced of her course. The beach was peaceful and inviting, free of seaweed, rocks, and people. It was still early enough in the day that the probability of anyone appearing was minimal. And she could hide her face under her towel if she had to. She checked the shark app again and found that her sighting had already been posted, along with the pictures. Her location was marked by a square with a red exclamation mark over it. She wondered if they would call her for details, though she wasn't sure what more she could add.

"Fine," she said and turned the boat for shore.

* * *

The section of Route Six between Orleans and Dennis was a thirteen mile, two-lane stretch of highway known as Suicide Alley, so called because of all the spectacularly fatal accidents that occurred there. Cars rocketed past each other at high speeds with only a thin yellow line separating them. At night, when people had had too much to drink or were just feeling a little depressed, a slight twitch was all that was necessary to produce a head-on collision with some other poor bastard, who had no time to react and nowhere to go if he did. Over the years, as more people met their demise, a puny median strip was installed. Then they stuck yellow poles in it. The poles did little to deter the new crop of drivers, who were sure they could operate their cars and their cell phones at the same time. The constant human carnage led the local authorities to reduce the speed limit to fifty miles an hour, but many people—terrified of death—drove much slower. So it was that Rob found himself in a long line of single-lane traffic, south of Orleans, crawling along at speeds approaching twenty miles per hour.

"It's eight o'clock for Christ's sake," Rob said.

"Cape rush hour," Danny said from the back seat, his leg propped up. The swelling was gone and his knee felt much better, but all it took was a few minutes of walking to cause the pain to return.

"Stop-and-go driving is not good for my poison ivy."

"Why don't you have someone look at it?"

"It's going away."

"Of course it is," Danny said, poking at his knee and yawning. Years had passed since he had gone more than a day without running. Lethargy was setting in and he felt himself becoming irritable. "When are you going to tell me what you were doing in Provincetown Monday night?" he asked.

"I told you. I went to dinner with a friend. We had too much to drink so I stayed at his place."

"So who was it?"

"You don't know him."

"You're not fooling around on Mom, are you?"

"Stop it."

"Come on, just tell me. I won't blame you."

"It was a male friend, okay?"

"You were fooling around with a guy?"

Rob honked his horn at the driver in front of him, who was staring at his cell phone while a stretch of road opened up ahead. "Come on, asshole!" he shouted at the driver.

"Did it have something to do with Dorothy Bradford?" Danny asked.

"What?"

"Your trip to Provincetown. You said the headquarters was up there. Did that woman ever write you back?"

Rob sighed. He wasn't really sure why he hadn't told Danny about the meeting. There was no reason not to. His reasons for going were noble, after all. "Alright, I'll tell you," he said.

"I'm not going to be shocked, am I? I am having surgery in a few hours."

Rob explained about the society meeting and his attempt to disqualify Katie's picture, or at least scare them out of using it. As he spoke, Danny's face remained inexpressive. Rob could just as well have been telling him what he ate for breakfast. "I guess I wasn't very convincing."

"You're not the threatening type."

"I know."

"So you got hammered and passed out in Maggie Mason's backyard?"

"I didn't pass out. After the meeting I went to get food with this guy I met there, the only other guy at the meeting. We drank more. I wasn't in any shape to drive home so he said I could sleep at his place."

"And did he take advantage of you?"

"Yes. I now know as much about being gay as I do about Dorothy Bradford."

Danny fiddled with his phone trying to find the Dorothy Bradford web site. "Did they post the picture yet?" he said.

"No, but they will."

"Who cares? No one's going to see it."

"I'm not worried about the site. The problem is that they're now convinced she's Dorothy Bradford, and they're going to come looking for her."

"And do what? Offer her a beer? Listen, tell Mom about it. As long as she knows what to watch out for she'll be okay. She's much better, you know. Yesterday afternoon we walked on the beach."

"You did?" Rob said.

"We kept our distance from other people but she was fine with it."

"Has she gone back on the drugs?"

"Nope. It's just her."

Rob looked at Danny in the rearview mirror and smiled. "You're a good son to your mom," he said.

"Not to you?"

"You're a constant embarrassment to me." The car behind him honked. Now it was Rob who wasn't keeping up with the traffic.

*   *   *

Katie brought the boat to the shoreline but didn't get out. She thought maybe she could just sit there for half an hour and then move along. Still, there was no one in sight, and Katie was at ease despite the unfamiliar surroundings. Her beach walk with Danny yesterday afternoon was, as Danny told her repeatedly, a big deal. "Be proud of yourself," he said. "I'm proud of you." She wondered what had changed that made it okay for her to walk calmly within a few yards of other people. Perhaps it was Danny's knee—she was more concerned that he might aggravate his injury walking in the sand than she was about her irrational fears. Maybe she just needed other things to worry about.

She hopped out and pulled the boat onto the sand, turning it around so that she could make a quick getaway if she had to. She grabbed her towel and sat down next to the boat. She ran her hand along the gunwale, wondering if the shark had grazed it. She scanned the water for any signs of the animal but there was nothing. No humans either.

Katie had almost fallen asleep, remarkable in itself, when she was startled by a dog barking. She popped her head up. The dog was a hundred yards down the beach. A woman was following close behind. She could tell it was a woman by the long skirt she was wearing. Katie wanted to hop in her boat and take off, but she had resolved to fight the urge to flee. She lay down and pretended to be asleep which, of course, she almost had been anyway. Though she didn't feel the need to, she placed the towel over her eyes. A minute later she heard the dog sniffing close by. She didn't particularly mind the dog but knew its owner would be right behind. When the dog licked her face she bolted upright.

"I'm sorry! He's very affectionate," the woman called. She was still several yards away but was heading straight for Katie. The dog bounded into the water.

"You should keep him out of the water!" Katie cautioned. Somehow the warning served to lessen the anxiety that was toying with Katie's insides as the woman drew closer.

"Oh, he's fine," the woman said. "A real swimmer!"

"I saw a shark out there a few minutes ago," Katie said. She pretended to shield her eyes from the sun but she was actually covering them. She had to figure out a way of getting rid of the woman as quickly as possible.

"Oh there are no sharks in the bay, are there?"

"There are," Katie said.

"Can I give you this?" the woman asked, pulling a leaflet from the bag she carried across her shoulder.

"No. Sorry," Katie said. She was not going to open her eyes for this idiot woman who did not seem to care that her dog was at risk of being cut in half.

"Do you have a dog?"

"No."

"If you're troubled you should get one. He will help you find God. I wrote a book about it."

"Okay. Thanks." Katie wondered if she looked troubled. She had often wondered how she looked when her anxiety levels were rising. She imagined her face turned red from all the blood pounding through her veins.

"What a lovely boat," the woman said.

"Thanks, but I would actually be a lot less troubled if you'd get your dog out of the water. Good luck with your book." Katie lay back down, hoping this would signal the end of the discussion. Thankfully, the dog started barking, which diverted the woman's attention.

"What is it, boy? Do you see a shark?" the woman said, heading toward her dog. Katie peeked to make sure she was leaving. She noticed a leaflet lying next to her in the sand. After a minute she took a deep breath and congratulated herself on surviving another test, this one with a stranger, possibly a lunatic as well. In any event, the woman's dog had served a purpose in surviving his swim. Clearly the shark had moved on. It would be safe for her to get back in her boat. She stood up, and there on the other side of the boat stood two women. One of them had both her hands clasped over her mouth, seemingly awe-struck, the other had her cell phone aimed at Katie.

"It's her!" the woman without the phone screamed. Unnerved, and in no mood to engage any more unhinged women in conversation, Katie grabbed her boat and pulled it into the water. The women followed.

"Can we please talk to you?" the woman said while her companion continued to record. Katie cringed. Had these women written a book, too?

"Sorry," she said, climbing into her boat.

"We know who you are!"

Katie pushed off. When she was a safe distance away she said, "Who am I?"

"You're Dorothy Bradford!" the woman said.

"Sorry," Katie said. "You've got me confused with someone else." She started to row away.

"Please don't leave! You're very important to us!"

The two women jogged down the beach, chasing after Katie as she made her way south. She wanted to move further away from shore but was still mindful of the shark. These two women reminded her of the swimmers who had come after her in the water and then disappeared. Had they also thought that she was this Dorothy Bradford woman? Or were these two women and the missing swimmers the same people? She knew she would have to say something to Rob and probably the police, too. She hadn't liked the detective who questioned her at all. The thought of having to talk to him again was troubling. Before she got too far away, she snapped a picture of the women on the shore, zooming the lens as far as it would go. The women didn't stop their pursuit, and Katie wondered if they would follow her all the way to the secret beach. Not wanting to risk having them discover her sanctuary, she adjusted course and headed further out into the bay, shark or no shark. She would keep rowing until the women were out of sight.

* * *

Danny's surgery was a complete success according to the surgeon. He showed Danny and Rob the before and after pictures to prove it, but neither of them could see anything to show that the two pictures weren't of the same blob of connective tissue. Whatever they were looking at in the after-picture, though, was smooth and shiny—no ragged edges.

Danny was given a pair of crutches and some Percocet for the pain. The doctor didn't think he would need them beyond the second day of his convalescence, but he should plan to keep the leg elevated and iced regularly for at least the next five days. Once the stitches were out and the swelling came down he could start physical therapy.

The day had grown sunny and warm, which meant everyone was at the beach and not on the road. The drive back was uneventful save for a family of turkeys that hopped onto Route Six in Wellfleet. Rob would have been happy to run them over but he was stuck behind three cars.

They arrived home late in the afternoon. Katie decided that Danny should spend a day or two in the cottage so he wouldn't have to deal with any stairs. Rob offered to stay with him so Katie could go up to the house. She said no. She wanted to take care of him.

Katie was in the yard when they pulled in, tinkering with the hoses that fed her vegetable garden. She immediately left the hoses and hurried over to open the door for Danny.

"How do you feel?" she asked.

"Actually I don't feel anything right now," Danny said.

"You will," Rob said.

Katie helped Danny out of the car. Rob gave him the crutches and they escorted him into the cottage. Katie noticed that Rob was hobbling a bit, too. "What's wrong with you?" she asked.

Rob shrugged. "Poison ivy," he said. "And sitting in the car for an hour."

"Let me see," Katie said.

Rob showed her his ankle. Whereas the blistering seemed to have subsided over the past few days it had now returned. His ankle looked angry and red.

"Well, it's infected," Katie said. "You need to get antibiotics and steroids."

"I'll go to the health center in the morning," Rob said. "Let's deal with Danny today."

"Jesus, I've got a family of cripples," she said.

Danny was still woozy from the anesthetic, so Katie put him in her bed. She set pillows under his leg, wrapped an ice pack around the knee, and left him to sleep.

"The doctor said the knee cleaned up nicely," Rob said when Katie came back into the living room. "He thinks he'll be good as new in three months or so."

"Oh, good. So the Olympic trials are still in the picture?"

"Yes!"

Katie shuffled pots and pans in the kitchen, trying to keep her mind distracted. But then she stopped and gave herself over to the moment to see where it would lead. She noticed the hair on her arms was standing up. Her skin tingled. She was excited, but not scared. She would try to embrace what came next, and not fight it.

"I had an interesting encounter on the beach today, after the shark," she said. She took her phone out of her pocket and showed Rob the picture of the two women.

"Who are they?" Rob asked, but had a feeling he already knew. The two women fit the Bradford profile.

"I don't know. They seemed sure I was some woman named Dorothy Bradford. They followed me down the beach, so I rowed out into the bay. By the time I came back in they were gone."

"I'm not sure I like the idea of you rowing out so far with a shark out there."

"The shark was less of a threat than these two. They were pretty aggressive. One of them was filming the whole thing on her phone. I thought they might have been the same two women who took my picture before."

Rob took a closer look at the picture. The women were too stocky. The *Dorothy Swimmers* were much smaller.

"It's not them," Rob said. He knew he was going to have to tell her about the society and her new status within it. "Are you okay for a long story?" he asked, not wanting to instill any panic attacks while she was looking after Danny.

"Yeah, I'm fine. I'll put this on, though." She picked up her blindfold and placed it over her eyes. "I'm actually relieved to have you and Danny here. There were so many nut-jobs on the beach. I wish I could have gone with you to the hospital." She stood at the counter, still keeping her distance, looking like the subject of a hostage video. "I'm ready."

Rob laid out the course of events, beginning with the email exchange with Maggie Mason and ending with the Bradford Society meeting. Katie stayed in the kitchen, but her attention was rapt on Rob's story. Rob was enthralled by the look of amusement on her face, what he could see of it. He had expected her to either be appalled or run from the room.

"So Dorothy Bradford was the woman you mentioned in that psychotic rant of yours on YouTube?" she said.

"Yeah. I was just kidding around, though. That's how Maggie Mason found me."

"And they think I'm her?"

"They're sure of it. Your picture made a big impression. You'll need to keep an eye out for them. They'll be looking for you."

Katie smiled at this. She pushed her blindfold up to her forehead and grabbed a spatula from the sink, holding it aloft. "All hail Dorothy!" she said. "Just like in *The Wizard of Oz*."

Looking worried, Rob said, "This doesn't bother you?"

"I think it's a riot. I'm a figurehead for a women's beer-drinking society. That sounds pretty good, doesn't it?"

"They do make good beer."

"You should have brought me to the meeting."

"Are you crazy?"

"You already know the answer to that."

"You know what I mean."

"I know this sounds weird, but I think I want to meet these people, Rob."

"How do you all of a sudden want to meet people?"

"I don't know." Katie sighed and put the spatula back in the sink. "I need to stop shying away from things. You know?"

"I do, and that's great, Kay, but you need to go slowly. Maybe spend time with normal people first."

"Normal people are terrifying. Does Danny know about this?"

"Yes."

"What does he think?"

"He thinks you can handle it," Rob said. "He's just like you, you know."

"Hopefully not *just* like me," Katie said, looking into the sink. One of her most rational fears was that her son might develop his own phobic behavior, crippling his life as she had crippled hers. He was the least fearful person she knew.

Rob's cell phone rang. He pulled it from his pocket and checked the caller ID. "Oh, shit," Rob said.

"What?" Katie said.

"Ridgeback."

"I'll bet he heard about Danny."

Rob accepted the call and said, "Give me one good reason why I shouldn't hang up on you, Ridgeback."

"I'm actually calling for your wife," Ridgeback said.

"Then you should call her." Rob looked at Katie. She folded her arms and narrowed her eyes. He couldn't tell if she was preparing to flee or pounce.

"I'm doing another story about the *Dorothy Swimmers*," Ridgeback said. "I've got this picture of the woman who they claim is Dorothy Bradford, and she looks an awful lot like Katie."

"What?"

"Look, Rob, I talked to Maggie Mason. She told me you were at their last meeting and tried to convince them this woman wasn't Dorothy Bradford. Seems obvious to me you were protecting your wife. Are you guys still separated?" Katie came into the living room and sat down next to Rob. He whispered to her that it was about Dorothy Bradford.

"Should I talk to him?" she asked.

"I'd rather we hang up on him," Rob said.

"Is she there?" Ridgeback asked. "Hello, Katie?"

Rob searched his wife's face for signs of panic. Katie shook her head, then got up and headed for the bedroom, though Rob believed she was going to check on Danny, and not running from her husband and his cell phone.

"You're wasting your time," Rob said into the phone. "Katie doesn't know anything about the Dorothy Bradford Society. If they want to believe she is Dorothy Bradford that's their business."

"It's interesting that both you and your wife are now wrapped up with the *Dorothy Swimmers* and this society, don't you think?" Ridgeback said. "Care to comment on that?"

"You're an enormous piece of shit, Ridgeback."

"Possibly."

"Always nice to talk to you," Rob said.

"How's Danny, by the way?" Ridgeback asked.

"Why?"

"I understand he had knee surgery today."

"How do you know that?"

"It's my job, remember?"

"Well he's doing just fine."

"Surgery a success?"

"Yes."

"How long is the recovery period?"

"Listen, he'll be ready for the Olympic trials so don't write any bullshit story that says he won't."

"Of course not! Why would I do that?"

"Are we done?"

"Hey, maybe I'll see you at the next Bradford Society meeting."

"Bye." Rob ended the call, glaring at his cell phone.

* * *

That night Rob relaxed on his sofa with a glass of scotch, and watched a double feature of *The Boys from Brazil* and *Marathon Man*. These were two of his favorite movies, both of which featured Laurence Olivier starring as a Nazi dentist in one and a Nazi hunter in the other. At the end of the *Boys from Brazil*, when the boy sets his Dobermans on Gregory Peck, Sidney rose from his slumber and pranced toward the screen, watching intently as the dogs shredded Peck's character into a forensic mess.

"Great scene, huh, boy?" Rob said. It was the first time the dog had ever taken notice of anything on television. When the scene was over, and Sidney had lowered himself back to the floor, Rob thought that maybe his next dog should be a more menacing breed, something he could set on intruders and journalists. Sidney got up again when Dustin Hoffman howled during the famous dental exam scene in *Marathon Man*. "Is it safe?" Olivier asked. Rob stared at his infected ankle, wondering if it would draw sharks, and knew it was not.

FOURTEEN

Black Eyes and Tee Shirts

Rob pulled into the Wellfleet Health Center early the next morning. He had been spending altogether too much time at doctors' offices and hospitals. This would be his third medical trip in the last week. This one was probably overdue, though. His ankle now looked like something out of a zombie apocalypse movie.

On the way, he had stopped at the cottage to see how Katie and Danny had managed the night before. He was pleased to find the two of them eating breakfast and looking chipper. Both had slept through the night without incident. Danny said the knee didn't hurt much at all and that he had only had to take one Percocet at bedtime. Rob told him about Ridgeback's phone call. Danny thought Rob should have told him his son would never run again. "I've been told I shouldn't bait the media," Rob said.

Rob checked in at the front desk, and was told to have a seat in the waiting room. "Shouldn't be long," the receptionist said. He nodded, wondering if he should ask the woman what her definition of "long" was, but discussing time with anyone on the Cape was pointless. He turned and looked for a seat, careful to avoid anyone who looked ill.

After he sat down, a man across the room said, "We meet again!" Rob knew who it was without looking. How had he missed him? Probably because Ridgeback's nose was hideously swollen and plugged up with cotton balls.

"Jesus, what happened to you?" Rob said, finding it oddly difficult to summon up the vitriol he had felt the day before. Ridgeback chuckled, and Rob expected him to say he had walked into a door or something. It was better than that.

"Tim Desmond," he said.

"Really?"

"I think I finally pissed him off."

"You? That's hard to believe."

"I know, right?"

"What did you say?"

"I asked him how he would feel when they started knocking down his house." Ridgeback poked at the swollen mess spreading across his face. "I was just kidding!"

Rob made a mental note not to cross Tim Desmond.

"Well, it probably serves you right."

"Not the first time someone took a swing at me. Though it is my first busted nose."

"Did you call the police?"

"Why? Waste of time. Desmond's not a bad guy really."

Rob propped up his ankle and noticed the coloring was similar to the welts on Ridgeback's face. "I met him," he said. "He showed me the house."

"He's not supposed to go in there."

"He wasn't living there." Rob was immediately sorry he brought it up. He had forgotten how easy it was to talk to Ridgeback. "Shit, you're not going to write about him showing me the house are you?"

"I'm done reporting on Desmond. I'll cover the board meeting tonight and that's it."

"You don't want to report on the demolition?"

"They won't make him knock it down. They'll slap a fine on him, which will be paid by the contractor, and he can move in."

"Wouldn't you rather write about that than the Dorothy Bradford Society?"

"Of course not! You met them. Tell me there aren't five or six good stories there."

A nurse came into the waiting room and stared down at her clipboard, clearly having trouble with the name she had to call. She read the first name and then as much of the last name as she could manage. A woman rose, finished off her last name for the nurse, and followed her back to the exam rooms.

Rob was careful with the next question. "Did you find out who the woman in the boat is?"

"Well it's your wife, isn't it, Rob?" Ridgeback said.

"Nice try."

"My editor won't let me put a name in there without a confirmation. We'll run the picture but refer to her as an unidentified woman. I think Don Hill knows who it is but he won't tell me. He's pretty pissed the picture got out. He thinks someone in his office leaked it." Rob couldn't imagine Don Hill being pissed. He was relieved at this news, though he had learned not to trust Ridgeback. Until he read the article nothing was sure.

"Is Hill making any progress?"

"He won't tell me. He did say that he's trying to establish if there was a personal connection between the *Dorothy Swimmers* and any of the society members. That includes the woman in the boat."

"What does that mean?"

"You know, scorned lovers, that sort of thing."

"Sounds like he's reaching, or watching too much TV."

"I think he's getting frustrated." Ridgeback looked down at the floor and noticed Rob's ankle. "Jesus! Your ankle looks worse than my face."

* * *

After thirty minutes of waiting, then five minutes of being lectured by the doctor, who threatened amputation more than once, Rob was given a steroid shot, antibiotics, and a pile of prescriptions. The doctor told him to stay out of the weeds and keep the foot elevated. Rest, ice, and the other letters were apparently not necessary.

Rob was discharged into the parking lot, foot intact, where he noticed a blue Prius parked next to his car. He stared hard at the empty driver's seat, sure that whoever had sat there was the prick who ran Danny off the road. Working up his inner rage, he ran back inside and scanned the waiting room for an older man. The room was full of them. Resisting the urge to call for the owner of the blue Prius, he went back outside, took a picture of the car, and texted it to Danny. "Was this the car?" he asked. Danny wrote back that he wasn't sure. It was the same model and color. Rob asked about the license plate. Danny hadn't seen it. He only knew it was a blue Prius and that the driver was a guy with white hair. He asked his father about his foot.

"They want to cut it off," Rob answered. He got in his car, propped the foot up on the passenger seat, and waited. He wanted to see the son of a bitch who owned the Prius.

A half hour went by, and Rob was becoming impatient. He had already done enough waiting for one day, and he still had to stop at the pharmacy. He played with his cell phone, trying to figure out how much data he had left in the current billing cycle. The month before, he had exceeded his limit by three kilobytes and the bastards charged him fifteen bucks. Having determined he had plenty of capacity left, he opened the Dorothy Bradford Society website, now bookmarked on his phone, and discovered that the picture of Katie had been added to the home page. There was a one word caption below that read, "Dorothy Bradford found!" A video link had also been added, which showed Katie on the beach, popping up from behind her boat, dragging it into the water and rowing away. This was surely the footage that had been captured the day before. Rob watched the video twice. The second time, he turned up the volume on his phone and could hear the two women behind the camera squealing repeatedly, "It's her! It's her!" One of them asked Katie to come back, that they needed to talk to her. Katie said nothing. The end of the video showed Katie disappearing into the bay as she rowed out of the camera's range.

Rob toggled back to the screen that showed his data utilization, curious to see how much he had used on the video. Before the screen refreshed, he heard a car door close. An elderly white-haired man, looking shrunken and frail, had somehow managed to squeeze behind the wheel of the Prius. The driver's seat was so far forward that it seemed impossible that anyone could fit in there. Rob stared hard, hoping the man would look over and see the hateful expression on his face. The man was busy, however, flipping through what appeared to be his own ream of prescriptions. "Fuck this," Rob said and got out of the car. He circled the Prius and knocked on the driver's side window. The man did not look up. Was he deaf? Rob knocked again and said aggressively, "Excuse me?" The man put down his prescriptions and tried to lower the window, but the engine wasn't on, if there even was an engine in a Prius. Puzzled that the window wouldn't go down, the man opened the door instead.

"Oh, did I forget something inside?" he said, figuring Rob for an employee at the health center. The man had a kind face. His expression was disarming, and Rob immediately regretted his decision to confront him. He cleared his throat, and wondered what the hell he was doing.

"Uh, no," Rob said. "I'm sorry, I thought you were someone else."

"I think that, too, sometimes," the man said, smiling.

"Listen, I'm sorry to bother you."

"It's alright," the man said.

"Looks like you're next stop is the pharmacy, too," Rob said, now feeling the need to empathize.

"Yes. I'm having to spend more and more of my time there these days. And I'm not looking forward to making that left turn onto Route Six. I'm not the driver I was."

Rob's face hardened again but he didn't have it in him to accuse the old man, who had started patting his steering wheel as if to smooth relations with his car. All the same, he let the man leave the lot first so he could follow him to the pharmacy and see whether he was able to keep the car between the white lines. The man drove slowly but his car did not drift.

* * *

Had the doctor said anything about not sitting in the sun while taking the medication? Rob couldn't remember, but he didn't care. The weather was too nice. To be safe, he would sit under an umbrella and wrap a towel around his ankle. He would also bring down a cooler, so he could prop up his foot while convalescing on the beach.

Since the tide was coming in, Rob planted the umbrella and chair further from the water. He didn't want to have to get up and move, given all the crap he had dragged down with him. He spent most of his time watching for sharks. The shark tracking app hadn't reported any sightings in the bay since Katie posted her entry, although she had been a mile south of there, and well away from the shore. There were plenty of people in the water at the public beach. No fins in sight.

Rob was about to nod off, when Helen Schantz wandered by. She stopped and stared at Rob, most likely trying to remember who he was. After a moment she said, "Did they ever find those people?" Perhaps Rob's chair, umbrella, and cooler had jogged her memory.

"Hi, Helen," he said, trying to be civil. He had abused enough elderly people today, though he wasn't sure anymore that Helen Schantz was elderly. He now thought she could have been his age. "You mean the swimmers?"

"Yes. Nobody else has disappeared, have they?"

"I don't think so. No. They're still missing."

"Well that's very peculiar, isn't it?" This sounded like a rhetorical question, but Helen Schantz appeared to be looking for an answer.

"Yes, very peculiar," Rob said.

"You know, I didn't think much of those policemen who were down here before. I'm not surprised those people haven't been found. Maybe if they brought in some real police."

"Like the FBI?"

"Well, I don't know about that."

Realizing he had an opportunity to make a point with Helen Schantz, Rob pulled the towel off his ankle and deliberately looked at the rash. "Hey, Helen, you want to see what poison ivy does to me?"

Helen Schantz shuffled forward and looked at Rob's ankle. Her expression remained indifferent, and absent any sympathy, she said, "How long are you here for?"

Rob sighed and put the towel back over his leg. "I live here year-round now, Helen."

"Oh. It can get very cold in the winter."

"I brought a jacket."

Helen Schantz gave Rob a tight-lipped smile, and continued on her way to a spot a few yards from where Rob was sitting. She was barely far enough away to be considered a separate party and not a beach buddy. "Please, join me," Rob said inaudibly, or so he thought. Helen Schantz looked at him. He waved. She didn't notice.

In addition to keeping an eye out for sharks, Rob was also on the lookout for Dorothy Bradford Society scouts, who were sure to be patrolling the bay beaches, in search of Katie, especially after the sighting and resulting video from the day before. It seemed clear that it was only a matter of time before two or three members got between Katie and her boat, and demanded to know what she had been doing for the last four hundred years. She would have to be especially vigilant now when leaving the cottage, assuming she didn't decide to remain holed up in there until the mayhem subsided.

Every beach walker was suspect, particularly the many women who passed by, usually in pairs, some bent on physical fitness, walking briskly with arms pumping, others meandering thoughtfully toward spiritual fulfillment. It was the first group that were more likely to be Bradford women, though they were searching for a savior, not fitness.

One particular pair of women caught his eye, one large, one slight, both wearing shorts and what looked to be matching white tee shirts with something stenciled on the front. From a distance, Rob could not see what the tee shirts said, but he had an idea. The large woman looked familiar. Her size and gait—she moved like a gymnast, seemingly defying gravity—gave her away. It was Rachel, the gentle Amazon who served as Maggie Mason's assistant. He pulled down the lid of his cap and thought to hide behind his book. But as he dug in his backpack, he wondered why he needed to hide. He liked Rachel, after all. There was nothing threatening about her, and she seemed to genuinely like him. Rob liked people who liked him, particularly women.

So for the second time that day, Rob did something out of character. He got up from his chair and walked over to greet the two women. He could now plainly see that the picture of his wife was silk-screened on their shirts, with "Dorothy!!!" printed below. He also now recognized the smaller woman as being Elaine Snow, the dimwitted society member who meekly presented the unremarkable picture of the kayaker at the society meeting.

"Rachel!" Rob called as the women approached. Elaine Snow checked up, slowing her gait warily, but Rachel became animated and waved.

"Hi, Rob. We were hoping we might see you around here somewhere," she said. "Though, we're really hoping to see someone else, too." She pointed proudly to the front of her tee shirt.

"They make quite a statement," Rob said, relieved to see that the quality of the silk screening was such that you couldn't really see Katie's face clearly.

"Did you see the video from yesterday?" Rachel asked.

"I did."

"Has your lawyer friend told you about it?" Rachel's expression was eerily omniscient. Rob had the feeling she knew exactly who Dorothy Bradford was.

"Um, no," he said. I haven't seen her for a few days actually."

"I think our girls managed to scare her off."

"Well, it's not such a great idea to run at her like she's a rock star or something."

"But she is a rock star!" Elaine Snow said. "To us, anyway."

"You're Elaine, right?" Rob said. "I remember you from the meeting." Elaine Snow dropped her head and stared at the sand, still clearly embarrassed by her performance. Feeling bad for her, he said, "I liked your picture of the kayaker very much."

"Thanks," she said. "I worked pretty hard to get it. Just as hard, if not harder, than the people who took the one on our shirts." She sounded bitter now.

"Come on, Elaine, nobody says you didn't." Rachel said. "Besides, if we see Dorothy today you can take an even better picture of her, right?"

"I guess," she said, looking out at the water now, hoping to see a row boat. She had a digital SLR camera with her. No cell phone camera for Elaine.

"Elaine, you go on ahead for a bit," Rachel said. "I need to talk to Rob about a personal matter. I'll catch up with you. If you see anything you can call me, okay?"

"Sure," Elaine said. And she left without saying goodbye.

Rob wondered what personal matter Rachel could want to discuss. She barely knew him.

"Elaine doesn't like the two women who took the Dorothy picture," Rachel said when Elaine was far enough away.

"She knew them?"

"No, but Elaine is our staff photographer, and Elizabeth and Roberta were brought in just for this assignment. So you can understand why she is a little miffed that they got the Dorothy picture, and she didn't."

"But Elizabeth and Roberta could be...well, you know." He found it strange to speak their names. He had referred to them as the missing swimmers, or the *Dorothy Swimmers*.

"Elaine feels like she could have gotten the picture without disappearing." Rachel folded her arms and looked at the water.

"This is where they went in," Rob said, pointing to the shore.

"I know." She grew pensive and Rob guessed the personal matter was going to be a difficult subject.

"What did you want to talk to me about?" he asked. "Without Elaine?"

Rachel smiled uncomfortably. "Listen, I'm not supposed to say anything, but I like you, Rob, and I don't want to see anything bad happen."

"What do you mean?" Rob asked. He reached down to scratch his ankle, but stopped himself. He needed to sit down soon.

"Some of our members are more aggressive than others."

"I got that from the meeting."

"I worry a few of them might try and grab your friend, once we find her. And we're getting close."

"You mean kidnap her?"

"Oh, I hope it doesn't come to that." Rob shot a panicky glance behind him toward the stairs.

Rachel's attention followed his. "She lives up there somewhere, doesn't she?" Rachel said.

"Look, are you serious about this? Do I really need to worry that someone is going to grab my..." He stopped himself and swallowed hard.

"She's your wife, isn't she?" Rachel said.

"Listen. I've got to go and sit down. My ankle is bad." He hobbled back to his chair and sat. Rachel followed him.

Helen Schantz was standing next to her chair, staring at the two of them, her hands on her hips.

"Who is Dorothy?" Helen Schantz asked in a demanding tone, eyeing Rachel's extra-large tee shirt.

"Dorothy Bradford, ma'am," Rachel said, not wanting to pass up the promotional opportunity.

"I don't know who that is." She looked at Rob for answers, but Rob had gotten out his cell phone. He was calling Danny, who was still at the cottage, to alert him to the threat.

Rachel continued her explanation, but Helen Schantz was not interested. "This has to do with those foolish swimmers, doesn't it?" she said.

"I'm sorry?" Rachel said. She sensed the woman was not worth her time, and sat down next to Rob.

"Helen, it's fine," Rob said, having hung up with Danny. "She's a friend."

"I'm glad you think of me as a friend," Rachel said, smiling now. "Did you call her?"

"I called my son. He's with her," Rob said, abandoning the charade. "She's a tough lady," he said. "Much tougher than I am."

"I know she is."

"What do you mean, you know?" Rob asked, now worried Rachel and Katie were friends, too.

Rachel cocked her head and pointed to her tee shirt.

"She's Dorothy Bradford, isn't she?"

"She's not Dorothy Bradford, Rachel. I've known her for thirty years." Rob looked over at Helen Schantz, who was still glaring at him and Rachel disapprovingly. "Sit down, Helen," he said impatiently. "Relax for God's sake."

"Look, I don't know that anything is going to happen," Rachel said, "I just wanted to alert you, so you can keep an eye out. You know?"

"Sure," Rob said. He stood now and gathered up his things. "I've got to go."

"Can I go with you?"

Rob struggled with the cooler and beach chair. "No. Not a good idea," he said.

"I'll carry your stuff. You have a bad ankle, remember?" Rob looked at the image of his wife, stretched over Rachel's remarkable bosom, and considered whether his initial reaction to her request was the right one. Perhaps by introducing Katie to Rachel, the society's extremists could be appeased, and the threat of a hostile first encounter avoided. Despite her size, there was nothing threatening about Rachel. She was the ideal liaison.

"If I take you, you have to promise me that you'll keep the others away," Rob said. "If she's going to meet with the members she has to do it on her own terms. And you can't tell anyone where she lives, or who she really is."

"She's Dorothy Bradford," Rachel said. She took the beach equipment from Rob. It seemed much less unwieldy in her arms.

"I have to call her first, and let her know we're coming. Make sure she's okay with it." While he dug for his cell phone, he told Rachel about Katie's condition.

"I used to be afraid of leaving the house," Rachel said.

"She's not afraid of leaving the house," Rob said. 'She's afraid of other people."

"Same illness."

"She's not ill, she has a condition."

"Sure," Rachel said.

Katie answered her cell phone, and Rob told her about Rachel. "She wants to come meet you," Rob said.

Katie didn't say anything.

"This might make sense, Kay," he continued. "It could put an end to these random beach encounters."

Katie said something to Danny in a muffled tone, and Danny said incredulously, "Here?"

"I'm worried they'll show up at the door one day," Rob continued. "It's probably better this way. And you'll like her." Katie remained silent. Rob expected she wanted to say yes, but needed to subdue the anticipatory anxiety first. He looked at Rachel and shrugged his shoulders.

Rachel pointed to the cell phone and whispered, "Let me talk to her."

Rob punched the speaker icon on the screen and held out the phone. "Katie, the phone's on speaker. Rachel wanted to say something."

"Hi, Mrs. Crosley," Rachel said, surprising Rob by not calling her Mrs. Bradford. "I know this is probably making you uncomfortable. I don't want to make you uncomfortable. There are a lot of people, me included, who are convinced that you're Dorothy Bradford, and really want to meet you. I want to find a way where you can meet them on your own terms, and not theirs."

After a moment Katie said, "Okay. Please come up."

Rachel smiled, overjoyed that her request to meet the great woman had been approved. She thanked Katie and said she looked forward to meeting her.

Rob ended the call and said to Rachel, "One condition."

"Sure."

"If she gets panicky, and it sounds like you know what that is, you leave right away."

"I understand."

"She might be wearing a blindfold."

* * *

Rob didn't want to have to explain about his family's living arrangements, so he bypassed the house and went straight to the cottage. He hobbled along on his bad leg, while Rachel followed close behind, loaded down with beach equipment like some oversized Sherpa. As they approached the cottage, Rob was surprised to see Katie waiting for them in the front yard.

"Wow," Rachel said as they neared. She stopped and gawked at Katie. She continued to cradle the cooler under one arm, with the chair and umbrella in the other. Katie was wearing jeans, work boots, and a tee shirt. Her hair hung loose over her shoulders. She looked formidable.

Katie stared, too. She was surprised by Rachel's size, and was at a loss to understand why she was carrying all of Rob's stuff. Then there was the tee shirt with her picture on it. The woman was so completely different from what she imagined that her anxiety was derailed.

"Rob, why have you made this poor girl carry everything up from the beach?" Katie said. Though Rachel was large, she looked quite young, and Katie's motherly instincts, rekindled by Danny's injury, took over.

"Oh, it's okay," Rachel said. "I offered. Rob's ankle is bothering him."

"Put it down there," Rob said, pointing to a spot by the cottage.

"I came outside because I didn't want us bothering Danny," Katie said, interpreting Rob's confused expression.

Rob picked up the chair from where Rachel had left it and snapped it open. "I hope you ladies don't mind if I sit down. Katie, this is Rachel. She's a big fan."

Katie said hello. She had decided against wearing the blindfold. Was she already tending to her image as Dorothy Bradford?

"I'm so happy to meet you," Rachel said, keeping a respectful distance. She was either in awe, or being mindful of Katie's disorder.

Rob settled awkwardly in the chair and rewrapped his ankle in the towel. Though he wasn't in the sun he didn't want anything landing on it and gnawing on the pus and blood beneath the infected skin.

"Put your foot up on the cooler," Katie said.

Rob did as he was told. He sensed something different about Katie's demeanor. She seemed less a person who needed to be coddled. Her gaze shifted from his foot to his face. She raised an eyebrow, scolding him silently for taking his foot to the beach. He felt he had somehow failed her.

"So, you met Rob at one of your meetings?" Katie asked, shifting her attention back to Rachel.

"Yes," Rachel said, clearing her throat, her voice having briefly deserted her. "We invited him to come after the news segment came out. I guess he came to try and convince us you weren't Dorothy Bradford."

"Well, I'm not. Am I?"

"We think you are. That you're somehow immortal."

"And what do you want from me?"

"Instruction, direction."

"About?"

"How to survive."

"I survive by avoiding other people."

"But you're not avoiding me."

"Only because I want you to tell your friends to stop looking for me."

"Come tell them yourself."

"You have to tell them, Rachel."

"But Rob already tried that, and it didn't work. They need to see you. If you don't come, they'll keep chasing you. That's what I'm trying to save you from."

Just then, a woman called out from the road. "Rachel, where are you?" the woman said. It was Elaine Snow. She had seen Rachel following Rob up the dune stairs.

"Who is that?" Katie said, mildly alarmed.

Rob scrambled from his chair. His first instinct was to chase down Elaine Snow and tackle her. Realizing he was in no condition to chase anyone, he stopped and pressed his forefinger to his lips, imploring Rachel not to answer. He thought Katie would have ended the conversation and run back to the house by now, but she stayed where she was.

"That's my friend, Elaine," Rachel whispered to Katie. "She must have seen us come up here."

"She'll want to meet me, too, right?"

"Oh, yes."

Katie hesitated, making sure she wasn't slipping. "So, go and get her," she said. Rachel ran out to the road to collect Elaine Snow.

Rob held up his arms in disbelief.

"Kay, what are you doing?"

"Meeting my people, I guess," she said.

"You're okay with this?"

"I don't know why, but I feel really calm right now." She looked at the sky. A lazy cloud had drifted in front of the sun. "Maybe I am Dorothy Bradford."

Rachel came back into the yard, dragging Elaine Snow behind her like a little kid soon for a bath.

"Rachel, you're hurting me!" Elaine Snow yelled.

Rachel let go of her and pointed at Katie.

"Look, Elaine. Look who it is."

Elaine was tending to her camera strap which had slipped down to her elbow in the frenzied few yards from the road. She looked up and squinted at Katie.

"Oh my God! It's her!" Elaine shouted. "Dorothy!" Star-struck, she fumbled for her camera and struggled to bring it to her eye. Here was her moment to capture the definitive picture of the immortal Pilgrim.

"Stop it, Elaine," Rachel said, grabbing her arm. "She's not a yeti."

Elaine Snow peered over the top of her camera but would not lower it from in front of her face. She wanted to be ready if Katie should bolt.

"Elaine is our photographer," Rachel said.

"Not the one who took the picture on our tee shirts, though," Elaine said, her voice shaking. "I would never take my camera in the water."

"You can take my picture," Katie said. "You've already got a bunch of them as it is."

Elaine Snow's eyes widened with anticipation as she prepared to start shooting.

"Not in front of the cottage!" Rob shouted, blocking Elaine Snow's view of his wife. He took Katie by the arm and moved her to the other side of Elaine so the cottage was now at the photographer's back.

"Rachel, come stand next to me," Katie said.

"Really?" Rachel said.

"Maybe if they see you and me together your friends will listen to you."

Rachel moved cautiously as she approached Katie's side. She had heard so many stories about Dorothy Bradford she wasn't sure what to expect. Was her body temperature forty-five degrees—the temperature of the water when she plunged into the bay? Did she have abnormally strong arms from four hundred years of rowing? It was not particularly hot out, but perspiration started to bead on Rachel's forehead. She took a deep breath and exhaled. Katie did the same, holding her breath for a moment and then releasing it slowly, hoping to keep her anxiety at bay. She took Rachel by the hand and pulled her closer. Rachel gasped audibly.

"What do you think, Elaine?" Katie said. "Do we look okay?" Elaine had the camera in front of her face but her hands were shaking. She couldn't steady the frame.

"Hold still" she yelled, but it was clear she was yelling at her hands, not at her subjects.

"I can take the picture if you want," Rob said, seeing the poor girl was on the verge of some kind of episode of her own. "You can be in the picture, too, Elaine."

"No! I have to take this!" she screamed, which only made her hands shake more.

"Wait a second," Katie said. She went over and put an arm around the troubled photographer. She recognized panic all too well.

"I'm sorry, Dorothy," Elaine said, her voice breaking, tears forming.

"Elaine," Katie whispered. "I'm as scared as you are."

"Oh, come on," Elaine said. "You? Scared?"

"I don't avoid people because I don't like them. I avoid them because I'm scared of them."

"Really?"

"Yes."

"Are you scared of me?"

"I was when I first saw you. I'm better now. How about you?"

"Better, too," Elaine said, nodding. "You're much nicer than I imagined."

"What did you imagine?"

"Oh, lots of things. You hear so many stories."

Katie returned to Rachel's side and smiled for the pictures. Elaine Snow took a bunch of them from different angles, kneeling at one point.

"Could you maybe not smile?" Elaine said after the first few shots.

"Why?" Katie said.

"You're supposed to look serious, like in the boat picture."

"Who says?"

"Everyone."

"Don't listen to her," Rachel said. "I think we're done with the pictures now, Elaine."

Elaine replaced the lens cap and inspected the camera, making sure nothing could compromise the valuable digital information inside.

"Thanks for the pictures, Dorothy," Elaine Snow said. "I really appreciate it."

"You can call me Katie."

"But your name's not Katie," Elaine said, now cradling her camera. "It's Dorothy."

"No, it's Katie," Rob said. "You two need to go and tell everyone that she isn't Dorothy Bradford. No more beach scouting parties and no visits to the cottage, okay?"

"You know we can't do that, Rob," Rachel said. She needs to tell them herself. Maybe if Maggie came by. Would that be okay?"

Rob had taken to putting all of his weight on his good foot, leaving the damaged foot to dangle like a poor cut of meat at a butcher store. He looked at Katie, worried she might say yes. "No," he said.

"Would you come to Maggie's house then?" Rachel said, now looking at Katie. "Maggie is the only one that will know for sure whether you're Dorothy or not."

"What do you mean, *or not*?" Elaine said. "Now that we've met her, it's even more obvious that she's Dorothy. And how come Rob's acting like he's Dorothy's agent or something? I thought you were just a friend."

"He's my husband, Elaine," Katie said.

"Your husband? He said she was just a friend," Elaine said, glaring at Rob.

"I lied."

"You're William! You're evil!" Elaine stepped behind Rachel for protection.

"Who's William?" Katie said.

"She thinks I'm William Bradford—Dorothy's husband," Rob said.

"He's not William," Rachel said, trying to pull Elaine out from behind her. "William is dead. Only Rachel survived, right?"

"Why do you think William is evil, Elaine?" Katie said.

Elaine crept back into view, eyeing Rob suspiciously.

"He abused you! He was awful! All men are awful!"

"This is nuts," Rob said, losing patience.

"Rob, you need to sit down," Katie said, ushering him back to his chair. He sat down, and Katie kissed him on the top of the head, to prove he was not evil. She turned back to Rachel and Elaine. "You can tell Maggie that I'll think about meeting with her, okay?"

"Oh, good," Rachel said. "She'll be happy to hear it."

"Now, I'm going back inside to look after my son. It was nice meeting you both."

Rachel and Elaine watched her go into the cottage, and then looked at Rob, seemingly at a loss for what to do next.

"Looks like we're done here," he said. "You know the way back to the beach, right?"

Rachel thanked Rob, while Elaine sneered at him. They headed to the stairs, and Rob followed at a distance, wanting to make sure they didn't hang around, though he didn't expect they would. Rachel was not the scheming type, and Elaine would want to start printing poster-sized enlargements of her pictures as soon as possible, for the next society meeting. No one would toss these captured images in the grass. He was hopeful the pictures of Katie's smiling face would disarm the Bradford women and steer them toward the next unsuspecting female with an oar in her hands. No woman who had been dumped in the bay and left to drift for four hundred years would smile.

Rob dragged his bloated ankle to the house, ready for an evening dose of antihistamines and antibiotics. He had an idea that it probably wasn't a good idea to add alcohol to the mix, but as with the sun, he didn't care.

FIFTEEN

Coolers and Trespassers

The prophylactics coursing through Rob's veins took hold over night. The next morning he woke to find that the swelling in his ankle had come down considerably. The angry red hue, pulsing like a glowing amber the day before, had also faded. He eased out of bed, putting equal weight on each foot, and felt no pain in the ankle. "Who doesn't love drugs!" he announced as he strode into the kitchen.

He found Sidney standing by the patio doors, staring vacantly into the side yard. The circuit in his brain that instructed him to bark or nudge his master in the armpit when he needed to go had come loose, so he sat by the door and waited for it to open.

"Hang on a sec, boy," Rob said, curious to test his ankle further. "Let me put on some shorts and we'll go down to the beach."

The morning sky was overcast but the wind was out of the south, making it comfortable for shorts and a tee shirt—perfect dog walking weather. Rob carried Sidney down, the dog waving his front paws as if he was actually descending the steps himself, and set him down in the sand. Sidney staggered a bit, found his footing, and set off toward the water.

It was still early, and with the cloudy skies the beach was deserted. The sand at the shoreline was undisturbed, no footprints, which meant Rob and Sidney were the day's first beach-walkers. There was a thrill in being the first one on the beach because if anything had washed up overnight he would be the one to discover it. Mostly the tide brought in plastic bottles and stray bits of clothing, but sometimes there were more interesting finds. The camera from the *Dorothy Swimmers* was an example. The seal head was another. Less so was the syringe tangled in seaweed. Rob no longer worried about stumbling on the remains of one of the swimmers. If they had died in the water some part of one or all of them would have washed up long before.

Rob was also pleased not to see any Bradford Society scouting parties combing the beach. He hoped that Rachel had at least been able to convince Maggie Mason to call off the search for Dorothy. They had found her, after all, and been able to open a dialogue. Surely Maggie wouldn't want to risk losing the opportunity for a second meeting because of the actions of some overzealous society members. But then, how much control did Maggie have over these women, particularly when they were drunk most of the time?

The first person Rob ran into was Betty Whitman, accompanied by her non-secular dog. Sidney fully ignored the other dog and planted his butt in the sand when he came around for a sniff. Rob wished he could plant himself in the sand, too.

As Betty came closer Rob saw the pained expression on her face. Had God somehow forsaken her? The dog seemed okay, bouncing around Sidney playfully, nudging his withers to try and get him to stand up and present his asshole for inspection. There was no bounce to Betty Whitman.

"Can I give you this?" Betty Whitman asked, offering one of her flyers half-heartedly. Her hand was unsteady and the flyer shook.

"Thanks but I already have one," Rob said. "We've met."

Betty Whitman scrutinized Rob more carefully and then looked over at Sidney. She dropped her hand to her side.

"Yes, I'm sorry," she said. "I remember your dog". She sounded completely off her game. Rob wondered whether to ask what was wrong but worried about the consequences. She looked back at him and managed an unconvincing smile. Was she fighting back tears? Sidney barked at Betty Whitman's dog angrily, telling him to get lost. The dog scampered away.

"Sidney, be nice!" Rob said.

"Well, both of us have now gotten yelled at, I guess," Betty Whitman said.

Rob flinched. "I didn't yell at you, did I?" he said.

"Oh, no, of course not. Sorry, I wasn't talking about you."

Rob imagined that Betty had approached someone further down the beach who had not responded well to her promotional campaign. Since he was heading in that direction, he decided it now made sense to ask. He didn't want to stumble on a band of assholes.

"Why would anyone yell at you?" he said, knowing the answer full well but figuring he would try and be sympathetic.

"I don't know," she said, sighing. "I don't think it was necessarily about my book." She watched her dog bound into the water, chasing after a gull.

Rob couldn't believe he was going to have to coax the information out of the woman.

"What do you think it was?"

"There were two men. They were unloading these coolers from a motor boat that had come up onto the beach. Zach started sniffing around like he always does, and one of the men yelled at me to get my fucking dog away from his cooler."

Rob winced when Betty Whitman said "fucking." Being a woman of God, he had not thought of her as the type of person who would use profanity, even if she was using someone else's words. She had also raised her voice in an effort to imitate the man's tone. Rob looked down the beach. He didn't see a boat.

"It's gone now," Betty said.

"Where was it?"

"In front of that new house," she said.

Rob nodded. He remembered the kid in the overstuffed vest who worked for Tim Desmond—Sammy Boland, the guy who got him his bait. "I'll bet it was a fisherman unloading his catch," he said. "Or maybe it was bait. They probably didn't want your dog getting into the fish."

"I guess not," she said.

"Well, hopefully your day improves," Rob said, wondering if the second guy on the boat had been Tim Desmond.

"I'm not usually so thin-skinned," Betty Whitman said. "But that man who yelled at me sounded like the devil himself."

"Guess he could use a dog," Rob said, remembering Desmond's dog had been done in by a coyote.

"Yes, he surely could," Betty said. "You're a kind man."

"People need to be nicer to each other," he said, aware now that his mouth was beginning to get away from him. Time to go before he got himself enlisted in another cause. He wished Betty Whitman well and continued down the beach, Sidney at his heels, in the direction of the devil.

* * *

Tim Desmond's new house had come alive. Windows were open, and outdoor furniture sat on the deck. The Board of Selectmen must have agreed to the fine after all, Rob thought. The house would stay where it was. Curious about the details, Rob waited to see if Desmond would come outside. After a few minutes he came onto the deck, carrying a large table umbrella. Rob waved. "Looks like good news?" he called.

"Yes, sir!" Tim answered.

Rob wandered over the short dune toward the house. "If you see any coolers, stay clear," he told Sidney, who was close behind. Sidney knew the house was a water stop. Tim came down to meet him at the side of the house, and Rob offered his congratulations.

"Thanks," Tim said. "Listen, hope you don't mind if I don't ask you in. The house is a mess right now. But when we're done we'll have a party. You're invited! Hey, tell me about the Bradford meeting."

Rob provided the details, describing the kegs of beer and the enlarged photos of the women who might have been Dorothy Bradford.

"Any promising candidates?" Tim asked.

"One."

"Was she there? What does she look like?"

Sammy Boland had come out onto the deck pushing a large gas grill in front of him. "Where do you want this, Mr. Desmond?"

"One second, Sammy," Desmond said. "Listen, I should probably get back to it. But next time you're out this way, stop by and we'll fish. Just got some new bait in this morning."

"I heard. Ran into a woman down the beach whose dog apparently got a little too close to the coolers. Said she got reamed out."

"Oh, no. Must have been the delivery guy. Sammy would never yell at anyone. I'll speak to him about it. Can't blame the dog, though. That menhaden sure does stink."

"Well, good luck with the move."

"The big stuff doesn't come until tomorrow. I'm just moving a few things over in my truck. I want to eat dinner out here tonight."

"Can't blame you. Hope the fine wasn't too steep."

"Doesn't matter. I'm not paying any of it. That's the contractor's problem."

"Was your buddy Steve Ridgeback at the meeting?"

"Oh, yeah." Tim grinned slyly. "I busted him up pretty good yesterday."

"I saw him at the Health Center afterwards. He told me he wasn't going to call the police," Rob said.

"Don't care. It was worth it." Tim shook his head. "Years of frustration, I guess." He shifted his attention to Sidney. The dog had started whining, and was eyeing Tim Desmond impatiently. "Oh, I'm sorry, buddy," Tim said, petting the dog. "Hey, Sammy, could you turn on the hose and bring it over here for the dog? See you soon, Rob, okay?"

He and Rob shook hands again. Sammy Boland came over and handed Rob the hose.

"It's on," he said.

"Thanks," Rob said, opening the valve and running water into his cupped hand for Sidney. "Don't let us keep you. We'll be going in a minute here."

Sammy Boland nodded but didn't move, as though he was worried about having the hose stolen. Feeling oddly uncomfortable, Rob introduced himself—they had never formally met.

"Hi," Sammy said. "I'm Sammy Boland." He dug into one of his bulging vest pockets and pulled out a card. "If you ever need any work done around your house, give me a call."

Rob looked at the card. There was a long list of available services listed beneath Sammy's name and number.

"I will," Rob said. "Tim has good things to say about you."

Sidney finished drinking, and Rob handed the hose back to Sammy Boland. He still didn't move, and Rob wondered if he was waiting for an offer of work.

"See you again soon, I'm sure," Rob said, coaxing Sidney back toward the beach.

"Okay," Sammy said. They didn't shake hands.

*   *   *

Rob arrived at the house, carrying Sidney, who had decided he was done walking. The car was gone, which was odd because Danny wasn't ready to drive yet, and Katie rarely took the car anywhere anymore. He went inside, set Sidney down by his water bowl, and checked the answering machine. The light was flashing.

"Where are you?" Danny's recorded voice asked. He sounded rattled. "I tried your cell phone, too. You need to get down here."

Rob hustled down the driveway and was greeted at the front of the cottage by a crowd of women, maybe twenty of them, waving signs and drinking beer. Someone had rolled in a keg on a wagon, seemingly manufactured just for this purpose. The signs showed new pictures of Katie, and now displayed her full alias, Dorothy Bradford. Some of the women looked over at Rob when he arrived. A couple of them hissed. Rob scanned the crowd for a familiar face. He didn't see Rachel or Maggie Mason, and there was no Elaine Snow to record the event. Katie wasn't among them either.

"You guys need to leave!" Rob called out. He wanted to add that this was private property, but decided not to be too confrontational. He was not Tim Desmond.

"He's William!" one of the women screamed.

"Go back to your whores!" yelled another.

Rob slipped past the crowd, wondering how much beer they had already drunk, and went inside the cottage. Danny was sitting on the couch, his leg propped up on a stool. He was banging on the thigh of his bad leg, looking exasperated, an expression Rob remembered from the boy's youth when he needed something but couldn't get it without the help of his parents. Katie was nowhere to be seen. He figured she was barricaded in her room. Then he remembered the car.

"Where's your mom?" he asked.

"She took off. Hopped out the window. These women are insane."

"The car is gone."

"She took the car?"

"Either that or someone stole it. It's not there." Rob fumbled for his cell phone. It had gone sideways in his pocket and was stuck. Cell phones had gotten too big. "How long have they been here?"

"Half an hour. I called the police."

"Good." He wasn't so sure this was good. He wanted to be supportive of his son, though. "You okay?"

"No."

"I mean your knee. Why are you pounding on your leg like that?"

"It feels good. My knee is fine." He adjusted the dressing, which consisted of an ace bandage wrapped around a bag of frozen peas.

"Was she upset?"

"She was confused," Danny said. "I almost thought she was going to go out there. Then she lost her nerve."

"She wasn't ready for this," Rob said. He was close to the point of ripping open his pocket. He took off his shorts instead, making it easier to dislodge the phone.

"What the hell are you doing?"

"My phone is stuck." As he worked to free the cell phone, he looked out the window. The women didn't seem to be following any particular agenda, other than standing in the yard and drinking beer. Most of them had set down their signs now. They were like visitors at a zoo, waiting for the tiger to come out of its cage. "Maybe we should tell them she isn't here," Rob said.

"Like they're going to believe you."

Rob won the battle with his shorts and the phone popped free. He began thumbing an email to Maggie Mason. Somehow he thought she wasn't necessarily aware of what was going on. He believed Rachel was sincere in her wish to prevent any further contact with Katie until Maggie had a chance to meet with her first.

"Are you texting Mom?" Danny said.

"Yes. I'm also sending an email to Maggie Mason."

"She's not out there?"

"I don't recognize anyone out there. I'm pretty sure this is the radical faction of the society. I'm glad Mom left."

"And what about me?"

"They don't care about you. Nothing personal. They don't care about me either."

Rob sent the text to Katie, asking her to call as soon as she could. Next he sent the email to Maggie. Soon after, two police cars—lights flashing—pulled into the driveway. The women picked up their signs and began chanting "Come to me, Dor-o-thy!" Officer Grainger and three other officers got out of the cars.

"Cops are here," Rob said. "I'm going out."

"Tell them not to shoot anybody," Danny said.

Officer Grainger took charge immediately, announcing that the women were trespassing, and that they would have to leave or be arrested. They also could not congregate on the road fronting the property without a permit.

"This is Dorothy's house!" one of the women argued. "We have a right to be here!"

Officer Grainger noticed Rob coming outside and walked over to him. "Hello Mr. Crosley," he said.

"Quite a mess, isn't it?" Rob said.

"We've got a van coming. Your son said they were trespassing. We'll take them away if they don't leave." Grainger noticed the keg now. "Are they drinking beer?" he said.

"They are," Rob said. "I don't think they're capable of doing much without it." He wasn't sure he liked the policemen's chances of cuffing twenty beer-drinking Bradford women.

"Is your wife at home, Mr. Crosley?"

"She left when they showed up. Went out the back door." There was no back door. She had climbed out a window.

"Anybody else inside?"

"Just my son." Rob worried Grainger was looking for a place to take cover should things get out of hand. Envisioning a siege, he felt something poke his thigh, and he jumped. At first he thought he had been struck by a projectile, but it was only his phone vibrating. He hoped it was Katie, but it was Maggie Mason instead, emailing to say she was on the way.

Officer Grainger remained at ease until the van pulled in a few minutes later. None of the women had left the yard, though the arrival of the van had clearly gotten their attention. Grainger looked over at Rob, eyes narrowed, thumbs hooked in his belt. Rob sensed he was looking for approval to proceed. He nodded.

"Last warning!" Grainger said. "Leave now or we arrest you and put you in the van. Your choice, ladies." Two more officers, laden with several pairs of handcuffs, came out of the van and opened the rear doors. The odds now seemed to tilt in their favor.

Rob watched as the women drew closer together, the keg serving as their nucleus. It was clear that they weren't going to cooperate. Rob stepped back, sensing trouble was imminent. They could have waited until Maggie Mason arrived—perhaps she could diffuse the situation—but after a few more beers, who knew what these women were capable of? Grainger and the other officers pulled out their billy-clubs, while the two men from the van, who were thankfully larger than most of the trespassers, started peeling the women off the Bradford cluster, one at a time, cuffing them, and escorting them to the van. For the most part, the women only protested vocally. A couple of them sat down when their turn came, but the policemen snatched them up easily. None tried to escape.

Half the women had been deposited in the van when a fourth vehicle arrived, this one unmarked. Rob suspected all of the town's police force were now on the scene, clearly a major event. Surely they had never arrested this many people at one time. Steve Ridgeback couldn't be far behind. The latest arrival was the inspector, Don Hill. Rob couldn't imagine why he was here. No one had been found face-down in the woods. What was there to investigate? Hill climbed inside the van, then came back out and walked over to the remaining violators. He was clearly looking for someone. After speaking with Officer Grainger he approached Rob.

"These women really seem to worship your wife," he said. "Looks like our boys have got things under control, though. Jesus, is that a keg? Never too early in the day, I guess. Though I'd be asleep inside of an hour."

Rob was irritated by Don Hill's cavalier attitude. He could have been watching a pair of referees breaking up a fight at a hockey game. "Are you looking for someone?" Rob asked.

"I am," Hill said. "Maybe you've seen her? Her name's Elaine Snow."

Rob nodded. "I know her," he said. "She was here yesterday, in fact." Rob explained the events of the previous day, and how he and Rachel were trying to prevent what was happening now anyway.

"Elaine Snow is a hard woman to pin down," Don Hill said.

"Did she do something?"

"Don't know. Could be." He folded his arms and turned away from the police action, which had all of a sudden becoming congenial—one of the officers chatted amicably with a woman he was escorting to the van—and looked at Rob directly. "Did she ever say anything to you about the missing swimmers?"

Rob pictured Elaine Snow's face, generally in a scowl anyway, but particularly so when the subject of the *Dorothy Swimmers* came up. "Yeah, she hated them. They took the picture of Katie. She didn't."

"She told you that?"

Rob knew where Don Hill's line of questioning was going. "Well, she hated the fact that they took the picture. She's their staff photographer or something."

"She's...um," Don Hill gestured toward a particularly burly woman who required both officers to get her into the van. "Little, isn't she?"

Rob figured he was talking about Elaine Snow and not the burly woman.

"Yes, little," he said. "I can't imagine her hurting anyone. Besides, I don't think she knew the swimmers. I don't think any of the other members knew them either."

"And you're a member now, too, I hear?"

"Honorary. They liked what I said on the news."

"I see," Don Hill said, his tone causing Rob some consternation. "So where's your wife?"

"I don't know. She took the car and left."

Don Hill sighed. "I'm sorry you folks have to go through this."

When the last trespasser was loaded into the van, one of the officers called over to Grainger and asked about the keg. "Bring it along," Grainger said, "but don't let them drink anymore!"

Don Hill watched as an officer wheeled the keg over to the van. A cheer rose up from inside. "Guess I need to go," Hill said. "I'm blocking everyone in."

"Are you any closer to finding them?" Rob asked.

"Can't really say, Mr. Crosley," he said. He started toward his car, but before he reached it, another one pulled in. The driveway was beginning to look like a border crossing.

The latest arrival was Maggie Mason. The officers immediately converged on her, telling her she needed to move so they could leave. Maggie wanted to see the women in the van first. She was told by Officer Grainger that she could see them once they were processed and released. She pleaded her case to Don Hill but he held up his arms and shook his head. Out of options, and not wanting to risk getting tossed in the van herself, she moved her car and let the convoy leave. Rob thought she might follow them, but she pulled the car back into the driveway. Rob thought about the beer. He wished the officers had left it behind.

"Well, this was unfortunate," she said, hurrying over to his side.

"How did they find us, Maggie?" Rob complained. "Rachel and Elaine were the only ones here yesterday, and I'm not sure Elaine knew what planet she was on, much less the street name."

"It wasn't either of them."

"You didn't tell them, did you?"

"Why would I do that? I wanted to meet with her first."

"Then how did they find us?"

Maggie Mason shrugged her shoulders. "It's a small town, Rob," she said.

"Listen, you need to tell your members to stay away from my wife," Rob said. "No more stalking." Rob stared at the spot in the yard where the women had huddled around the keg. He had lost sight of what had touched off this chain of insanity.

"Is she here?" Maggie said, looking toward the cottage.

"Your members scared her off. She's gone," Rob said. He made it sound final, like she wasn't ever coming back.

"That's what I thought."

"What do you mean by that?"

Maggie Mason cocked her head. "It's what she does. When she gets hemmed in, she runs away. I'm sure you know this. Why do you think she hopped off the Mayflower in the first place? "

"Will you stop with the Mayflower shit," Rob said. "Why can't you just be a friendly, boring historical society? Leave my wife alone."

"We want the same thing, Rob." Maggie Mason turned and started toward the house. Rob worried she meant to go inside.

"Where are you going?" he asked.

"She built this place, didn't she?" Maggie said, looking up at the roof.

"She builds everything."

"Can I look inside?"

"No. My son's in there recuperating from surgery. Besides, I've had enough Dorothy Bradford Society for one day."

"Well, I need to get to the police station anyway. Hey, were there any press here?"

"Seems like there are always press here. None today. So far."

"Did you see the article in the Gazette this morning?" She hurried over to the car and grabbed the paper off the passenger seat. Rob followed, making sure she kept her distance from the cottage. She held up the front page to show off the picture of Katie in her boat. "Pretty neat, huh?" Maggie said. Rob looked at the caption under the picture. To his relief, Katie's name wasn't there. Instead it said, "Local paddler or Dorothy Bradford?"

"How is this a page one story?" he asked.

"You should read it," Maggie Mason said. "You can keep that copy. I have a bunch more in the car. Wait; one more thing." She reached into the car and grabbed a pen. "This is my cell phone number." She scribbled the information on Rob's copy of the newspaper. "Call or text me when she's ready to meet, or if you have any more trouble, but I don't think you will. It's important that I meet with her as soon as possible, though. Make it happen, Rob."

Rob watched Maggie Mason drive away. A ringing silence remained, like the aural residue at a rock concert after the band leaves the stage and the lights come up. A stab of fear followed, the feeling, again, of being unseated from reality. He looked into the trees, wishing the wind would come up and rustle the leaves. Somewhere, an insect screamed. Rudderless, Rob stuck the paper under his arm and went back into the cottage, hoping his son could provide some ballast.

* * *

Danny had repositioned himself in a chair by the window. From there, he had watched the action in the front yard. He shook his head when Rob came inside. Rob collapsed on the sofa, looking a bit overwhelmed.

"You okay?" Danny asked. The question nearly pushed Rob to despair.

"This thing has gotten out of hand, hasn't it?" he said, trying not to sound defeated.

"The police did their job. I was actually impressed with how they handled the situation. Who was that woman who just left?"

"Maggie Mason."

"So that was her. Did she know about this?"

"I'm not sure. She says she didn't, but I don't trust her. I told her to get her members under control." Rob flipped open the paper and looked at the iconic picture of his wife. The pictures of the two *Dorothy Swimmers* were also on the front page, as was an empty box with a question mark inside, designating the male swimmer. The byline for the article read, "Where are they?"

"More coverage?" Danny said.

"Ridgeback strikes again. I haven't read it." He flipped the paper over to Danny. He had no stomach for gonzo journalism right now.

"Local paddler?" Danny said, reading the caption.

Rob closed his eyes and searched for calm. It wasn't noon yet, but he could have used a drink. Unfortunately, Katie didn't keep anything alcoholic in the cottage.

"Did your mom call?" he asked.

"Not yet."

"We should try her again."

Danny grabbed his cell phone off a side table and dialed his mother. She didn't pick up, so he left a message letting her know she could come home. He set down the phone and started reading the article. "Hey, listen to this."

"What?" Rob said, worried his name was somehow going to resurface.

"There's a description here of Dorothy Bradford that Maggie Mason supposedly wrote twenty years ago. There's a description of the boat, too. Wow. Creepy shit. Sounds just like Mom."

"Oh, fuck that," Rob said, hopping off of the couch. "She's making stuff up. Or Ridgeback is. It's bullshit." Rob went into the kitchen and started rifling through the refrigerator. "Listen, Danny, you want to go get some lunch?" he said, disappointed with the contents of the refrigerator. "Get some fried clams and beer? You can walk now, can't you?"

"Sure, but we don't have a car, remember?"

"Shit." Rob stared blankly at the refrigerator. He considered the options. "I've got beer up at the house. I'll go get it and bring back some food, too. I wish they'd left the keg."

Outside, Rob was met at the end of the driveway by the news team who had first stalked him after the *Dorothy Swimmers* disappeared. It was a dangerous time to face the media. Rob was in a chaotic mood, and besides being irritable and hungry, he was particularly disposed to sarcasm at the moment. There was no keeping his mouth shut.

"You guys are late!" Rob said.

The greasy-haired cameraman peered up the driveway, looking for something to film.

The newsman arched his eyebrows sensing opportunity nonetheless. "What did we miss?" he asked. "We heard the police were here."

"Right here in this very driveway."

"Is it okay if we film?"

"What, now you're asking? Do you need my permission?"

"No." The cameraman shouldered his equipment and started recording. Rob was pretty sure he hadn't looked in a mirror since yesterday.

"Tell us what happened here today, Mr. Crosley."

"News, gentlemen. Innocent people, guilty people. The long arm of the law. A lesson in civics."

"The police were here?"

"They are everywhere. They're watching us now."

The cameraman looked up from the viewfinder. The newsman looked behind him.

"Don't worry!" Rob said. "You're safe! I will protect you."

"This guy is nuts," the cameraman said, continuing to film.

"And who are these innocent and guilty people?" the newsman asked.

"All of us. On any given day we can be innocent or guilty of something. I, myself, threw a pine cone at a turkey this morning."

"Have you seen Dorothy Bradford?" the newsman asked.

"She is gone! Sailed across the bay in search of her people. Go to Plymouth. Your story is there."

"She went to Plymouth?"

"I would look there first. Boston is another possibility. Maybe the Commonwealth of Virginia!"

"Virginia?"

"Hey, would you guys give me and my son a ride into Wellfleet? We want to get some lunch."

SIXTEEN

Bike Lanes and Monuments

Later that afternoon there was still no word from Katie. By the fourth unanswered call, Rob thought to check Katie's bedroom to see if she had forgotten to take her cell phone with her—she had left in a hurry. A faint buzzing noise came from the chest of drawers. He found the phone sitting behind a picture of Danny. The phone bounced around as it rang, spitting out some electronic version of a jazz riff while Rob's name flashed on the screen.

"Piece of shit," Rob said, stifling the urge to fling the phone across the room. He had to stop taking out his frustrations on inanimate objects. Though he was still upset with the Bradford women who had shown up that morning, he was just as angry with his wife for running away and not taking her phone. Where had she gone this time? She would necessarily head for someplace isolated, he knew, but it was nearly impossible to hide from other people on the Cape during the summer season. He thought she might have taken the back roads to Wellfleet and disappeared into one of the sparsely populated islands. Or what if she had gotten onto Route Six and, because of her anxiety, and not having driven in over a year, veered into oncoming traffic?

Rob needed to do something. He thought about riding his bike into Wellfleet to see if the car was parked along one of the dirt roads that wound through Bound Brook and Griffin Islands. But then what? Was he going to plunge into the woods where the poisonous vines grew to the size of beanstalks? He knew she was capable of surviving in the woods. She had done it before when they lived in Boston, and the world got too close. She would sometimes escape into the woods for a few days, living like a hermit, not returning until she felt she could manage. But in those instances, he knew where she was. She took her cell phone with her. Rob decided to take a more measured approach to finding his wife. He called the police.

* * *

The phone rang longer than Rob expected. It was not yet five o'clock. When someone did pick up, it was not the desk sergeant who answered, but Don Hill. He explained that they were short-handed at the station. Rob wondered if the desk sergeant had been sacked. Perhaps she was the one who had leaked Katie's photo.

"What can I do for you, Mr. Crosley?" Don Hill asked. "Did some more of those Bradford women show up?"

"No. But my wife hasn't come home yet, and I can't get in touch with her."

"Doesn't she have a cell phone?"

"She left in a hurry when the crowd showed up, and forgot to take it with her. She hasn't driven in over a year. Look, she never goes anywhere during the summer, too many people."

"What about that beach of hers? Maybe she went there."

"No, you can't get there by car. I don't think you can walk there either."

"Ordinarily I'd say it's too early to be concerned," Don Hill said. He paused, and Rob worried he was going to make some comment about what circumstances warranted an immediate call to the police, like when someone went for a swim and didn't come back. But, oddly, he didn't seem to be in the mood for conversation. "Listen," he said, "give me a description of the car and the license plate number and we'll have our officers keep an eye out for it." Rob provided the information, pleased that he had remembered to keep a photo of the license plate on his phone, since he could never remember the number. Don Hill told him not to worry and thanked him for calling.

After ending the call with Don Hill, Rob was plagued by another numbing bout of loneliness. Katie was gone again, Danny had moved out to live in the cottage, and Sidney barely recognized him anymore. He scanned the apps on his phone as if one of them might be intended to lend comfort. He thought he heard a car pull into the driveway but it was only the wind rattling through the trees.

* * *

The next morning Rob was awakened by a carpenter bee hovering just above his head. The thing was the size of a drone, and sounded like one, too. He was on the deck, still waiting for Katie to return, and had fallen asleep in one of the recliners, a bottle of scotch nearby. He had been sure she was waiting for nightfall, when the roads emptied, and she could comfortably drive home. There had been no stars out that night, and the sky was particularly black. For such a congested area during the day, the outer Cape became a moonscape at night. The scotch slowly disappeared from the bottle, and Rob had passed out. The tidal wave returned to his dreams, but this time there was a swarm of sharks preying on the panicked victims of the disaster. They popped their heads out of the water and screamed for help.

Rob sat up. He checked the driveway, just to be sure. Still no car, and no car down at the cottage either. His head was throbbing, his mouth was dry, and his wife was still missing. Sidney was staring at him from inside the screen door, waiting to be let out. Rob got up and opened the door for the dog, who hopped out and immediately took a dump on the deck.

Rob got a paper towel and launched Sidney's turd into the pines. Then he took four ibuprofen, drank a quart of water, wolfed down two chocolate donuts, and fed the dog. Next he washed, dressed, and collected some essentials into a backpack. He put Sidney on his leash, then went outside and freed his bicycle from the shed. He walked his bike and the dog down to the cottage.

"Are you here?" Rob said stepping inside, dragging Sidney behind him.

"In here," Danny said.

Rob walked into the bedroom to find his son hunched over on the bed, yanking the stitches out of his knee.

"Should you be doing that?" Rob said.

"What?"

"Taking out your stitches?"

"Relax," Danny said. "The doctor said I could." Danny snipped the last stitch and pulled the thread from his leg. "Are you going camping?" he said, seeing his father's backpack.

"I'm biking up to Provincetown."

"To see your boyfriend?"

"Don't be an asshole. I'm going to find your mother."

"On your bike?"

"Listen," Rob said, tugging at the straps on his backpack, "After your mom moved out of the house and came down here to live, I promised myself that if she ever left again I'd go after her. I kick myself every day for letting her leave. Besides, she took the car."

"She'll come back when she's ready, Dad," he said. "She doesn't want to be found right now. Besides, where are you going to look?"

"Maggie Mason's to start. I want to make sure she doesn't have your mom tied up in her basement."

"Don't be ridiculous. She's out in the woods somewhere. Or on the beach."

"Unless a couple of Bradford women grabbed her. She could have been followed when she left yesterday."

"Are you taking the dog with you?" Sidney had lain down on the floor, the leash snug around his neck.

"He's staying here with you," Rob said, dropping the leash. "If you hear from your mother, you call me, okay?"

"What do you have in your backpack?"

"Jesus. When did you say you start your physical therapy?"

"Tomorrow. I'll need a car, though."

"We'll get you there. Watch the dog."

* * *

Lately, Rob had taken to riding his bike more often. While he continued to run, he now preferred biking as a form of exercise—it was less demanding on his aging joints. Two hours of biking would not leave him crippled for two days after. He could ride twenty miles, stop for food and beer, and then go another twenty miles. There was no shame in taking a rest when you were cycling. If you were running, you only stopped if you were injured or dead.

The day was cool and overcast, perfect weather for a search and rescue operation. The dreary conditions also meant there would be a throng of cheerless motorists driving to Provincetown to eat, shop, and fight for parking. When Rob entered the narrow bike lane on Route Six, the cars were crawling along at a rate of speed not much greater than what he was managing on his bike. This was good, because it somewhat reduced the risk of getting knocked into the weeds. In any event, Rob had attached a side-view mirror to his handlebars so he could keep an eye on the traffic coming up behind him. He also wore a bright yellow shirt and had attached a flashing light to the back of his saddle.

Because of the backpack, some of the slow-moving tourists assumed he was on the last leg of some trans-continental journey, and shouted inanities like "You're almost there!" and "Keep going!" Rob waved politely—better not to anger the guy operating the heavier machinery—and adopted a more aerodynamic form to impress them with his cycling prowess. One passenger rolled down the window and asked Rob if he knew where Provincetown was.

* * *

Rob did know where Provincetown was, and when he got there it was a mess. Pedestrians and cars were everywhere; many of them not moving. He was glad to be on his bike. Had he driven he probably would have made a U-turn and gone home. The chances of Katie being at Maggie Mason's house were slim. But he had to do something, and this was the only known destination with any potential, however small.

Rob stood outside Maggie Mason's front door and listened. What did he expect to hear? Muffled screams?

Someone on the street, a local evidently, who knew whose house it was, yelled, "Looking for Dorothy?"

Rob turned, threw up his hands, and said, "Yes!"

"She's dead!"

Assholes were everywhere.

Rob finally knocked on the door and listened some more. He heard no noise, no sound of approaching footsteps, so when the door opened he was surprised to see Rachel's imposing figure. She beamed at him, and unlike most every other Bradford Society member whom he met, did not look past him in search of his wife.

"Hi, Rob! What a nice surprise," she said graciously, opening the door all the way now so he could come inside. "What brings you here?" Rob stepped into the foyer. The living room was to his left and the dining room on the right. The rooms were large and had lots of places to sit. They were empty now, and there was a stillness about the house—dust particles danced in the shafts of sunlight which had just broken through the clouds.

"I was wondering if Katie was here," he said sheepishly. Rachel closed the door behind him, and led him into the living room.

"There would be a crowd of people here if she was," Rachel said. "Did she say she was coming?"

"She took off yesterday, after the little demonstration on the front lawn, and I haven't seen her since." Rachel's expression tightened into a grimace. Rob hadn't seen her displeased before. She seemed irritated.

"They shouldn't have done that," she said. "I was afraid something like that was going to happen. I'm sorry it did and that your wife ran off. I guess I'm not surprised she's stayed away, but she hasn't called?"

"She forgot her phone."

"Where else do you think she might be?" It occurred to Rob that he was divulging useful information to the enemy, but he didn't think of Rachel as an enemy. She seemed to regard Katie as something other than an immortal Pilgrim.

"Probably in the dunes, camped out somewhere."

"That is exactly what Dorothy would do," she said, the smile returning to her face. "That's probably what she did after she fell from the Mayflower—found a spot in the dunes and then found a way to survive, on her own. I'll bet this isn't the first time your wife has run off like this."

"It's not. She's actually very good at it."

"So you don't need to worry, right? Hey, I'm being a bad host. Wait here." Rachel skipped noiselessly out of the room. The woman seemed to defy gravity.

While she was away, Rob wandered through the living room, staring at the stuff on the walls. Most of it was the usual Cape art fare—dune scenes, sail boats, and birds. On one wall, though, was a series of photographs of women, most of whom looked gaunt and unhealthy. Some had bruises on their faces. Some had track marks on their arms. Rob looked closer and saw that each photo had a name beneath it, just a surname—Susan, Denise, Kathy. The photographer's name was also shown—Sammy Boland. Wasn't that the guy he had met at Tim Desmond's house, the handyman with the vest and the business card?

Rachel returned with two mugs of beer and handed one of them to Rob. She made a toast. "Here's to Katie's imminent return," she said, raising her mug, then downing most of the contents. Rob joined her. Though it was before noon, he was glad to have been offered the beer. He was thirsty from the bike ride and, like the Pilgrims, he found it easier to deal with life's ordeals when he had a little alcohol in his veins, though there may well have been some left from the night before.

"Tell me about these pictures," he said. "These women don't look so good."

"They're heroin addicts," Rachel said. "Or they were. Denise is one of our members now."

Rob looked at the picture of Denise, thinking he might recognize her from the one time he had been at a membership meeting. She didn't look familiar, though he suspected she might look very different now.

"And the photographer is Sammy Boland?"

"Have you seen his stuff before?"

"Not sure. Is he just a photographer? The Sammy Boland I know has a handyman business."

"That's him. He does work for Maggie, too."

"Where is Maggie?"

"Not sure. Out somewhere."

"Do you live here with her?"

"A few of us do," she said. "Until we get back on our feet. Denise lived here for a while, too.

Rachel finished the rest of her beer. She smiled and looked away, and Rob wondered what had happened to Rachel that landed her here. She didn't look like anyone who had ever been a drug addict.

"Would you like me to help you look for her?" she said.

Rob shook his head. "Isn't that what you've been doing?" He didn't mean it to sound harsh, but it came out that way.

Rachel winced.

"Sorry," he said. "I've been a little on edge."

"It's okay. I guess we all want to find her. But it sounds as if she doesn't want to be found right now."

"Unfortunately."

"More Dorothy."

Rob finished his beer and checked the sides of his mug to see if anything was moving.

"You okay?" Rachel asked.

"No. I'll have another."

"Of course you can have another, but that's not what I meant," she said.

Rob knew where she was going, but didn't know how to answer. He was okay under the circumstances, but he was not okay in general. He bounced the mug around in his hands. Or the mug bounced itself around. He wasn't sure which.

"Hey, have you ever been to the top of the monument?" Rachel asked, sensing Rob needed a diversion.

"No."

"Come on, let's go then. Great for lifting the spirits."

"I'm doing that now," Rob said, holding up his beer. He wasn't interested in climbing the monument. He was sure the thing was unstable. What he wanted to do was find his wife, and if he couldn't do that then he wanted to drink. But Rachel bolted through the door, without looking back to see if he was following. There would be no argument.

* * *

Rachel scampered up the steps inside the monument, exhibiting all the glee of a child at an amusement park.

Rob had no chance of keeping up. He had to stop at one point and swallow the beer that had jumped back into his mouth. So much for staying in shape, he thought.

"Isn't it beautiful?" Rachel said as Rob arrived at the top, struggling to catch his breath. He was struck by the intensity of the wind, much stronger here than at the base. The parapet wall that ringed the top of the monument had the look of a battlement, as if Massachusetts infantrymen had been posted here at one time to watch for invading warships. Iron grates now filled the gaps, each containing a cut-out where people could aim their cameras. Rob spied the gargoyles protruding ten feet below him. They seemed out of place in a New England fishing town. He looked to the south and followed the shoreline on the bayside, running past his house and bending back towards the mainland. Further to the east, he could see the ocean beaches of Provincetown and Truro.

"Can you see her?" Rachel said, pointing toward the dunes along the ocean. "I'll bet she's out there."

Rob squinted. He had forgotten to grab his sunglasses out of the car. What he thought was a large bird, turned out to be a small commuter plane, banking over the dunes on its final approach to the airport. Sunlight played off the fuselage in bright flashes, and it looked like it might burst into flames, like an ant under a magnifying glass. A gust of wind slammed into the north face of the monument and Rob thought he felt it sway. He grabbed onto the iron grate.

"You know, there was a time when we weren't allowed to have any contact with Dorothy," she said. "It was an unwritten rule that you couldn't disturb her."

"Can you reinstate that rule?"

"Maggie decided it wasn't enough. We're not just some fan club. Dorothy is a part of us. The problem is, some of the members are a little too anxious, like the ones who came to your cottage yesterday. Maggie is having a hard time keeping them in line."

"That's what I'm worried about. That some of them kidnapped her and are holding her somewhere."

"We'd know about it if they did. They're all loyal to Maggie. She's done a lot for us. She'll do a lot for Katie, too."

"Katie?"

Rob felt a vibration in his leg and was sure the monument was shuddering in the initial stages of collapse. He turned to run for the stairwell when he realized it was only his phone that was vibrating. Anxious it was news about Katie, he excused himself and headed into the stairwell after all. He would never hear a word in the wind.

"Hello, Mr. Crosley?" It was Officer Grainger calling, Rob could barely hear him.

"Speak louder!" Rob shouted, plugging his ear against the sound of the wind.

"We found the car."

"Where?"

"Head of the Meadow Beach parking lot." Grainger said. "Looks like the car was there all night. Lots of condensation still on the windows when we found it. No sign of your wife."

Head of the Meadow Beach was an ocean-side beach in North Truro. You could walk several miles north from Head of the Meadow toward Provincetown and find nothing but sand, beach grass, and the occasional dune shack. Rob and Katie had hiked it together before.

"She must have wandered off into the dunes somewhere," Rob said.

"Nothing out there."

"That's the way she likes it."

"Listen." Crosley cleared his throat, and Rob became anxious there was more to the story. "Your wife wouldn't do anything foolish, would she?"

This made no sense to Rob. Katie had stayed out all night, and not called him or Danny. Wasn't that foolish enough? "What do you mean?" he asked.

"You know. She was upset. She drove to the ocean, parked the car and then disappeared."

"Are you asking if she would kill herself?" Grainger didn't answer. "Jesus. She's on the beach or in the dunes somewhere. She does this all the time." This was an over-exaggeration, of course, but Rob didn't want the police toying with the idea of a suicide. Steve Ridgeback would have a field day.

"Sorry, I had to ask."

Rob thanked Grainger and ended the call. He went back onto the observation deck and told Rachel the news, though he didn't tell her where the car had been found.

"You want me to go with you?" she said.

"Uh, you can't. I came here on my bike."

"Really?"

"No car, remember. You don't have a car, do you?"

"Maggie has the car. Sorry."

"Okay, well." Rob made a sweeping motion with his arm to indicate it was time to go.

"You don't mind if I stay up here, do you?" Rachel said.

"No," Rob said, wondering if she thought he was incapable of finding his way back down the stairs.

"Say hi to her for me." Rachel said. "Tell her to come and visit us soon, okay?"

* * *

Rob pedaled hard out of Provincetown. Head of the Meadow beach was not far, just a few miles. He rode past Head of the Meadow Road and got off at Highland Road, where he could cross under Route Six and get back on heading north. Making a left turn from Route Six onto Head of the Meadow Road was sure death.

Before getting back onto Route Six, his phone rang again. He stopped right away, hoping it would be more news of Katie, or perhaps Katie herself, but it was Steve Ridgeback's name that flashed on the phone. Rob groaned and took a sip from his water bottle, eyeing the blanket of poison ivy growing along the side of the road. Ridgeback was sure to be writing about yesterday's Bradford demonstration at the cottage. After the fifth ring—how many before voicemail picked up?—he answered.

"Where are you?" Ridgeback asked. "Are you in the car?"

Rob only wished.

"What is it, Steve?" he asked.

"I hear Dorothy Bradford is in Plymouth. Care to elaborate?"

"Where did you hear that?"

"From you. You're on YouTube again."

"Oh, great. Yes, she's in Plymouth. You should head there now. You don't want to miss out again."

"Hah! I was getting a CAT scan yesterday morning, otherwise I would have been there."

"Too bad. They had beer. What's wrong with you?"

"I got popped in the face, remember? Black eye, broken nose? They wanted to be sure nothing had come loose in my skull."

"And?"

"Negative!"

"Shocking."

"So tell me what happened yesterday."

"I'm busy right now, Steve."

"Looking for your wife?"

"Christ, you probably know where she is. Why don't you tell me?"

"Plymouth?"

"I'm hanging up."

"She's the woman in the picture, isn't she?"

"Well, I guess that's no secret now, is it?"

"Her name will be in the Gazette tomorrow. I wanted you to know so you don't lose your shit."

"I'm really hanging up now."

"Was there any direct confrontation between the Bradford people and your wife? Just tell me that."

"No. She went out the window and managed to elude them."

"As far as you know. There might have been one or two of them in the car with her."

"I'm sure you'll write that. Dorothy Bradford car-jacked by Pilgrims."

"Of course! Perfect lead, Rob."

Rob ended the call and hopped back on his bike. The beach parking lot was only a few minutes away.

* * *

The sky had cleared, and despite the hoards in Provincetown there was a line of cars waiting to get into the lot. Rob moved into the opposite lane, gliding past the idling vehicles. Many people had gotten out of their cars and set off on foot, loaded down with chairs and boogie boards, leaving a designated driver to wait for a parking space to open up. The sun was directly overhead now and the pavement quivered with heat. There was little breeze. Someone blasted heavy, bass-laden rap music from their car stereo. The sound waves rattled the metal tubes of Rob's bike.

He found the car in one of the spaces at the front of the lot, closest to the beach. This meant that Katie had arrived sometime late in the day, after most people had packed up and left. Rob opened the trunk and was relieved to find that the survival kit was gone. Since the day they bought their first car, Katie insisted that they keep a kit in the trunk, in case they became stranded or had to escape some kind of invasion. This was, of course, exactly what had happened yesterday. The kit contained canned food, water, a blanket, flashlight, toilet paper. He checked the front seat for a note, some indication of her intentions, but there was nothing. As Danny had said, Katie didn't want to be found.

Rob chained his bike to a fence post, just next to a large sign that covered topics such as dogs, litter, rip tides, hours of operation, and the requisite warnings about seals and sharks. Among other things, it said that great white sharks were predators, and should be considered dangerous.

He walked to the beach, unsure of what to do next. The tide was out and the waves were strong, stirred by some offshore storm, breaking acutely in the distance and rumbling onto the beach. Katie had probably hiked north, into the barren, wind-swept dunes of North Truro and Provincetown. He headed in that direction, but once he got beyond the sign designating the point at which the life guards ignored you, he stopped, daunted by the vastness of the panorama. The boundaries between sand, sky and water blurred, creating some kind of post-apocalyptic conflation.

Unlike the bayside, vegetation on the ocean beaches had mostly been stripped from the faces of the dunes. The only things that were visible, besides sand, were the exposed roots of the grass and plants that sat on the crests, and the occasional pipe protruding from the upper part of a dune—the vestiges of some vacation home snatched by the sea. He saw a few blankets and beach chairs, and some beach-walkers in the distance, but he couldn't be sure which way they were walking.

There was also a small boy, perhaps nine or ten, wearing only a bathing suit and a baseball cap. He was by himself and was erecting some kind of human sculpture made from rocks, sticks and seaweed. The boy was staring at Rob. He did not seem startled or afraid, and continued with his art project.

"Did you lose something?" he asked, ramming a stick into what appeared to be the ass-end of the effigy.

Rob kept his distance, mindful of how adult males could sometimes be perceived in when approaching small boys.

"I did," he said.

"Is it your dog?"

"My wife, actually."

"How do you lose your wife?"

Rob shrugged. "That's a very good question."

"Do you like this?" the boy asked, pointing at the sculpture.

"Sure," Rob said.

"I think it's a piece of shit." The boy picked up a stick and started whacking at the effigy, strewing its various parts across the sand.

"Language," Rob said, remembering his conversations with a young Danny about when it wasn't okay to use profanity.

The boy continued to pound on the remains of his creation, now exhibiting a ferocity that Rob found unsettling.

He walked back to the car and got in, laying his head back against the headrest and closing his eyes. Bright lights popped on the back of his eyelids, dancing in waves across his eyeballs. Exhaustion had set in, from having passed out on the deck the night before, and then cycling up and down the Cape, not to mention climbing the Pilgrim Monument. A car honked behind him. He lifted his head and turned to see an impatient driver making wild hand gestures. Rob shook his head and motioned for the driver to move on. He wasn't leaving yet.

Rob slumped lower in the seat, keeping his head out of view from the next anxious space hunter, when he saw a woman walking from the beach onto the parking lot. She was attractive and had a certain independence, he thought, that would have made her an ideal Dorothy Bradford candidate. As she came closer, he realized she already was.

"Katie!" he shouted, jumping out of the car. She waved cheerfully and quickened her pace, as though she was being picked up at the airport.

"You're here!" she said, coming right up to him and kissing him on the lips. He nearly fell over, conditioned over the last few years to be careful of spontaneous affection with his wife. "I'm sorry I forgot my phone. You probably left a ton of messages."

A large group of assorted parents and children passed by, thrilled to be out of their cars. They said hello, and Katie smiled and said "hi." She would normally have bolted for the car, or at least shied away, but Rob saw nothing of the usual apprehension in her face with so many people close by.

"Jesus, Kay, we were worried about you. Are you okay?"

"Better than okay. So how did you know where I was?"

"I figured the beach parking lots were a good place to look." He didn't want to tell her about his call to the police. It almost seemed an overreaction now.

"You knew what I was doing, right?"

"You guys leaving?" a driver yelled—another tourist in search of deliverance. The driver didn't wait for a response. He turned on his turn signal and waited. Though there would necessarily be another open spot somewhere—the lot attendant didn't let a car in until one left—this guy wanted this spot, at the front of the lot.

"We should go," Rob said, now more uncomfortable with his surroundings than Katie was, if she was. She seemed completely at ease. Parking lots had typically been virulent breeding grounds for Katie's panic attacks.

Rob unlocked his bike and threw it in the back of the car. He opened the door for Katie, then walked casually to the other side, making the guy with the turn signal wait a little longer, and got behind the wheel, happy to be leaving, happy to have recovered his wife and car.

"So where were you? Where did you spend the night?" he said, tearing down Head of the Meadow Road toward Route Six.

"Slow down, Rob. There are a lot of people walking here."

"Sorry. Force of habit, I guess." He always drove fast when Katie was in the car, wanting to get her home before panic set in. He glanced over at her, waiting for an answer. Her hair was loose, and the wind scattered it about her face. Her hands, usually folded in a defensive posture, now wandered playfully, one hand testing the wind and the other tapping out some internal rhythm. She reached over and squeezed Rob's leg. He looked closer, just to make sure he hadn't picked up the wrong person.

"What happened to you out there, Kay?" They were at the stop sign now, waiting for traffic to clear so he could make the left turn onto Route Six. He took a chance, and leaned over and kissed her. "I just kissed you, for Christ's sake. You didn't pull away. You didn't flinch. Something happened."

She smiled. "I met some people," she said. "Living in one of those dune shacks."

"What people?"

Katie leaned forward and checked the traffic streaming up the Cape. "Make a right turn, Rob, then turn left somewhere. You're never going to get across this traffic."

"You're not going to tell me?"

"I will. Just give me some time to process what's happening. I haven't felt like this in a long time."

"Are there Bradford people involved?"

"I'm beginning to think all women are Bradford people," she said.

Growing frustrated with his wife's reticence, and sure that Maggie Mason had somehow been involved, Rob peeled out onto Route Six, making the left, though just barely. Katie squealed in delight.

"Those Bradford people chased you out of your house," Rob said, accelerating.

"I wasn't chased out of the house." She was playing with her hair now, securing it in some form of braid. "I decided to leave. I wasn't ready for them. I am now."

"What does that mean?"

Before Katie could answer, a police car came up from behind, lights flashing. Rob was going well over the speed limit. His head started to throb again. He pulled into the bike lane, as far over as he could. Cars zipped by in the left lane, making no effort to slow down. The officer had effectively blocked off the right lane with his cruiser, leaving the lights flashing. Rob watched in his rearview mirror and saw Officer Grainger pop out of the car.

"Hello, Mr. Crosley. I see you found your wife," Grainger said, coming alongside. "Everything okay Ma'am?"

Katie smiled and leaned forward to get a full view of the policeman.

"I'm very well, Officer," she said. "Were you looking for me, too?" She gave Rob a quizzical look.

"The parking attendant let us know when you left the lot. She was watching the car for us."

"Are you okay there, Officer?" Katie said. "I don't want you to get sideswiped.

"It's fine. They'll hit my car before they hit me." Grainger checked the traffic anyway. A car sped past and a passenger yelled "Coppers!" out of the open window.

"Thanks for keeping an eye out," Rob said, relieved that he had not been stopped for speeding.

"You do need to slow, Mr. Crosley."

"Yes, sir. Guess I was just glad to have my wife back."

"Where are you heading now?" he asked, peering into the backseat as though there might have been a cache of contraband.

Rob was put off by the question. Was it any of Grainger's business? Was he being surveilled?

"Home!" Katie answered.

* * *

The rest of the ride home, Rob explained himself, and his call to the police. He thought that Katie might have scolded him for taking such drastic measures, but she was sympathetic, and told him he had done the right thing.

When Rob pulled into the cottage driveway, he saw a woman sitting on the front steps. She was by herself. A small backpack sat next to her. She was crying.

"That's the photographer," Katie said, showing no signs of alarm at the sight of an unannounced visitor.

"Elaine Snow," Rob said. "What the hell is she doing here? Where's Danny?" He popped open the door and jumped out. "I'll get rid of her. The cops said they would arrest anyone who came back. Stay here."

"Don't be silly," Katie said, and got out of the car as well. When Elaine Snow saw Katie approaching, she got up from the steps, threw herself into her arms, and started to sob. Rob tried to extract the photographer but Katie pushed him away.

"I'm fine, Rob. It's okay."

"Are you here alone, Elaine?" Rob said, looking into the trees that surrounded the cottage. Elaine Snow continued to sob inconsolably.

"Elaine, why don't you come inside and tell me what's wrong?" Katie said.

"Do you think that's a good idea?" Rob asked.

"Go find Danny and tell him I'm back, okay?"

"You sure?"

Katie nodded and turned Elaine Snow back toward the cottage. Rob watched as she ushered her inside, like a mother tending to her distraught child. From inside, Elaine Snow wailed, "Oh, Dorothy, please help me!"

SEVENTEEN

Yellow Tape and Frisbee Games

The car was gone again the next morning. Rob experienced a moment of panic, then remembered Danny's physical therapy appointment. Danny had taken the car. Rob was on the deck, checking the yard for turkeys, journalists, and Dorothy Bradford Society members. There were none of these, though a fox—gray and hungry-looking—stood motionless in the driveway, staring curiously at Rob, much like Sidney did when he wanted to be fed. There was no sign of Katie yet, who was usually out in the garden early in the morning. After yesterday's histrionics with Elaine Snow, he wondered whether the girl had spent the night. He had called Katie that evening to make sure everything was okay. Apparently, Elaine had been tracked down by the police and brought into the station for questioning. Don Hill had found her. "They let her go, and she was so upset that she walked here," Katie told him. "They actually thought she might have done something to the swimmers, since they were hired to take my picture and she wasn't. What's wrong with the police? She's just a girl, for God's sake."

Rob was tempted to walk to the cottage, but thought better of an unannounced visit, even though Katie seemed to be in the midst of some form of recovery. He had seen this before. His wife's condition would markedly improve after one of her disappearances, and she would eagerly start doing the things she had been prevented from doing, thinking she was cured, only to have a major panic attack knock her down, like a two by four slamming into the side of her head, pushing her into an even deeper seclusion.

Rob went back in the house, instead, and tried to assemble some sort of plan for the day. Sidney was there, too, eyeing his empty dog dish. Rob filled it and added water to soften the food, making it easier for Sidney to chew with the few teeth he had left. Strange gummy, squishing sounds now emanated from the dog's mouth when he ate, a process that required a great deal more effort than it had before. Sidney examined the bowl and then looked at Rob. The dog would not eat his food until he was sure nothing else was being offered. Rob peeled an orange, which was of no interest to Sidney, and he began gumming his wet food.

"I have fed the dog and eaten an orange," Rob announced as he dropped the peel into the trash. His wife was tending to her flock, his son was rehabilitating his knee, and his dog was noisily eating his breakfast. Rob took a mental inventory of the house, trying to think of some project he could busy himself with, something to repair or alter. Perhaps there was something on-line he needed to buy? He could go for a run. He could pick weeds out of the driveway. He decided, instead, to ride his bike into Truro Center, and pick up the new copy of the Gazette, the one that would have Katie's picture in it.

He read the article while standing in line with the intelligentsia at the town store. It didn't shed any new light on the Bradford story. Katie's picture, now with her name, was reprinted alongside a picture of the demonstration in the front yard of the cottage. There hadn't been any news cameras at the house, and Rob wondered how Ridgeback had gotten the shot. Maybe he had contacted the DBS and bought the photo from one of the demonstrators. All the same, Rob was pleased that Ridgeback clearly established Katie as the victim, driven out of her house by a group of zealous fanatics in search of a savior. Unfortunately, he also mentioned that Rob was a member of the organization, and that he had suggested his wife was somewhere in Plymouth. And then, in typical Ridgeback fashion, he crossed the line, and reported that Katie Crosley had left her husband to live in a one-room cottage, implying that Rob was somehow complicit with the Bradford Society in driving his wife from her home.

"Son of a bitch," Rob said out loud. The woman in front of him turned around and asked if he was alright.

"You know, I try not to read newspapers when I'm on vacation," the woman said. "Defeats the purpose."

"Good," Rob said. "Next time I'm on vacation I'll keep that in mind." The woman made a face, looking at him as if he had just belched violently, and turned back toward the cashier. Rob shook his head, and noticed a man grinning at him from over by the display of sunscreen products. Was he empathizing?

* * *

He got home, and all was as he had left it, though Sidney had finished eating and retreated to his closet. With no other good ideas of what to do next, he did what he always did—the reason he had moved out here in the first place—he went down to the beach.

The bay looked like a lake. The air was calm, the tide was still, and there were no waves. Blankets and umbrellas had yet to be spread and planted. Only a few beach walkers were out. Rob set up his chair, dropped his towel and book, and decided he would walk, too. He found that there was usually something new to be seen or heard when he walked the beach early in the morning. Today would be no different.

When he reached Tim Desmond's house he assumed the yellow tape that had been stretched along the dunes was meant to keep people away from the nesting sites of the shore birds—more concern for endangered species. It wasn't until he saw the officer on the deck of the house that he realized the yellow tape had "crime scene" printed on it. Had the town board changed their minds? Were the votes miscounted? Rob went as close to the house as the tape would allow, trying to figure out what was going on. He did not see Tim Desmond, or anyone who might be his wife. There were only the police. He watched until one of the officers spotted him and waved him off. The officer was not wearing a Truro police uniform. He had on a dark jacket and dark pants. Rob moved away but kept an eye on the officer. When he turned around, the large block letters on the back of his jacket were plainly visible. They read, "DEA."

When the DEA agent went back inside Rob crept back to the yellow tape. Why had he moved in the first place? If the police wanted people to stay further away from the house then they should have placed the tape further away. He expected there was more to see on the other side of the house, but the dunes blocked the view. After a few minutes of inactivity Rob got out his phone and called the police station. The desk sergeant answered. A different voice, though, sounding very new and eager to please.

"Listen, I'm on the beach, near the Desmond house, and I see police tape and DEA agents," Rob said. "Can you tell me what's going on?"

"Well, there was quite a stir here this morning," she said. "I wonder if that's what it was about. There's nobody else at the station right now. Only me. Anyway, I'm not allowed to give out any information concerning police business. Can I take a message?"

Where was this woman three weeks ago? Rob wondered. He called Steve Ridgeback next.

"I'm waiting outside the house right now," Ridgeback said. "Looks like our friend may have been mixed up in the drug trade. Man, I'm really going to enjoy writing this story."

Rob thought back to his encounter with Betty Whitman, and her account of the three men who had yelled at her on the beach, somewhere close to Desmond's house. Did the igloo coolers hold something other than fish?

"Is Desmond there?" Rob asked.

"No, they hauled him off earlier. They're searching the property now. Listen, I've got to go. One of the investigators is coming out."

Rob wondered if the investigator was Don Hill. Would he be involved with the DEA? He had heard there was some type of drug task force on the Cape that included local officials. Why would Desmond bring illegal drugs onto a property that was under so much scrutiny, especially one that already looked like it was owned by a drug lord? Maybe he kept the drugs in his other, less ostentatious house. Tim Desmond didn't seem like a drug lord, though. He seemed like a fisherman.

Eventually, two other beach-walkers stopped and asked Rob what was going on. They were young, maybe still in their teens, a boy and a girl. Rob wondered what they were doing out of bed so early in the morning. Perhaps they hadn't bothered to go to bed in the first place. He told them only that it was some sort of police action. The girl took out a cell phone and considered whether the events warranted a video recording.

"I'll bet it's a murder," the boy said.

"Don't think so," Rob said, quickly squashing any rampant speculation. "I saw a DEA agent on the deck. Looks like a drug bust."

"What's a DEA agent?" the girl asked.

"A drug agent, stupid," the boy said. And then they both had their cell phones out, snapping photos of the house, and furiously tweeting and texting the shocking news. Rob watched as they became totally consumed by their virtual realities, oblivious to him and each other.

"Do you live around here?" Rob asked, but neither of them responded. He frowned. "I had diarrhea this morning," he said. Still no reaction. Their total distraction was stunning. He resumed his surveillance of the house, but the crime scene was as vapid as the millennials. Eventually, he abandoned the yellow tape and resumed his walk, thinking he might see something new on the way back. But when he returned, an hour or so later, the rear of the house was still quiet. He ran into the millennials again, heading in the opposite direction, and made to wave to them, but they avoided eye contact. They probably hadn't bothered to look at him when they first met either. "What's a DEA agent?" he mumbled. He was going to miss Tim the fisherman. What would become of his house now?

* * *

As he neared home, it appeared the sprawl from the public beach had spread much further than usual. Rob's chair, which had been the only piece of equipment on the beach when he left, was now barely noticeable, engulfed by two large beach parties. One group had arranged their chairs in a circle, like covered wagons, carving out a space nearly twenty feet in diameter. In the middle of the circle, overweight adults horsed around, telling stories and laughing too hard. The other group displayed no sign of symmetry, scattering towels, chairs, wind screens—there was no wind—and umbrellas around haphazardly. Off to the side, a bunch of younger adults played various games with Frisbees, bean bags, and sand darts. In the water, a young man yelled for one of the women on shore to bring him a beer, insisting that drinking alcohol was the only thing he was good at, and that his balls had shriveled to the size of peanuts. Without any wind or waves, every word was audible. It was mayhem.

Rob arrived at his chair, hopelessly overmatched by the chaos around him, and considered whether to move further down the beach or simply go back to the house. One of the large men in the circle was dancing now, much to the amusement of the others. Perhaps, Rob thought, he should tell them about the drug bust, and see if they all got up and ran down the beach to watch. The dancing man fell down and began rolling in the sand, much of which clung to his lotion-covered skin. Feeling nauseous, Rob folded his chair and decided to surrender. There was simply too much unwelcome insanity on the beach today. As he broke through a heated game involving a Frisbee and two small trash cans—apparently the idea was to get the Frisbee into the cans—one of the contestants became particularly distracted and eyed Rob closely.

"Dude," the guy said. "Aren't you the Beach Freak?" The guy was directly in Rob's line of sight, making it impossible for him to duck the question and assume he was talking to somebody else.

"Sorry?" Rob said.

"The guy on YouTube, right? Dorothy Bradford? You're fuckin' hilarious, Dude."

Rob shuddered. One of the other Frisbee players started chanting "Beach Freak!" as if he was at a cage match or something. All four of the competitors now approached him.

"When are you going to start posting more stuff, man?" the first guy said. "Where's Dorothy now?"

"You need a website, Dude, or a twitter feed or something."

"Podcast!"

"Podcast, Dude."

Rob was sure no one had called him "Dude" before. It seemed clear that the four of them were not going to return to their game until he gave them some kind of acknowledgement.

"I know the guy you're talking about," he said, "but I'm not him."

Thrown off by Rob's recalcitrance, the Frisbee players looked at one another and tried to work out an appropriate response.

"I get you," one of them said. The others nodded and extended their fists.

"Really, it's not me," Rob said.

They looked at him anxiously and continued to offer their fists. Rob had no idea whether this was meant as an apology or a sign of respect. He shrugged and bumped each one, bringing an end to the encounter and sending them back to their game, but not without a final chant of "Beach Freak!"

Relieved, he continued his escape, but soon came upon Helen Schantz, who was planted menacingly at the bottom of the stairs.

"Hi," Rob said, unsure as ever whether he was the root of the annoyed expression on the woman's face.

"Are these people your friends?" Helen Schantz asked, motioning toward the hoard behind him.

"Never seen them before," Rob said.

"This is what happens when people rent out their houses," Helen Schantz said.

"I couldn't agree with you more," Rob said, glad of the opportunity to commiserate.

"You don't rent out your house, do you?"

"No, Helen. I wouldn't have anywhere to live if I did." He smiled, hoping she might grasp the humor, but the woman was incapable of recognizing sarcasm. He changed the subject. "Are you just coming down now?"

"Yes, but this won't do. Where will I sit?"

"Head down the beach," Rob suggested, despite having rejected the alternative himself. "Plenty of room that way."

Helen Schantz emitted a labored sigh and started walking, not bothering to say goodbye, though she never did.

"Good luck," Rob said. He turned to head up the stairs, checking first to see if anyone was heading down. No one was on the steps, but there was someone at the top. She was not looking at the view, as most people at the top of the stairs did. Her head was down instead, her eyes locked on the steps in from of her. Katie was taking chances.

Two summers had passed since Katie last came down to the beach in the middle of the day, and the beach was certainly nowhere near as crowded the last time. She had not yet moved from the top of the stairs, but Rob could tell she was determined to do so.

"Look at you," Rob said, having quickly trotted up the stairs before she could summon the courage to start down. He wasn't sure this was the day for her to test herself on the beach. She smiled, looking a bit uncertain of herself, and unglued her eyes from the stairs.

"There you are," she said.

"You weren't thinking about going down there were you?"

"Is it always like this now?"

"Never. This is total bullshit."

"I was thinking of taking my boat out."

"Now? You do that in the morning."

"I know," she said. She cocked her head to the side and looked at Rob's chair. Given the rush to extract himself from the beach mania, he had forgotten to wipe the sand off the metal braces. There was a calmness in her eyes, a tranquility that mirrored the stillness of the bay. "I'm done with it, Rob," she said.

"It?" he said. This was a stupid thing to say. He knew what she meant.

"I know you think I'm moving too quickly, but I'm not jumping back in all at once. Every day a new challenge."

"This is today's challenge?" Rob looked down at the circle people. They had made a hole in their formation so the sand-covered idiot could go wash himself off.

"Maybe I should wait until it's a little less crowded," Katie said.

"That's a good idea. I didn't want to stay down there either. I went for a walk, then decided to come up. Even Helen Schantz is walking further down the beach, and she never does that." He told her about the apparent drug bust at the Desmond house, as if that might further dissuade her. Katie looked back toward their own house as though there might be police activity there, too.

"So, what time did Elaine leave?"

"Late," Katie said. "Rachel borrowed Maggie's car, and came over and picked her up. She stayed for a while and we talked. She was really upset about the demonstration. I guess there's a small group of members who sometimes set their own agenda. They have the same objective though."

"You."

Katie smiled. "Rachel told me about your visit to the monument," she said. Rob thought about the wind, and how he had hung onto the railing for fear he would be blown into the bay. "I agreed to meet with them."

"Them?

"The members."

"But I thought you were going to meet with Maggie Mason first?"

"We'll go early. I'll sit with her for a while before the meeting."

"I think that's a bad idea, Kay. There was a hoard of them here two days ago and look what happened."

"I wasn't ready then," she said. She reached over and brushed some of the sand off his chair. "Will you come with me?"

Rob looked across the bay, to the spot at the top of the monument where he was perched with Rachel the day before, holding on for dear life. He remembered how unsettled he had been at the society meeting, and all the beer it took for him to stand up in front of the rowdy Bradford women. The rabid attention might prove devastating to Katie. She was not a big beer drinker.

"Listen," she said, reading his doubts, "I need to do this. I was told I've been suppressing Dorothy; that the reason I have these weird memories is because they're not mine, they're Dorothy's. I try to suppress them, but I can't. I panic. I know it sounds ridiculous but it works for me. I'm not afraid when I'm Dorothy Bradford."

"Did the people in the dunes tell you this?"

"They suggested it. Think of it as my stage name," she said. "An acting career. I'm not adding schizophrenia to my medical condition."

"That's what I'm worried about, your medical condition." Rob became a little too demonstrative and dropped his chair. It clattered off the wooden stoop and fell into the bushes.

"No!" Katie yelled as Rob reached to pick it up. She snatched the chair out of the shrubbery and held it away from Rob. "I'll wash this down back at the house."

"Thanks. I missed it," Rob said, seeing the poison ivy beside the path.

"Hey, listen," Katie said. "How about if I come up to the house for dinner tonight? If you don't have other plans that is."

"When do I ever have other plans?"

* * *

They ate mussels and pasta with crusty bread and lots of wine. Danny told them about his physical therapy and the recuperation timeline. "Four weeks and I can start running again," he said flexing his atrophied leg.

Sidney was flexing his legs, too, staring up through the glass tabletop, wondering why the plates of food didn't all fall to the floor. At first, Rob watched Katie closely, looking for signs of anxiety, but she didn't avert her eyes from her family, other than to watch the sun setting over the bay. Her hands wandered around the table, discarding mussel shells, pouring wine, and sneaking pieces of bread to Sidney. After a time, Rob relaxed, forgetting about her illness, and able to enjoy having his family together in one room. He was enchanted by the serenity in his wife's face, an expression he had nearly forgotten. He had not forgotten how much pleasure he took in her happiness.

Rob didn't want to sour the occasion with talk of the Tim Desmond story, but after the dishes were cleared and he had ushered Katie down to the cottage—he kissed her at the door!—he came back to the house and turned on the late news to see what coverage there was of the drug bust. Danny was asleep on the sofa, having allowed himself a few glasses of wine, too, and Sidney was sacked out in his closet. There was a cool breeze drifting through the windows, and no signs of the invisible biting insects that sometimes infiltrated the screen meshing and wreaked havoc on Rob's exposed flesh. Rob poured some whiskey and listened to the news team report the story of the drug raid at the California-style house on the bay.

"Two kilograms of heroin, and other narcotics, with a street value of a quarter million dollars, were seized from a Truro home this morning in a raid coordinated by the Cape Cod Drug Task Force," the newscaster reported. There was film of Tim Desmond and his wife being led from his new house. They both had a look of total bewilderment on their faces. "Recently obtained information led the investigators to the Desmond house." They cut to a field reporter, whom Rob recognized from his own run-ins with the media, and there was Don Hill, too, being interviewed. Don Hill said that he believed that the Desmonds were major heroin suppliers on the Outer Cape. The newsman asked how they found them, but Hill wouldn't go any farther than to say that they had received a tip.

"Do you find it strange that a major supplier would build a house like this?" the reporter asked.

Don Hill looked at the house and shrugged. "I find it strange that anyone would build a house like this," he said.

There was no mention of the recently resolved zoning issues, or the fact that the Desmonds had just moved in. Rob had hoped they would talk about what would become of the house. Undoubtedly the Desmonds would go to prison. Did they get to keep their stuff? And what if the police found the D*orothy Swimmers* buried in the dunes close by? Were they somehow connected to Desmond, too? Had they seen something they shouldn't have?

Rob watched the first half of *Schindler's List*—he was too tired to get through the whole thing—then went to bed. He lay awake for a while, anxious that he might soon be sharing his bed again with his wife. He tried to remember how they made love. What was it she liked? Where did they start and where did they end up? He fell asleep and had a vivid dream of hundreds of seals lying dead on the beach in front of Tim Desmond's house. Desmond was there, too, picking his way through the carcasses, carrying an igloo cooler. Katie stood on the shore, next to her rowboat. Desmond loaded the cooler into the boat, and she hopped in and shoved off, heading into the bay. Desmond spread a blanket and lay down on the beach. Soon he was indistinguishable from the dead seals around him.

EIGHTEEN

Kool-Aid and Maidservants

The next issue of the Cape Cod Gazette was fat with stories about the Desmond drug bust. Steve Ridgeback wrote the lead story, tagging Desmond with the pseudonym, *Beachfront Drug Lord*. He also wrote an opinion piece—though most of Ridgeback's articles seemed to be opinion pieces—in which he said that "Everyone was so caught up in Tim Desmond's zoning battle that no one noticed all the smack that was funneling through the house."

There was also an arrest of the boat owner who ran the stuff across the bay from Boston. The police had yet to find any evidence connecting Desmond to the *Dorothy Swimmers*. A thorough search of both of the Desmond properties yielded no clues. The day after the arrest Don Hill stopped by the cottage to show Katie a picture of the drug-running boat and asked if she had seen it on the day she saw the swimmers. She had not. Rob was there, too, and he told Hill about his encounters with Desmond. He also shared the story about Betty Whitman and her dog, who may have stumbled upon a drug delivery on the beach. Don Hill wrote down Betty Whitman's name and thanked them. On the way out he apologized to Katie for showing up unannounced and said that he hoped his visit hadn't been too difficult for her. Katie told him she was doing much better and that he was welcome to stop by any time, though she did scold him for his treatment of Elaine Snow. "You never know," Don Hill said.

Meanwhile Katie continued to tackle new challenges. She experienced some occasional bouts of anxiety but they were manageable. One afternoon she went down to the beach with Rob, the next she drove to the town store, and after that she worked in her wood shop while Rob and Danny were upstairs. She even had a conversation on the beach with Helen Schantz which lasted for almost half an hour.

"Did she know who you were?" Rob asked.

"Not sure. I reminded her I was your wife but that didn't seem to help."

"What did you talk about?"

"Poison ivy and heroin."

There was no sign of the Bradford Society women either, and little discussion. Rob wondered if Katie had decided to let the Dorothy thing go, perhaps deciding she didn't need the alter ego after all. She hadn't said anything more about meeting with the members, and he hadn't wanted to ask. *Ignore it and it will go away*, Rob thought. Hopeful that the society may have found a new Dorothy, he checked the web site, but Katie's picture was still there. There was also an announcement of a meeting with a special guest. All members were strongly encouraged to attend.

Rob went down to the basement, bringing the laptop with him. Katie was busy building a pair of bar stools for the kitchen island. She was gluing the pieces together now, so the power tools were idle.

"Did you see this?" he asked, showing her the web page.

"Is that the meeting announcement? Rachel called me about it this morning."

"You're the special guest?"

"Very special."

"Jesus. So you're really doing this?"

"Dorothy Bradford lives."

"What are you going to do?"

"I'm going to go."

"I mean when you get there."

"Drink beer. Talk to the ladies."

"You don't like beer."

Katie wiped some excess glue from around a joint. "A lot has changed about me," she said.

"They're going to lose their minds, you know. Your picture alone nearly caused a riot."

"You'll come, too?"

"It's tomorrow?" The date and time were right there on the web page, but calendars were of little consequence to Rob anymore. He seldom knew what day of the week it was.

"Too soon?"

Rob found himself studying the picture of Katie again. He was mesmerized by the image every time he saw it, just as the Bradford Society had been mesmerized. That it may have been shot by someone using a waterproof camera while treading water made it that much more intriguing.

"I guess it's better not to have too much time to think about it," Rob said.

"That's what I thought."

"But if you're feeling uncomfortable tomorrow we don't go, okay?"

"I'll be fine."

"Maybe you could wave to them from a second story window or something."

"Like the Queen?"

"You would have some separation."

"I'll have you and Rachel to protect me. Remember, we need to go early so I can talk to Maggie before. Get comfortable with the place."

"Did Rachel tell you about the bonnet?"

"The what?"

"They'll ask you to wear a bonnet. You know, like the Pilgrims did." Rob remembered that Maggie had given him a bonnet to give to Dorothy. He thought he might have drunkenly tossed it in a dumpster somewhere in Provincetown.

"Do they all wear them?"

"Yes."

"I'm not wearing a bonnet."

"Good. You'd look like Hester Prynne or something."

"A marked woman."

"Exactly."

* * *

When Rob told Danny about the meeting he was apprehensive. After the demonstration at the cottage he was less sure about his mother becoming involved with the Bradford Society.

"You don't think they're going to feed her Kool-Aid or anything, do you?" he said.

"Beer," Rob said.

"What happens when they find out she's a fraud?"

"I expect they'll stone her to death," Rob said.

Danny gave his father an annoyed look and sat down to put on his running shoes. "Don't be nonchalant about this when you're up there," Danny said. "Stay close to Mom."

"What do you think you're doing?" Rob asked, pointing to the shoes.

"Relax. I'm only going to walk around in them for a while." Danny stood and rocked back and forth. "I'm going to tell Mom she shouldn't go. I've decided these women are lunatics.

Eventually they'll move on and find a new Dorothy and Toto, or whatever the hell it is."

"I think she really wants to do this, Danny. Something happened to her on her beach adventure. I've never seen her so determined. Kind of like you before a race."

That night, over dinner, Danny had no luck. He could be much more persuasive than Rob, given his elite jock mindset. But Katie was just as stubborn as her son—she was set on being Dorothy Bradford.

"I'm proud of you, Mom, for wanting to do this, but I don't think these women are worth the effort," Danny said. "And you don't know how many of them will be there. Fifty? A hundred?"

"One person can be more terrifying than fifty," she said. "Look, I'm not jumping out of a plane. I could have a panic attack tomorrow, but I could just as easily have one right now, too."

"Those maniacs are more terrifying than we are," Danny said.

"That's not fair," Katie snapped. "You don't know them."

Was she now a defender of the Dorothy Bradford Society? Danny wanted to point out that she didn't know them either, except for Rachel and Elaine. He backed off, seeing he had annoyed his mother. Rob was gnawing on an ear of corn, but froze when Katie scolded Danny. Katie had exhibited another dormant behavior—he and Danny had become so careful not to upset her.

"Fine," Danny said. "You don't need my permission anyway."

"You need to start running again," Katie said, sensing her son's frustration.

"Tell me about it."

* * *

The next morning Katie rowed to the secret beach. Rob wondered if she would come back in time for the meeting, or come back at all. She could suffer a bout of anticipatory anxiety and lose her nerve. But she returned at three o'clock, as she said she would, and was ready to go by four. She wasn't quite sure what to wear. She hadn't gone to any sort of social event in years, much less one where she was the guest of honor. In the end she stuck with jeans and a tee shirt, and let her hair hang loosely around her shoulders.

"Will this work?" she said to Rob, presenting herself for inspection.

"I don't think it matters what you wear," Rob said. "You could walk in there with your tits out and they'd still lose their minds."

Traffic was heavier than usual on the way to Provincetown. Added to the time it took Rob to clean the turkey shit off the windshield, they had already lost fifteen minutes. Since Katie had told Rachel she would come early to meet with Maggie, she suggested that Rob drop her off before parking the car.

"You sure you want to walk in there alone?" Rob said.

"Rachel will be there."

"Do you know what you're going to say? Your story, I mean?"

"Sort of."

"They'll want to know if you were pushed into the bay, if you fell, or if you jumped. If you were pushed, then who pushed you? Did you hop in a rowboat and escape to the shore? How are you still alive, and why?"

"Don't worry, I'll give them a good performance."

He stopped in front of the house and turned on his flashers. "We can still turn around, Kay," he said. Rob was starting to wonder if he was more anxious about the meeting than Katie.

"I'm good," Katie said patting her husband on the arm. "Go park."

"You should ask Rachel if there's a room in the house you can go to if you need to, you know, escape."

"I could."

He waited until Katie went inside, as if he was dropping off a kid at a play date. Rachel answered the door and gave her a hug. She waved to Rob. He made a quick U-turn and headed for the parking lot, wanting to get back as soon as possible. He was worried about how she would fare with Maggie Mason.

Rachel answered the door when he returned. She was alone. "She's with Maggie," Rachel said, leading Rob inside.

"Take me to her," Rob said, looking into the large rooms on the first floor. They were empty.

"Maggie said she wanted to meet with Katie alone. Katie was okay with it. She said to tell you she was fine."

"She's been saying that a lot lately. What are they talking about?"

"What they're going to do at the meeting, I imagine."

"Did you give her some beer?"

"I did."

"Don't let her drink too much, okay? She's not a big drinker. You don't want a drunk Dorothy."

"A little drunk is okay," Rachel said, intoning the society's creed. "Where's your mug?"

"Shit. I forgot it."

Rachel got him another, and filled it from the keg set up in the backyard. There was already a healthy crowd there, more than fifty people. Rachel thought they might see upwards of a hundred. Everyone knew who the special guest was.

"So what does Maggie have planned?" Rob asked, swigging beer.

"Not sure. She's been pretty tight-lipped since I told her Katie had agreed to come."

"Is that like her? To keep you out of the picture?"

Rachel frowned. "It's her call," she said. "My job was to get her here." She adjusted the keg, the same mobile contraption Rob had seen at the cottage. A second keg, which Rob supposed was there to accommodate the larger crowd, sat on a table close by. "Listen, Rob, you need to call her Dorothy tonight, okay? I mean, you can call her Katie with me, but around the other members we have to use Dorothy."

Rob shrugged. "Sure. She came here to play the part. As long as I don't have to be William. He doesn't seem to be real popular here."

Rachel laughed. "No, William is dead. Only Dorothy is immortal. You're at least the second husband she's had."

Rob quickly finished his beer and refilled the mug, thinking about the other men Katie might have married. "Anything else I shouldn't do?"

"Don't kiss her."

"What?"

"Don't hug her, and try not to touch her either."

"Why?"

"A lot of the members don't like the idea of a man being with Dorothy."

"Is she supposed to be a lesbian?" he said.

"It's a point of contention."

"I'm only here if Katie needs me."

"Dorothy."

"Her, too."

* * *

By five o'clock Rob had already developed a Bradford beer buzz. As at the last meeting he was largely ignored by the members, but on this occasion there was a much greater sense of anticipation in the air. Women huddled together with their beers, and spoke in excited tones. Many of them were already seated, wanting to have the best views when the great woman arrived. There were no lines at the kegs. Everyone's attention was on the back door of the house. Rob hunted for Jeff Hansen but didn't see him. He knew that Jeff didn't think much of the Dorothy Bradford charade, but he did appreciate the beer.

As the time wandered past five, Rob became concerned that Katie might have had an attack and possibly sequestered herself somewhere in the house. If she had, wouldn't Maggie Mason have come out to find him? He pulled out his phone and texted Katie. As he did, he overheard two members talking about what they thought was in store.

"I hear she's dressed as a Pilgrim," one said.

"She is a pilgrim," said the other.

Rob was certain that Katie wouldn't agree to wear any type of costume, even after drinking a beer or two. He kept an eye on his phone, waiting for her reply to his text. One of the women was now looking at him suspiciously.

"You're the husband, aren't you?" she said. It would have been easy to play games with the woman, but Rob decided this was not a good idea. Since they hadn't found a seat yet, he thought they might be two of the less radical members.

"I am," he said.

"You said she was your friend at the last meeting."

"I was protecting her. She wasn't ready for this."

The woman nodded and smiled. "You're a good husband then," she said. "Her first husband was not."

"Thanks," Rob said, happy to hear he was a better man than William Bradford. Clearly, it was a night of celebration, not recrimination. The women moved away without any further word and went to find seats. So did the rest of the few remaining members still on their feet. Rob checked his watch. It was now fifteen minutes past five. Maggie Mason's backyard had gotten eerily quiet. It was as though someone had dimmed the lights. But there was nothing happening at the back door to suggest that someone was about to emerge. Was Maggie Mason habitually fifteen minutes late? Rob's heart rate was quickening. He hoped Katie's was not.

And then Maggie came out, Rachel at her side. Katie was not with them. Her picture was, though, set on an easel, as it had been at the previous meeting. Rachel found a seat. There was nervous mumbling from the audience, perhaps sensing that they were about to be stood up again. Maggie did not appear concerned, though. On the contrary, her expression was one of complacency. She was about to make good on her promise to deliver their deity. She rang the ship's bell to signal the start of the meeting.

"Hello, everybody," Maggie said. Rob noticed that Maggie Mason was not wearing her bonnet. Since this was only his second meeting he had no way of knowing if the missing bonnet was significant or not, but it seemed as though a number of the members had noticed, too. Maggie Mason smiled and took a deep breath. She looked at each corner of the yard, establishing eye contact with her audience, but everyone was looking past her, straining to catch a first glimpse of Dorothy Bradford. Many of them had their phones out, ready to record the big event.

"Where is she, Maggie?!" someone called out. "Where's your bonnet?"

Maggie held up her hands. "She is here," she said. "She is finally here. I have brought her to you."

In his borderline drunken state, Rob wanted to interject and argue that *he* had brought Dorothy to them. Hell, Rachel deserved more credit than Maggie Mason.

"I have been looking for Dorothy for thirty years," she continued. "There were times when I thought we were close, but she would slip away. But today she is ours. This is truly the greatest achievement in the history of our society."

Rob belched loudly. No one turned to look. They could not be distracted.

"Breath, Katie," Rob said, feeling he could now talk to himself in full voice without anyone noticing, or caring. There was something comforting about giving voice to his thoughts, more so when no one was listening. It occurred to him that he was not in a good spot for Katie to see him when she came out. He felt it was important for her to see a familiar face among all the unfamiliar ones. There were two sections of seats in the yard with an aisle down the middle. Rob moved into the aisle and stood toward the rear, directly in Maggie Mason's line of sight. The excitement emanating from the women seated around him was nearly as stirring as the beer. The dread he had felt before was now replaced by the same nervous energy he experienced when he was in a packed stadium watching Danny line up for a race. Rob leaned in, turning his head slightly, as aware of what he was hearing as what he was seeing. He set one foot in front of the other and rocked back and forth, as if he was the one waiting for the gun to sound.

"Dorothy Bradford!" Maggie Mason said, and everyone shot out of their seats like missiles from their silos. Rob threw up his arms triumphantly, brandishing his Bradford beer mug. He was about to shout out his wife's name, but checked himself and yelled, "Dorothy!"

And then, there she was. She opened the screen door and stepped into the yard—no Pilgrim costume, no bonnet. She paused for a moment to take in the scene in front of her. This was the moment that would have overwhelmed her in the past, but she saw nothing threatening here, only acceptance. Women were now weeping and hugging each other. One hundred cell phones were held aloft. Rob's arms were still up, his eyes on his wife. Were they welling with tears? Katie saw him and smiled. Maggie caught sight of him, too, and signaled for him to get out of the aisle. He wiped his eyes and went to refill his mug. Katie had not disappointed.

The general frenzy continued for what seemed like five minutes. Several women tried to approach her, but Maggie and Rachel kept them back. Katie went over and stood by her picture while she waited for the ruckus to subside. She made no effort to silence the members and no effort to speak over them. When the crowd did quiet, at Maggie's beckoning, Katie remained quiet as well.

Rob worried she was becoming anxious and would turn back to the house. And perhaps that would be enough. The members had seen her, after all, in the flesh—the four hundred year-old Pilgrim woman was real. Maggie Mason moved toward Katie, perhaps to goad her into performing whatever it was they had choreographed. Katie held up her hand though, signaling Maggie to stay back.

"It is best if no one gets too close to me," Katie said, her voice booming, betraying no discernable anxiety. "Otherwise you might lose me again."

"No!" someone shouted. "We won't!"

"You're among friends here," Maggie Mason said, and sat down in the front row.

"Thank you for inviting me," Katie said. "I have already met a few of you, and I look forward to meeting the rest. Oh, and I apologize for not being at home the other day when some of you showed up in the yard, but as I said, I do not react well when a group of people comes after me." Katie became momentarily distracted by two women in the front row who were holding on to each other in a rapturous way. "That is how I ended up in the bay." Everyone leaned forward in their seats sensing they were about to learn the answer to their most important question.

"Tell us what happened, Dorothy!" someone cried. "Who came after you?"

"I am not sure," Katie said. "But I did not jump. I did not fall. Someone pushed me." A collective wail rose from the audience.

Rob choked on his beer before he remembered that this was an act. His wife was playing a role, or at least he hoped she was.

"She was pushed!" a woman in the front row screamed, turning to address the crowd. "I knew it!"

"Who was it, Dorothy? Who pushed you? Your husband? It was William, wasn't it?"

"Not my husband," she said. "My husband loved me." This admission produced an even stronger response. William Bradford was vilified by much of the society, and was thought to be the root of Dorothy's ills.

"Everyone, please!" Maggie said. "We must hear Dorothy out. Everything we have believed to this point has been just that, beliefs. Now comes the truth!"

"William Bradford was the bravest man I ever met," Katie said.

Rob tried to think of a time when he was brave. There was never an opportunity. His life was seldom threatened. These were different times.

"If he had been on the boat at the time, he would have rescued me," Katie continued.

"He abandoned you!" one of the William-haters shouted trying to salvage the moment.

"No," Katie said. "He was on shore, scouting for a place where we could live. All of us. He was my husband but he also cared greatly about our people. They would not have survived without him."

"You survived without him!"

"Did I?"

Another gasp.

"She's a ghost!" someone yelled. More general mayhem ensued, the various factions of the Dorothy Bradford Society arguing the evolution of the woman before them. When the bickering did not subside, Maggie Mason motioned to Rachel, who stood up, shoved two fingers in her mouth and let out an ear-piercing whistle that quickly brought the meeting back to order. Rob wondered why Maggie didn't ring the ship's bell instead.

"Why don't we let Dorothy tell her story?" Maggie said. "And not put words in her mouth."

Rob leaned against one of the kegs. He wondered if Katie had enough strength left to tell her story, whatever it was. Was she making this up as she went along? Or was this the story Maggie Mason wanted her to tell?

"Who do you think pushed you?" someone in the front row asked.

"I guess that is a fair question," Katie said. Even Rob wanted to hear the answer to this one. She paused. Her attention drifted back to the two amorous women in the front row. Rob now had the impression that she was working this out as she went along, thinking on her feet, an impossibility when she was having an attack and adrenalin was swamping her heart like gas flooding an engine.

The backyard was deathly silent now. All eyes were on her. Was death in the cards?

"This may be hard for some of you to hear, but it is the only explanation I have," Katie said. "Remember that the men, or most of them anyway, were on a scouting expedition. So most of the people on the boat at the time were women and children."

Rob glanced at Maggie Mason, who seemed as enthralled as everyone else. Was this story new to her as well?

"There were two young maidservants on the boat," Katie continued. "Some people thought they were sisters but they were not. They were attractive, but had not married despite the advances of the single men on the boat, and some married men as well."

"Pigs!" someone yelled, but she was quickly shushed by the crowd.

"They kept to themselves when they were not working," Katie said. "They were not friendly except with each other."

"Were they witches?" someone said. Maggie Mason scowled at the woman who had offered the indictment. "Sorry," the woman said. Witchcraft was apparently a sore point among members of the Dorothy Bradford Society.

"One day, after we had anchored in the bay, I went down into the hold to get some flour. There, among the few stacks of supplies we had left, I saw the two women embracing each other. They were kissing." Katie paused, knowing this last piece of information would need time to be absorbed.

"Where the fuck did that come from?" Rob mumbled to himself. He assumed that a number of the members were lesbians, including the *Dorothy Swimmers* themselves. How would they react to this twist in the story? A troubled silence ensued, followed by clapping, and then some cheers. Perhaps these two fictional Pilgrims would now be lauded as America's first lesbians.

Katie went on.

"They saw me and immediately stopped what they were doing. I was in shock, as I had never seen two women behave this way before. My first thought, I admit, was that they were either witches or were under the spell of witches. They told me they had drunk too much beer and lost their heads, but I knew they were lying. We were nearly out of beer, and what was left was carefully rationed. They asked that I not tell anyone and said that they would never do it again. I turned and left the hold without saying anything."

"They loved each other!" someone said. "Men were shit!"

"I do not know about that," Katie said. "But later that same day I was out on the deck looking to see if William was returning. The deck was slick with ice, and as I leaned over the side I felt a hand on my shoulder. At first, I thought it was someone trying to keep me from losing my balance, but it was not. I was given a hard shove, and I tumbled into the water."

"Those bitches!"

Katie paused again. She looked toward the back of the yard and found Rob lurking. She gave him a sly smile, a sign that she was enjoying herself. Still, Rob worried she was setting herself up for trouble with the lesbian story. Maybe this was her intention? To place doubt in the minds of the members and perhaps shift their allegiances?

"And you're sure of this?" Maggie asked once the backyard quieted.

"I cannot be sure since I did not see who pushed me," Katie said. "I must have passed out when I hit the water. It was so cold."

"Well, we do know now that you were pushed."

"Yes. But I have no idea who else could have done it. You can imagine what would have happened to those girls if I had said anything."

"What were their names?" a woman at the back of the assembly yelled, sounding skeptical.

"Why do you doubt her!?" another woman yelled. Several others voiced their agreement.

Maggie stared down the woman, who risked becoming an ex-member of the society in short order.

Katie narrowed her eyes.

"Alice and Catherine," she said.

Rob knew there was a manifest of the Mayflower passengers. He got out his phone and pulled up a list from the internet. There was, in fact, a list of servants but the names Alice and Catherine were not among them.

"Did you drown?" a woman in the front row asked, ready to move past the treasonous show of defiance. "Are you a ghost?"

"I do not think so," Katie said. "I came to sometime later. The tide had pushed me onto the shore. I looked for the Mayflower but it was gone."

"So, your William left you for dead?" the woman in the rear shouted. With that, two other members—the stocky variety—collared the trouble-maker and began to hustle her out of the yard.

"Wait a minute!" Katie said, holding out her hand, palm forward. "This is not the way we should handle things. This woman is entitled to her opinion."

"Yes, please let her go," Maggie said. The two women released the agitator, who started in again.

"Maybe he was having an affair with one of these maidservants," the woman said. "Maybe William told her to push you off the boat. Or maybe it wasn't one of these women at all." Another faction of the membership expressed their approval of this position.

"Why is it so important that William be the one to blame?" Katie asked. There was a fire in her expression now, similar to the one displayed in the picture. Everyone fell silent, worried they had stirred Dorothy's wrath. They did not yet know what she was capable of.

"Because it's what we have believed for thirty years," the agitator said, now more demure.

"I think we should move on," Rachel said, popping out of her chair. The meeting was spinning off in a direction no one had expected. "Dorothy told us she was pushed into the bay and that she survived. We'll never know for sure who pushed her so let's just leave it at that, okay?"

"I agree with Rachel!" Rob called out, standing in the aisle again. All turned their heads in his direction, and he was immediately sure he had said something out of line. But the silence was broken by a smattering of applause, and soon everyone was clapping for Rachel's suggestion.

Katie walked to the keg and filled her mug. All eyes followed her. "You folks sure do make good beer," she said, looking in Maggie's direction, trying to ease the tension. "So what else can I tell you?" Several women jumped up and called out their questions, giving the meeting the frenzied feel of a press conference. Katie pointed to a woman in the front row.

"We want to know why you're still alive," the woman said. "And have you aged at all since you fell off the boat?"

"She didn't fall," the woman next to her said, "She was pushed."

"Right. Sorry. Since you were pushed?"

"I have some gray hair," Katie said. "So I have aged a little, I guess. Maybe the time I spent in the water that day slowed the aging process. The water was very cold."

"How did you survive?"

"The natives who lived here showed me how to grow crops—corn, tomatoes, carrots. Things like that. And I knew how to make beer from corn."

"Why aren't you wearing the bonnet?" a woman from the back yelled.

Katie smiled at this. She looked at Maggie Mason and provided the explanation of the bonnet's disappearance. "I always hated those things," she said. "We were made to wear them to keep our heads covered. They are a reminder of the constraints that men placed on us." In an instant, all pulled off their bonnets and tossed them on the ground.

The questions continued for another thirty minutes and, to Rob's surprise, Katie had answers for all of them. Most were about the legends that surrounded her, like her supposed ability to resurrect the dead from the bay, which she quickly dismissed as a myth. She admitted that she spent a lot of time paddling around the bay, but had yet to come across anyone floating in the water. Of course, for the first three hundred years or so there were few people on the Outer Cape to run into in the first place. Plenty of people died in the monstrous storms on the oceanside but she was seldom over there, and never in her boat.

She was so convincing in how she handled the audience's questions that even Rob began to think she was Dorothy Bradford. He thought someone might ask her about him and maybe other husbands she had had over the centuries, but no one did. William Bradford seemed to be the only male they were concerned with, some more than others. And no one asked about the *Dorothy Swimmers*, the lost women in the bay whom Rob had announced to the world were snatched by the four hundred year-old Pilgrim standing in front of them.

Throughout the question and answer session Maggie Mason stayed mostly quiet, reveling in her defining moment, comfortable in knowing that her members were embracing this woman she had brought them, seeing her as the one true Dorothy Bradford.

"What a day!" Maggie said, deciding it was time to bring the meeting to a close. Rachel started clapping and the members joined in. "At last, our very own Dorothy Bradford!" This got everyone out of their seats again. Maggie gave Dorothy a mug and made her a member of her own society. Rob thought Katie might go straight back into the house, avoiding what was sure to be a crush of women around her—the thing that had driven her out of her own home a few days before—but she stayed to meet the members, all of whom wanted to hug her and get their pictures taken once they had cleared the tears from their eyes.

As everyone crowded around Katie, the agitator went to the kegs and filled her mug. She was standing there by herself, and Rob thought to feel sorry for her. She was, after all, the woman who was trying to do exactly what Rob had meant to do at the last meeting—expose Katie for the fraud she was. He walked over to console her.

"I admire your courage," he said as she drank her beer. She nodded, not bothering to look in his direction, keeping her focus on a point beyond the backyard. She filled her mug again.

"You're not off the hook yet, William Bradford," she said, and wandered back toward Dorothy.

"I'm Rob! Remember?"

While his wife continued her performance, Rob wandered over to the tree where he and Jeff Hansen had spent the last meeting and, checking for any new ivy that may have sprung up since, sat down. He was trying not to get too drunk since he had to drive home later. He watched the throng at the front of the yard, knowing Katie was in there somewhere, and wondered how she could possibly cope with so many people bearing down on her. How could she escape if she needed to? He hoped the crowd would start to thin out, but no one left. They had been looking for Dorothy Bradford for so long that they weren't about to let her from their sight now. They filled their mugs and some broke off into smaller groups, but all kept their eyes on Katie. Some sat back down in the chairs, others sat on the grass close to where Katie stood. Rachel stayed at Katie's side, the dutiful steward, while Maggie Mason accepted congratulations from the members.

When Katie headed back to the house, seeing she needed to leave before anyone else would, the agitator approached her and said something that clearly startled her. Seeing the encounter, Rob got up and ran towards Katie, concerned the woman had somehow threatened his wife. Rachel was close by and she stepped in and pushed the agitator away. The woman said a few more things as Rachel took Katie inside. It did not appear that anyone else was close enough to hear what was being said.

Rob banged through the back door and found Rachel alone in the kitchen. "Where is she?" he said.

"In the bathroom. She's fine."

"What did that woman say?" Rob said, looking out the window.

"More nasty stuff about William Bradford. We're going to have to work on improving William's image, I guess."

Rob sensed that Rachel's job would now include the maintenance of the myth surrounding his wife, deflecting anything that might detract from Dorothy's legend.

"Why don't you go and get the car, and I'll bring her out when you pull up," Rachel said.

The walk cleared his head. Rob freed his car from the lot, and pulled up to the house. Rachel and Katie were waiting outside. They embraced, Katie becoming lost in Rachel's enormous wingspan, and said their goodbyes.

"So how are you feeling, Dorothy?" Rob asked as he pulled away from the house, careful to dodge the human diversity wandering in the street. It was getting harder to tell male from female. "You were amazing. They love you."

"Well, not all of them. Not yet anyway. Can we turn off the air conditioning?"

Rob turned off the fan and opened the windows.

"Don't let that bitch ruin the evening. You were fantastic."

"She's not a bitch. She's got as much right to believe William was to blame as I do in blaming the two maids."

"How did you come up with that story? What did you call them?"

"Alice and Katharine. A revelation I had when I was on my beach walk."

"Which was?"

"The two women I met were partners. I saw them kissing and it sparked a panic attack."

"So, you're homophobic, too?"

"No. I'm not homophobic, too. Asshole."

"Sorry."

"The sight of the two of them kissing stirred up a suppressed memory that's apparently at the root of a lot of my anxiety. At least that's what I believe."

"From the Mayflower? There weren't any maids named Alice or Katharine on the Mayflower. I checked the manifest."

"Alice and Katharine were two girls I went to camp with. They were in my tent." Katie made a guttural noise, like she was coughing up a bad piece of meat.

"You didn't like them?"

"They mostly ignored me. They stayed up all night talking about their bodies. They practiced kissing a lot. One of them told me that if I said anything to anyone about it she'd kill me." Katie leaned her head out the window and into the breeze.

"Well, she was just being a bitch, right?"

"I didn't know what to think. I was thirteen. I was terrified."

"You never told anyone?"

"No. Just the ladies on the beach. They thought there was probably an earlier memory, too. A Dorothy memory I couldn't deal with because it seemed like it didn't belong to me. They would tell you I did see two women kissing on the Mayflower, and that they did shove me in the bay. Who knows? I was actually feeling a bit nervous up until the point where I told the story."

"Were they at the meeting? The dune girls?"

"I didn't see them. They might have been."

Rob pulled onto Route Six, careful to keep his speed at fifty. He had no chance of passing a sobriety test in his present condition. They drove past the dormant harbor, the last of the day's sunlight flickering in the ripples like dying candlelight.

"So what happens now?" he said.

Katie reclined her seat, closed her eyes and took a deep breath. She saw the Mayflower, anchored in the bay, ice bumping up against the hull. She exhaled. “Now I am Dorothy Bradford,” she said.

NINETEEN

Lobster Rolls and Sand Darts

The following day brought two new developments. First, a new picture of Katie was added to the Dorothy Bradford Society's web page, and second, Sidney dug a hole in the yard and lay down in it. Rob stood over the hole and asked Sidney what the hell he thought he was doing. Sidney lay on his left side, but his right eye was open, focused, as much as either of the dog's eyes could focus on anything anymore, on the man standing over him. Rob had started to wonder if Sidney still knew who he was. The dog had taken to wandering around the yard in a state of bewilderment, searching for landmarks, stepping in one direction then turning and stepping in another, waiting for something to trigger one of his decaying senses.

"He looks like you when you're trying to figure out which smoke detector is beeping," Danny said. But Sidney didn't seem to have any idea of what he was looking for. Perhaps a hole to crawl into? It had been a long time since Sidney dug a hole. He did it a lot when he was younger, wreaking havoc in the garden beds, particularly on hot days when the cooler dirt beneath the surface offered some relief. Was this what he was doing now, or was he making his own funeral arrangements?

Rob knelt down and petted the dog. Sidney raised his head to make sure there wasn't an offer of food being made. Seeing none he lay his head back down and made a low grumbling noise. Rob called the vet, who assured him that dogs did not generally dig holes when they were ready to die. More likely, he was just hot. Still, with all the wildlife roaming through the backyard, Rob was not comfortable leaving Sidney alone in the hole, given his diminished ability to escape or defend himself. He didn't want to disturb him either. The dog had worked too hard digging the hole, only to be yanked out of there by a vaguely familiar human. Rob grabbed his laptop and a lawn chair, and sat down next to Sidney's hole.

It was while he was sitting next to the hole that Rob opened the Bradford Society web page and got a look at the new picture of Katie. There was a drawing of William Bradford next to her picture—the long dead husband. The caption announced Dorothy's revelation that she *may* have been forced off the boat by two women—no mention of their sexual preferences—and that her husband, William *may* not have been involved.

Rob fumbled for his phone and called his wife. After they had returned from the Bradford Society meeting, she spent the rest of the evening alone in the cottage, preferring some alone time to recover from all the attention she had received. Though she had been able to corral her anxiety, it was still quite an effort affecting her new persona. Rob first told Katie about Sidney's hole, and she wondered if they should take him to the vet. But Sidney's vet anxiety was as strong as Katie's people anxiety, and Rob was sure the trip would kill him. "If it's his time, it's his time," Rob said. "Let's leave him be. He's not in any pain."

Katie was aware of the changes on the web page. Maggie had called her earlier that morning to let her know that she was going to place emphasis on the word, "may" in the account to placate the William-haters. A few of them had come up to her after the meeting and wondered if they had found the wrong woman. Why would Dorothy say that William Bradford was a noble man? There were no noble men, as far as they were concerned.

"You still sure you want to be Dorothy Bradford?" Rob asked her. "I get the impression that the William-haters are the more militant members."

"They are a minority," Katie said. "They need to be educated."

Rob listened to his wife drift back into character. Her voice took on the unyielding tone he had heard the night before. As Dorothy, she enunciated her words carefully, and didn't use contractions. "William could not have pushed me," she said. "He was not on the boat. I can still see those two girls kissing in the tent."

"The tent?"

"I mean the hold."

"Hail Dorothy," Rob said.

"Rachel and Maggie are coming over to discuss next steps. They are bringing a few of the members with them."

"When?"

"Tomorrow."

"Will there be beer?"

"I imagine," Katie said. "We do not seem to do business without it." Rob said that he might stop by to say hello.

When lunchtime rolled around, and Sidney had given up his hole, looking oddly rejuvenated from his time underground, Katie suggested that she might be ready to go out for lunch. This would be her next big challenge, she decided, and she was craving a lobster roll. Rob was thrilled. He loved going out to lunch, but hadn't had anyone to go with, owing to Katie's phobia and Danny's strict dietary regimen.

Traffic was bearable on Route Six, as were the crowds at the restaurant. It could have been a weekday in September rather than the height of the summer season. Katie showed no signs of discomfort as she munched happily on her lobster roll. Rob ate a plate of fried clams. He wondered if anyone in the restaurant would recognize her. The local papers had featured Katie's picture a number of times now in conjunction with the stories about the missing *Dorothy Swimmers.* Though she was also known as Danny Crosley's mom, most people had never seen her, given her infrequent excursions to public places. Now she was known and recognizable as Dorothy Bradford.

The lunch was pleasant, and they weren't disturbed until Steve Ridgeback walked into the restaurant. His hyperactive reporter's eye instantly picked them out, and he walked over to greet them.

"Isn't that the reporter guy?" Katie said, seeing Ridgeback first. Rob turned to look and swore under his breath.

"Rob and Katie Crosley!" Ridgeback said, sounding pleased to see them. "Or is it Dorothy Bradford?"

"Don't be an asshole, Steve," Rob said.

"Hey, that's not fair," Ridgeback said. "I'm not the one who named her that." Katie smiled, still savoring her lobster roll.

"Well, I'm Katie Crosley right now, Mr. Ridgeback."

"Call me Steve, okay? I'm not that big a deal. So what's up with you two? Are you back together again? I can't remember the last time I saw you out together. Come to think of it, I don't think I've ever seen you out together."

"What do you mean, back together again?" Katie asked, looking at her husband suspiciously. Rob shook his head.

"Rob told me you were separated," Ridgeback said.

"We are doing just fine, thanks," Katie said, comprehending Rob's tactic.

"And how is Danny?"

"He is also doing well," Katie said. "He should start running in another week or two."

Rob had forgotten how nice it was to have Katie around. She was the more vocal of the two of them and could be expected to do most of the communicating, relieving Rob of the pressure to make small talk.

"Well that's good news," Ridgeback said.

"What are you in such a good mood about?" Rob said.

"My article about the heroin bust has been picked up by a national news syndicate. I'm going to celebrate with a cheeseburger and a milk shake."

"I should have gotten a milk shake," Katie said.

"What's going on with Desmond?" Rob asked. "Have they been able to tie him to the swimmers yet?"

"No. They haven't found a thing, and nobody is talking either."

"But they still think Desmond was behind it?"

"They've got nothing else to go on. If this lead dries up, I'm not sure where else they can look. Maybe Dorothy Bradford really did grab them." Ridgeback grinned at Katie, but she was not to be bothered. "You know, I would love to interview you, Katie, about all this Bradford business." Rob started to object but Katie cut him off.

"What do you want to know?" she said.

"Really?" Ridgeback said eagerly.

"Really?" Rob said, less eagerly.

"Fire away," Katie said.

Ridgeback flipped open his notepad—always close at hand—and pulled over a chair from another table.

"What are you doing, Kay?" Rob whispered. "You know how this guy writes. He'll make you out to be a lunatic."

"It's part of the job," Katie said. "I'm doing my part for the DBS. You did."

"And look what happened to me. You know they refer to me as the Beach Freak now?"

"Who is "they"?

Ridgeback sat down across from Rob and Katie, and scribbled a few words in his notepad. Rob noticed the bruising beneath Ridgeback's eye—the residue of the Tim Desmond haymaker.

"What about your cheeseburger?" Rob asked.

"This comes first," Ridgeback said. "The cheeseburger isn't going anywhere." He looked toward the kitchen, as if to make sure they weren't about to run out of hamburger meat. As he turned back to face Katie, he blurted his first question. "Do you believe you're Dorothy Bradford?"

Katie took her time. "The Dorothy Bradford Society believes I am. I'm willing to accept that role."

"So you're just playing Dorothy. You're not four hundred years old?"

"I'm four hundred years old when I'm Dorothy Bradford. I'm much younger the rest of the time." She gave Ridgeback a sly grin. She was not going to tell him how hold she was.

"So I'm not talking to Dorothy right now?"

"Dorothy doesn't eat lobster roles," Katie said. "You sure you don't want us to order you your food, Steve? We could send Rob."

"I've got to order it," he said, flipping through his notes. "Too many variables." His notebook was large and dog-eared. Rob thought it was curious that he carried the thing around with him. "You never know who you'll run into!" Ridgeback said when Rob asked him about it. "Here's the thing I don't understand," he went on, getting back on topic, "Initially, you seemed to go out of your way to avoid these people, which I can understand. Rob here went to a DBS meeting to try and convince them you weren't Dorothy Bradford, and when they showed up on your front lawn you ran away and disappeared for two days. What changed? Why are you now happy to be Dorothy Bradford?"

Rob leaned in, as anxious to hear Katie's answer as Ridgeback was.

"I guess it sounds odd, doesn't it?" Katie said, poking at a piece of the roll left on her plate. She glanced at Rob. His face had tightened, and his leg bounced up and down under the table. He was afraid she was going to tell Ridgeback about her condition. "Let's just say I was convinced by some of the members. I was put off at first. These are very strong-minded women, and they've been looking for Dorothy for a long time."

"But what's in it for you?"

"Have you ever done any acting, Mr. Ridgeback?" Katie said. "Gone on stage and had everyone in the audience look at you, hang on your every word? And then when you're done, they stand and clap?"

"Ego trip?"

"Maybe."

"You enjoy being Dorothy Bradford. I like that. I'm going to make that the byline, "Being Dorothy Bradford." Ridgeback finished scribbling in his notebook and then glanced at Rob. "So," he said, "Are you guys moving back in together, or what?"

"That's between me and Katie," Rob protested, worried what Ridgeback would write in any event.

"We're getting there," Katie said, grabbing Rob's hand.

"I asked that question as a friend, by the way, not as a reporter," he said.

"Horseshit," Rob said.

Ridgeback tapped his pen on the open page of the notebook and said, "I'm not always a reporter, you know." His expression became somber, and Rob wondered if Ridgeback had any friends. Before he could ask his next question, his cell phone rang. He took the call, but got up and wandered toward the back of the restaurant, leaving his notebook on the table.

Rob swung his chair over to get a better look.

"Stop it, Rob," Katie said.

"I can't read any of it anyway. Let's hope this story doesn't get syndicated, too. I'm glad you didn't say anything about your health."

Ridgeback came back and hurriedly gathered up his things.

"Breaking news?" Rob said.

"New development in the Desmond story," Ridgeback said.

"Is it about the swimmers?"

"Don't know yet."

"So, we're done?" Katie asked.

"For now. I've got some more questions but they can wait. I can only write so many articles at a time! Hey, after this one I'll have written articles about your whole family!"

"Poor guy," Katie said, watching Ridgeback leave in a hurry. "He never got his cheeseburger."

* * *

That afternoon, as Rob got ready for the beach, it occurred to him that he might want to ask Katie if she wanted to go, too. He had stopped doing this a while ago—she said no most of the time, and the two of them went about their lives as any separated couple would, only sometimes sharing their experiences, and then only after the fact. He called her now and shared his plans. Did she want to come along? She told him to go ahead and that maybe she would come down later. He ended the call, feeling oddly relieved. He had developed his own independent routine, and realized that the time he spent alone on the beach had become an important part of his day. They had, after all, just gone to lunch together. That was a good first step. Perhaps tomorrow they could go to the beach. They had to learn how to be a couple again.

The beach was markedly quieter today. The circle party—apparently a hit and run affair—had thankfully not returned, but the game-playing youths were back, now competing in some form of sand dart game. "Dude!" one of them called out as Rob came onto the beach. He worried some type of interaction would be necessary, but the communication was meant only as a greeting. Rob raised his hand in greeting, like a pope or a royal, to show he wasn't ignoring them. He moved well out of range of the darts and dialogue—why did millennials have to shout when they spoke?—and set his chair close to the water.

The wind was up, and the tide, which was heading out, was choppy. He did not have to put his foot in the water to know it was a Jesus! Day. The water looked frigid. He sat and stared at the bay, and before too long the head of a seal popped up, no more than ten yards from shore. He had hoped the half eaten seal that had washed up a few weeks before was the only one to patrol the area, but he knew better. A replacement had been found. Maybe this one would be gutted as well.

Rob was beginning to nod off when Danny plopped down next to him. Rob was surprised to see him on the beach. Walking down the stairs was still something of a challenge.

"You're doing better," Rob said.

"They went easy on me in therapy this morning," Danny said. He picked up rocks and started chucking them in the water. "Is that a seal?"

Rob looked where Danny was pointing. Was it a different seal?

"Unfortunately."

"So, I've got some news."

"You do?" Rob's thoughts went right to the *Dorothy Swimmers*. Had Danny found them at the therapist's office, or perhaps heard news from Steve Ridgeback?

"My coaches want me to move back to Boston to finish therapy, and stay there to train."

Rob watched the seal easily disappear into the water. It had not been dragged under. "What did you tell them?"

"I told them I'd think about it," Danny said. He began massaging his quad muscles.

"You should go," Rob said. He knew a large part of the reason Danny stayed on the Cape was to look after his mother. For a long time, his was the only company she could tolerate. He knew Danny was still worried about her.

"I don't know. I like the therapist I'm seeing here."

"You don't have to look after your mom anymore. I can do that now. Go to Boston and run in circles."

"You don't want me around anymore?"

Rob shrugged. "You know, your mother and I never wanted to have kids."

Danny sighed and launched a rock toward where the seal had been. "I haven't told Mom about this yet," he said. "So don't say anything."

"She would tell you to go, too."

"Yeah, I know. Hey, Mom told me you went to lunch today," he said. "How was that?"

"Great. Until Steve Ridgeback showed up."

"She told me she let him interview her."

"The guy should give us a cut of his paycheck for all the interviews our family has given him."

"I really don't like this Dorothy Bradford thing," Danny said. "And now she's parading herself in front of the press like…"

"Like me?" Rob said. Danny shrugged, or nodded, Rob wasn't sure which. "Listen, it's the reason she's doing so well. If being Dorothy Bradford allows her to live her life, then why fight it?"

"As long as she doesn't forget about being Katie Crosley," Danny said, wrestling with the idea of his mother and father being alone together. "I'm going for a walk." He raised himself up, keeping most of his weight on his good leg. "They tell me walking in the sand is good therapy for the knees."

"Good therapy for everything," Rob said. "Check on the Desmond house. See if they've dug up any bodies."

"Sure," Danny said. He moved slowly down the beach, at one point poking his foot in the water and yelling, "Jesus!" Rob found it strange to see his son cover ground at such a deliberate pace, but his stride was no longer labored, and he wasn't checking his knee every thirty seconds. The physical therapist had told him that the muscle mass in his right thigh would come back quickly, after which he could start running again. Rob had started thinking about traveling with Danny to the winter and spring events leading up to the Olympics next summer. It had been a challenge getting to the meets while he was working, but now there was nothing preventing him from going. Perhaps even Katie could come along, too. Barring a relapse, it seemed entirely possible.

A short time later, two of the sand-gaming youths rushed past Rob and hurdled into the water, arms and legs churning. Apparently the water portion of their beach Olympics had begun. After a few yards, though, they popped their heads out of the water and one of them yelled, "Do you see it?" Rob scanned the water for the seal. There it was. He had been here before. So had the seal. Or maybe it was another seal.

"Hey, guys!" Rob called, using his millennial voice. Should he have addressed them as "dudes"? "You shouldn't swim after the seal!"

One of them turned and said, "Is it against the law or something?"

The other one said to his buddy, "Dude, that's the beach freak. He knows shit." Abandoning their pursuit they headed back to shore.

"Sorry guys," Rob said when they came out of the water. "Seals attract sharks."

"Here?"

"Yeah."

"You've seen them?"

"No, but my wife saw one just a few days ago, not far from here."

"Dude, you saved our lives!"

"I wouldn't go that far."

"Does this mean we shouldn't go in the water?"

"You can go in," Rob said, sounding like the father of eight-year-olds, "Just stay away from the seals."

"See," one of them said to the other. "The guy knows his shit."

"So what do we do if we're in the water and a shark comes by?"

"Keep still," Rob said. "It will go away."

"But what if it's attacking? Like on YouTube?"

"Go for the eyes or the gills."

"Awesome. Where are the gills?"

Rob drew a picture of a shark in the sand and showed the youths where the gills were located. He assumed they knew where the eyes were but added them just in case.

"The other thing you can do," Rob said, "is always make sure to go in the water with a slower swimmer."

The youths looked at each other and processed this new information. One of them got the joke.

"Hah, hah!"

"Hey, dude, I'm going to grab a couple of beers," the other one said. "You want one?"

Rob was inclined to turn down the offer, but he did want one, so he said yes. One of the youths bolted over to their encampment and returned with three red cups of beer. They stood by the water, drank their beers, and watched for seals. The youths asked Rob more questions about the bay. Why did the tide go out so far? Why were there no big waves on the bay? Had anyone ever swam across it? And where could they find Dorothy Bradford? Rob pointed toward the Pilgrim Monument and said they could find her right out there, but that sightings were pretty rare.

"What do we do if we see her?" one of the youths asked.

"Stay away from her," Rob said. "Treat her like a shark."

The youths finished their beers, thanked Rob again for saving their lives, and returned to their beach collective. Rob watched as the two of them chatted with their buddy dudes, sharing the wisdom they had gathered.

The youths were idle now, strewn across their blankets and towels, suddenly seeming older. Rob checked the stairs, on alert for Helen Schantz, but it was Katie he found there, again standing at the top. She stood motionless, clothing and hair buffeted by the wind. He waved but she did not see him. She was not looking down at the beach—her sights were set on the bay. He wanted to call out to her, but knew she wouldn't hear him over the wind. He waved again. "Come down, Katie." He danced around a bit, trying to grab her attention.

"Beach freak!" one of the youths shouted exuberantly. He had deployed his cell phone and was recording Rob's latest antic. Rob stopped and threw up his hands.

Katie's gaze remained fixed on a point beyond the shore. He assumed she was dealing with her inner turmoil, perhaps summoning up the courage to start down the stairs, but when he turned to see what she was looking at, he saw a large wooden ship anchored in the bay. He became still now, too. Where had the boat come from? He had been looking at the water only a few minutes before, and there were no boats to be seen, certainly none of this size. What's more, this boat was anchored, the sails on its masts furled. Rob examined his cup. Had the youths spiked his beer?

Katie came down the steps at last. Now that the youths were at rest, the beach was much less threatening.

"Where did that boat come from?" Rob asked her as she approached. "All of a sudden it was just there."

"It's the Mayflower," Katie said.

TWENTY

Blackberries and Claw Hammers

Katie was not wrong. Rob found the boat on line, and learned that it was, in fact, a smaller version of the Mayflower, recently constructed and christened "Little Mayflower." The boat, which was available for charter, was mainly powered by wind, but also had an engine on board that allowed it to motor around the bay, probably explaining how the ship had appeared so suddenly. Rob texted Maggie Mason to see what she knew about it. He even wondered if she had chartered the boat herself, but surely the expense had to be prohibitive. Maggie had heard of the boat, but had no idea why it was anchored off Provincetown. "We have no real affection for the Mayflower, real or otherwise," she told him.

"No real affection?" Rob said to Katie reading her the text. "There wouldn't be a Dorothy Bradford Society without the Mayflower. There wouldn't be any pilgrims either."

"That ship was a nightmare," Katie said, taking on her Dorothy persona. "We were glad to be rid of it."

*   *   *

By the next morning the ship was gone. Rob stood on the deck with his binoculars and scanned the horizon, not seeing anything other than fishing boats. He thought of the antagonistic woman at the society meeting who had called him William, and wondered what she and the other members would think if he chartered the boat and invited everyone on board for a cruise around the bay. With plenty of beer, of course.

The turkeys were taking a cruise of their own around the front yard, hunting for whatever it was they ate. They worked their way from the driveway to the house, lined up in a formation that was probably designed to protect the young, though Rob couldn't imagine that these idiot birds had any idea what a predator was until it snapped their necks. "Fuck you, birds," Rob said, wondering if Maggie Mason had any affection for turkeys. Did the Dorothy Bradford Society have Thanksgiving?

After the last bird wandered off the driveway, the man with the ear phones reappeared, plucking blackberries off the bushes and popping them in his mouth. Like the turkeys, he seemed oblivious to his surroundings.

"Fuck you, too," Rob said as the man moved further into the yard. He thought to yell at the guy, who clearly had no regard for private property, but decided to confront him instead. This was a time to be brave, like William Bradford.

He went outside and took up a position a few yards behind where the man was picking. Rob cleared his throat a few times and put his hands on his hips. He wondered what the guy was listening to in his ear phones. He wore a tee shirt and a bathing suit, and was of an indiscriminate age, possibly anywhere between thirty-five and fifty years old. He carried a

Tupperware container, where he deposited the berries that didn't go into his mouth. The man pulled his head out of the bushes and turned around. Seeing Rob, he smiled and once again flashed the peace sign.

"Hello, again," Rob said.

"Have you tasted these?" the man said. "They're amazing."

"Yes," Rob said, lying. He didn't like blackberries. "Maybe you'll leave some for me?"

"Sorry," the man said. "I follow the bushes and lose track of where I am. I have to keep an eye out for the poison ivy, too. I'm real allergic."

Rob's mood softened. The berry man was a fellow member of the poison ivy society. He could be forgiven, like someone who had lost a limb. Rob introduced himself and learned that the man was a summer resident who owned a house up the street. They swapped stories about steroids and anti-itching creams, and the man offered Rob some of his blackberries. Rob declined, though. Even if he had liked them he wasn't going to eat anything that hadn't been washed first.

"Hey, you're the guy who's wrapped up with those swimmers who disappeared, aren't you?" the man said.

"I'm the last one who saw them, I guess," Rob said, but this wasn't true either. Katie had been the last one to see them.

"They never found them, did they?"

"Not yet," Rob said.

"It's been a month, hasn't it? They're gone. Too bad. Listen, I'll try to keep out of your yard, but if you see me wandering in again just yell, okay?"

"It's alright," Rob said. "To tell you the truth, I don't really eat them anyway. But please don't send your friends. Okay?"

"I got you!" the man said and flashed the peace sign. Rob nearly did the same.

* * *

Feeling buoyed by his diplomatic coup with the blackberry picker, Rob decided to go for a run, sensing that his mind and body were in sync, or some such horseshit. Sidney stared at him while he got dressed, prompting Rob to go through the mental checklist of morning dog chores. Sidney had crapped, peed, eaten, and taken his medicine. There was nothing undone. "What?" Rob said to the dog. Sidney's focus did not waver. Rob got down on the ground and ran his hand gently over the dog's flanks. Sidney lay down and made a low purring sound. Even in his old age he still needed attention every now and then.

As Rob started his run he noticed the unfamiliar car parked in front of the cottage. He jogged over and stuck his head inside the cottage, to find Rachel and a few other women sitting in the living room with Katie. They were drinking beer. It was not yet ten o'clock.

"Hi, Rob," Rachel said. The other women smiled politely.

"Going for a run?" Katie asked.

"Yeah. But I wanted to see who was here first. Hello, ladies."

Katie introduced them, rattling off each of their names as though she had known the women for years. None of them scowled at him. They appeared to be from the bloc of members who could accept a man in Dorothy Bradford's life, William Bradford or otherwise. Either that, or they were happy to learn that he lived across the street. Maggie Mason was not among them.

"Stop by when you're finished," Rachel said. "We should have some beer left." Rob said that he certainly would. After checking with Katie to make sure she was okay—she was—he headed off on the long slog up and down Truro's hills.

* * *

It was still early, and most vacationers had yet to haul themselves out of their rented beds. Rob began running and immediately wanted to stop. Despite his positive frame of mind, his legs and lungs felt as if there was no blood circulating through them at all. He pressed on for a mile or so, thinking that once he warmed up he would feel better, but it wasn't happening. "Fuck it," he said, and slowed to a walk. Danny always told him to listen to his body. He was listening to his body.

He came to an unpaved road that led to some of the larger homes along the beach, including Tim Desmond's. Curious to see if the house was still cordoned off, he turned onto the road and headed in that direction. He had never been down the road before. There were signs marking the driveways, but the homes were mostly unseen, set well off the road, behind the pines and scrub. The air was very still, and the morning sun was muted by the trees. The neighborhood had an abandoned, sinister feel to it, as if the people who lived there had been driven off by a pack of wolves.

As he got closer to the water, the trees gave way to open terrain, and he found the Desmond house. Though it was set back from the road by a hundred yards or so, it was in plain sight, surrounded only by dune grass. The yellow tape was gone.

He stared at the house for a while, wondering where the drugs had been hidden, and how they were distributed. Did Desmond have dealers who stopped by, or did he meet them someplace else? He wondered if the house would be put up for sale, and how much it would go for. Would the heroin bring down the asking price?

Feeling exposed, Rob decided to walk home along the beach, rather than retrace his steps and risk getting mauled by wolves. Since there was no public beach access here, he needed to walk across the Desmond property to get there. Believing the house was empty he set off to do just that, when he heard a voice.

"I'm not used to seeing you on this side of the house!"

The voice came from behind him. He turned to find Tim Desmond walking down the drive of the house across the street.

"Tim?" Rob said, thinking at first that Desmond had somehow escaped. "I didn't expect..."

"To see me here?"

Desmond was walking quickly, and Rob took a step back. He looked around for a tree to hide behind. He could run if he had to. He was dressed for it.

"Relax," Desmond said. "I'm not the thug you think I am." Desmond stopped a few feet from Rob and held up his hands in mock surrender.

"Did they let you go?"

"They never should have arrested me in the first place. It wasn't me."

"It wasn't?" He almost sounded disappointed. "But they did find heroin here, right?"

"They sure did." Desmond dropped his head. Rob could see now that the guy was exhausted, and perhaps traumatized, too. "First a zoning violation and then a drug bust. I think this house is cursed."

"Somebody planted them?"

"Come on," Desmond said, heading for the new house. Rob surmised that he had been in the old house across the street. "I'll show you."

Desmond led Rob into the house and down to the basement. It was not finished, except for a workshop on one end. The dehumidifier kicked on, and Rob almost tripped over his feet. There were plenty of tools spread across the workbench that would have made excellent murder weapons.

"Here," Desmond said, pointing to a spot on the floor. There was nothing there. "He kept them in a freezer that used to be right here."

"Who?" A couple of photographs hung over the spot where the freezer had been. They were of shorebirds, though the beach was in the background and the water in the foreground. Whoever had taken them was in the water when he did.

"Sammy Boland. Can you believe it? I've known him since he was a kid. He had the drugs brought right up to the beach in a fishing boat. They stuffed the heroin inside the fish. He brought them down here and stored them in the freezer."

Desmond picked up a tool that Rob didn't recognize. He had thought he could identify most hand tools, from the extensive collection Katie kept in his own basement, but he had no idea what this was. It didn't look like it could do much damage.

"What the hell is this thing?" Desmond said, flipping it over before tossing it back on the bench. "I set this place up just for him, even though no one was supposed to be in here, and told him he was free to use it for his own projects, too. I guess I should have said, *lawful projects*."

"Where is Boland now?" Rob said, looking around, worried the guy might be lurking, wielding a claw hammer.

"They're looking for him. You haven't seen him, have you?"

Rob shook his head. "Not since the last time I was here." He looked more closely at the bird pictures, hoping to draw Desmond away from the tools. "Did Boland take these photos?"

"Sure," Desmond said. "Another of his professions—photographer, caretaker, drug dealer."

"Does he take a lot of pictures in the water?"

Desmond looked at the photos. "Was he in the water? I guess so."

Rob told him about the pictures he had seen at Maggie Mason's house—the gaunt, destitute women.

"Probably his clients. Piece of shit. I wonder how many kids have overdosed on the drugs from my basement."

"How did the police figure it out? That it was Boland?"

"They arrested the boat owner, too. He told them Sammy was the guy. That he only used the house as a place to keep the drugs until he sold them."

"So you're in the clear?"

"Well, they don't want me to leave the Cape. Not that I haven't thought about it. If I wasn't a pariah before, I sure as hell am one now."

Rob stared at the floor, not sure what to say. He wasn't thinking about Tim Desmond's image problems, though, he was thinking about Sammy Boland's water photography.

* * *

Rob successfully extracted himself from the cursed Desmond house, and having found his legs, jogged back home at a leisurely pace. Desmond had thanked him for stopping by, saying that he needed all the friends he could get. Were they friends? Rob supposed so, as much as he was friends with anyone.

When he arrived back at the cottage he thought about sharing the Tim Desmond news with the Bradford women. Would they care about Tim Desmond? Perhaps they knew Sammy Boland, though, from the pictures in Maggie Mason's house.

He went inside the cottage and helped himself to a beer. A couple of the women nodded when he came in. One of them was sharing a picture on her phone of a woman who had once been presented to the society as a Dorothy Bradford candidate.

"She looks a little pale," Katie said, looking at the phone. Rob leaned over her shoulder to see a picture of a woman wearing what appeared to be a tight, skin-colored top. On closer inspection he saw that she was nude from the waist up.

"That picture was shown at one of our meetings last year," Rachel said.

"They thought she was Dorothy?" Rob said.

"One person did anyway. The picture was voted down, but by the end of the meeting a few of the members had taken their shirts off."

Rob studied the other women and wondered if any of them might have been included in that select group. Probably not.

I'm the only one here who has seen Dorothy Bradford's tits, he wanted to say, and probably would have if he had one or two more beers in him. "So where's Maggie?" he asked.

"She's on her way," Rachel said. "Bringing some of the other members with her, including some of the William-haters."

"Here?" Rob said, shooting a worried expression at Katie.

"I told her to bring them," Katie said. "They need to get over William."

"As long as there are no demonstrations in the yard," Rob said. The other women in the room stared hard at Rob. Even Katie's expression soured. Only Rachel appeared vaguely sympathetic.

For a brief, unsettling moment, it felt as if Rachel was the only familiar person in the room. Rob sensed that it was probably time to go back up to the house. Before he did, he grabbed a second beer, while Dorothy Bradford launched into a tutorial on survival tactics. This seemed to be of particular interest to the other women. They wanted to learn how to rely on themselves, the way Dorothy had. Katie was certainly qualified to do this, but so were many women. The difference, Rob knew, was that none of them had survived alone in the wilderness for four hundred years. What he really wanted to know was whether Sammy Boland had taken his wife's picture, and if he did, why his camera had been found washed up on the beach.

* * *

Rob was tired from the run, what little running he had done, but he carried Sidney down to the beach anyway. The beach was uncluttered, and he was able to relax and watch the water, also uncluttered—no seals in sight.

He tried to remember what the male *Dorothy Swimmer* had looked like, the one with the camera. He had been wearing sunglasses and a bathing suit. He had a pair of binoculars. What else? He was about the same age as Sammy Boland; that much Rob could attest to. He wondered if he should call Don Hill. Would he be interested? *There are lots of birds out here,* Don Hill would say, *and lots of photographers who like to take pictures of them.* Maybe; but how many of them get in the water with their cameras and sell heroin when they're done?

Sidney hobbled around in circles, staring into the distance, again trying to decide if these were new surroundings. Rob had read on the internet that dogs seldom died on their own, unless they were hit by a car. They got sick and reached a level of discomfort where an injection was the only humane answer. Rob didn't dwell on this but knew Sidney's time was not far off. He had gotten the name of a vet who would come to the dog owner's house and euthanize the animal there, saving the dog and the owner the indignity of having to sit in an unfamiliar, off-smelling room, waiting for death. Rob thought it would be nice if this alternative was available to humans when his time came.

After two hours of uninterrupted beach time, he headed back up the stairs, stopping at the small platform halfway up to catch his breath. He set Sidney down and rubbed the cramps in his legs. He was woefully out of shape, running-wise. Or out of shape altogether. As he was poking at the veins bulging out of his calf, Sidney emitted a labored "woof" behind him. It was one of Sidney's more human noises. It was the noise he made when he fell. Rob turned and, sure enough, Sidney had managed to step off the platform and tumble onto the dune. The drop was only a foot or two and the sand had cushioned his fall. Sidney had an amused expression on his face, as though he had intended to launch himself onto the dune. He lay on his belly, resting in a thick patch of poison ivy.

"Shit!" Rob said, loud enough that a few people at the public beach below looked up at him. He had always known that if he dropped anything into the grove of ivy below the stairs, it was gone forever. Irretrievable. Sidney did not move. He seemed happy to lie in the toxic hedge. There was no way he could haul himself up the dune. And if he tried, he would more than likely tumble back toward the beach, and get caught up in the bushes below.

Rob thought about grabbing the dog and sprinting back to the shower, where the two of them could douse themselves in cold water. His mind spun, searching for alternatives. He dug for the cell phone in his knapsack—Dorothy Bradford would come to the rescue. He was about to hit the "call" button when Helen Schantz appeared, coming down the steps toward him. She had that curious look of uncertainty on her face, the one Rob was used to seeing whenever he ran into Helen Schantz.

"Oh dear," Helen Schantz said, having caught sight of Sidney.

"He fell," Rob said, sounding helpless. He was. "I'm calling Katie to come fish him out." He wanted to explain to Helen Schantz why he couldn't rescue the dog, to make a point, but before he knew it, the woman stepped into the ivy, let Sidney sniff her hand—he didn't growl— then picked him up and hopped back onto the platform.

"Follow me," she said, starting up the stairs. Stunned, Rob did as he was told. The woman had his dog.

Rob had never been to Helen Schantz's house, or even close to it, for that matter. He had only ever seen the bits and pieces he could spy through the trees, trying to figure out what the woman was up to, other than spying on him. She carried Sidney to the far corner of the house, where she kept the hose. She put down the dog and held him by the collar, then turned on the hose and gently washed him down. Sidney strained a little; he didn't like getting wet, but after a few seconds he settled in and accepted the situation, as though he knew it was necessary.

"There," Helen Schantz said, turning off the water. "Will he follow you back to the house?"

Rob was shocked by his wet dog's appearance. It had been some time since he had given Sidney a bath. The muscle atrophy and loss of weight had shrunk the dog down to the size of one of those malnourished foxes that ran across his yard.

"I think so," Rob said. Sidney couldn't find the energy to shake off the water. He stood panting in the puddle that formed around him. Rob considered drying him off with his towel, but thought better of it. "Listen, thank you, Helen. This was very kind of you."

Helen Schantz smiled, only for a moment, perhaps the only time Rob had seen her smile. Was there hope for her after all? She continued to look at Rob, unmoving. There was something else on her mind.

"I saw those two women," she said. "The ones who didn't come back. I saw them in the grocery store in Provincetown. They had on hats and sunglasses, but I knew it was them, from their pictures. I called the police."

Rob didn't think much of Helen Schantz's story. The woman could barely see, after all. Maybe she harbored some small amount of guilt for their disappearance, too, and saw their faces in every pair of young women she encountered.

"Did the police come?" he asked, now trying to get Sidney moving toward home.

"They said they would but I don't think they did. They're not very capable."

"I don't know about that, Helen," Rob said. "They just made that big heroin bust." They had arrested the wrong guy, of course, but Rob didn't bring it up.

"Awful business," Helen Schantz said. "At least we know they're alive. I'm going to try again to go down to the beach."

Rob felt stung, as if he was to blame for interrupting her last attempt, which, of course, he was. He thanked her again and caught up with Sidney, who had started toward the house, spent from his ordeal under the hose. Rob wondered how many calls the police received from people claiming to have seen the *Dorothy Swimmers*. Probably a lot less now that news of their disappearance had faded to the margins. He tried to remember their names but could not.

* * *

Back at the house, Rob put on a pair of rubber gloves and washed Sidney and himself in the shower. When they were both dry, he deposited the dog in his closet, where Sidney passed out immediately. The day had been a massive ordeal for the dog.

Rob went onto the deck and checked for any signs of activity at the cottage. Maggie Mason's car was still parked in the drive. The yard was empty; there were no women milling around plotting some heretical folly. He heard a laugh, then saw Maggie and Katie step outside and walk to Maggie's car. Rob was glad to see the meeting was over and that Maggie was leaving, but then Katie got into the passenger seat. Rob checked his cell phone to see if there were any messages from his wife, but there were none. What was Maggie Mason up to now? He thought to call Katie and ask where they were going, but he had a better idea.

He had never tailed anyone before. How far was a discrete distance? Maggie Mason had no reason to believe anyone was following her so she probably wouldn't even notice. And as a passenger Katie had no reason to look behind her. Maggie headed into North Truro and took the car onto a secluded dirt road. They were not far from the ocean there, and Rob thought that perhaps they were heading to the seaside home of some major benefactor, if the Dorothy Bradford Society had such a thing. Someone had to pay for all that beer. He hoped that was all it was, a courtesy call, so he could turn around and go home. But as the dirt road turned to sand and the houses fell away from the scrub, he had the feeling this trip was something different. He parked the car in a turn-off and continued on foot. A tailing car would certainly attract attention beyond this point, and it didn't seem like Maggie Mason's car could navigate the road much further anyway. Concealing himself also became more of a challenge, but then someone once told him that people who had no reason to think they were being followed seldom turned around to look. He moved cautiously.

He hoped Katie knew where Maggie Mason was taking her, and that this wasn't some sort of a surprise. He couldn't quite figure what it was about Maggie Mason that made him suspicious. She didn't seem to fit the profile of a cult leader, someone whose zealotry was absolute. Did she see Dorothy Bradford as an immortal or simply an ideal? Were her views purposely tempered to appeal to a broader range of members? Rob needed to know what Maggie Mason had in store for Dorothy Bradford, and whether his wife would follow her regardless.

The small rustic cottage that appeared over the next rise was, Rob assumed, one of the several dune shacks that dotted the Provincelands. Supposedly built from the flotsam of old shipwrecks, the shacks were popular among writers, painters, and recluses. Katie and Maggie Mason were standing outside the shack, talking with two other women. Rob figured that these were the women Katie had met on her beach trek. He crouched down behind a row of scrub pines. He strained to hear what was being said, but was too far away. As he inched further into the vegetation, looking for ways to improve his position, something leafy brushed his calf and he jumped back, grabbing his leg as if he had taken shrapnel.

"Shit, not again!" he said, writhing in the sand. Why was it that whenever he was spying on people, he always ended up in poison ivy? He looked closer at the vines, but didn't see any berries. The leaves were in groups of four, not three. He was lucky this time, but kept an eye on where he was kneeling anyway, as if something menacing might shoot out of the sand at any minute.

He was frustrated that he couldn't hear what the women were saying. He watched their faces, Katie's in particular, to gauge the mood. They appeared happy, and gave the impression that they all knew each other. He started to wonder if Maggie had been at the first meeting, too. They started for the beach and Rob took the opportunity to get closer. There was a spot on the dune, overlooking the path to the beach, which was protected and offered good, nontoxic cover. He got there ahead of them and got a clear look at the two women. The day had grown overcast so there were no sunglasses to hide their eyes. They wore shorts and tee shirts, exposing enough of themselves for Rob to notice their perfect skin. Could it be? Or was he just as paranoid as Helen Schantz? He got out his phone and took a picture. Then he tried to search for a picture of the *Dorothy Swimmers* on the internet, but there was barely enough reception for a phone call, much less a download.

He crouched down as they passed by, any number of conspiracy theories running through his head. If these were the swimmers, why were they hiding, and what was Maggie Mason's involvement? Did Katie know they were the swimmers? One of the women spoke loudly now, and Rob could hear her clearly as she put her arm around Katie and said, "We had so much fun when you were here before." Katie smiled and said something that Rob couldn't hear. The women continued onto the beach and headed north. Rob stood up, and when the women were far enough away, he approached the shack and tried the door. It was not locked. He stepped inside. The large single room had a bed, a table and chairs, and a small kitchen. There was nothing lying out, nothing that might give away their identity, like a purse or a wallet, maybe a Sammy Boland photograph. He thought to call Don Hill, but as seemed to always be the case where Rob and the police were concerned, he waited. He wanted to talk to Katie first.

TWENTY-ONE

Brainwashing and U-Turns

Rob waited in the cottage for Katie to return from her meeting in the dunes with Maggie Mason and the two other women. He didn't say anything to Danny, not wanting to implicate his son, too.

"The whole family knew where the *Dorothy Swimmers* were," Ridgeback would write, "and chose not to alert the authorities." He checked the internet picture of the two women, and compared it to the picture he had taken earlier. It was difficult comparing head shots against full body shots taken from a distance, but there were enough similarities, skin included, to conclude that the women at the dune shack were the *Dorothy Swimmers.*

Maggie Mason dropped Katie off, but she did not go inside. Bradford business was apparently now concluded for the day. Rob peeked out the window. Katie was waving to Maggie as she drove off, probably on her way to recruit some new dues-paying members, or to spread more lies about the two missing ones.

"What are you doing down here?" Katie asked as she came inside. It was unusual for him to be in the cottage when she wasn't around. He couldn't claim to be fixing anything since she did all of that herself, and better than he could anyway. He didn't have to make up an excuse though, he planned to come right out with it.

"I was worried about where Maggie was taking you, so I followed in the car," he blurted.

Katie tilted her head to the side and looked at him quizzically. She had gotten used to being stalked, but not by her husband.

"What did you think was going to happen?"

"I don't know, but I don't trust this Maggie Mason," he said. "Who were those two women you were with?"

"Jesus, Rob, were you hiding in the grass?"

"Yes," he said, averting her glare, something he had not had to do in a while.

"They were the women I spent the night with on the beach. The women who helped me. Liz and Bobby."

"Why didn't they come here to see you?"

"They don't have a car."

"Maggie could have picked them up and brought them over," Rob said. "Look, there's a reason they're hiding in that shack. Here." He held up his phone and showed her the internet picture of the two women.

"That's them," she said, unmoved.

"Katie, they're are the missing swimmers! Liz and Bobby--Elizabeth and Roberta."

She took the phone from him and looked more closely. "How can that be?" she said, fingering the screen to enlarge the image.

"You didn't recognize them?"

"The only time I ever saw them was in the water. And the pictures of them in the water. I never saw these pictures."

"They didn't say anything about it?"

"No. Not a word. They told me they'd seen me before but didn't say when. I figured they were just another random pair of women out looking for Dorothy Bradford." He could see she was getting flustered. Her Dorothy Bradford persona was under attack. She sat down on the couch, hands folded in her lap. He could tell her mind was racing, a clear indication that this was all new to her, and he wondered if the turn of events might stir up a panic attack.

"I'm sure there's some explanation," she said. "Why would they cover this up?"

"I think it's got something to do with the photographer, and I'm pretty sure I know who that is, too."

Rob told Katie about Sammy Boland, the bird pictures, the heroin in the fish, and Tim Desmond's release.

"The photographer was a drug dealer? Are you saying that Liz and Bobby were wrapped up in this, too? That doesn't make any sense. What do drugs and Dorothy Bradford have to do with each other?"

"Maybe drugs and Maggie Mason? She has some of Boland's photographs in her house."

"No. That can't be right." She glanced toward the bedroom.

"Are you okay? You want me to leave?"

"No. I'm just confused."

"Me, too."

"Maggie said they were recluses. She didn't want me to tell anyone about them."

"Wait, Maggie was there, too?"

"They called her after we met. She came over that night. We drank lots of beer."

"What else?"

"She taught me some exercises to help manage my anxiety. I'm using some of them now. She said that if I let Dorothy Bradford out, my fear would disappear. We spent the night on the beach and watched the meteor showers. By the morning, I could see certain events in the past pretty clearly, like the one where I'm falling from the deck of a ship but never hitting the water, like I'm suspended in mid-air." She looked down at the floor as if it was the surface of the bay. "Splash," she said.

"She's obviously brainwashed you."

"Let's not crucify her yet. Whatever she did, it may have cured me. She's helped a lot of the women in the society."

"Are they all phobic, too?"

"A lot of them were abused—by husbands, parents, boyfriends. A few of them suffered debilitating anxiety like me. It's the reason they all hate William Bradford. They think he abused Dorothy."

"But you don't believe that."

"I've never had negative feelings about him. My memories are all good ones."

"You have memories of William Bradford?"

"Yes."

Rob pulled his head to one side, kneading a cramp that had developed in his neck. Could he be jealous of a long-dead Pilgrim? If Katie was letting Dorothy Bradford "out," where did that leave him? He went over to the refrigerator and looked inside, wondering if there was any beer left from the morning meeting.

"You think they were really recluses, or just hiding out in the dunes?" he said, not finding anything drinkable except an odd-colored juice. "What are they up to?"

Katie leaned over and grabbed the phone out of her bag. "Let's find out," she said. She put the phone on speaker and waited for Maggie to pick up. She was still in her car.

"I'm on Route Six!" Maggie Mason said, using the hands-free, yelling into the wind. "I might lose you!" In her best Dorothy voice Katie asked if Liz and Bobby were the *Dorothy Swimmers*. For a few moments they heard nothing but the sound of wind and traffic. Then Maggie said, "Is Rob there?" Katie said that he was. "I'm turning around! I guess it's time I told you what's been going on." And then the call was dropped.

"Did she hang up?" Rob said.

"I think we lost her. But she's coming back here."

"With some answers, I hope."

"That's what she said." Katie got up from the couch and went into the kitchen where she started shuffling things around, looking for distractions. Rob was having trouble reading his wife. He couldn't tell if she was anxious or disappointed, or maybe just mad. "Jesus, Rob," she said, after moving the napkin dispenser from one end of the counter to the other. "What have I gotten myself into?"

TWENTY-TWO

Bay Breezes and Breweries

Maggie Mason never showed up at the cottage. Katie called her twice more but got her voice mail both times. She checked with Rachel to see if she knew where Maggie was. "I'm having a hard time lately keeping track of her myself," Rachel said. Katie asked her if she knew anything about the dune shack.

Rachel said that Maggie had rented them out in the past for visitors and therapy retreats, but she wasn't aware that anyone was staying in one of them now. "Why?" she asked. "Did you meet her out there?"

Katie said that she had, but didn't mention anything about the two other women.

"They're up to something," Rob said. "I'm going to call Don Hill."

"Let's wait," Katie said. "I want to talk to Maggie first. We can go to the police tomorrow if we haven't heard from her. In the meantime, let's stop off at the dune shack tonight on the way to dinner."

"I waited to call the police the last time I saw these women, and got shit for it."

"I know. But they aren't criminals."

"Sammy Boland is."

* * *

It was Danny's last evening on the Cape before heading back to Boston, and Rob and Katie were taking him out to dinner at a small out of the way restaurant in Provincetown, beyond the reach of most tourists, a place where Katie would feel comfortable. Danny was told he could start running within the next week or so, but it would be under the watchful eye of his coaches and the team doctor, and only on a treadmill at first. He knew he couldn't afford any more setbacks if he was to be at his best for the Olympics.

"Where are we going?" Danny asked as they turned off Route Six and headed into the dunes.

"I've been trying to track down Maggie Mason," Katie said. "I think she might be at this place. I want to check quickly."

"Why would she be avoiding you?" Danny said. "You're her girl."

"The great and powerful Dorothy," Rob said.

"That's Oz again," Katie said.

"What?"

"Oz was great and powerful."

They arrived at the small parking area, the shape of which had already changed in the few hours since Rob had parked there before—the dunes were constantly in motion. Katie wanted to walk to the shack on her own, but Rob wouldn't allow it.

"You're leaving me here alone?" Danny said. "What if the large women come and get me?"

"You're not allowed to make fun of them," Katie said.

"I'm serious!" Danny said. He lay down in the back seat and got out his cell phone. "No signal!" he shouted as his parents made their way up the road.

They found the shack empty. The door was locked, and from what they could see of the interior the women appeared to have left altogether. Rob and Katie walked to the beach, to make sure the two women weren't camped out by the water, but no one was there. No umbrellas or beach chairs either.

"I think Maggie got them out of here," Rob said. The wind whipped down the beach. Katie tied up her hair to keep it in order for dinner.

"She's afraid we'll go to the police," she said.

"We are going to the police," Rob said. He saw the disappointment in Katie's eyes. Maggie Mason had been her miracle worker. "We didn't really know the woman," he said, putting his arm around her. They walked back to the car.

* * *

After a quiet dinner they stopped at Maggie Mason's house to see if anyone had heard from her. Rachel said there was still no word and that she was starting to get worried. Rob tried to coax Danny to come inside, if for no other reason than to taste the beer, but he declined, saying he was still traumatized by the hoard of Bradford women who had trapped him in the cottage. "They didn't even know you were in there," Rob said.

Danny lay down in the back seat again. He had become fond of lying down whenever there was an opportunity to do so. He said he was too full from dinner to drink beer anyway. "Not to mention the fact that I'm training for the goddamn Olympics."

After obliging the other women who were in the house, thrilled by Dorothy Bradford's surprise visit, they went into the backyard to talk. Without the DBS members milling around, the expansive lawn looked more like an abandoned fairground than a backyard. They sat down with their beers and Katie told Rachel about her visits with Liz and Bobby, and the call to Maggie earlier in the day.

"Well, I guess she finally did it," Rachel said.

"Did what?" Rob said.

"Maggie always talked about orchestrating some big PR stunt. Maybe this was it."

"You're saying she faked their disappearance for publicity?" Rob said.

"If she did, it worked," Rachel said. "A lot more people know about us now." Rachel shrugged and managed a feeble smile.

Katie said nothing, her expression tightening in anger. There were few people she trusted—she may have given her trust to Maggie Mason too quickly.

"I know," Rachel said, seeing Katie's displeasure. "It's not good." She groaned and stared into her beer. "So what now?"

"We have to tell the police," Katie said.

"What will happen to them?"

"I don't know."

"Do we have to tell them?"

"Yes. Tomorrow morning. You should let the board know."

"Do you think any of them knew?" Rob asked.

Rachel shook her head. Rob could see she was rattled by the news. Perhaps her own confidence in Maggie had been shaken, too. Rachel set her mug on the ground—another sign of turmoil—and rested her chin in her palms.

"We should probably get going," Rob said. He had never been comfortable with the sadness of women.

"Wait for me in the car," Katie said. "I want to sit with Rachel a little while longer."

Rob wandered back to the car, forgetting for a moment where he had parked. When he got there, Danny was still lying in the back seat.

"I've already had three guys stop to ask if I wanted company," Danny said.

"What did you say?"

"I believe I said, no. One of them called me a bitch."

They sat for half an hour. Rob tried to convince Danny to get out of the car so they could wander around a bit while they waited for Katie to return, but he wasn't interested.

"Provincetown has become a zoo," he said.

When Katie arrived back at the car, Rob was sitting on a bench next to the car. Danny was still lying down in the back seat.

"Everything okay?" Rob said.

"She's scared Maggie may never come back," Katie said. "Or that if she does, she'll be hauled off to jail."

"And the Dorothy Bradford Society crumbles."

"Maybe. But the house is also their home. Rachel lives there, remember. Without Maggie, where do she and the other residents go?"

* * *

The next day, they were back in Provincetown to drop Danny off at the Boston ferry. They got there as the boat arrived, and Danny hopped out of the car and joined the long line that snaked down the pier. Rob got out, too, and stood with Danny for a few minutes, as though his twenty-three-year-old son needed supervision, when, in fact, he only wanted to put off saying goodbye. Katie stayed in the car. There were too many people coming and going for her to hold her own. Particularly bothersome were the two men who had come off the ferry and stopped next to the car, fumbling through their luggage frantically.

"You packed everything that was on the bed, right?" one of the men said.

"Yes, it's all in there."

"The sunscreen, the costumes, the shoes?"

"Yes, darling, it's all there."

"What about the stuff on the kitchen counter?"

"I got that, too."

"You didn't."

"What?"

"You forgot something!"

"What, darling?"

"Derek, you forgot everything for the bay breezes. Now the weekend is ruined!"

Derek slumped, exasperated.

Katie looked away, hoping the quarrelling couple would regroup and find a way to salvage the weekend somewhere else.

She calmed herself by focusing on the boats docked at the pier, one of which happened to be the Little Mayflower. She wanted to get a closer look, but could not bring herself to get out of the car. She worried that Maggie Mason's charade might have jeopardized her recovery. She didn't want to find out in this throng of summer tourists.

The line of people were now boarding the ferry. Katie watched her son bound up the gangway, his knee almost fully healed now. He turned and waved as though he was boarding a steamer headed for the Paris Olympics, which, in a way, he was. Katie waved back. From where he stood, he wouldn't see her.

There was still no word from Maggie Mason. Rob thought she might have driven the two women back to their home in the western part of the state. But that didn't explain why she wasn't returning anyone's calls, or why she hadn't come back to the cottage the day before to explain to Rob and Katie what she was doing harboring *The Dorothy Swimmers*.

"It's weird how that Mayflower boat is everywhere all of a sudden," Rob said to Katie as they drove south toward the Truro Police Station. "Maybe it's here for you." He looked at her, but her mind was elsewhere.

"Should we be going back to Boston with him?" Katie said, missing Danny already.

"Maybe later," Rob said. "You're not ready for that now. Besides, we don't have anywhere to live." Though he was sad to see Danny go, he was also glad to be relieved of the burden of responsibility that came with offspring, even after they reached adulthood. The U.S. Olympic Committee could take care of him now, or at least keep him from getting run down by weaving Priuses.

"We could sell the cottage and buy a place in town," Katie said, less trusting of the USOC than her husband.

"That means living with me."

"We all have to make sacrifices," she said.

"We won't need to sell the cottage," he said. "We'll rent it out, like we planned."

"I guess," Katie said.

* * *

There was no one at the front desk when they arrived at the Truro Police Station. Had another desk sergeant been let go? Katie and Rob sat down and waited for someone to appear. The first person to come out was not a police officer but Steve Ridgeback.

"The Crosleys! Of course!" he said. "Well, I can't leave now."

"What are you talking about?" Rob said.

"Something's going on, but Inspector Hill won't tell me. I think they found *The Dorothy Swimmers*. Did they find *The Dorothy Swimmers*?" He looked at Katie, presuming she was now more knowledgeable about Bradford affairs than Rob.

"If they did, why wouldn't they tell you?" she said.

"Exactly!" he said. "They're suppressing important information."

"Why would you think that?"

Don Hill came out next, appearing disgruntled that no one was at the front desk. He grabbed something off the desk, then spoke to Rob and Katie without looking at them. "You have a very convenient habit of showing up here when I need to speak to you," Don Hill said. Rob assumed he was talking to him. This was Katie's first time to the police station and Ridgeback had just been kicked out. "Come on back."

"I'll wait here," Steve Ridgeback said. "Take your time."

They sat in the conference room and Don Hill complimented Katie on how well she seemed to be doing. "Glad to see you out and about, Mrs. Crosley," he said. "Listen, I have some questions, but why don't you go first since you came to me. Sorry there was nobody out front to greet you, other than our friendly newspaperman."

Rob showed Don Hill the picture of the two women. He and Katie laid out the course of events and Maggie Mason's disappearance. Rob also brought up the Sammy Boland photographs he had seen.

Don Hill listened thoughtfully but displayed only muted reaction to the Crosley revelations. He asked no questions as the story unfolded, remaining strangely silent as though the events being described were not news to him.

"The whole thing was a publicity stunt," Rob said dramatically, trying to elicit some kind of response from Don Hill. "And Sammy Boland was in on it."

"How do you know Boland was involved?" Hill asked.

"The photos in Tim Desmond's basement. And Maggie Mason has some of his pictures. They know each other. He's an accomplished water photographer."

"That doesn't mean he was the photographer who took your wife's pictures," Don Hill said. "Can't jump to conclusions here." Rob shrugged his shoulders and held out his hands, palms up. It sounded like a perfectly logical conclusion to him. "But..." Don Hill continued. "You raise a very plausible theory."

"I do?" Rob said. He shot a sideways glance at Katie. "Wait...What do you mean?"

"We picked up Maggie Mason yesterday afternoon. That's why she never showed up at your place. She's being held in Barnstable."

Katie slumped and closed her eyes.

"You doing okay, Mrs. Crosley?" he asked, still mindful of her condition.

"So, faking a disappearance is a crime." Rob said. "Did you arrest the swimmers, too?"

Don Hill checked the door to see that it was closed, and to make sure that Steve Ridgeback hadn't wandered back to eavesdrop. With no one out front to monitor the waiting room it was a distinct possibility.

"We're not holding her for the disappearances," he said, "though there will be consequences for that, too. A lot of money was spent on that search."

"Oh shit, there's more?" Katie said. "Sorry for the language."

"Oh, yeah," Don Hill said.

Now it was Rob who looked at the door. He expected they were about to hear the news that Ridgeback wanted to hear. Don Hill leaned forward and folded his hands on the table. Rob had the sinking feeling that he was once again under suspicion—and Katie now, too, for that matter. Rob's leg was bouncing up and down under the table, causing the floor to creak. Katie reached over and grabbed his thigh, making him stop.

"Did you two drink any of the beer at the Mason house?" Don Hill asked.

Rob was caught off guard by the question. He stammered, afraid that he might somehow be implicating himself if he admitted he had. He looked at Katie. It was time for her to save him.

"Yes," she said. "We did."

"Did Maggie Mason ever tell you how it was made?"

"She didn't tell me," Katie said. "I know they made it themselves, though."

"They didn't tell me either," Rob offered, though Don Hill's attention was now clearly focused on Katie. There was something vaguely sinister in his expression. Rob's heart was pumping fiercely. He worried Katie would wilt, but her expression was almost as intense as Don Hill's. He guessed he was now sitting next to Dorothy Bradford.

"Are you aware that Maggie Mason was a psychiatrist?"

"Yes," Katie said, answering as though she was on a witness stand, offering no information beyond what was asked of her.

"Did she ever tell you why she stopped practicing?"

"No."

"What's wrong with the beer?" Rob asked, finding his nerve.

"Maggie Mason was buying drugs." Don Hill eased up now, sharing information rather than interrogating.

"Drugs?" Rob blurted. "Jesus, was it heroin? Did she put heroin in the beer?" In a startling moment of idiocy, he checked his arm for track marks.

"Not heroin," Don Hill said. "LSD. She had several tabs in the car, and we found more in her house."

"You were at the house?" Katie said.

"We searched it late last night."

"And the women who live there?"

"They're in custody now, too."

"Oh, no," Katie said.

"We also found a brewery in the basement, along with several kegs of beer. We confiscated the beer and are having a sample tested now. We're pretty sure she was micro-dosing the LSD."

Rob was having trouble processing the information. He stared at Don Hill as if the man was bleeding from the mouth.

"You with me?" Don Hill said.

"No," Rob said. He needed to have it explained. He had been told not to jump to conclusions.

"She puts LSD in the beer, Rob," Katie said.

"I get that."

"Small amounts," Don Hill said. "Not enough to trip on, unless you drink a lot of it."

"Why would she do that?" Rob said, thinking of all the beer he drank, especially the night of the first meeting, when the Pilgrim Monument looked as though it might collapse on top of him. He continued to inventory parts of his body, looking for overt signs of drug addiction.

"I'm told it induces a state of euphoria. Reduces anxiety. When she was practicing psychiatry, Maggie Mason was a big proponent of its therapeutic applications. She was caught using it on her patients. She did some jail time and had her license revoked. Judging by your present condition, Mrs. Crosley, she may have been onto something."

"What was the concentration?" Rob asked, as if the answer would mean anything to him. There were so many questions running through his head he didn't know which one to ask first. He blurted out the one that involved the fewest number of words.

"We don't know yet," Don Hill said. "Still waiting on the test results. It's possible, I guess, that there might not be any LSD in the beer, but I doubt it. She didn't serve anything else, did she?"

"No. Always beer," Rob said.

"It was definitely the beer," Katie said. She looked up at the peculiar light fixtures over the conference room table, wanting to make sure the bulbs weren't moving. It reminded her of the meteor showers she had seen that night on the beach with Maggie, Liz and Bobby. She wondered if the shooting stars were all imagined.

Rob was about to ask if LSD had a taste, if it could have enhanced the flavor of the beer, when he sat upright and said, in a moment of inspiration, "Boland sold her the LSD, right? That's the other piece of information that ties them together, isn't it?"

"Again, we can't jump to conclusions, Mr. Crosley, but we did find LSD when we raided the Desmond house. It's certainly a good possibility."

"So where is he?"

"We're looking for him. We'll find him."

"And Liz and Bobby?" Katie said. "Where are they?"

"No idea," Don Hill said. "We actually stopped looking for them a few days ago."

"So, how did you know their disappearance was a hoax?" Rob said. "Did Maggie Mason admit it?"

"Nope. She hasn't admitted anything yet."

"So, how did you know?"

"I didn't. I do now, though."

"Really?" Rob was elated that he had now finally become an asset to the Truro Police Department.

"I'll need that picture you took of the two of them, and the location of the dune shack. Listen, do me a favor and don't share any of this with Steve Ridgeback, or any other journalist for that matter. No videos, Mr. Crosley."

"Of course not!" Rob said, sounding like Ridgeback.

Don Hill eyed him judgmentally.

"Understood," Rob added in a calmer tone.

"Inspector, I'm worried about the women you arrested at the house last night," Katie said.

"We haven't arrested them yet. We're holding them for now."

"You don't think they were involved with this LSD business, do you?"

"We don't know yet."

"Can I ask you what Steve Ridgeback does know at this point?" Rob asked sheepishly, inducing another icy stare from Don Hill.

"He knows that Maggie Mason has been arrested for drug possession."

"OK. Thanks."

"Listen, you two weren't involved in the hoax?" Don Hill said, causing Rob's leg to start bouncing again. "Were you?"

"Of course not," Rob said indignantly. Katie shook her head.

"Had to ask." Don Hill got up from his chair, signaling an end to the meeting. "Well, thanks again for stopping by and sharing your information," he said. He led them out to the reception area, where Steve Ridgeback was still waiting, scribbling something in his notepad.

"No more news here today, Steve," Don Hill said.

"I was hoping to get a quote from Dorothy Bradford," he said.

"Not now, Ridgeback," Rob said, hustling Katie out the door. Ridgeback persisted, following them outside.

"Did you know Maggie Mason was involved with drugs?" he asked. "What kind of drugs were they? Was it heroin? Did she buy it from Sammy Boland? Where are the Dorothy Swimmers?"

* * *

When they arrived home, the "large women", as Danny called them, were once again assembled in the front yard of the cottage. Rob wanted to drive up to the house and avoid them, but Katie insisted that she meet with them. "They're probably scared," she said.

"You can't tell them anything, though," Rob said. He pulled into the driveway and the women pressed toward the car. Notably absent was the mobile keg. The Bradford women were without their psychedelic beer. The mood was anxious and subdued. Without their mugs the women didn't seem to know what to do with their hands. Many of them folded their arms over their breasts. Rob got out of the car first.

"What did you do?!" one of the women shouted angrily, looking directly at Rob. He was going to close the door but stepped back behind it for cover, as if he was an outlaw under siege. The women huddled closer together, sneering at Rob, but when Katie got out of the car all of them shifted their attention to her. Katie told them what she could, that Maggie had been arrested for drug possession, and that the four other women from the house, Rachel included, were being held under suspicion.

"They took the beer!" another woman said, throwing her arms in the air. Rob crouched down behind the door assuming a more defensive posture. Perhaps Danny was right to be afraid of these women who were possibly more dangerous sober.

"Was there something in the beer?" someone said, looking at Katie and then the other women for answers.

"Somebody put drugs in the beer," the woman who had initially accused Rob said. "I think it was him!" She pointed at Rob. He now recognized her as the agitator from the last meeting, the one who called him William.

"It wasn't Rob," Katie said. The women demanded to know who the informer was but Katie said she didn't know. A lie, but she couldn't say she did know and then not tell them. The agitator insisted that she was covering for her husband. Rob had heard enough.

"Come on, ladies," Rob complained angrily. "I'm a member here, too." Tired of taking shit on his own property, he came out from behind the car door and slammed it shut. Some of the women stepped back, seeing the anger in his expression, afraid he might become violent. "Are any board members here?" he said. Three women held up their hands. "You need to decide what to do, not Katie, and not Dorothy either." None of the board members said anything. It seemed clear they were uncomfortable meeting, much less making any decisions, without Maggie.

"Tell us what to do!" a woman said, more demanding than pleading.

"It's not up to me," Katie said, figuring the woman was addressing Dorothy Bradford. "You're welcome to have the board meeting here if you want."

Rob grimaced. He would have preferred that they leave, but he had been the one to suggest that the board take action. It was no matter, they held the meeting on the front lawn, and it lasted all of five minutes. The three board members, who constituted a quorum since there were only five members in total, one of whom was Maggie, decided that the chairwoman would serve as the acting president in Maggie's absence. She would drive down to Barnstable and try to meet with Maggie, and see about Rachel and the other housemates. That was it. Satisfied, or unwilling to hang around without beer, the women disbanded and left the property.

*   *   *

Up at the house, Rob was greeted by a line of pungent dog turds on the living room floor, plus a puddle of pee that had found an incline and run toward the kitchen. He couldn't be sure that Sidney was losing control of his bladder and bowels. It may have been simply that the rudiments of house-training had escaped him altogether. Rob cleaned up the mess while Sidney, instead of sulking off into a corner and hiding, sat close by and watched. For all Sidney knew, Rob could have been cleaning up his own shit.

He took the dog outside anyway, thinking it might be time to get some doggie diapers, and after nudging him onto the grass, saw the news crew lurking at the bottom of the driveway. "Christ," he muttered. Like sharks in the bay, they smelled blood. Figuring they were looking for Katie, he ran down to cut them off, keeping in mind Don Hill's admonition. No videos.

"Mr. Crosley, we were hoping to talk to your wife!" the newsman said, the same guy with the same greasy haired cameraman. Rob figured this was their third of fourth visit to the house. They knew their way around.

"Why?" Rob said. "Has something happened?"

"We were wondering if she would like to comment on Maggie Mason's arrest, or the Dorothy Bradford Society being a front for a large-scale drug operation."

"What?" Rob said, annoyed. He wanted to fire back but this was exactly what the newsman wanted. Say something outrageous to elicit a response. The cameraman stood ready to run the video.

"We knocked on her door but she doesn't appear to be home. Has she moved back in with you? Or is she still in

Plymouth?" The newsman smiled. Rob wanted to smash the guy in the face, much like Tim Desmond had done with Steve Ridgeback.

"Go look for news somewhere else," Rob said.

"How about an Olympic update?" the newsman called after him. "Can we talk to your son?" He was back in Boston by then but Rob wasn't divulging any more information to the press. He waited until they got back in their van and drove away, then went back up to the house.

* * *

The exchange with the Bradford women had unsettled Katie. It was still a challenge to get her bearing when unexpectedly faced with a large group of people. But more than that, she had sensed a loss of faith with these ladies, a level of doubt and suspicion directed not only at Rob but at her as well. Though she hardly knew any of them, she realized their opinion of her mattered. They seemed particularly vulnerable now, with their leader in custody for possession of narcotics and God knows what else. She felt she had something to offer them other than stories, real or unreal, about Dorothy Bradford. She could help them, as they—micro-dosed beer and all—had helped her.

The cottage seemed a small and lonely place now. Rob was up at the house, Danny was gone, and Rachel—the one Bradford Society member she felt close to—was being held by the police. Katie had been alone for several years now, but never lonely.

Needing to do something constructive, something to take her mind off of Bradford politics and legal woes, she grabbed a hammer and some nails, and walked to the beach stairs, thinking she might flip a couple of treads that were showing signs of wear. The weather had become overcast and cool, and the beach was deserted. The water was not. The masts of the Little Mayflower became visible before she got to the top of the steps. The boat was anchored a few hundred yards off shore, sitting motionless in calm waters.

Katie left the hammer and nails, and ran down to the beach, where she pulled her boat into the water instead. The tide was coming in but it still only took her five minutes to reach the ship. All of a sudden, she felt particularly strong. She turned every so often to see if anyone on board had noticed her, but the ship seemed eerily quiet, almost deserted. She came alongside and found the rope ladder she had spied earlier in the day when the boat was moored at the pier in Provincetown. She assumed it was a rope ladder, but it could have been some decorative bunting, draped over the side to enhance the Pilgrim effect. It looked like one of those things you saw soldiers struggling to climb in Army recruiting videos. Whatever it was she thought it looked sturdy enough to hold her. She wrapped a corner of the ladder around one of the oarlocks to secure the boat, then stood up, holding onto one of the ladder's rungs. She yanked on it to make sure it was secured. The climb was not a long one, maybe ten feet. The ladder was wide enough that she could stay clear of the rowboat, giving her a clear path to the water if the rope structure gave way. The lines creaked as she stepped off the boat and gave over her weight to the ladder. She stayed in place for a moment, until the creaking stopped, then continued.

As her eyes came up to deck level she stopped again to see if anyone was there. Toward the stern the deck ramped upward. The aft section was the highest point of the ship. Katie was at the low point, in the ship's mid-section. She saw signs of habitation—deck chairs, books, cocktail glasses, beer bottles, binoculars—but no one was on deck. Katie thought of her story about the two maids on the original Mayflower, and wondered if everyone on the Little Mayflower went below to grope each other as well.

Katie pulled herself onto the deck. As with the cottage a few minutes before, she found no comfort in the solitude here. It felt like some alien invader had snatched everyone off the boat and whisked them away in the hold of their own craft. There was nothing familiar about this place. She turned and looked toward shore. She had been this far out before, but not at this elevation, always near water level. She could see their house on the top of the dune, the steps leading down to the empty beach below. At that moment she might have been alone in the world.

"Excuse me!" someone called from behind her. A man dressed in khaki pants and a flowy, billowing shirt—a uniform perhaps?—was coming quickly toward her. A second man wearing the same get-up was close at his heels. "*Who* are you?"

Katie climbed back over the rail, looked over her shoulder, and said, "You know, I'm not really sure." Then she jumped.

The plunge was exhilarating. She shrieked and closed her eyes, pointed her toes and pulled her arms in tight to her body. She thought the water would arrive much quicker than it did. She peeked to make sure it was still below her and that she hadn't entered some void created by the acid remnants in her brain. And then she was in it, the noise of her entrance muffled by the water flooding her ears. She went into the water as vertical as she was when she left the deck. In no hurry to get back to the surface, she waited until coming to a stop before unfurling her arms and legs. She opened her eyes—the water was much clearer than she expected—and was surprised at how far below the surface she was. She could see the length of the Little Mayflower's hull with her little rowboat alongside. She kicked and pulled herself to the surface, coming up alongside her boat, still securely lashed to the rope ladder.

"Lady, are you alright?" one of the crewmen called out to her. "What were you doing up here?"

Katie pulled herself into the boat and freed the oarlock from the ladder. No one had ever called her "Lady" before, as if she was some addled housewife trying to parallel-park on a busy city street. "Sorry, just curious," she said, pushing off. "Give my best to the captain!"

"I'm the fucking captain," the man yelled.

*   *   *

"Did you see the Little Mayflower out there today?" Katie said. She had come up to the house for drinks and dinner, and to watch the news. Rob expected Don Hill would have to tell the press what was going on sooner rather than later otherwise risk misinformation being spread by the press.

"Yeah. I don't really understand what goes on there," Rob said. "They seem to spend a lot of time not sailing."

"I rowed out to have a look."

"That's pretty far out, Kay."

"I was fine. The water was calm." She was drinking a standard issue beer, no foreign substance. It had begun to rain and the lateness of the season further dampened the daylight. "I went on board," she said.

"No you didn't," Rob said thinking she was kidding, but he knew better. Katie went on to tell him about the two crew members running toward her, and her feet-first plunge into the bay. Rob had to take a few moments to process the events. It had been a day full of surprises. "Why?" he asked.

"Maggie Mason told me to do it. Another PR stunt." Rob nearly fumbled his whisky onto the floor. Even Sidney looked up, emitting a low reproachful growl. "Now I'm kidding!" she said.

"Jesus, Kay, the Dorothy Bradford Society is in ruins, Maggie Mason is in jail, and you're making jokes. I figured you'd be a bit more depressed."

"I actually feel pretty good right now, drinking my over-the-counter beer."

"Was that what you planned to do? Jump off the boat?"

"Not initially, but when I got up there I knew I wanted to. When those two guys rushed me, I went."

"Just like Dorothy?"

"Dorothy fell. I jumped. She's gone."

"You're letting her go?"

"She served her purpose. Along with Maggie Mason and her LSD." She sat down on the floor next to Sidney and scratched him between the ears. "I can't let her go entirely though."

They turned on the local news and listened as the anchor reported on the "sensational story of Maggie Mason," providing details of her arrest, the *Dorothy Swimmers'* hoax and the distribution of LSD to the unsuspecting members of the Dorothy Bradford Society. Don Hill had given a briefing at a news conference that afternoon, reporting that the lab results confirmed the presence of acid in the beer. No mention was made of whether Maggie acted alone or if others were involved. Elizabeth Tanner and Roberta Stevenson were alive, and were believed to have left the Cape. Before closing the segment, the anchor said, "And just when you thought this story couldn't get any more bizarre, an unidentified woman climbed onto a replica of the Mayflower this afternoon and jumped off."

The captain of the ship was interviewed and said, "It was the damnedest thing. She came alongside in a small rowboat. Climbed up the rope ladder. Jumped the minute she saw us."

"Any idea who it was?" the reporter asked.

"Dorothy Bradford," the captain said.

The anchor came back on and said, "But unlike Dorothy Bradford, this woman survived." Then they cut to a commercial for hemorrhoid cream.

* * *

After dinner, and too many drinks, Katie decided to spend the night with Rob in the house. The cottage suddenly seemed a remote and lonely place, much like the Little Mayflower had before she was rushed. She wondered if her brain, conditioned by the LSD, had agreed to mute the fear of other people in exchange for some other irrational terror. Perhaps she would now become afraid of being alone, or something less consequential, like spiders or turkeys. Regardless, she knew she would always be wary of other people. Other people could slander you in the press, run you down with a Prius, lace your beer with LSD, or knock you off the second story of a home construction site. But none of these people were Rob. None were Danny.

She was not yet, however, ready to sleep with her husband. She could climb into bed with him, and did for a little while, resting her head on his shoulder, but knew it would be impossible to fall asleep. She spent the night in Danny's room, still in disarray from his departure that morning, and slept soundly. Sidney followed her downstairs and slept on the floor next to her, abandoning his closet. Her dreams were of sitting in an Olympic stadium.

TWENTY-THREE

Deck Nails and DVDs

When Rob woke up the next morning he remembered that remarkable things had happened the day before, he just wasn't immediately sure what they were. He reached over on the bed and found the familiar empty space, then remembered that Katie had lain there briefly the night before, but left to sleep in Danny's room. Had she made it through the night, or crept back down to the cottage? He also recalled her saying that she didn't want to be alone anymore. Certainly that was remarkable. Then there was the smell of fresh-brewed coffee wafting through the house. Rob had given up trying to program the machine anymore since its reliability was shit. Danny couldn't have made it unless it was Father's Day, or Rob's birthday, neither of which was the case. And then he remembered the other significant event—Danny had left to go back to Boston. His home was somewhere else now.

Rob wandered out of the bedroom in his underwear, curious to take inventory. Katie was sitting on the deck, chatting with another woman. The woman's back was to Rob, a good thing since he was naked, except for the underwear which was bunched up in his crotch. Katie spotted him through the glass doors and smiled. The other woman turned to look, but Rob knew who it was before she did. Her size gave her away. Rachel waved before her head came around. When it did, and she saw what the bedroom had spit out, she covered her mouth and whirled back around. Rob went into a defensive crouch and scampered back to the bedroom. "Sorry!" he yelled.

Where was Sidney? He thought hard about this while he brushed his teeth. He expected the dog had hobbled out of the bedroom when he heard Katie in the kitchen. But Sidney hardly heard anything anymore. Had he gone downstairs to sleep with her? Katie would have had to carry him down. The stairs were no longer surmountable in either direction for Sidney.

"Sorry again," Rob said as he came onto the deck. "I didn't know we had company."

Rachel got up and hugged him. She had on her Dorothy Bradford tee shirt.

"I'm just glad to see you guys."

"I'm glad to see you, too," Rob said. "Both of you." He smiled at Katie in the way someone smiles at his partner the morning after a night of sexual frolic—had there been sexual frolic?—and spotted Sidney lying comfortably under her chair. With Katie back in the house, there could be no doubt about whom the dog preferred to shepherd when the flock was apart.

"They let Rachel and the other girls go last night," Katie said. "What an ordeal."

"Were you able to go back to the house?" Rob asked.

"No," Rachel said, frowning. "The police locked it up and strung tape around it. We couldn't even get our stuff. At least not yet anyway." Rachel and the other girls had spent the night at the house of the board chairman, who had dutifully waited for them to be released.

"And Maggie?"

Rachel didn't answer right away. She looked exhausted. She poked her sandal at a deck nail that had sprung up from a plank.

"Jesus, Rob," Katie said and scampered into the kitchen to grab a hammer out of the drawer. "I thought I told you to take care of this." She banged the nail back into place and started hunting for other toe-gashing threats.

"That's your department," Rob said, patting the re-secured nail with his foot.

"I'm trying not to think about Maggie anymore," Rachel said, clearly not willing to forgive the LSD therapy, and the PR hoax.

"So what happens now?" Rob said watching his wife dart around the deck. "Katie, come sit down, will you?" She had found other nails to bang on. Whether she was around other people or not, certain things still pushed her to distraction.

"Done!" Katie announced, sitting down, but still clutching the hammer, ready to pounce if another nail sprouted. "Rachel thinks the Dorothy Bradford Society won't survive without Maggie," she said. "I don't either."

"There's no one else who can run it," Rachel said. "The board means well, but they're only there because they have to be."

"And no one knew about the LSD?"

"No one. It's kind of hard to believe we've all been on acid for the last three years. Should I be worried about long-term effects? I may never drink beer again."

"Don't be ridiculous," Rob said, trying to imagine life without beer. "Can't someone else make the beer? Without the LSD?"

"Maggie made the beer. She had help, but she ran the operation. I bought most of the ingredients. Except for one."

"You should be the new president, Rachel," Rob said. "You could do it. I'm sure we can find someone who can make the beer. You can't have a Dorothy Bradford Society without beer. It's a gift from God, for Christ's sake."

"Rob, forget about the beer," Katie said.

"I've got some in the refrigerator. You guys want any?" The women stared blankly at him. It was not yet nine o'clock. "We are discussing the future of the Dorothy Bradford Society, aren't we? Official business?"

"Listen, I have an idea," Katie said, tapping the hammer on the armrest.

"Is it about the beer?" Rob said.

Katie rolled her eyes. "Rachel, excuse us for a minute." She grabbed her husband's hand, and led him into the house. In the kitchen, she told Rob her idea, wanting his okay before she made the offer to Rachel. It was his cottage, too, after all.

"If it means you'll move back into the house, then yes!" Rob said. He was getting his wife back at last. He hugged her spontaneously, without thinking. "You're okay?" he said. Touching had been difficult for Katie, hugging impossible. No more. They were rejoined.

"I can stay in Danny's room until I'm ready to sleep in the same bed with my idiot husband," she said. She kissed him on the cheek and tapped his thigh with the hammer, still in her hand.

"Do I have a loose nail down there?"

*   *   *

The plan was for Rachel to move into the cottage as soon as possible. Katie would move her things back to the house over the next few days. In addition to becoming Rachel's home, the cottage would also serve as the new meeting place for the remnants of the Dorothy Bradford Society, and also a place where troubled women could stay for a day or two. Katie and Rachel would build a one-room addition onto the cottage where visitors could sleep. "A place where they can gather themselves," Katie said.

Rachel was overjoyed. She told Katie and Rob that the halfway house—Maggie's house—was always the thing she liked best about the Dorothy Bradford Society, more than the beer or the Dorothy hunting. Rob asked what would happen when Maggie came back, after the justice system was through with her. Katie shrugged and said they would deal with it when they had to. Rachel didn't think there would be anything left for her to come back to.

"What about Dorothy Bradford?" Rob asked. Katie and Rachel looked at each other.

"A part of you will always be Dorothy," Rachel said.

While Katie and Rachel hashed out their plans, Rob went down to the beach. Despite the condition of the water, which had become choked with seaweed overnight, the usual crowd huddled around the entrance to the parking lot, while one or two smaller groups fanned out onto the quieter stretches of beach. Only one person was below. He didn't recognize her at first, but she belonged there.

"Hi, Helen," Rob said, stopping in front of her chair. She was wearing jeans, a work shirt, and a baseball cap. She looked like she was going to drive a truck somewhere.

"Oh, hello!" Helen said, going to the trouble of getting out of her chair.

"You don't have to get up."

"How is your family?" she asked. "And that dog of yours?"

Rob was stunned by her graciousness. Still no names, though. "They are all fantastic, Helen. Thanks for asking. And thanks again for rescuing Sidney the other day."

"That was nothing," she said, waving her hand. "Beautiful day, isn't it?"

"Indeed," Rob said. When had he ever said "indeed?" Still, it was a spectacular day in every respect.

"Are we done with those swimmers now?" she asked.

"We are," he said. He might have said "we are indeed."

"So they were never really lost at all?"

"All a hoax, Helen."

"I won't think of them again. And I hope I never see them again." She straightened her hat, tugging on the lid with one hand and smoothing the back with the other. "I am meeting Katie later. She's going to show me how to build a wood rack." She smiled at him and nodded. Helen Schantz was genuinely excited.

Rob was genuinely in shock.

"Seriously?"

"I need a place for my wood. That's why I'm dressed like this. You know, I've never built anything before." She sat back down in the chair, closed her eyes, and dreamed happily of neatly stacked rows of wood. Helen Schantz had wood?

Rob sat down a few yards away, feeling less threatened by his neighbor. Perhaps there was hope for Helen Schantz after all.

A short while later, two middle-aged men and two women, trudged past him in single file. They marched like infantry, giving every indication that there was plenty more ground to cover before they could plant their umbrella poles in the sand. One of the men was tasked with towing one of those beach carts that held all of their gear—chairs, umbrellas, an igloo cooler or two. The others carried back packs. Despite their intensity, each of them smiled and said hello as they passed.

Rob said hello twice. Four times would have been idiotic, though it might have insured a greater distance of separation. No matter, they soldiered on for another fifty yards before stopping. Their preferred configuration was the same as their mobile formation—a line parallel to the shore, giving ten yards to allow for the incoming tide. They opened their umbrellas, set out their chairs, stripped off their shorts and shirts, sat down, and began tapping on their phones. Rob stared for a moment, beginning to worry the world was becoming a place where people could not function without technology. Still, their umbrellas were not lined up symmetrically. They had said hello. There was hope for these people, too.

The next person to come along was a single man who, from a distance, appeared to be smiling. Rob wondered if the guy was drunk, or perhaps challenged in some more permanent way. As he got closer Rob could read the man's tee shirt which said, "Trust me, I'm a journalist."

"Ridgeback?" Rob said.

"I thought I might find you down here," Ridgeback said. He was dressed for the beach and carried a chair and a small beach bag.

"Are you here for the beach or another story?"

"I'm here to see you, Rob. I feel like our relationship has been strained by this Dorothy Bradford business. Now that it's almost over I thought I would come by and make amends."

"Almost over?"

"Here, I brought you a peace offering." Ridgeback reached into his bag, pulled out a DVD and handed it to Rob. "Have you seen it?" The DVD was *The Great Escape.* "Classic World War Two movie. You're still into that, right?"

Rob turned over the box—he had not seen the movie—and began reading about the film. Everyone in the cast was dead. The movie was nearly as old as he was. "Thanks," he said.

"Okay if I sit?"

"Sure." Rob was feeling sociable, maybe forgiving, too. Ridgeback could be amusing when he wasn't being a journalist, though Rob expected part of the reason Ridgeback had come was to keep the Olympic conduit open. "How did you know I would be down here?"

"A hunch. I make my living on hunches." He unloaded his bag, opened his chair and sat. "Look, there's a seal."

"You sound surprised."

"Hey, you'll never guess what happened to me yesterday afternoon."

"You won a Pulitzer?"

"Not yet," Ridgeback said. "I was body surfing at Ballston Beach. Went there after I finished writing my article on Maggie Mason. I was out pretty far, trying to ride the bigger waves. As I was getting ready to catch one, something bumped my leg. I let the wave go and reached down to make sure my leg was still there. Then I saw the shark circling back. It went right past me and headed out to sea."

"Jesus."

"I can now say I survived a shark attack."

"Is it an attack if they don't bite you?"

"Of course! It rammed into me! I fended him off. The story will be in the next Gazette. They closed the beach for the rest of the day."

"Wow," Rob said. "Seems like you're getting attacked a lot lately. So what does your Maggie Mason article say?"

"Nothing you didn't hear from Don Hill yesterday."

"How do you know what Don Hill told us yesterday?"

"I don't, but he came out with all of it in his news conference. Wouldn't give me the exclusive. One surprise after another, huh? LSD in the beer? Jesus. What was that like? Did you see psychedelic colors? Listen to Beatle music?"

"It was just beer to me, but it seemed to have helped Katie."

"Helped her to believe she was Dorothy Bradford."

"Maybe. But she's not afraid anymore. No more than anyone else, anyway. She can function again." Rob glanced back toward the foursome further down the beach. Some of them had put down their phones and were figuring out what to do next.

"Maybe we should all be taking the stuff," Ridgeback said.

"I'd settle for just the beer," Rob said.

"Well, you can keep making that, can't you?"

"Maggie made the beer."

"She must have had a recipe written down somewhere. Maybe Don Hill found it."

"Fine, but who's going to make it?"

"You. You said you were looking for a hobby. Go make acid-free Bradford beer." Ridgeback picked up a rock and tossed it into the bay. "What do you do down here without any waves?"

The waves were actually bigger than most days, but they were of no use to body-surfers. Rob watched a small bird scamper along the water line. He had seen thousands of these things but had no idea what they were. It looked like one of Sammy Boland's photographs, taken from the opposite direction.

"They're still out there aren't they?" he said, looking at the water.

"Who?"

"The *Dorothy Swimmers*."

"Out there? In the water?"

"You know what I mean."

"You'd have made a great journalist, Rob," Ridgeback said. He picked up a clump of dried seaweed now, and examined it as though it was an alien life form.

"The thing I can't understand is why anyone who was dealing in illegal drugs would risk all that attention? Does that seem strange to you?"

"You want to find out?"

"Is this what you meant when you said it was *almost* over?"

Ridgeback smiled. "I got a call from Maggie Mason's attorney this morning. She wants me to write the story about the hoax. I'm going to meet her tomorrow in Barnstable."

"You already wrote an article."

"That was just based on what Don Hill said. This is going to be the good stuff."

"Is it wise for her to do that before the trial?"

"The attorney said she wasn't going to answer any questions about the LSD. Just the hoax. Anyway, never look a gift-horse in the mouth, right? I wondered if you and Katie would like to come with me. Thought you might be interested."

"Is this another gift-horse? You already gave me a DVD."

"I'll drive."

"I'm not so sure Katie has any interest in seeing Maggie Mason right now."

"I can understand that, I guess. So it'll just be the two of us, then, and Maggie Mason. And her attorney."

"Does she know I'll be there?"

"No. But you're a member of the society, right? You're coming to pay your respects."

"Maybe I'll bring beer."

"Of course! Hey, was that Katie who climbed onto the Little Mayflower yesterday? They said the woman was in a small rowboat."

Rob smiled. "I have no idea what you're talking about."

"Come on, Rob. We're off the record here."

"The captain said it was Dorothy Bradford. Let's go with that."

TWENTY-FOUR

Maggie Mason and Dorothy Bradford

Steve Ridgeback was an awful driver. Rob spent most of the trip down to Barnstable trying to keep out of sight, sure that someone would pull a gun and open fire. Ridgeback drove too fast, tailgated and honked at cars that were moving too slowly. The honks weren't short toots either, but sustained blasts, issued with the full force of the heel of Ridgeback's palm, driven hard into the middle of the steering wheel. He swore continuously, usually calling out offending drivers by their license plates. *New York Fuck* was one of his favorite slurs.

Rob had been right about Katie. She intended to visit Maggie Mason at some point, but wasn't ready to go now. "Besides, this is Steve Ridgeback's interview," she said. "You go. I need to get started on the addition anyway." She and Rachel were heading to the lumber yard to order materials.

Rob was relieved to be out of the car as they walked into the Barnstable Correctional Facility, already thinking of ways he could avoid having to get back in it. They were led to a room with two doors and a narrow line of windows at the top of one wall. The room was bare except for a table and four chairs. The table had metal rings attached to the surface for the purpose of attaching a prisoner's manacles. Maggie Mason wasn't wearing manacles, though.

She was brought in with her attorney. The accompanying guard escorted Maggie to a chair and then announced that they had fifteen minutes.

"What?" Steve Ridgeback said, sounding much the same as he had sounded behind the wheel. "I was told I would have an hour!"

"Sorry," the attorney said. "We only just found out about it a few hours ago ourselves. But Ms. Mason has graciously written out a statement that we will leave with you. If you have follow-up questions, you can send them to me."

"Wonderful," Ridgeback said sarcastically, flipping through his notepad, picking out the most important questions.

"Hello, Rob," Maggie Mason said. "I didn't know you were coming. Is Katie here, too?" She wore a dark blue prison uniform that made her look like a nurse. On the back of the shirt it said, *Sheriff's Inmate* in white lettering.

"Just me," Rob said, not caring to explain why Katie hadn't come.

"Here is Ms. Mason's statement," the attorney said, handing Ridgeback a folder.

"Well, I'm going to ask some questions," Ridgeback said hurriedly.

"Of course," the attorney said.

"Where did you get the LSD, Maggie?"

"I'm sorry," the attorney said. "As I told you over the phone, Ms. Mason won't be answering any questions about the narcotics in question."

"Oh come on. Why am I here?"

Maggie Mason put her hand on the attorney's hand in a maternal way. Rob thought the attorney was easily twenty years younger than Maggie. He could have been her son.

"I want you to write about the *Dorothy Swimmers*, as you call them, Mr. Ridgeback. I'll answer any questions about that."

"Will you talk about your prior experiences with LSD? You had your medical license revoked for treating your patients with low doses of LSD, and did some jail time, too, right?"

"That's right." Maggie said. "I had some great successes with the medication."

Rob watched the attorney. The man was rocking in his chair, looking as if he was suffering from stomach cramps.

"We can't talk about the narcotics, Mr. Ridgeback," the attorney said.

"But her prior experiences are all a matter of record, aren't they?"

"So you don't need to waste your time asking her about them, do you?"

Ridgeback sighed heavily. The guard, who was standing by the door to the prisoner's area, checked his watch. Rob started bouncing his leg up and down. Katie wasn't there to stop him.

"Who was the third swimmer?" Ridgeback asked.

"Sammy Boland," Maggie Mason said. This was news, of course, but no one was surprised.

"The same Sammy Boland who is wanted for drug possession?"

Maggie looked at the attorney. He nodded.

"Yes," she said.

"And you're aware that LSD was one of the drugs found when the police raided Sammy Boland's workshop in the Desmond house?"

"Nope!" the attorney cut in. "No questions about LSD, Mr. Ridgeback. One more time and I'll terminate the interview."

"Jesus, why did you bother inviting me?"

"To write about the *Dorothy Swimmers*," Maggie Mason said calmly.

Rob noticed that Maggie Mason's disposition was no different than it had been the previous times he met her. She didn't seem bothered to be in prison, though it wasn't her first time.

"How do you know Sammy Boland?"

"He does maintenance work for me at my house. It' still my house, isn't it?" she said, looking at the attorney. He nodded again. "I also have some of his photographs."

"Birds?"

"No. He took some very striking pictures of some of the women who have stayed in my house."

"Patients?"

"Yes. If you prefer."

"They weren't patients," the attorney said. "They were residents."

Steve Ridgeback continued to hammer away at the source of the LSD, and Sammy Boland's likely involvement. Rob knew that even if Ridgeback didn't get Maggie to admit that she bought the drugs from Boland, he would probably write that she did, or at least strongly intimate it. Rob was less interested in Boland's involvement with drugs. He wanted to hear about the hoax, and how they had targeted Katie.

Finally, Ridgeback, tossed out his Hail Mary. "I'm going to write that Sammy Boland sold you the LSD. It seems obvious to me, and I expect you're holding back to preserve some leverage with the prosecutor. Would I be wrong to say so?"

"We're done," the attorney said. "Guard?" He signaled for the officer to take Maggie back to her cell.

"How much time do I have left?" Maggie said.

"Five minutes," the officer said.

"I have more questions," Ridgeback said.

"I'd like to talk to Rob now," Maggie said. "Alone."

"I can't leave you alone," the guard said.

"I understand. Why don't you take Mr. Ridgeback outside, and see to the rest of his questions?" Maggie said to the attorney. He leaned over and whispered something in her ear, then stood.

"I thought this was my interview," Ridgeback said.

"It's over," the attorney said.

Rob looked at Ridgeback and shrugged. "I'll catch up with you," he said, though he would have been glad if Ridgeback got in his car and went home. He would happily take the bus, or a cab.

The attorney looked relieved to be leaving and taking Steve Ridgeback with him; clearly he didn't consider Rob a threat. After the door closed Rob wondered if he was meant to ask questions now. Maggie folded her hands on the table and closed her eyes. Was she meditating? He looked at the guard, who was looking at nothing, waiting for the last five minutes to tick down.

"Many years ago," Maggie said, her eyes now opened and fixed on Rob, "I had heard stories about Dorothy Bradford, and found them quaint, in a folksy, Cape Cod sort of way. One day, I was walking on the beach, not far from where you live, when I saw a woman in a row boat. This was unusual, because it was December and the weather was cold. You rarely see any boats in the winter. The boat was not far from shore and I could see the woman pretty clearly." Maggie Mason's eyes became animated now, widening to the point where they might have popped out of their sockets. She began rocking in her chair, moving her arms back and forth. "The boat flew through the water so quickly that I almost thought there was a motor on board. She was alone, completely in her element, rowing so effortlessly. There was no noise either—no sound of the oars dipping into the water, or the bow carving through the waves. She was not wearing a hat, and her long hair flew behind her." She stopped moving her arms, and her eyes settled again. "Her strength and calmness were so intoxicating. I followed her along the shore, as best I could, but she moved further out and then disappeared. I hoped I would see her again, but never did."

"Until Katie?"

"Until Katie. Your wife has two people inside her, Rob, but they're really the same person. She is Katie Crosley, but she's Dorothy Bradford, too. She's been suppressing Dorothy all her life. That's the reason for the panic attacks. Imagine if memories kept popping into your head that weren't yours. Memories that were foreign and alien, almost as if they were plucked from a dream. She tried to suppress them but couldn't. She panicked."

"You really believe that?"

"It's more important that she believes it. It's how she gets through this."

"How's she going to believe she's Dorothy Bradford without the LSD?"

"I can't talk about the LSD, remember?"

"You could have told us, Maggie, that you were drugging us."

"Time's up, Ms. Mason," the guard said. He came over and took Maggie's arm, helping her up from the chair.

"Please say hi to Katie for me," Maggie said. "Make sure she takes care of the ladies, though I know she will. And call her Dorothy every now and then, okay?"

"Why the hoax, Maggie?"

But she was at the door, being hustled back to her cell.

"It was all for Dorothy," she said as the door closed behind her.

* * *

Ridgeback and the attorney were in the middle of some heated exchange when Rob caught up with them outside the building entrance. Ridgeback was going on about something to do with Maggie's plea hearing. The attorney was standing with his arms folded in front of him, a painful looking frown on his face. Rob expected he would look the same, once he got back in Ridgeback's car.

"So, what did she say?" Ridgeback said, releasing the attorney from his clutches.

"She told me to say hi to Katie. She wants me to call her Dorothy every now and then. She told me the story of when she first saw Dorothy Bradford."

"Hey, maybe you should have her plead insanity," Ridgeback said to the attorney. The attorney grunted and headed back inside the building.

They walked to Ridgeback's car. Rob looked at the other cars in the lot, wishing one of them was his. He wondered if, perhaps, there was some way he could sit in the back seat, or maybe climb in the trunk.

"Here," Ridgeback said, handing Rob his keys. "Would you mind driving so I can read Maggie's statement?"

"Really?" he said, sounding like a kid who had just gotten his learner's permit.

They wound their way back to Route Six, and Ridgeback opened the folder.

"Read it out loud," Rob said.

"I won't understand it then."

"What are you talking about?"

"I can't understand anything I read out loud. I feel like I'm giving a speech."

"Well, at least tell me what it says."

Ridgeback read for a while, then looked up, long enough to comment on the traffic. "Watch out for that Delaware dickhead up there," he said. "I think he's texting." He went back to reading.

"So?"

"She starts off with the history of the society. Nothing new here. They worship Dorothy, and believe she is still alive. They've recently begun looking for her." He read some more. "Liz Tanner and Bobby Stevenson are friends of Maggie's, who vacation on the Cape during the summer. They're big Dorothy believers, and spend most of the summer visiting bay beaches on the Outer Cape, searching for her. Last month, they spotted a woman in a rowboat, a couple of times, who fit Maggie's description of Dorothy, but weren't able to get a good picture of her on their cell phones. They told Maggie about it and she said she knew a local photographer who could help."

"Sammy Boland."

"Apparently they always saw her at that same time of day—around 4:00 pm. Boland thought they should get in the water to take her picture. They tried a kayak at first, but the woman turned away when she saw them coming. Then they tried swimming to her, hoping she wouldn't notice them until Boland had taken the pictures. The first day they swum out, they didn't see her. The next day, they did. Boland also thought the pictures would be more dramatic if he took them at water level."

"Like his fucking birds."

"They parked at Desmond's house."

"When?"

"The days they were camped on your beach."

"Why?"

"I don't know. It's hard finding parking in the public lots."

Ridgeback read for several more minutes without commenting. Rob sensed he had come to the good part.

"What?" Rob said. "What happened next?"

"The wind came up. The temperature dropped. They got the pictures. Boland took a few of the women swimming toward Katie's boat. Then he got the money picture of Katie."

"And?"

"And then Bobby started having a hard time. They had been in the water for half an hour. Cramps, maybe hypothermia. The tide was coming in, but the current and the wind made it difficult for them to get back to shore. Boland and Liz were able to pull Bobby along, but she collapsed when they got to the beach. They pulled her out of the water."

"Boland took a picture of that, too. Liz pulling Bobby out of the water."

"Why would he do that?"

"I think he likes taking pictures of damaged women."

"Anyway, the current had pushed them all the way back to the Desmond house. Because of Bobby's condition they got her back to the car and Boland drove them home."

"The dune shack."

"Maggie let them stay there. She owns it apparently."

"So why didn't they go back and get their stuff?"

"Boland went to pick it up the next morning, but when he got there he saw two guys and a police officer poking around. He took off."

"Why? He could have cleared up the whole thing, and we wouldn't have had to go through all this shit."

"Boland doesn't want anything to do with the police. He would have had to explain everything, including parking at Desmond's house. His opium den."

"So why didn't the women call the police?"

"They called Maggie, instead. She told them to wait. She wanted some free publicity. They told her about the pictures, which Boland had shown them on the camera. And then Maggie had the idea that Boland should dump the camera in the bay to make it look like they had disappeared. Boland didn't care since there were no pictures of him on the camera. Nobody would know he was involved. The girls, though, would have to go into hiding, since they could be identified."

"They were pretty much in hiding already, living in that dune shack."

"Both of them are estranged from their families, so they didn't have to be concerned about overwrought parents. Bad childhoods, I guess."

"Typical Bradford material."

"Maggie officiated at their wedding."

"Lovely."

"The rest is about Dorothy, or Katie, I guess. How she came upon Liz and Bobby on the beach outside their shack. And then Maggie came over."

"She told me about that."

"It gets a little weird."

"What do you mean?"

"Katie gets freaked out when she sees Liz and Bobby kissing. Runs to the beach. Maggie follows, calms her down. Tells her she's having Dorothy Bradford flashbacks. They see shooting stars. They must have been drinking the LSD beer, I guess." Ridgeback cleared his throat and read directly from the text, "Millions of people believe in God, and many of them say that they have seem him. Is it such a stretch to believe in Dorothy Bradford, or to say that we have seen her?"

"Who said that?"

"Maggie. It's the last line of her statement."

"Amen."

* * *

Rob pulled into the driveway, and asked Steve Ridgeback if he wanted to come in for a beer. He declined, saying he had another Dorothy Bradford article to write.

"And probably not the last one, either," he said.

"Listen, Steve, go easy on the Bradford ladies, okay? There's no villain in this story."

"What about Sammy Boland?"

"Heroin has nothing to do with the society."

"Maybe. I'll bet a few of the ladies bought heroin from him at some point in their lives."

"You can't write that. You don't know."

"And what about Maggie Mason?"

"She didn't hurt anyone."

"When did you become a guardian of the Bradfords?"

"I'm a member, remember? And I happen to be married to Dorothy Bradford."

Katie was still out with Rachel, but Sidney was at the door when Rob came in, eyes wide and tongue wagging expectantly. Rob's first thought was that the dog had gotten into something, like a box of decongestants, or a tube of steroid cream. There was nothing lying on the floor, though. Sidney was apparently having a good day.

He took the dog down to the beach. Sidney actually went down the steps himself, vaulting the last three.

"Jesus, Sidney. You'll hurt yourself."

The sky was overcast, and the water was still infested with the soupy seaweed that had invaded the day before. Sidney went straight to the water and sniffed the mounds of brown and green salad that had accumulated on the shore.

Rob had been so enthralled with the dog that he hadn't noticed the two women sitting by the water until Sidney wandered over—his stub of a tail wagging—to say hello. They wore pants and sweatshirts, and were huddled together as if it was cold out, which it wasn't.

"What a cute dog!" one of them said.

Rob strolled over. At one time, people, women in particular, used to fawn over Sidney all the time.

"Is he a puppy?" the other one said.

Rob could see the women's faces clearly now, and he was immediately reminded of the *Dorothy Swimmers.* They were the same age, and looked similar enough that Rob couldn't be sure it wasn't them. He hesitated for a moment, and probably stared long enough to suggest that something might be off about him.

"Far from it," Rob said, finally. "He's fourteen."

"No!"

They played with Sidney for a while, until he got winded and wandered off to lie down in the sand. The women got up and thanked Rob for letting them play with the dog.

"I'm Rob, by the way," he said, hoping they would share their names.

"Nice meeting you, Rob," one of them said.

Not to be deterred, Rob said, "You're not looking for Dorothy, are you?"

The women exchanged curious glances.

"Sorry, who?"

"Dorothy?"

"I don't think we know any Dorothys, do we?"

They looked at each other and shook their heads.

"Sorry," one of them said.

"That's okay," Rob said. "I think I've confused you with somebody else."

He waved, just to demonstrate he wasn't completely insane, and the women headed toward the public beach. He took out his phone and checked the picture of the *Dorothy Swimmers.* These two women, he decided, were not Liz and Bobby. Liz and Bobby had disappeared again.

Sidney was back at the water, though he wasn't sniffing the seaweed. His attention was focused on something in the water instead. Rob looked up and saw what he thought was a swimmer wearing a white bathing cap, about ten yards off shore. Why would anyone want to swim in this shit? But the head was moving too quickly to be a swimmer, darting below the surface and then popping back up. On closer inspection he saw that it was not a human, but a seal that had managed to get its head tangled up in a white piece of refuse. He was reminded of the Dorothy Bradford bonnet, the one Maggie Mason had given him for Katie to wear, and which he had stuffed into a dumpster somewhere in Provincetown. Rob decided it was just a plastic bag, but he couldn't be sure. He wondered if the bag, or whatever it was, was wrapped around the seal's neck, causing the animal distress. If the seal washed up on shore would he try to save it?

The low-tide rock was now peeking out of the water, dripping with seaweed. Rob was looking right at it when the hatted seal scooted out of the water and came to rest on the surface of the rock. The seal arched its back, pointing its nose and tail toward the sky in a U-shape, as if it was the main attraction at SeaWorld. It held this pose for some time, more than a minute, then barked and dove back into the water.

Acknowledgements

Thanks to Linda Cashdan for editing the manuscript and providing valuable perspective. Thanks to my parents for introducing me to the Cape in my early years. Most of all, thanks to Ellen for her love and support.

About The Author

Paul Ehrenreich grew up in Belmont, Massachusetts. He lives in Bethesda, Maryland and Truro, Massachusetts with his wife and their dog. *Out With The Tide* is his first novel.

Made in the USA
Middletown, DE
10 June 2021